ABOUT THE AUTHOR

Timothy Nils lives in London having grown up close to its centre. After a career as a systems consultant in manufacturing industry that saw him work in many countries across Europe, he now devotes his time to literary and historical pursuits that fascinated him as a student and young adult. He is married with two children and has a dog called Pontus.

AT THE NEXT SPRING

TIMOTHY NILS

First published 2023

ISBN 978-1-7397099-3-8

The author acknowledges permission by Faber and Faber Ltd to quote
from 'Selected Poems T. S. Eliot' by T. S. Eliot

This novel is entirely a work of fiction. Any resemblance to persons living
or dead is purely coincidental. Any character or incident identified with
public places, private or public institutions is purely imaginary and does
not imply, impute or claim any association, view or behaviour with such
places and institutions or any of their personnel past or present.

Page design and typesetting in the UK by pblpublishing.co.uk

Author's Note

The acronym COBRA stands for Cabinet Office Briefing Rooms (A) and is the place where the UK Government meets to discuss and to plan for specific national crises. Its better-known counterpart in the US is the White House Situation Room.

GCHQ stands for Government Communications Headquarters and is the UK's intelligence, cyber and security agency. Its counterpart in the US is the National Security Agency.

UCL & LSE (University College London, London School of Economics) are constituent colleges of the University of London.

ISS (Institute of Strategic Studies): a 'think tank' devoted to international affairs.

ICBM (Intercontinental Ballistic Missile): missile with nuclear warhead.

CIA & MI5 (Central Intelligence Agency, Military Intelligence 5) of the United States of America, and the United Kingdom of Great Britain and Northern Ireland, respectively.

The Venona files (or papers) refer to a US intelligence project that decrypted Soviet communications in the 1940s.

Delos is an island at the centre of the Cyclades in the Aegean Sea. Mythic birthplace of the Greek gods Apollo and Artemis, it is now a World Heritage Site.

Sixth form: the last two years of secondary education in the UK (except Scotland) for 16 to 18 year olds. It equates to the 11th and 12th grades in the US.

Acknowledgements

I would like to thank my family and friends for their support, patience and fortitude in the time it has taken to research and bring this story to fruition. In particular, I would like to thank my daughter for her sharp eye for idiom and dramatic tension as she read drafts of this work.

My thanks too to Paul Baillie-Lane for his cover design and graceful responses to my fastidious tinkering.

To Andrew Lowe and Rebecca Millar who, as professional editors saw earlier drafts of this novel, and whose feedback and encouragement helped to light the way ahead.

While this story is the product of my own imagination, it has benefited from the insights and learning of many specialists in literary, historical, and classical studies. I am indebted to their expertise.

Who bid thee go this way to be rid of thy burden?

From 'The Pilgrim's Progress', by John Bunyan

PART ONE

PROLOGUE

London, England
3 December 2019

The voice spoke again.

Larry Antony kicked the bedsheets aside and stumbled to the floor of his hotel room. He stood up, obedient to the ethereal command. A trickle of blood ran down his leg, darkening as it settled on the rug beneath his feet. He looked away, drawn once more to the glare of a fierce, inquiring lamp. He screwed his eyes and raised his hands like a shield. 'Goddamn you,' he screamed. 'I've told you guys everything. Everything … that I can.'

Naked, and alone, he fell to his knees and wept, begging his nightmare to end.

The voice summoned him once more. He rose, wiped his eyes and crossed the room to a chair by a simple, wooden desk. Trembling, he sat in front of the lamp. He glanced down. His confession was still there. His anguished words forced by an endless torment that racked his brain. And faces that scowled and drifted towards him. And a light that stayed constant.

He picked up the pen and steadied his hand. *October 2* he wrote, feeling things would soon be okay. The words were coming, and he could remember … people and events. He lifted his eyes as the faces fell back—stationed against the walls of his room. He nodded and lifted his hand in a friendly gesture. It was official now, he thought. Like a tribunal, a tribunal of the mind. Smiling, he put the pen down and spoke to the ghostly delegates instead. 'Must be a couple of months ago, now, gentlemen. Met with the British … a little after I got back from the States. I think it was near London Bridge. In some kind of security suite. High up. With sloping glass windows.' He sat back in his chair. 'It was my first meeting with their intelligence team.' Larry watched as the lifeless faces weighed his words. He was telling the truth, they agreed.

Another voice spoke. But calmly. And from behind. Larry didn't turn, but it was still okay, he thought. Just routine. Just preliminaries about the Brits and who they were. He leant forward, speaking again. 'Correct, James Ellison, sir. A senior UK official. And one of their juniors. A rookie called Felix. Felix Leighton. Joint intel. Washington and London.' He sat upright. His eyes fell on the confession. The voices in his head wanted more.

'The CIA was out of it.' He looked around. His words caused a sudden stir. 'I mean, Carter … their liaison guy. He'd messed up. They had to pull him out.' The faces reared. Larry tensed. 'It was *my* assignment, dammit. My boss … he said so. He promised me.'

Larry grabbed the armrest of the chair. He was too anxious. Too loud. Too helpless, he realised. He counted over and over, waiting for his inquisitors to settle down. And his pulse to slow. He relaxed his hands.

A voice spoke. 'Who are the main conspirators? What are their intentions?'

Larry picked up his pen and returned to his confession. *Three students*, he wrote. *Art history. University College London, England.*

A second voice demurred.

'I mean, at first there were three students.' He bit his lip. The eyes sharpened. He lowered his head and wrote again. *Two males. Francis Eggar. Age twenty-one. Alex Rowdesley. Twenty. And the girl. Jane Shere. Brits. Young Brits. Radicalised. Forbidden studies. Hostile to the world order.*

Larry leant back, sneering at the words on the page. The faces nodded. He was doing okay. Doing his job. He drew a breath, feeling his pulse settle down. He was ready for more. 'Yeah,' he said, dropping the pen and folding his arms. 'Kind of dumb guys,' he added, sitting upright. Talking aloud. 'And some kind of weird science. And the occult. The crazy occult.' He laughed and threw his arms in the air. 'I mean, they want to screw the world and start over again. Like they know the secret. The origin of America. The day it all began.' He stood up, but the second voice interrupted.

'The fourth student, Mr Antony, you haven't spoken about the fourth student.'

'Pardon me.' Larry sat down and retrieved the pen. The pen touched the page. He wrote. *The fourth student. Name of Addings, Richard Addings. Nineteen years of age. Literature. Freshman. No evidence of radicalisation.*

The eyes exchanged glances. Tell us more.

November 7, Whitehall, London, he wrote. *Kind of like a palace.* He crossed out the words. But the eyes noted. Watching. Silently. *I mean the fancy room. And all the mad, pagan signs. Just like the zodiac.* The eyes turned. Warily. The pen jumped off the page.

A voice probed. 'You mean the British Foreign Office?'

'Yeah, the Locarno Room.' Larry lowered his head. 'I meant to write that,' he mumbled. There was a silence. He glanced around the room. A shuffle of feet unsettled him. Like journalists comparing notes. And eyes watching. He sat still, clutching the hotel chair.

The noise subsided. He breathed again.

And then another voice. A sterner voice. 'Are you a patriot, soldier?'

'Yes, sir. Special Forces.' He nodded affirmatively. 'Proud folks.' Larry raised his hand as if waving to his mom and pa. He smiled. Just like a family homecoming, he recalled.

The first voice interrupted. The questions continued.

'No, sir. There were only two meetings with the British. October second and November seven. Intelligence briefings. Classified.' He smiled. He'd be okay. They'd let him sleep, now. And go back to bed. He closed his hands, hiding blood under his nails.

'And nothing else?'

'Pardon me?'

'Were there no other meetings, Mr Antony? Meetings with others while you were in London? A young man, for instance? An informant who knew about the fourth student?'

Larry shut his eyes. He swallowed. He had to play it cool. 'You mean the kid? Well, kind of casual,' he admitted, looking around once more.

The eyes conferred.

'You know how it is with the Brits and building rapport.' He tried to slow his words. His body shifted. 'Jesus … these jerks. They need a few beers sometimes. To loosen up.' His words fell on silent stares. He sat up. Trembling, he felt cold. 'I mean … off duty, sir.'

The voice sharpened. 'You're on oath, soldier.'

'There were no other meetings. No way.' Larry looked back at the confession on the desk. The kid was lying. Trying to drag him deeper. Trying to dodge the blame. Larry pushed it away. 'The CIA was not doing its job,' he bawled. 'We needed leads, goddammit. It's a dirty business.' He checked the room. The reaction stayed muted. Maybe they understood. But wouldn't say. He closed his eyes, clenching his fists. Flecks of blood fell to the floor. 'The assassination … the killing. It was in London. By the river. Embankment Gardens.' Larry paused. He opened his eyes unnerved by the heavy silence. And a throbbing in his veins. 'A detail accompanied me. We found the target. The detail was armed. Glock 26, 9 mm. But I didn't agree. It was too public. There were people. Students. Near a café. Someone would see.

He dropped his head. And stared at his hands.

The voice resumed. 'You were a college boy too, Agent Antony.'

Larry swallowed. Another tack. Soft guy. Hard guy. They're sweating me. Stay calm, he thought. He looked up. 'Math and cryptography. Great years.'

The voices conferred.

'No, sir. Stayed clear of the fraternities. Keeping focus.'

The voice probed.

Larry looked away. 'That is correct. To my knowledge, there was no invitation. Not from the fraternities. As I said, I stayed clear. Keeping focus.'

The voice sharpened. 'You're a loner, soldier.'

Larry froze. The eyes stood out against the glare of the table lamp.

'You're working freelance. Admit it!'

'No, sir. I'm working for my country.'

The words echoed around the room. Papers shuffled. Larry hid his face, frightened by the confession.

'Look at me. Your boss has called you a fantasist. You've endangered the mission. The students are at liberty. The world order is threatened.'

Larry stood. Shaking.

'Sit down, soldier!'

There was more talk. And accusations. His inquisitors formed a circle.

'No, sir. I don't believe in Satan. No way.' Larry crossed his arms. He shook his head as they circled.

The voices stayed silent.

'The way I see it, you've just got to make up your own mind. I mean, like the stories in the Bible.' He shuddered. 'And the commandments.'

There was movement. And anger.

'It's not true,' he screamed. 'The kid's lying. I don't want the secret.' He seized the confession and waved it in the air. He grabbed a page, and sweeping his arm across the desk, wrote furiously. *We went back. To the riverside gardens. The target was still there. Male. Forty. Dark haired. Light build. He saw us and turned to flee. I gave the order. There was a shot. And then another, close up, as he staggered and fell amidst the dark leafy shrubs close to the Thames.* Larry lifted his head. The circle was complete. He dropped the pen. The voices slipped from his mind. The faces from the constant light.

Larry sank his head into his hands and sobbed. 'I hate the kid. I hate Satan.' He opened a drawer at the side of the desk and reached for an instrument stained with blood. He pushed back the chair and stood. His hand shook. Sweat rolled down his skin. He turned, and fixed his eyes on a strange spiralling shape, a glyph that beckoned from his bedroom wall, telling him things. In his head. Taunting. Mocking his fleshy bulk, his nakedness, his extra pounds.

He looked down. White boxer shorts lay trampled beneath his feet. Spread like a cloth to soak his blood. His remorse. His sacrifice. He lifted his eyes, drawn once more to the winding curve. Following its shape. Round and round. Slipping deeper within its thin, sinuous arms ready for its instruction.

It whispered its command in a sly, lascivious breath.

Larry opened the scissors. He raised his hand. Snapping and slicing the air. Cutting the threads that whirled and danced around the room. Around his mind. His head. His body. That tightly bound his skin. His feet. His shins. His thighs. Cutting and slicing. Higher and higher. Laughing. Cutting. And shaking.

But then … nothing. The bleak, bleak emptiness … of nothing.

His eyes drifted up towards the wall. He stared. The spiral had gone.

Larry dropped the scissors. Blood settled between his toes. Colouring his nails a soft crimson red. Making patterns on his feet. Warming his thighs. Consecrating the cloth.

* * *

'Mr Antony, sir. Are you okay? Mr Antony. Please open the door.'

Larry drew back. The night porter? He snatched his shorts from the floor and stuffed them into a drawer. He grabbed a pair of pants. 'Yeah. Hang on, I'm okay. Just a dream.'

'Mr Antony. Would you please open the door? I insist you open the door. Or I must call the police.'

'Hold on. Hold on there. I'm dressing.'

Larry reached the door. He edged it ajar, his hand trembling to keep it still. 'Jesus. That was some freaky dream. Like I was in hell or something.'

The porter drew back. 'I am sorry … but a guest has reported noises. And screaming from your room.' He shifted his eyes.

Larry switched on the light and opened the door. 'Look for yourself.'

The porter stepped forward and looked around. The curtains were drawn. A bottle of bourbon sat on the desk. And alongside the lamp, sheets of paper covered with notes. The Stars and Stripes lay draped across the dishevelled bed. 'You are alone?'

'Yeah. Sure thing.' Larry gestured to the table. There was only one glass by the bottle.

The porter stepped back. 'We ask our guests … to respect the privacy of others, Mr Antony.' He paused, focusing his thoughts. 'I am sorry to disturb you. But there was … concern.'

'Like I said. Just a dream.' Larry closed the door and turned the lock. He leant hard against the door, counting as the porter's steps withdrew. A sweat eased his weight to the floor. He pulled his knees towards his chest and placed his hands around his feet. Mixing the red between his toes. Cold and alone. Begging the dark for sleep. And forgiveness. He lifted his head and stared back at the wall.

The glyph had returned.

1

'You'll shudder at the thought, Richard. But make us a promise, will you? You won't lose heart and turn away?'

I'd met Francis and Jane by chance soon after the computer network had crashed. They were third-year students on a four-year degree course at University College London. I was a fresher, straight out of school. I'd opted to read English literature and, during my first-year, a free study option that was supposed to sharpen my academic insights and widen my circle of friends. Our paths crossed in a quiet conference hall not too far from where I'd expected to enrol on a damp, breezy day at the start of October. The hall was hosting an exhibition on sixteenth-century drawings and prints, and I had little else to do but hang around until the IT problems had been sorted out. Francis and Jane came up to me and introduced themselves. They talked to me about the artists Dürer and Da Vinci, asked me about my degree, and whether I was interested in European Renaissance studies.

And then Jane came up with an idea. 'Why don't you join our tutorial?' she said, reaching for my arm.

Art history? Really? I was intrigued. We grabbed a coffee nearby, and in no time they'd sketched an outline of the central campus, told me about their tutor, Dr Hatherleigh, and their unusual course module, and then explained how to find his rooms in one of the terraced streets not far from the uni. They mentioned an entry code for the front door, but didn't want to write it down. Oh, and access to the third floor was by stairs or an odd-looking lift with a long gallows-like pulley. But don't worry, Francis had said, we all get used to it. As for the studies, they were full of ideas and suggestions, offered me a few tips on an interview with the tutor, and agreed to meet later if their other commitments allowed. So, Art History B, I thought. Let's go for it!

The lift rose to the third floor, where it clattered to a halt. There was an odd, heavy silence once it stalled. I slid back the inner and outer gates and stepped on to the polished parquet flooring. I looked around. A glazed ceramic vase with rural scenes sat on the white-painted windowsill to my left. On the adjoining wall, a mirror hung, set in a carved gilded frame. And beneath that, under a moulded dado rail, a period-style table with brass handles on the drawers.

Oh shit, I thought, closing my eyes. I'd screwed up in places like this before. At Oxford. Ten months before … and an experience I was still trying to put behind me.

I closed the lift gates, silenced my phone after adding the security code to my list of contacts, and then stepped over to the mirror to tidy my hair. I still had a free option to sort out … and a promise I'd just made to Jane.

The tutor's study lay ahead. A soft light filtered through a door left ajar. I headed towards the room, my steps more of a whisper compared to the racket that had emerged from the lift. After knocking on the door, I asked for the tutor by name, giving my own, Richard Addings, as my introduction. I waited for a response before pushing it wider. A sudden curiosity drew me in. I looked around. I was alone.

The light shone from a table lamp positioned on a large mahogany desk. There was an old-fashioned charm about the place; more a drawing room in a country house than the dull cubicles of learning I'd hurried through when visiting the university six months earlier in the year. I stepped forward, my presence hardly betrayed by the soft, green carpet beneath my feet. The entire room, I noticed, was stacked with books, lining the walls like sandbags against a tide. Others were gathered in small piles around the room. And another on the table, crammed with a dense print and strange-looking symbols. But not a screen. Or even a keyboard in sight.

There was a slight eddy of air. I heard the door close sharply. Someone had entered the study behind me.

'If you want to arrive unannounced, young man, you had better climb the stairs.' The voice caught me off guard. I turned, although still spellbound by all the books. 'They are splendid, aren't they? I have been collecting for many years. My field is very specialised. In fact, many are quite rare.'

In his arms, the tutor was carrying several large books on which he'd balanced a delicate-looking device. He paused a few steps from me. I stayed still, drawn to the strange mechanism.

'It's a spherical model of the solar system,' he explained. 'Lots of complicated gearing. And such a beautiful adornment to the study of natural philosophy, wouldn't you say?'

I nodded, but still nervous about my intrusion. 'It looks … ingenious. Is it old?'

'Prague, 1590. The castle is a wonderful place, you know, with a magnificent library, museums and galleries. And once the best art collection in Europe.'

I nodded again.

His eyes scanned me from the top of his wire-framed glasses. 'Now forgive me, young man. I should have asked you to take a seat.' A glance landed on a sturdy, carver chair set back from his desk. 'Please.'

I did as directed, but moved the chair closer for our conversation.

Dr Hatherleigh was a silver-haired academic. Close to sixty, he was of medium height but with a heavy build. A chubby glow to his face softened the years and hid the contour of his jaw. Jane had mentioned that he'd spent a whole lifetime in the department and held the esteem of others in his field. He was thoughtful and always considerate, she'd said, could be brisk and incisive at unexpected moments, and wasn't shy of a little drama if it helped liven a debate. But right now, I felt relieved by what appeared to be his easy-going attitude despite my unexpected appearance in his room and a precious device that threatened to slide to the floor at any moment. Another glance forestalled the danger, prompting me to reach forward and clear a space on the desk.

Dr Hatherleigh placed the books next to an office-style phone. A message light called for attention. Hatherleigh ignored it. He sat in his chair, but after a moment's reflection, removed the planetary model from the books and set it in front of me. He pointed his finger at one of its shiny brass orbs. 'This orb represents the sun. Rather remarkable, don't you think?'

The model was concentric. Like rings within rings. And the Earth was fixed at the centre in accordance with medieval thinking. I smiled, but sidestepping its distraction thought it would be better to explain my presence in his room. 'I've come about the art history module, Dr Hatherleigh.'

'I'm sorry?'

'The art history module. Jane Shere and Francis Eggar. I met them earlier. They said I should talk to you about my free study option.'

'Jane and Francis?'

'Er, yes. That's right. They're third-years.'

His gaze narrowed. 'And your own name, young man?'

'Oh, Richard Addings. They recommended your course to me, Dr Hatherleigh. Art History B, in particular.' I pushed back my hair and smiled again.

'Art History B?' he queried, frowning as he raised a hand to his chin. 'You are sure of this?'

'Er, yes. Jane was specific. She said it would go well with my other studies. I'm studying English literature, Dr Hatherleigh.'

'Really? But I haven't taken students on that programme for two years, Mr Addings.' He leant back in his chair and folded his arms. 'There are people in the university who want to see my tutorials shutdown altogether, whatever your other studies, Mr Addings.' A bemused stare dashed any prospect of appeal. His attention returned to the planets as he moved them to the side of his desk.

I was ready to sink. This was almost as bad as Oxford.

'I can, if you wish, speak to my colleague Dr Arbetta concerning the Art History A course.' Dr Hatherleigh adjusted his glasses before checking some paperwork containing names. 'One of his candidates has withdrawn, so you may be able to join his programme. If he is agreeable, that is.' He turned back to me. 'Now, if you are studying medieval literature, then I am quite sure it would be a suitable match. I think the Flemish School would be appropriate.' He nodded to himself. 'Or maybe the early perspectivists.'

'To be honest, I'm more early modern than medieval.' I grinned back at the tutor, not sure if my reply was much help.

'Then in that case, the high or late Renaissance, would be the better choice, I think.' He broke eye contact as he scribbled something down.

Maybe the interview would have been easier if I'd waited at his door instead of just strolling in. I glanced at the rows of books on the shelves surrounding us. Heavy-looking volumes with gilded spines. Pioneering works in their day, I supposed. And then at an old French clock sitting above a marble fireplace, quietly setting the mood. Oh, guys. You'd been so sure ... when we'd met and talked, letting one thing lead to another, even slipping off for a friendly coffee and chat. Had I forgotten something to win over the tutor? I stared up at the ceiling. A light hung from the fancy plaster of petals and thorns. And as I lingered on its meaning, something that Jane had mentioned flitted back into my mind. I looked across the desk. 'I have … always admired Albrecht Dürer, Dr Hatherleigh.'

'Dürer? Yes, a great artist.' He continued to write.

'It's, er … fascinating how his work tells us about the world we live in.'

'Indeed, Mr Addings.'

'I know it has suffered a lot from, er, uninformed criticism but I have always been intrigued by his work, the "Triumphal Arch".'

'Really?' He raised his head. Our eyes met.

'I have always thought its detail, its, you know, enigmatic iconography even …' I was searching my brain for Jane's enthusiasm for the piece when she and Francis found me puzzling over it earlier in the day.

Dr Hatherleigh placed a finger to his cheek. He looked curious.

'I would not disagree with you. Emblemata offer a vital perspective on surface appreciation, Mr Addings, and suggest a more profound interpretation of the underlying subject matter.' His expression relaxed as he spoke. 'The best critics have always stated this.'

If only I could build on this, I wondered. 'I have the same experience, you know, with literature, Dr Hatherleigh. How sad that the reader stumbles, er … blindly, through Spenserian allegory or the strange language of the Metaphysical poets and their friends.'

'The Metaphysicals, you say?'

'The untiring champions of the intellect,' I said, remembering something my sixth-form tutor had told me at school.

For a few moments, we shared the measured beat of the clock.

'You said earlier that my course was *recommended* to you?'

'Yes. By Francis and Jane …' I was now sitting upright.

He studied my face. 'And your sixth-form subjects, Mr Addings?'

'English literature. Maths. And Classical Studies. All grade A.'

'Hmm.' He placed a finger once more to his face. Slowly, his stare dissolved. 'The tutorial programme is not without challenges, you must understand. The focus of our work is often … subtextual.'

I nodded. 'My friends explained.'

'And your wish to join my class is your own decision?'

'Yes, Dr Hatherleigh. My decision alone.'

A thoughtful silence followed. I crossed my fingers and hoped.

'We cover the geometry of Euclid in depth and specific contributions by Fibonacci and Pacioli.'

My pulse raced. This is it.

'Your mathematics should help you there. Some Latin or Greek would be useful, of course, since we study several ancient commentaries on original texts and drawings.'

I swallowed. 'We studied some primary sources at school, I remember. I can always catch up in my own time.'

'As you wish. But I can supply translations of the latter if the texts are too advanced for you.' He gestured with his hand towards the books. 'They are mostly eighteenth and nineteenth century, young man, but always faithful to the originals. More contemporary translations, I fear, often stifle the idiom.' He paused before continuing in a less indulgent tone. 'Now, the so-called occult sciences … in the current curriculum, these studies form an important part of our historical investigations. They will probably be new to you.' He paused, expecting confirmation.

'Yes. Completely,' I said, edging a little closer.

'We go much deeper than the allusions you may already be familiar with in your poets and writers.'

I swallowed again.

Dr Hatherleigh retrieved a business card from his desk. 'Please, take this. It will confirm your bona fides. You should apply for membership of the British Library. Ask for Ms Lopez. She will help you with the more obscure publications.'

I took the card. More careful smiles.

'I am sure you will find my course helpful regarding your other studies in literature. Like Ariadne's thread,' he proposed, 'and Theseus amidst the bewildering labyrinth of the legendary King Minos.'

I settled back. It was an interesting allusion. Renaissance poetry is full of strange myths that often puzzle the modern reader. But with a bit of background in the intellectual sources that inspired such writers, I reckoned it wouldn't be too difficult to add a dash of flair to an essay or even to shine at one of the deeper-meaning English seminars. And *that,* was a thread I could happily pursue.

Dr Hatherleigh clapped his hands, reminding me of the arrangements for enrolment. I asked for the course registration code.

'Yes. Registration. The ever-watchful bureaucracy.' He slid open a small drawer to his left and cast his eyes over the contents. 'I have not had occasion to use it of late, so I had better confirm it for you. The A option is C178, but you have *elected* to take B, which is … C173, Mr Addings.'

He signed a short letter of introduction, writing the course code alongside his signature. After a slight hesitation, he ticked a box confirming an admission test and added today's date after checking his wristwatch. 'There. You should say that you were interviewed by Dr Julian Hatherleigh, 2 October. That will be sufficient.'

He passed me the letter of acceptance.

'Your friends …'

'Oh, Francis and Jane.'

'Yes. Did they touch on our need to be a little … circumspect about matters we investigate in the tutorials?'

'You mean the occult stuff?'

'Indeed, I fear we are rather friendless amongst the departments these days. There is a lot of unsympathetic scrutiny of our studies. Even, I'm told, by the security services.' He allowed me a moment to ponder the implications of this. 'And so, it is necessary for us to refer somewhat obliquely to much of our work. In order, one might say, to allay the suspicious and *untutored* mind. Much like your poets, Mr Addings.'

I wondered at what he might mean, but I wasn't turning back now. And while I could imagine that some material was challenging to orthodox opinion and might even upset a few people from time to time, my only real fear was the sheer breadth and complexity of it. I had a lot of work to do. I nodded, acknowledging the gentle hint.

A pensive look settled across his face. He slid the planetary model towards me, as if it was a parting gift.

'To follow the Copernican revolution,' he declared, 'we must first consult the Ptolemaic model.'

'I'm sorry?'

'The modern world is the recipient of many influences, Mr Addings. It is governed by a very precise mechanism, and one not always explained by the conventional sciences or accepted by modern political theories.' He spoke with a quiet emphasis. 'There are many secrets concerning its origin, when and where it was created, and much speculation about its future,'—his finger slid down the brass orb of the sun—'and the part that anyone of us might play in shaping its destiny.' He withdrew his hand. 'It is a subject we shall return to in our tutorials.'

'You mean … like those mystery schools of ancient Greece?' I asked, my eyes straining and widening at the prospect.

'And other schools of thought up and down the ages. We are not alone, I suspect, in this endeavour.'

Hatherleigh studied me for a moment. Was there still something else?

But it was nothing, only my date of birth. 'The twenty-third of September,' I replied. The autumn equinox, he commented. 'I'm supposed to be a Libra,' I added, stealing a smile. It prompted a further question from him.

'Are you familiar with Plato's "Timaeus"? His wonderful work on the creation of the gods and the cosmos?'

But before I could say no, our attention was drawn to the message light of his phone, which was now flashing vigorously. It seemed the right moment to conclude the interview, and so Dr Hatherleigh rose from his chair. I followed, moving towards the door as he led the way. His parting comments had a hint of his earlier spontaneity. 'I shall post a notice of our tutorials and reading list outside the main library. I know it's convenient for students when taking lunch.' His hands then leapt up in mock horror. 'I'm afraid we have little use of the university websites or the inane, frivolous gossip of their social media.'

I left his room, the door closing behind me as I slipped down the stairs, wondering about this strange dimension to my study of poetry and plays. Anyway, that was my first-year studies sorted out, I decided. Just fingers crossed now for the rest of the day's registration.

I followed the streets back towards the campus; and as I walked, feeling upbeat and rather relieved, I thought of the funny old lift, the books, and even the friendly ticking clock. Along the way, I paused and looked ahead. A brief shower of rain had come and gone, freshening the air and sharpening the light. In the near distance, I could see the university's Senate House soaring skywards, looming high above London's Bloomsbury like a great slab of Portland stone— its crisp, modernist lines probing quite different horizons to the ghostly contemplation of stars.

Hatherleigh's critics might laugh and scorn, ridiculing his fondness for antiquity and all those odd beliefs about legends, cosmos, and time, but none of that was my concern. I'd just turned nineteen. I was ready for my own adventure. A new chapter in life. New friendships. New freedoms too … as the long and lazy count of student days beckoned ahead of me.

Francis and Jane had said something about celebrating the outcome of my meeting with their tutor. And I pretty much owed them—and the German Renaissance for that matter—a round of drinks or at least a few words of thanks. I threw my jacket over my shoulder, and with a quicker pace, headed back to the exhibition hall and the curious artwork that had caught my attention: Dürer's dark and extravagant 'Triumphal Arch'.

2

Felix Leighton, a young official fast-tracking his career at the Foreign Office, pushed back in his chair towards the security console. He ran his fingers across the keypad, entering all but the last of the familiar commands before turning to two older colleagues in the room.

'I can set the video and voice capture to begin at three this afternoon, guys. Or we can wait for the two other gentlemen from the US State Department, if you prefer.'

Felix's proposition was unanswered. His immediate superior at the Foreign Office, James Ellison, a career diplomat in his late fifties, was busy writing. He had heard his younger colleague, for sure. It was the usual consideration from Felix, ever mindful that any private exchanges would be part of an official record. But other matters preoccupied James at that moment, particularly those two new faces who would soon join their deliberations. He raised his head, acknowledging his subordinate's suggestion, but gave no obvious response to the young man's proposal.

Felix turned to William Carter, a lean, suntanned American from Massachusetts who had spent thirty years in the CIA. He coughed, hoping to draw William's attention as the American gazed through a sloping glass window high above the London skyline not far from a riverside that once teemed with ships and dockers' nodding cranes.

'The security protocol, sir?' asked Felix, his outstretched hand still poised to complete the codes at the console.

'Hey, let's do it,' said William, as he swung around and faced the room. 'Let's capture it. For the politicians. And the analysts, Felix. And don't forget those policy wonks. They'll want to crawl all over it.' William punched the air, but a downbeat smile belied the mood of his gesture.

Felix relaxed his hand. He reached instead for a Foreign Office briefing.

James glanced up from his notes. 'Do I detect a vein of cynicism in those remarks, William?'

William shrugged and turned back to the window.

James reread his notes, his train of thought unsettled by William's frivolity. For the past two years, he had worked with his American colleague chairing an obscure diplomatic initiative devoted to matters of common historical interest. The so-called 'destiny question'.

'What floor are we on, guys?' asked William, shifting the conversation.

'The forty-second,' replied James, still reading his notes.

'Is that British or American?'

'British.'

'Forty-two.' He glanced back over his shoulder. 'It's a long way down, James. To the sidewalk.'

'Yes, I believe it is.' James lifted his head for a moment, sensing a restlessness in his colleague's demeanour.

'Hey, Felix,' asked William, switching attention to the younger man, 'has your boss ever told you how he and I first met?'

Felix stopped reading. 'Wasn't it at the Institute of Strategic Studies? Nearly thirty years ago?'

'Is that what you told him, James? The ISS.'

'I told him we were both interns at their offices near Covent Garden before they moved to Arundel House by the Thames. And that our paths crossed later in Latvia and Stockholm.' James looked up from his notes. 'I think it was … twenty-nine years ago.'

'Yeah, I remember. We got caught up in that business … who was it now?'

James let go of his pen. 'Kalinsky. A Balt. With an academic background.'

'Kalinsky. Dr Josef Artur Kalinsky. I remember. He was into publishing and collecting old books.'

'Books?' said Felix, looking quizzically at his boss.

'Rare book trafficking,' explained James. 'And forged manuscripts. Especially after the Berlin Wall came crashing down.'

William flared with a sudden enthusiasm for the story. 'Just imagine … There was this guy, he could speak four or five languages, was as charming as your James, giving the runaround to European intelligence services because of some dusty, old art books and a few papers he'd put together with his buddies.' William placed his hands on the back of a chair. He leant forward. 'And guess what, Felix? We'd checked in at the same hotel as this guy in downtown Riga! Where were we, James?'

'Just by the old castle.'

'Yeah, that's right. I remember those dreary paintings. They probably wanted the books as well. You know what, guys? Someone should make a new spy movie. Just like those Cold War features they used to show when we were young.'

James thought back with a subdued affection for those days. He still remembered many of the events and players, and the unfolding drama, the wild speculation, even the extraordinary claims by historians and scientists. And at a deeper level, the surreal fears that something bizarre and uncontrollable might happen across the world, leaving his own government's plans in disarray. He turned to William, making light of his thoughts. 'If they made a film of it, it would surely mystify the audience.'

William shrugged. 'I guess you're right there, James. It all sounded like a lot of hocus-pocus to me.'

Felix looked agog at the disclosure. 'And so what happened? To Kalinsky.'

'Nothing happened, Felix. Nothing at all,' replied William. 'While your James and I were beset by egomaniacs and paranoid staffers back home convinced that this Dr Kalinsky guy had made some kind of discovery about the destiny of the world, he just disappeared. Before we were accused of letting him escape.'

'Did you? I mean, did he?'

James looked gravely at Felix. 'We followed him to Sweden, but he vanished in Stockholm's Old Town during a snowstorm, taking whatever secrets he had with him.'

A tranquil silence descended on the room leaving James to wonder why, after so many years, his friend had now chosen to recall these events and their inconclusive outcome. But more immediate matters curtailed his thoughts. Gathering his papers, he broke the silence. 'William, your colleagues from the US will join us shortly. I think Felix and I will be better hosts if we might learn something more about them.' A tightened smile suggested the need for a more serious approach to their conversation.

William took a seat at the table. Felix reached for a notepad and pen.

'Okay, James. What would you like to know?'

'They're from Washington, I believe?'

'Yep. Both connected to the State Department. The old man's called Warren David Dudley. Maybe you've heard of him. He's the boss.' William turned to Felix. 'Known for his fiery temper.'

'And his assistant?' continued James.

'Yeah, his sidekick, Larry Antony. Wait, make that acolyte, Felix. Shifty college guy itching to run his own show on this side of the Pond. Screwed up, if you want my opinion.'

James folded his arms. It wasn't much, he thought. Even a little flippant.

'And you'd better remember Warren runs his own church. Stateside. Big on the "end times" and "the rapture". And check out the foundation he has here in London. Website and TV channel. He's also a friend of the president. Threw the kitchen sink at his last campaign according to the media.' William was now grinning broadly.

It wasn't what James wanted to hear, nor was he sure about William's restless behaviour. James pondered the implications of this. The regular pre-meeting briefing from Felix had been thin on substance. He felt ill-prepared for his new visitors and anxious that events might soon be beyond his control. He needed William to stay focused and lend his support. But he also had a more delicate matter regarding security breaches at the University of London—breaches that were troubling his own superiors at the FO.

'I'm inclined, William, to be insistent on a matter which both you and I have discussed several times.' He paused, fixing his eyes on his friend. 'You know Her Majesty's Government's position on this.'

William stretched back in his chair. 'Oh, James, so you've got to kick some ass. Not your style, surely, *old boy*?'

Felix cringed, rereading his notes.

The American's facetiousness shocked James, but he kept his composure. He reworded his proposal. 'William, forgive me, but the university vice-chancellor has threatened to go to the prime minister. The constant disruption of their computer networks is making his position intolerable. There are endless complaints from tutors and students alike. Is this not a matter for our committee to pursue, in view of the underlying historical sensitivities?'

William eased himself from his chair and turned again to the plate-glass window at the end of the room. He stared out as a dark cloud threatened rain over north London, mulling his thoughts. He turned back to his colleagues. 'James, what would you do if you wanted to get out of this business?'

For a moment, James wondered if he had misheard, but William pressed the question. 'No, serious. If you really wanted to get the hell out, what would you do?'

Felix closed his eyes as if fearing a sudden escalation.

But after a pause, James's deeper sensibilities prevailed, and he replied in a soft, disarming tone. 'I would teach. My tutor at Cambridge used to say that I might make a fine don one day.'

'Yeah. But teach what? Politics? History? Art?'

'I would teach literature. Milton. John Milton.'

The words crystallised a new thought in William's mind. He spoke aloud as if to a much larger assembly. '"Paradise Lost"', he exclaimed with a sense of public grief.

'"Paradise Lost", indeed. And "Paradise Regained", William. Milton completed a sequel wherein the meek and the just inherited the Earth.'

William looked at James. 'I've heard of "Paradise Lost". But "Paradise Regained"?' He laughed, 'I didn't know. I was a history major.'

Felix shifted in his chair.

Yet William's reflection dissipated the unease, and, in a slow-motion gesture, a gentle smile spread across his face. 'There's one thing I want to share with you guys. At least before you read it in one of those dull, official communications.' James and Felix exchanged glances. 'You know, my wife Hailey, and daughter Mary, have both returned to the States.'

'Isn't Mary starting college?' asked James, trying to sound cheerful.

'Yep. She's off to Harvard to study medicine.' There was a brief flourish in William's voice. 'Well, as I was going to say. You guys in Whitehall have put up with me for two years now. All that hectoring by a brash American. All those crazy demands and mispronunciations, Felix.'

Felix smiled, acknowledging the charge.

'Listen, guys. I'm moving on. There's lots happening back at the Agency. You know how the boys in Langley like to shake things up. So that's it. I'm out. Period.'

James lowered his eyes, replying in a voice tinged with emotion. 'I'm sorry, William. Things will never be the same without you.'

William declined to stay. He had promised to phone Hailey as soon as the meeting was over. James understood. The men rose and shook hands in a hurried and muted farewell before William, with a sigh, slipped away.

James avoided his young assistant's eyes. Like William, he, too, felt drawn to the tinted glass and the sweeping vistas. The last few minutes had been both unforeseen and unwelcome and would mean a change in tactics for the rest of the day. There was much still to discover and much that their new American colleagues might insist on. Like the release of data. Sharper surveillance. And even, he feared, direct action. The very things he had so far been loath to agree. The prospect did not please him. And yet, in recent weeks, there had been unsettling news. Reports from the university. From the British Library and British Museum. Old faces gathering once more. New recruits. A new enterprise underway, perhaps? His thoughts turned back to Stockholm and the elusive trail. And Kalinsky. And he wondered. He must look older now. A new identity. A new disguise. James drew a deep breath and stared through the dark, transparent glass. The forty-second floor, he mused. Yes, it is a long way down, my old friend.

No matter, he would handle the American gentlemen and whatever might arise. He smiled to himself, a little less anxious at the risks that now lay ahead. He turned to his colleague. 'Felix, our visitors may prove rather difficult.' James raised a hand to his chin. 'I am not altogether sure that we understand one another's positions. Or how we should proceed. The Americans, I fear, will be quite forceful.'

Felix looked away. His eyes fell once more on the security console.

3

Dr Hatherleigh placed his hand on the outer orb of Saturn and gave it a gentle push towards the side of his desk. His gaze lingered on each of the planets in turn as Jupiter bowed to Saturn, Mars to Jupiter, the Sun to Mars, and Venus to the Sun. Mercury, the messenger of the gods, the guardian of souls, the patron deity of thieves, commerce and trickery, sped his way, with forward and backward motions, between Helios the Sun, and Artemis, the chaste goddess of the Moon. The Earth, rock-solid at the centre of this medieval cosmos, looked up, forever troubled and beguiled by the wandering spheres.

Francis and Jane remained still as they followed their tutor's action.

Dr Hatherleigh turned his head. 'I'd just got back from seeing Otto at the British Museum, when I found him sneaking around … fascinated by the books. I then told him to sit down, Jane, where you're sitting now.'

'We spotted him at the exhibition, Julian. In Senate House,' said Jane.

'He was gazing into a Renaissance print. One of those ghastly ones by Dürer.' Francis stretched out his right leg and rotated his foot.

Jane moved closer to Hatherleigh's desk. 'He seemed at a loss when we found him, so we asked him for a chat. Over coffee.' She loosened a silk scarf around her neck and placed it on her lap.

'Well, you did a good job on him, Jane.' Dr Hatherleigh leant forward. 'I offered him Lionel's programme to see how he'd react. But he wasn't interested. Art History B, he insisted. So, I ticked the box.' He tore a page from a notepad alongside the phone. 'I'd better review the tutorials. We don't want the vice-chancellor threatening us with sanctions or suspension again.' He scribbled his thoughts on the page before turning back to Francis and Jane. 'How about one next week and another around mid-November, say the nineteenth?'

'But not Wednesday, Julian, I'm busy,' said Jane. 'Friday would be fine.' She turned to Francis, but his attention was elsewhere.

'The eleventh it is, then. And the nineteenth in the following month.' He made another note. 'Francis?'

'I'm listening.'

'Perhaps you could leave a message on our notice board for Richard. The one outside the refectory.'

'And what are we studying?' Francis held his foot steady.

'Plato's "Timaeus". And the destruction of Atlantis.' Dr. Hatherleigh glanced briefly towards his bookshelves. 'I have discovered some new insights into the text that we might share with Richard.' Francis and Jane nodded. 'By the way, there's been a major incident in the IT department.'

'Oh?' said Francis, now fumbling with his left shoe.

'Complete disaster from what I hear. I saw the registrar dashing around the quad with lists of names and courses. What it means for enrolment, I wouldn't care to say.' He shook his head, still unsure at the implications.

Francis re-threaded a lace. 'In that case, it explains why we found Richard alone in Senate House.' He raised his foot to test the tightness of the shoe.

'Well, I'm glad we did,' said Jane, tucking her hair behind an ear. 'But the question is: will he cooperate when he learns what we want him to do?'

'Why not? He'll have no choice. That's always been our intention.' Francis lifted his heel to the chair and retied the lace with a sudden irate vigour. He placed his foot down. Satisfied by the endeavour, he shifted his chair forward. 'So, what does Otto think, Julian?'

'If he's the man for the job, then he wants us to act before the end of the year. That's what he said. All Otto needs are the coordinates showing where the modern world began and the day on which it started.'

'And then Richard can pull the plug on it.' Francis cast his eyes around the room.

'But we still have to be sure before we draw Richard deeper,' said Jane. 'He's got to buy into our vision. I couldn't bear it if he turned back at the very end.'

'I couldn't, either,' said Francis. 'You know that. Not after what happened last year at the end of summer.' He reached for Jane's hand. She smiled, squeezing his hand gently.

Dr Hatherleigh rose from his chair and crossed the room. Returning with a silver tray, on which he had placed a pot of tea, a small jug of milk, and three porcelain cups and saucers, he placed the tray alongside the planets. A small plate of biscuits complemented the refreshment. He served the tea before returning to his chair.

'Maybe you should run over the interview, Julian,' said Jane. 'Tell us how it went with Richard.' She raised her cup and saucer, glanced again at Francis, and then sipped from her cup.

'Well, I thought he was an affable young man. And you were right about the untidy hair and teenage looks. He called you Francis and Jane as though you were old friends.' Dr Hatherleigh glanced towards the biscuits, urging their enjoyment with a gesture of his hand.

'Did he talk about his experience at Oxford, Julian?' asked Francis, reaching for a chocolate-coated digestive.

'No, not at all. Just his studies at A-level. And his grades. And what you must have told him to say about Dürer.' Dr Hatherleigh lowered his cup to the saucer. 'Though I'm not sure his Greek or Latin are up to very much.'

Jane turned to Francis. 'He didn't say much about himself in the refectory, if you remember. Checking his phone while asking about the course. I hope he'll settle in.'

'He's a first-year, Jane. Once he understands what will happen, he'll fall into line. He has to,' replied Francis.

'Exactly,' said Dr Hatherleigh. 'So I mentioned the myth of Theseus and Ariadne to him. I think he picked up on that.' Dr Hatherleigh lifted the teapot and poured another cup. 'Naturally, I asked him if it was his own decision. And he said it was.' He helped himself to a biscuit. 'It was the only time he looked me straight in the eye, you know.'

Francis nodded.

'But did you discuss destinies?' asked Jane. 'And how they will change.'

'For the whole world, I said. Origins and futures. And whatever part we play. When we do, that is.'

'And was there any reaction?' asked Francis.

'Mystery schools. That's what he said. But I did say that he should keep some of these things to himself, what with the university council and others making life difficult for us. Anyway, I passed him off to all those busybodies in Enrolment.' Dr Hatherleigh removed his glasses and checked the lenses. He breathed gently on the glass before rubbing it with a soft cloth he kept on his desk.

'I know he'll do what we want,' added Francis. 'His fate is as much tied up in this as is ours, but we still need to play our part as well. Get him on his feet. Help him with his confidence. That's our role in all this.'

'Or just lead him by the nose. Otto doesn't care how you do it, so long as he gets to where he has to go, and knows what to do once he arrives there.' Dr Hatherleigh returned his glasses to his face.

'There's a whole list of changes he's working on, Francis. Politics. Economics. History. You know how it is, how long he has waited to see his plans fulfilled.'

'Yes, Julian, I do,' said Francis, turning to Jane. 'And not just a bright, radical future. But a past that we will dismantle. And con-figure once again.'

4

I stood in front of the 'Triumphal Arch'.

It really was a mass of pompous detail, I decided. No wonder the critics had slammed it. Jane had said that the Holy Roman Emperor Maximilian had commissioned it in 1512. This was during Dürer's middle period, which would become notable for his study of Saturnian melancholy. I expected to learn a lot more about *that* during Dr Hatherleigh's tutorials.

I wasn't trying to bluff my way with the tutor. My interest in his art history option, at least as Francis and Jane had described it, was real, even if it had mixed roots. At sixth form, I did a little sketching and became curious about the technical challenges in Renaissance art, especially when I started to grapple with the problems of distance and perspective. As I read up on it, I soon found that the subject was a natural complement to my A-level studies in maths and even classical history. And then I found a connection to my English studies too, since there were often good visual clues to the many classical allusions in poetry and drama of the same period. But until I'd arrived at uni, I hadn't given any thought to exploring it further, even though I still had to sort out my free study option while wanting to avoid another English genre like the pastoralist tradition. That's when I bumped into Francis and Jane, eyeing me as I tried to make sense of all the nonsense in the Dürer print.

'You look completely puzzled by it,' Jane had said. 'Would you like to study it?'

'I'm not really sure,' I'd replied, as we moved closer to the sprawling work.

The whole woodcut extends twelve feet by ten. It imitates an imperial Roman arch with three gateways and a massive, decorated superstructure that rises, tier after tier, above each of them. No one could build it. And when you see it, you just want to shake your head, hardly knowing where to begin with the story it tries to tell, and which, I would soon learn, was an account of Maximilian's dynasty and life. Jane hopped from one mad panel to another, describing historical scenes, classical motifs, and, finally, a symbol from ancient Egypt that was stuck on to the front of the cupola. Francis, in a less flattering voice and an accent I couldn't quite pin down, scoffed at the underlying pretensions. It's quite dull, he complained. Colourless and scrawling dark print. And the hieroglyphics that Jane enthused about were all bogus, he'd said, invented by a charlatan in the late Roman period called Horus Apollo.

Jane was undeterred and then focused on the three walk-through portals that give a kind of presence to the arch. They represent the virtues of fame, honour and nobility, she'd declared. Francis shook his head, underscoring the gesture with a long, calculated yawn that earned him a friendly dig in the ribs from Jane. She pretended to be cross. 'Francis, please. Maximilian claimed descent from Osiris, the god of rebirth,' but even Jane couldn't help a smile flitting across her face.

I'd followed Francis and Jane to the nearby refectory. And while they'd ordered the sandwiches and coffee, I'd reflected on our chance encounter after checking my phone for messages. I was intrigued at how they talked so effortlessly about Dürer's woodcut. Jane like a tutor and Francis the laid-back critic, even if the work looked quite nuts to me. But as they discussed their studies telling me about their small, almost intimate, tutorial group, I wanted to rub my eyes. This was the academia I could feel at home in, or at least allow me to get back on my feet, after the disaster at Oxford. So, it wasn't long before the pastoralists slipped out of my mind like fading airs on some distant shepherds' flutes. And that's when Francis drew his map. And Jane said to make sure it was the Art History B course.

I'd told them not to worry if they couldn't get back to the exhibition by three. They'd wanted to hear how I got on with Hatherleigh, but had mentioned some other things that might keep them away. It didn't matter since we'd agreed to meet a few days later at a nearby pub, and I still had a few things to do myself, not the least being to complete enrolment after the morning's non-event at registration. If I didn't get that done, I wouldn't get to the student accommodation people for my appointment. And if that was the case, I'd be sleeping on somebody's floor for the night. Or going home prematurely.

I waved goodbye to Dürer and the exhibition in Senate House and headed off towards the registration desks at UCL. I had a ten-minute walk to the quad and my uni precincts.

'Are you lost?' A stranger, with his hair tied back in a ponytail, approached me with a friendly smile as I paused, suddenly, in the courtyard. He held a wad of loose papers close to his chest.

'I'm sorry …?'

'You seem distracted. Are you a new student at the university?'

'Yes. First day, actually.'

I'd stopped just after the gatehouse, puzzled by two small build-ings to my left and right. They had pepper-pot roofs and protruded from the ground like objects without a purpose. I must have missed them earlier in the day in my excitement to enrol. The stranger was anxious to enlighten me.

'Well, these very quaint buildings you see here,' he said, in a fastid-ious manner, 'were observatories. There was considerable interest in astronomy. In fact, we were the first secular university in the country.'

'Really?'

He stepped back. 'Vivien Weekes. Senior tutor. Department of History.'

Ready to slip away, I grinned apologetically, but looking more earnest, he reached forward and tugged my sleeve.

'Do you sing? We don't mind a little rustiness. We have a wonderful local choir.' He flashed the wad of papers at me. 'We're doing Walton. And his oratorio "Belshazzar's Feast". Do you know it by any chance?'

'No, I'm sorry. I'm doing English literature. I've got to register now.'

'Oh, well. Another time.' He thrust a leaflet at me with a sigh and breezed away as quickly as he'd appeared. I slipped the leaflet into a pocket, a little bemused by the encounter.

I crossed the quadrangle to the main building and entered by a side entrance. The next stage of admission was in the Old Refectory, which lay hidden behind the portico and a stone stairway that dominated the quad. A line of students tailed back to the South Cloisters. This was where I had started a few hours earlier, before dumping my bag and wandering off to Senate House and its exhibition of sixteenth-century drawings.

A steward, wearing a UCL T-shirt, checked that I'd brought some identification and then handed me a bag of freshers' week goodies. She said that the admission queue would take another hour or so, but less if the network came back up in the meantime. I took my place in the line and peeped into the bag. More leaflets and a discount voucher, I noticed, as well as a campus plan. And a list of must have apps for my phone that I briefly examined. I popped the tutor's leaflet in for company.

Student enrolment had ground to a halt earlier, prompting me, and others, to head off and find something else to do. Some kind of incident had happened overnight in the IT department, we'd been told, and the only update since was that the police were now present on site. A guy in the queue mentioned hackers and trojans as we waited. I didn't care—my mind was on other things, anyway.

The queue drifted forward, so I readied myself for registration. Like other new undergraduates, I had completed all the pre-enrolment activities during the summer. The next step was proof of identity, a bank transfer to cover the fees or, in my case, a letter of sponsorship from the student-finance people funding my three years of study. With that done, enrolment would be straightforward. Except, I had to explain Art History B, and the little matter of its non-existence or whatever Dr Hatherleigh was getting at when we met earlier. I reread the letter of introduction—it was difficult to make out the course code the tutor had scribbled on it—until a commotion ahead of me diverted my attention. A female academic was interrogating the line of students.

'Literature. English literature. I'm looking for two students,' she declared, as her gaze shifted along the queue. I made myself visible, ready for an introduction. The academic took the lead. 'Good afternoon. I am Dr Fisher. And you are?'

'Richard Addings, Dr Fisher.'

'Ah, Mr Addings, I think I missed you earlier. If you were here, that is. Your first day instructions were emailed to you last week. We were due to meet at twelve.' The tone was admonitory. It sounded like detention.

'Yes. I'm sorry. I've been having my own problems accessing emails. And then all the problems this morning.'

She looked at me, unsure of my reply. But then her tone relented. 'Well, our computers have been going up and down all summer, so I suppose it is possible that others are experiencing similar frustrations.' She studied her paperwork before returning to me. 'I see you have opted for my seminar course on Shakespeare's contemporaries. Do you have any leanings amongst this distinguished crowd?'

'The University Wits, Dr Fisher—the dramatists Greene, Lyly, Marlowe. And Thomas Kyd.'

'Interesting. But I'll only grant you Marlowe and Kyd from that group since the best of the other two are earlier, and if we discuss them, it's only as background. Perhaps you'd like to recall some other writers with whom you are familiar?'

My mind went blank, so I tried a different literary genre. 'The Metaphysical poets … like JD. I mean John Donne.'

'Well, I grant you the term *wit* is common to both your choices, Mr Addings.' I could sense a hint of sarcasm. She must think I'm showing off. 'What else have you read?'

'Songs and Sonnets.'

'Of course you have. You wouldn't be much of a metaphysician, otherwise.'

'The satires and the elegies,' I added. 'I did an essay at school.'

Dr Fisher made a note on her paperwork. 'Good. There's a lot of stimulating and complex material for seminar work. I did my doctoral dissertation on Mr Donne. In Canada. Where I'm from.' She looked again at the paperwork, freeing my attention.

The admissions staff had opted for a slimmed-down procedure that helped to speed things up, though my own situation might take a little longer since my free study choice was very much last minute. I looked around, half wishing that Francis or Jane would appear. Ahead of me was the IT guy and two more freshers. I checked the time and the progress of the queue. I had about forty minutes left to think of something to say about Hatherleigh's course and still make it to the housing office. But I wasn't off the hook with the English tutor.

'And what have you read of Herbert or Vaughan?'

'Sorry?'

'The divines, Richard, and such poems as "The Temple" or "The World". Donne had several successful imitators, you'll find.'

'Yes. George Herbert and Henry Vaughan,' I said. 'They're a bit later than Shakespeare, though.' I remembered how my A-level teacher at school had dedicated a whole week to the poetry of religious experience. Herbert was a friend of Donne, and Vaughan was a disciple to Herbert. My memory unloaded a few prominent poems to the tutor, though not always by the authors I attributed.

'There is much more, too. Start thinking about metaphors within the different poetic forms of Mr Donne. You might get your first assignment on this next week. If you are curious enough to check your email, that is.'

She studied the university paperwork again, shuffling the papers to show irritation with the makeshift arrangements. I wondered if she had quizzed all her students so briskly and whether this was what I could expect in her class. It felt a lot less cosy than art history. She set off in pursuit of the last of her wayward brood. Best of luck, I thought.

The ad hoc arrangements continued to work well. ID. Funding. And a new photo for my security pass. But then the administrator queried my free study option with her colleague. The course code being unreadable, she checked a printed copy of the academic catalogue. Nervously, I listened to their exchange. I decided to speak first. 'C-one-seven-three. It's part of the art history options.'

'Who is in charge of the programme?'

'I think it's Dr Arbetta. But I saw his colleague this morning. Dr Hatherleigh.' I referred again to the introduction letter.

Her colleague found an entry in the catalogue. 'It's Art History A. It should be an eight, not a three at the end.' And that was it. I was now a student at University College London. The rest of our exchange covered advice on the next library tours, information about the technology service desk and various undergraduate support services, plus a reminder to complete full IT registration once the system was back up and running. We concluded with a perfunctory smile and a good luck with my studies before they mentioned the student society reps outside in a temporary marquee in the quad for the freshers' fair.

I was about to check out the societies when I heard a voice call my name. It was a guy called Josh. I'd spoken to him briefly just before the computers went down. Like me, he'd headed off from the confusion, opting to register—in his case—on an engineering course, once things were better under control.

'Just registered.' I waved a leaflet on sexual health as a token of admission.

He eased his headphones around his neck. 'Did you sort out your study options, then?'

'Yep,' I boasted. 'Courses all sorted, but I got a real grilling by one of my tutors.'

'So, what are you doing?' Josh asked.

'English lit. Sixteenth-century writers to start with. I'm also doing something on art history.'

'You mean painting and landscapes?'

'Yeah. It's supposed to help with the literature. Covers lots of Renaissance themes. Background stuff like the classics, bits of early science. And the black arts, it seems, though I'm supposed to keep quiet about that.'

'Listen, I'm looking for my girlfriend. She's called Sophie. She's studying economics.'

He took out his phone and showed me a photo of them both on a recent summer fling. They were laughing, carefree, on an Aegean island, I reckoned, with arms around each other. She was pretty, I thought. Shoulder-length hair and flashy sunglasses that matched her lively, suntanned face. Lucky guy.

'She said she'd be upstairs in the main library, but when I got there, it was crawling with police. I wasn't allowed in.'

'In the library?'

'Yeah. They told me to come back later. I tried to call her, but her phone must be off.' He made an affectionate grin at the photo before returning the phone to his pocket. 'So, if you see her, I'm at the squash court in our hall.'

'OK. Give me your number.'

We exchanged numbers before Josh sauntered off, though I wasn't sure I'd be of much help if I asked around. But I tried to remember her face.

I still had a bit of time before my appointment, so I wandered over to the student society tables in the marquee where I enjoyed a free cup of coffee and a dried-out veggie sandwich. There was more information on freshers' week events, including campus gigs, club nights, and a boat party on the Thames. The best deal was to get a discounted pass and go to the lot. If you could drink that much. I was given a sprinted update on the political scene, ongoing causes, social media contact pages, and the need for action and engagement. It was the right moment to ask about the accommodation office before the conversation got a bit too deep for me. 'Oh, it's not far,' said my friendly activist. 'Just off the campus in Malet Street. But hurry, it can be a hassle if they screw up.'

'Thanks,' I said, and slipped away.

My repeated applications for a room near the central campus had failed. There were several halls of residence in the immediate vicinity, some in elegant terrace buildings—after all, this was Bloomsbury. In a mixture of hope and desperation, I'd applied to each one of them, but with no success. Instead, I had been asked to attend an interview with a housing adviser. I retrieved my bag from the Cloisters and hurried to the accommodation office with as much haste as its bloated condition would allow. And then, with one final effort, launched myself up the stairs to the fourth-floor reception.

I'd saved enough breath for a cry of help.

'Hi. I'm Richard Addings. Completely homeless, I'm afraid.' My bag fell to the floor, though I still hoped I had cause to be cheerful.

A young lady turned towards me. 'Sorry, we're just getting the system back. We'll get you sorted before we close.' She smiled before turning to her colleagues who were whispering to each other while staring at their screens. There was a look of consternation on their faces.

I settled into a plastic-moulded chair with my bag alongside me. A low-level table to my left contained a scattering of brochures showered with young, happy faces. So long as I had somewhere decent to stay, and maybe not too far away, I was pretty sure I'd soon be sharing their mood. I didn't know why I'd been overlooked since neither Josh nor his girlfriend seemed to have had any problems getting rooms. I picked up a brochure and flipped through the photos. Degree awards and graduation. Where would I be in three years from now? Working or studying? Travelling? New mates? Maybe even a partner?

I glanced around. Another ten minutes before the housing staff cleared off for the day. I still had my fingers crossed, but checked the time with dwindling confidence. I wondered again at those smiley faces amidst a more acerbic turn of thought. Then the lady who had spoken fleetingly when I arrived broke away and crossed towards me. She had a list of names in her hand, but was shaking her head as she approached. I stood up, fearing the worst.

'I don't know why you're not in one of the student halls. You are a first-year undergraduate, aren't you?'

'Yep, English literature. I thought a room in Bloomsbury sounded cool. You know, with all the literary associations.' I was still eking out my ration of cheerfulness.

'Well, there are usually hundreds of rooms in the accommodation blocks, but I'm afraid you're not even on the waiting list, Richard. So, it won't be Bloomsbury.'

Great. So much for Virginia Woolf. 'Okay. Is there anywhere else? Otherwise, I'll have to phone home.' I was feeling pissed off already.

'I'll talk to my colleague. He handles the other London locations.'

'Thanks, I'm sure I can wait.' I sat down again.

I was tempted to land my feet on the glossy magazines, but then thought better of it. Three of her colleagues got up to leave and appeared to share my lack of humour. As they slipped past me, someone mentioned a meeting called by the vice-chancellor.

The day was losing its friendly lustre. It had gone well to begin with. Option sorted out, a good brush with my English tutor, and even new friends. But now … nowhere to live. So maybe this was the flip side to the day's good fortune. I was resigned to calling home when the young lady's colleague, a much older, heavier-looking guy, threw me a lifeline. There was a buzz about him that appeared to be at odds with the conversation I feared I would have.

'Do you know where Drury Lane is?'

'No.'

'All right, do you know your way around Holborn?'

'Not really,' I confessed.

'Well, have you ever heard of Covent Garden?' His voice rose as if he might need to explain north and south to me as well.

'Yes, of course.'

'Well, you're just around the corner. The piazza will be like a backyard, mate.' He glanced towards the young lady. 'I'll take him there, Sandra. Should be back within the hour.' He turned to the door. 'Come on, grab your bag, young man. Someone's paid for your taxi.'

5

We jumped into a waiting black cab.

Frankly, I didn't care who'd paid for the taxi. And if it had been the price for a room near Covent Garden, I would have found the money myself. We raced down Gower Street and past Bedford Square, and then weaved our way through the maze of one-way streets that make up this odd, varied patch of nineteenth-century London. I clung on as we worked through all points of the compass.

It took fifteen minutes to arrive at an old block of flats, close to the Strand in the centre of London. It stood three storeys high and comprised several self-contained flats that overlooked a bare, charmless courtyard steeped mostly in shade. And yet the block was solid-looking, and for some would once have been a step-up in the world. A reconditioned plaque mentioned its construction as part of a social improvement project some ninety years before. The university housing trust now owned it.

'They're just right for students. You're a lucky guy, getting this address. Usually, they're for third-years or post-grads.'

I wasn't going to argue. Covent Garden was a two-minute walk from my room.

The accommodation adviser had introduced himself as Eddie. He knew the area well as he'd grown up in the streets nearby as a kid and pointed out old haunts as we jerked around inside the cab. ''Course in them days ...' he said (more than once), 'they still had the old fruit and veg market but like many families they'd moved on after the market closed and local rents got too high.' He still missed it.

Eddie paid the driver with three crisp twenty-pound notes he removed from a buff-coloured envelope amidst a clutch of other papers in his hand. Someone had written my name on it. There was no change, Eddie turning aside as if the payment had been prearranged. It was a lot for a short journey, even with the allure of the West End. But no matter, I wasn't paying.

We crossed the courtyard and made for a common entrance that served the flats. A faded sign, high against a wall, insisted *No ball games allowed,* though the open space was now bereft of any noisy youngsters. Eddie flashed a keycard at the security panel and we both stepped inside to the ground-level hallway. The stairwell rose to my left, where small, external windows were set midway between the floors. A weak, natural light filled the adjacent hall while low-voltage light bulbs hung ready to combat the hours of darkness. It made the paintwork of the wooden doors and skirting look heavy and dull. The air was still and stale.

'There's no lift, I'm afraid.' We turned towards the steps and a stone surface worn by generations of acquiescent feet. I lifted my bag, holding it in both arms, and marched up behind him. But Eddie wasn't racing away. He grabbed the wooden banister, careful to manage his own ascent. 'Your flat is one of two up at the top. There's only one on the ground, and a utility for washing clothes.'

We paused on the first floor. Eddie took a breath. There were two students on this floor, he said. One of them studied public administration and the other something to do with law or economics, but he couldn't really remember. We clambered up. The guy on the second floor was also a third year, but was doing history. That's where I'd find the wireless router for the block. The other flat was unoccupied.

I asked about overnight visitors. Friends. Girls, even. 'Just don't turn it into a harem,' he said, flitting his eyes. There were rules about guests, he added, but with no regular warden on site … But then he mentioned the guy in the flat next to mine.

'He's a post-grad. Psychology. You know, all that funny mind stuff. Pretty sharp though, when it comes to the university rules.' Eddie drew a deeper breath as we reached the top of the stairs. And then in a quieter voice, 'If you ask me, I'd say he's a bit of a loner. Don't think you'll see him much.' Eddie opened the door to my flat, handing me the room key and the security card for the common entrance. 'This is it, young man. Better make yourself at home.'

The flat comprised a bed-cum-sitting room with a small, modern-looking kitchen alongside, and a decent shower with a loo. A window provided a flood of light compared to the dreary hall and stairs we'd just climbed. I nodded, satisfied by the newly decorated walls, the high ceiling, and the extra sense of space. And a bookshelf, I noted, deep enough for any art history fanatic. A retro-style radio sat on its own, ready to bare its soul or gossip aimlessly.

Eddie gave me a checklist of items to sign for. I scanned it, noting some other things I hadn't seen or had overlooked in the cursory inspection. There was a microwave and a fridge. A study desk by the window, new bed linen, and a vacuum cleaner in the utility room shared with the other floors. I'd find a mailbox for the flat on the ground floor for all the rubbish that came through the letterbox. It all sounded fine to me, and I couldn't think of anything else to ask about. Not even my good fortune.

Having signed off the checklist, there was the residential agreement to complete. I filled out the sections on my degree course and student ID before handing it back. Eddie donned a strong pair of glasses and checked the details.

'So, you plan to spend three years studying books and paintings?'

'And a few other things, I hope.'

'That'll cost you.'

'The albatross of debt,' I moaned. Next came the direct debit for the accommodation.

'And then, when you're done with studying. What then?'

'Not sure. Have to get a job, I suppose.'

Eddie took the signed papers and placed them into the empty envelope. He glanced around as if memorising details of my room. He turned back to me. 'When I was your age, most students wanted to change the world. 'Course, in them days you never had to pay for your studies.'

'But many more of us are studying now,' I said, lifting my bag on to the bed.

'I know. And we can't seem to fit you all in the halls on campus. But you haven't done too badly.'

Eddie moved towards the door and, as he had shown me in, I now showed him out. It was like crossing a threshold. But before he left, a final thought occurred to me. 'The chaos this morning, with all the computers going down …'

'Yeah. It was a bit of a shock.' Eddie looked drawn.

I stepped back, puzzled by his remark.

'Best check your email for any updates. I don't want to gossip.' Eddie stepped into the hall but then turned back as if there was something more to add. 'Nearly forgot. If you have a problem with any of the fittings, or the washing machine downstairs, it's better to talk to the guys on the first floor rather than the history or psychology students. Otherwise contact the housing office. Good luck with your studies.'

He hurried down to the ground floor, holding his reading glasses and the envelope in his hand. I heard the main door close with a hard, unruly bang that sent a shudder up the floors. The rest of the house stayed silent. For now, I was alone. I closed my door and looked around the room. Empty shelves, empty drawers. I felt I was trespassing in a kind of unfamiliar space. Like a shadow fearing to fall. But enough, I thought. I had to unpack and settle in.

My bag, with a little resistance, held all the clothes, books, and gadgets I wanted for my first week at university. Mum had fretted that it still didn't seem big enough for a whole new world of experience, reminding me of the things I'd taken for granted at home while inserting fond reminders in my bag lest I somehow forgot where I even lived. 'But I'm not gone for good,' I'd said. 'I'm less than an hour away by train. And there are shops. And I can cook the basics.' But I agreed anyway to phone her and my little sister when I had the time. And that reassured her. I think.

I started to unpack. Clothes, sports stuff, laptop, an old set of headphones, toiletries, and a razor I now used twice a week. I found a home for everything, determined to dispel the odd feeling of detachment about the place. That left the shelves. I'd resisted the temptation to bring too many books with me, selecting just a few old favourites and those on the reading list for my course. They formed an uneven bedrock at the bottom of the bag. The first out was Ovid's 'Metamorphosis'. If you had to choose one classical source for Elizabethan drama and poetry, that was it—though I wondered what Hatherleigh might think of the modern translation. There were two books on metaphysical poetry, an anthology of John Donne's poetry, the 'Iliad', a novel I'd started but hadn't finished, and then another anthology of poems that took me by surprise. I wondered why I'd packed it. 'Selected Poems' by T. S. Eliot. It had been a peace offering by my maths teacher before I'd finished up at school. We'd had some lively discussions on algebra and poetry in class, not always seeing eye-to-eye. I sat on the bed and flipped through a few familiar poems. 'The Waste Land'. 'The Hollow Men'. 'Prufrock'. Eliot's lines could sound pretty cool, I remembered. At least when they weren't so obscure. And always something more below the surface. Ovid, too, got a plug in 'The Waste Land' and the grim tale of the young Philomela. Her violation. Mutilation. And a sister's revenge. Myths seem to serve a sorry purpose in the arts, mimicking the world's wantonness and pride. 'A mirror to ourselves', as my English teacher liked to say. And a warning. I'd heard 'The Hollow Men' before I ever read it in a film clip from 'Apocalypse Now'. And once was enough. My mind drifted back. We'd all left the cinema subdued. The horror still lingered. And then 'Prufrock'. I should learn it by heart, my teacher declared. As a punishment. For my obstinacy. I didn't, but some lines stayed with me … 'the muttering retreats, of restless nights'. I lifted my eyes from the page. And 'do I dare?' I put the book aside. The silence was making me pensive. I moved to the window and looked down at the street below. People coming and going. Some holding hands.

My phone buzzed, rescuing my mood. It was Dad, eager to talk. 'Yep!' I said. 'Everything's fine.' A new start, Dad. Not like Oxford. And tell Mum I wore my jacket and that I've sorted out my free study option and have a place to live. Covent Garden. Do you remember the theatre we went to? Oh, and thanks for the extra cash. I'll need it for freshers' week. Yeah, there are gigs and events on every day. It's going to be busy. Not sure I'll have time to study. No, only joking. And I met my tutor. Actually, I've met them both. Art history. Completely different characters. Oh, guess what? A guy with a ponytail asked me to join a choir. He's doing a composer called Walton. Yeah, I think so. But you never know, Dad. There's a lot to learn.

Dad sounded relieved. But added that he, too, might have to start anew. I'd stayed silent as he talked about his work, but he promised to ring at the weekend if there was any more news. 'And take care, son,' he'd said before ending the call. I tossed the phone on to the bed. Mum was right about the bag. I'd need more clothes after freshers. And I needed to get something to eat. Like now. And for tomorrow morning.

I wrote a short shopping list, itemising a few essentials plus a few cans of beer. I checked the size of the fridge, the kitchen cupboards. Tested the microwave. Turned on the shower. Getting to grips with regular domestic routines was now part of landing on my feet. Dad would agree. And the other guys in the block must have managed it already. I listened again for any stray sounds. Nothing. But maybe I'd see a light on when I headed down the stairs.

I was about to leave when I remembered the router. I powered up my laptop. With the IT issues sorted, I was soon on the university website. Eddie had mentioned an email, so I refreshed my inbox. A stack of ten messages lined up. Three over a week old. Several were from the admin team, including the accommodation halls. I already knew what they'd have to say. Nothing from anyone else, though. I waited, and then hit the update button again. And then again, thinking of the long faces back in the housing office. The update paused. A message from the vice-chancellor's office appeared. *To all students and staff*, it declared, in a dark, standout font. I read it slowly and with a sense of unease. There had been an incident in the IT department during the early hours of the morning. An employee of the university had died. The police were investigating the matter and next of kin had been informed. I stood up, unsettled by the news. In my head, an odd, echoing rhyme mocked the unhappy words. 'Here we go round the mulberry bush, the mulberry bush…. on a cold and frosty morning.'

I grabbed my jacket and hurried out. The day, I reckoned, had been ill-starred after all.

6

The Committee on Historical Matters was known only to a small circle of officials in Whitehall, London, and to their distant counterparts in Washington, DC. The most recent audit, by the British Foreign Office, had said little about the committee's plans and had stayed coy about its operational past, noting just a few treaties, an occasional conference and a solitary royal visit as evidence of its continuity since 1912.

An interest by the White House in 1947 led to US collaboration and a reorganisation of the committee's brief on a co-managed basis. It played a small part in post-war agreements between the British and American governments, often as a harmless-sounding codicil to matters of more economic consequence. But the intensification of the Cold War eclipsed its work, and the Space Age shifted ambitions to different frontiers. The Kennedy Administration ignored it. It had no bearing on Vietnam, China, or the Middle East. It drifted into obscurity, with officers on its American side drawn from foreign-relations committees or from military and intelligence staff who'd already served more conspicuous assignments elsewhere. The renewed attention of Pennsylvania Avenue was, therefore, something of a surprise to the Whitehall authorities, and, for James, an unwelcome anxiety as he prepared to meet his visitors in the same room that William had not long vacated.

James and Felix stepped forward as the two American gentlemen, dressed in almost matching dark-blue Brooks Brothers suits, entered the room. After a nod from James, Felix led the party to the table.

James closed the door before joining the others. He watched as his new colleagues settled in, deploying laptops, phones, and pens alongside two copies of a report stamped with the sharp-eyed American eagle. Warren Dudley, he noted, was the shorter of the two. A little overweight with straight, thinning hair pushed back across his scalp, and, in his early sixties, twice the age of Larry Antony. James studied the older man's face. Hardened, he fancied, by tough political campaigns. William's grin came back to him. The 'end times', remember. And he knows the president.

James shifted his eyes, catching Larry Antony unawares in his sight. A college guy, with hair trimmed neatly. Physically larger. Controlled posture—tense, even. With alert, anxious eyes. The FO briefing had said more. Maths and cryptography. The usual background on family and friends. A difficult schooling. Nothing, though, about a church. Or a fundamentalist leaning. James watched as Larry drew an arm across his laptop, causing a pen, caught by the sleeve of his jacket, to roll to the floor before he reached down, and retrieved it without comment.

A polite cough by James drew everyone's attention. 'I could arrange for refreshments, gentlemen. Coffee and sandwiches per-haps—it is a little late for lunch, I fear.'

'No. That won't be necessary.' Warren gestured to the bottled water on the table. 'This'll be fine. We have another engagement later. In town.' He turned to his colleague. 'Once we're finished here.' Warren picked up the reports and squared the edges on the table.

'As you wish,' replied James, turning to his left. 'In that case, Felix, would you start the video-recording? Once we are live, I will con-firm the attendees' names and status.'

Warren's stare sharpened. 'I think in the circumstances that won't be necessary. These are matters of great sensitivity for my government.' His attention switched to Felix. 'My brief, young man, is direct from the State Department. You do understand my position?'

Felix retreated, turning to his boss for guidance.

'Forgive me,' said James, affecting surprise. 'But it is an established protocol, Mr Dudley.'

Warren stared at the control panel. 'Carter said nothing about this.'

'Really?' James's eyes widened. 'And yet I believe both sides have benefited … from a verbatim record.' He smiled, letting his hands hover over the briefing paper as if unsure how to proceed.

Warren glowered. He turned to Larry. 'The hell do we need any reminders from the UK government.' He reached for his phone. 'We need Washington to sort this out.' He locked eyes with James.

James pursed his lips and, after a short, deliberate pause, slid his chair back from the table. Felix swallowed as James gripped the arm rests, ready to rise.

Larry turned to his boss. 'Maybe I can write-up … a summary, guys. Like something between ourselves … If that kind of helps everyone.'

'Perfect,' declared James, amidst an icy silence. 'A written summary, then.' He pulled his chair forward. 'Felix, would you please assist Mr Antony with the note taking? I'm sure Mr Dudley would like us to begin as soon as possible.'

Felix nodded.

Warren Dudley looked down at the bald eagle, heading the first page. 'This report, gentlemen, concerns one of London's academic institutions.' A temper leant an edge to his words. 'It has shocked the secretary of state. And it has caused the president much misgiving about the British connection.' Warren shifted the report to the centre of the table. He leant forward, resting on his arms. 'Our analysis shows that a small group of students, assisted by the academic staff, have uncovered information that poses a threat to

America's destiny.' He reached for the bottle of water and filled his glass. 'I am talking, sir, of an existential danger to the world if they are allowed to exploit their discovery.' Warren paused as Felix completed his notes.

Felix looked up.

'I see,' said James, glancing at his colleague's words.

Warren drank from his glass. 'The secretary of state has agreed to let me share an important confidence on this matter with your government, James.' Warren lowered his eyes. He placed his hands together. 'It is our belief, gentlemen, that this information relates to an event in North America … an event that occurred during the outset to your country's colonial times.'

'You mean before 1783?' asked Felix, looking around the table.

'Long before,' answered Larry with a grin.

James eased back from the table, recalling for a moment what he knew of this elusive event himself. An intrepid journey long ago. A date clouded in mystery. A longitude and latitude that marked the birthplace of the modern world like a coordinate in an astrologer's chart. The very secret that he and William had pursued across the frozen Baltic all those years ago. He glanced once more at the report, pausing for a moment to choose his words. 'I am surprised,' James declared, 'very surprised, that Mr Carter has shared none of these concerns with me.'

Felix winced.

'Carter was not doing his job!' Warren slammed his hands on the table. 'The CIA is blind to these people, blind I tell you.' He took the report and lifted it in the air. 'We have Larry and his team of analysts to thank for identifying this group. The UK government *must* take this seriously, James. Our futures are at stake.' Warren thrust the report at James, his face reddening as he glared across the table.

James retrieved the report. For a moment, he was disinclined to speak as he chafed at Warren's rebuke. The swift retreat of William had left him exposed. Warren would expect more cooperation from Whitehall. There were legal issues to consider, and questions about the latest intelligence. James snatched a glance around the table. Warren, he could see, had reached once more for his phone.

'I think your analysis on this matter will cause great interest in government circles, Mr Dudley.' Warren turned to Larry as James reflected on his words. 'I accept … that the situation has become … more pressing.' James swallowed but, with more urgency in his voice, turned to his colleague. 'Felix, would you underline my concerns, please? In the record. This report must be discussed with the foreign secretary.' He turned to the younger American. 'We are in your debt, Mr Antony.'

Larry Antony acknowledged the compliment with a smile. He reached for the bottle of water.

James turned to the summary at the beginning of the report. 'I see a mention here of a connection with the Bank of England.'

'Yeah. Just come on the radar,' said Larry. 'He's an old guy. Specialises in rare books. Has links with other contacts in northern Europe as well as the London students.'

'Books, you say … and European contacts.' James looked up from the page. 'He may well be an outpost of the Karlstad ring,' he added, conscious that he was raising expectations in the room. He turned to Felix. 'Release the documents we have on this Scandinavian operation to Mr Antony. It's the very least we can do in the circumstances. I will clear it with the Cabinet Office.'

The Americans exchanged glances.

'I'd sure appreciate any information that you guys have on that network,' said Larry, shifting forward in his chair. 'Their coded transmissions reference some pretty unusual texts when constructing messages. Oftentimes, I feel I'm wading through the whole of Western literature, trying to match a key to the encryption.'

James picked up the observation. 'Felix, you've done some work with our experts regarding this group.'

'Yes, GCHQ.' Felix glanced down at the report. 'The cypher alphabets are right shifted against the standard set of letters by inserting keywords from a literary text. This realigns the letters into new matching pairs. It's quite primitive compared with modern algorithms.' Felix looked at Larry. 'And easily decipherable.'

Larry shrugged, flipping his pen back and forth between his fingers.

'And there's no pattern in their choice of keywords. Just the occasional clue regarding the literary preferences of whoever is constructing the code.'

'You seem to have a handle on this literature stuff,' said Larry.

'Yes.' Felix paused, turning to his boss. James nodded. 'They are especially fond of English Renaissance texts when choosing keywords. We've identified lines from Shakespeare and others, and verses from the Bible.' Felix paused. 'The Psalms are a great favourite.'

'Crazy guys,' muttered Larry, still holding the pen.

'But a real difficulty,' continued Felix, 'is that many of these texts are not yet digitalised. This hampers our work. Though a feel for a writer's interests and friends can help when we are trying to narrow down their sources. And,' he joked, 'and expertise in dead languages as well.'

Larry shook his head, quietly amused. He placed the pen next to his laptop.

'Sorry, did I say something?' Felix's face paled.

'No, no. You're doing a fine job. Just reminded me of my time at cypher school.' Larry shifted back in his chair. 'I did my thesis on old Soviet signals traffic. Early Cold War code breaking. I'm a math major.' He smiled again before turning to his boss.

'Yes,' replied Felix, looking back at Larry. 'But other messages are more complex. And use multiple cyphers. Including one-time pads drawn from an agreed text.'

'Sounds just like the Soviets. As I said, you're doing a fine job.'

Felix looked away.

James helped himself to a glass of water. 'I will, of course, speak to the foreign secretary, but in the meantime, we shall assist as best we can.' James squared the report and placed it amongst his own papers. 'Felix will support from our side. Consistent with operational guidelines.'

Warren tapped his fingers on the table before reaching for his phone. He returned it to his pocket. 'James, I'd like to thank you for this response. It will reassure the secretary of state.' He shifted his gaze. 'And we'd like to welcome young Felix to the investigation. The Psalms are my favourite too.'

James handed his business card to Warren. 'I will need to confirm security clearances.'

Warren nodded. 'The embassy will send the usual affidavits, James.'

A final, nervous handshake concluded the meeting's business. James and Felix gathered their belongings and headed back to the Foreign Office in London's Whitehall, leaving the Americans to their own deliberations.

* * *

Larry closed his notebook. He checked his wristwatch. It was 5 p.m. The small conference room, he thought, was a little less stuffy now that the others had left. He refilled his glass from the bottle of water. But the meeting had gone okay … and the Brits … kind of lightweight. But the codebooks would help. At least their junior had cut a swathe through all that poetry crap. Larry lifted his glass and shot a glance to his boss. He'd made it to first base, at last. And with William Carter out of the way … He drank again, thinking of his favourite bourbon.

The old man stirred from his stooped position. He drafted a short note and slid it along the table, covering it with his hand.

Larry glanced towards the security console before reaching for the note. He paused before reading the content. The students' courier? it asked. Larry picked up his pen. He steadied his hand. The target had been identified, he wrote. The operation to eliminate him would follow. He slid the paper back to his boss and looked away.

7

The end of freshers' week saw the last of the induction events—a lecture outlining the English literature studies programme over the next three terms. I'd already opted for the Renaissance Literature module and another with a linguistic angle. Hatherleigh's course would have to fit in somehow, but with the emphasis on self-study and with my choices being fairly distinct, I reckoned I'd get by with the different workload.

The lecture finished a little after midday and, with a few chance companions, I had lunch in the refectory before heading off to my flat in Drury Lane. The weekend was at hand, and I was ready to wind down before catching up with Francis and Jane for a drink later in the evening—assuming they hadn't forgotten, since none of us had shared any phone numbers when we'd met a few days before. At three, I set out for Covent Garden, taking with me the handouts from the lecture and a book of poems. I'd have a lazy read in the sun. Snap the odd photo or just drift here and there, watching the street acts or browsing the stalls in the nineteenth-century arcades. I grabbed my jacket and phone. But before I left, I slipped a short note under my flat neighbour's door, and the history student's, saying hello, who I was, and see you around. I continued down the stairs and then out the main door of the block of flats. No ball games, I remembered.

'From Chaos came the goddesses, Night and Earth, and the god of Darkness.' The words broke above the lively bustle that animated the square. 'From Earth … Sky and Sea.' A young man, posing like an ancient god, called out his lines in some wandering street theatre. Curious at the activity, I sauntered over.

The actors had drawn a small crowd of onlookers in front of the local parish church called St Paul's, known for its association with theatre land. It was a classy choice, with the portico and columns working as a backdrop to their tale. The pagan god continued: 'And then came the great race of Titans. Castrating the Sky. And seducing the Sea.' We edged back as his friends rose to their feet, looking kind of proud and invincible. 'Saturn,' he proclaimed, with his arms held high and his gaze skyward, 'ruled supreme.' Nervous laughter filtered through the rest of us as the sun dazzled our eyes.

The tempo changed, and the young man's voice became more anxious. 'And then rebellion flared. The War in Heaven raged. And the Titans fell.' Another guy, a younger lad, brandishing a large wooden scythe, plodded wearily in front of the crowd. A fleeting shadow swept across our heads and sunlit faces.

I knew the story from school. Hesiod's Golden Age had ended; the Age of Iron had rudely begun. Only the hardy and the cunning could survive its onslaught. It was a favourite theme with my English literature teacher during my sixth-form studies at school.

The Greek poet Hesiod's 'Golden Age', he'd explain, was a metaphor for a lost world. It constituted the perfect, uncorrupted existence, and with its end, a new and fragile start. As a foundation myth, it underpinned the grim realities of life and the vague promise of good times to come in nearly every political culture—our modern world, he reckoned, being no exception.

As for the loss of innocence, I couldn't recall all the discussions we'd had at school about that, at least not the political aspects of its loss. But sometimes, they'd arise from a clever allusion in the line of a poem. Other times, I'd stay silent, puzzling instead over stress patterns and rhyme schemes in the text while ignoring things more profound as the conversation broadened. But I think we all reflected on our teacher's flashes of despair at the state of the world, even if I joked at his angst when safely out of his class.

Of my friends at school, I was close to three. We used to hang around together, and encourage each other's efforts and plans. I also did maths and classical history, which my English teacher claimed would help train a fine Renaissance mind. But only literature would teach us to think, he'd say, although we hardly ever discussed it with the other teaching staff. While I'd ended up studying in London, Simon and Becky had gone to study at Durham, where they were reading social sciences. In our last year at school, they were into Neuro-Linguistic Programming, and irritated the teacher with what he called 'facile contributions' to his class. Anna was brilliantly deductive. And when she freed herself from chemistry practicals, describing ominous-sounding substances she'd been blending, she'd still treat a poem to a 'scalding analysis'—our teacher's word—teasing us with interactions and explosive confrontations. It stirred emotions in me too and I often fancied her, hoping to see her at her college in Oxford once we had both settled in at uni. And I was … kind of back on my feet.

My maths teacher called me stubborn and vaguely idealistic. Ready to spurn the real world just to swan around the narcistic pools in academia. She would talk about probability functions and behavioural equations, and I would joke about the fate of the hero. Or the dilemma of a Prince Hamlet. Sometimes she'd call me flippant.

There was a lull as the street theatre rearranged its act. I checked my phone for messages and then skipped through a few items of news. There was nothing on the police at the uni or even the death mentioned in the email, so I headed to a first-floor café in the old market building that had a balcony overlooking the square below. Settling at an empty table by the balustrade, I ordered something simple to eat and drink. I decided to try some sketching, using a blank page from a handout that I'd picked up earlier in the day.

The balcony offered a good view of the church. St Paul's looked modestly grand in a plain but classical style. And its compact but imposing facade leant a quiet composure to the piazza. It would be an easy draw, and with the sun edging away, I did a quick outline of the building. But then I paused. Something I wasn't expecting caught my eye. Behind the columns supporting the portico, there appeared to be an entrance to the church. The architrave stood out boldly. But strangely, there was no door. Just a wall. And a commemorative plaque. And as I wondered, sipping my coffee, a sudden commotion in front of the church grabbed my attention.

A group of guys had pushed their way through the crowd towards the actors, shouting and jeering, until the onlookers fought back. A short scuffle was followed by a stand-off before the jeerers moved on, still gesturing and taunting as they left the square. The interruption lasted mere minutes, but in the confusion, I'd lost the inclination to draw.

'You are a student of the classical form?'

I turned, curious to see a stranger, a man of late-middle age, addressing me directly. 'Er no, not really,' I replied, trying to stem my surprise. His eyes shifted warily between my drawing and the street below. 'What I mean is that I have just started my own studies. At UCL.'

He smiled. 'The university. I too am very fond of books and learning.' He looked again at my sketch.

'I'm planning to read English literature. The Renaissance especially.' I placed the sketch alongside my book, as if to play down its attraction. I reached for my coffee.

He ignored my attempt to change the conversation. 'The pediment is a little disordered in your drawing, no?'

I acknowledged with a smile. It's only a sketch, I thought.

'The angle, I suggest, is stronger.'

'I was trying to catch the overall proportions. The Greek temple is nicely balanced. And harmonious. I used to draw them at school.'

'The pediment, yes. And the portico … perhaps. But the columns are of the Tuscan order rather than the Greek and are distinguished by their simplicity. In the myths, they are the gateway to Arcadia. To a lost innocence. And nature's gentle, ceaseless rhythms.' He paused as if reflecting on this idealised vision before adding, with more urgency, 'And in your studies of the Renaissance, do not neglect to read Alberti or Pacioli. You will surely learn the secrets of harmony.'

His gaze returned to the piazza—mine to the columns of the church. The actors, I noticed, had gone, leaving their discarded garments on a step.

'Maybe the gods should have fled into the temple,' I suggested, hoping to conclude the subject on a light-hearted note. His response was even more earnest.

'But not by the east. Behind the portico lies a bricked-up facade. And behind that, the altar. It is only from the west that you may enter the church.'

'I didn't know,' I replied, feeling less sure of my drawing and now wondering about the harmony. The bricked-up door only added to the confusion, I decided. But then a noise to my left interrupted my thoughts. Three guys, a little older than me, had camped themselves at a table alongside the balustrade, pushing the chairs aside to stretch their legs. I turned back to the old man, but he'd already gone. I'd meant to ask him about Alberti, or the other guy he'd mentioned. But it was time for me to leave anyway, so I folded my drawing, flicked a few crumbs of food from my fingers, and drained the rest of the coffee in my cup. I popped over to the till with my debit card.

'You had a slice of cake?'

'Yes, with the coffee,' I replied.

'Only one slice and one coffee?'

'Yep, only one of each.' I smiled, realising I hadn't spent much.

'But you were here awhile,' he said, studying my face.

'I would have left earlier … but for the disturbance in the piazza.'

'Ah, yes, the disturbance.'

As he spoke, I saw an old print fixed to the wall behind him. Drawn at a distance, it showed Covent Garden in a historical setting. The café owner noticed my interest.

'The print is by Mr Hollar. Mr Wenceslaus Hollar. 1647, I think it says.'

'Is that when the square was built?'

'The square was developed by Inigo Jones. A little earlier, I believe.'

Many things in the drawing had changed. But not the portico. At some point, the square must have been rebuilt but today's buildings echoed the original, and a bleak-looking Arcadia—the rustic garden of the stranger—was still there, hidden at the rear of the parish church.

'But you cannot enter by the east,' I declared.

He glanced at the print. 'Ah, the door. So, you know about the forbidden door.'

I smiled, as if sharing a secret. Yet the word *forbidden* intrigued me.

I settled the bill, still curious about the afternoon's encounters, but now ready to catch up with my friends. I'd left my jacket with my phone at the table, though it hadn't deterred the three other guys from spreading out after I'd gone off to pay. One of them was thumbing through the book I'd left behind, too. Some lines had caught his attention, and, surprising his pals, he rose to his feet as I returned to the table. He read and sneered at the words as I waited, trying not to look annoyed. '"Blasted with sighs and surrounded with tears. Hither I come to seek the spring ..."' He whimpered extravagantly to the amusement of his mates. I recognised the poem, but then he stumbled on the words before skipping ahead and looking at me sharply. '"But O, self-traitor, I do bring the spider love."' And in a lower voice declared, '"And that this place may thoroughly be thought, True paradise I have the serpent brought.'" His friends laughed, and he took a bow at my expense.

A few tribal gestures rounded off the performance before the guy clowning around asked. 'Do you understand this stuff?'

'Well, kind of. They're poems, guys, by John Donne. And I'm a student. Donne's part of my course. Look, I need the book for my class.'

'So, what's your name, then?' he said, hanging on to the poems.

'Would you give me the book, please? I need to go.'

'What's your name?' He turned to his friends. 'The pretty boy hasn't got a name, guys.'

'My name is Richard. And I need it for my studies. Please.'

'Please …' he mimicked, waving the book at me like a treat for a dog. He turned to his pals. 'The pretty boy's holding back.' He waved it again. Our eyes locked.

I would have turned away, but he thrust the book back at me. The other jerks were still laughing.

I grabbed my jacket, checked that I still had my phone, and went back to the short flight of stairs by the till. At the top of the steps, I paused and turned to the café owner. 'The man, the stranger?' I asked. 'The one who came to my table and spoke to me. Who was he?'

The owner shook his head. 'He works in the City. That's all I know.' And so I left just as another young guy hurried down the stairs ahead of me, hiding his face under a hood.

I stepped out into the street, only a few yards from the church and its implacable-looking portico. The mood was once more care-free and relaxed. Musicians had come back to the piazza, filling the spaces abandoned by the harmless troupe. A new crowd was ready to be coaxed and entertained. The sun shone. People laughed. And the old man was nowhere to be seen.

I headed off to meet Francis and Jane.

8

I found the pub alongside a narrow, low-roofed passageway that connected two quiet side streets a minute's walk from the Covent Garden piazza. It was a three-storey, redbrick building with plate-glass windows and pretty flower baskets that dangled from iron fixtures to the front of them. The pub was well known and added a splash of character to an otherwise drab, twisting alley that comprised the backsides of adjacent structures. I'd checked its website and read something of its history, including a bust-up between two rival poets in the late seventeenth-century. The affair didn't seem so improbable after my own awkward exchange earlier, so I slipped the collection of Donne's poems into a pocket and out of harm's way. I heard Jane's voice as I entered a traditional-looking and fairly busy bar. It was a little after 5 p.m. and I was ready for a few friendly beers.

My new friends were sitting at a table where the natural light ceded to the duller glow of the internal lighting. Francis was writing numbers in the boxes of a grid he'd drawn on a blank sheet of paper. I found a chair opposite the bench they were sitting on and cast an eye over his handiwork. Interesting, magic squares, I thought. Hadn't seen them in a while.

'They're awfully nerdy, I know, but Hatherleigh teased us with them today,' explained Jane. 'Francis has already cracked two of them.'

Jane sneaked a smile as I, with another glance, caught a base-four and base-five square that had been neatly solved on the page.

I'd studied them as an amusement during my maths A-level classes but remembered how you either tired of them or became obsessed trying to solve them. The most perfect arrangements were called 'diabolic' for reasons I couldn't quite remember. 'I'm working on a six-square teaser,' explained Francis.

'You know there are lots of solutions,' I said.

'One'll do. I spent less than twenty minutes on the others. But the sequencing's not the same this time.'

As Francis wrestled with the combinations, I suggested a different approach. He didn't resist and slid the sheet of paper towards me. Relieved, he offered to buy a drink as well. 'We've got another friend joining us soon. We think you'll like him.'

Francis headed to the bar. I turned to Jane, curious about Hatherleigh's thoughts on the magic squares.

'Well, Richard, we were talking about beauty and harmony. And if they had a mathematical explanation. Like the Platonic solids. Or the sculptures of ancient Greece.'

I frowned. It sounded a bit of a leap. 'But don't we just make up our own minds about beauty, Jane?'

'And that is what Hatherleigh challenged us to say—whether we agreed it was innate to the human mind or whether it was an external property in nature. Like the colours of a rainbow or the perfection of a magic square.'

I glanced at Francis's work. The elegance couldn't be denied, but I wasn't convinced about the aesthetics. I thought of a gentle way out. 'Didn't someone like Aquinas reckon it was a spiritual thing, anyway?'

'And Aristotle. And Augustine.' Francis had returned with my pint and a packet of crisps, which he split open on the table for everyone to share. '"Poetics", Richard. And "The City of God",' he declared.

It was sufficient authority to bring the subject to a close, so I took off my jacket, found a pocket for the discarded brainteaser, and then handed the jacket to Jane. I mentioned the book in passing as she placed it on their own neat pile of clothes beside her. And then we all smiled at one another, conscious that we'd skipped a few preliminaries.

'Well, Richard, we're glad to see you.' Francis thrust out his hand.

'Pleased to be here.' We raised our glasses. 'But, you know, I worried you might have forgotten since I didn't get your phone numbers the other day.'

'Oh, that's because we don't have any,' explained Jane.

'You're kidding?'

'No. Hatherleigh calls them a "pestilence quite unsuited to the academic mind" and Francis and I can't abide them. We're shocked at how people see them as friends. That's why we have only a landline in our flat. It's much more civilised.'

I retreated, open-mouthed. Jane lifted a pocket diary from the table and placed it inside her handbag, underlining the point. 'So Hatherleigh wasn't joking about the noticeboard either?' I asked. But they missed my words as their attention fell on a sudden movement near the door. They were both smiling in anticipation.

'So, where's *my* pint, then?' a voice called from the doorway.

A guy with straight, longish hair, a two- or three-day-old shadowy beard, and hands thrust in his pockets made his way towards us, before looking comically miffed at the absence of a drink.

'You're late, so I had to hand it over,' said Francis as though I'd muscled in on the beer just a few minutes before.

But his friend shrugged. Pulled off a sweater that was part-zipped to the neck, found another free chair, and parked down beside me.

'Hi,' he said, grinning and lifting his head, 'I'm Alex. Alex Rowdesley.'

'Richard … Addings.' For a moment, I felt thrown by his buoyant manner. 'Are you studying with these guys?' I asked.

'Yep! All bloody night sometimes.' His eyes rolled as if there was much more to tell. But then his tone dropped. 'We sort of live the subject, Richard. The ground we're covering is very demanding. And our tutor is helping … with some fundamental research.' Alex stretched out his arms, finding space that a moment before had been at a premium. 'Isn't that right, guys?' He yawned while flicking a glance to the bar. Francis headed off once more as Alex turned to me. 'So how did this lot rope you in, then? It's a bit off the beaten track for most people.'

Jane interrupted. 'We met Richard at Senate House, Alex. On an enrolment day. There was an exhibition on Dürer and Da Vinci. And after talking, we suggested he see Dr Hatherleigh.'

Alex stayed still, waiting for my own words. I let go of the pint and edged closer. 'I'm doing English literature at UCL,' I explained, 'but actually, I'm interested in Renaissance concepts … you know, ideas about man and his relationship with the cosmos … the nature of reality …'

He frowned, before slipping into a friendlier grin. I paused, and we both laughed. Okay. I sounded a bit pompous. 'Alex, it's hard work digging away at poems full of obscurities and hidden meanings. And anyway, your Dr Hatherleigh seemed … more relaxed. Not in a mad rush. Not like the literature tutor I met on my English course. And I had a free-study option to sort out.' I reached for the crisps.

'You've made the right choice, Richard. I was just wondering at your innocent enthusiasm.' He glanced at Jane. 'But don't worry, mate. We'll look after you. And those deep insights.' Alex ran his hands through his hair and yawned again. Jane smiled at him before removing his sweater from the table.

Francis returned with the pint for Alex and another two bags of crisps, and a leftover lunch-time snack for himself that he'd scrounged from the bar before they'd got round to binning it.

Jane steered us back to the tutor as Alex took a thirsty gulp. 'Why don't we ask Richard about his visit to Dr Hatherleigh?'

I looked up. 'You were so right about the lift, Jane. What a racket.'

'You didn't get trapped, did you? It's really annoying when it breaks down.'

'No, not at all.' I brushed aside the danger, recalling only its Siren-like fury as it wound its way to Hatherleigh's floor. 'But he wasn't in his room when I got there.'

'Really? We tried to get in touch before you arrived. How disconcerting.'

'So, I entered. And, my god, the vast array of old books. Where do they all come from?' Jane flicked a glance at Francis. Alex smiled at my nerve. 'But then he found me, so I recalled your names. And I talked about the Dürer drawing. Just as you'd said.'

'Oh, he's passionate about them,' said Jane.

'Then he mentioned Euclid and two other guys. And then … some occult stuff. Which I said was new to me. But he seemed rather anxious, though … about his course and the uni.'

Francis cast a wary eye at Alex, stilling any remark that might pre-empt his own. 'And well done,' he said. 'I can see that you must have impressed him, Richard.' He leant closer, before continuing in a quieter voice. 'What we study is a kind of philosophical investigation, focusing on the origin of things.' He settled back, forsaking the confidential air. 'It was common amongst radical Renaissance thinkers, but hardly at all with the authorities or the church.'

'Or even tolerated.' Alex jumped in, making a slicing gesture across his throat.

Francis cringed. 'At various times, Richard, these groups either disbanded or went underground. But not everything was lost. And they concealed some of their discoveries in the more obscure texts and drawings of the period.'

I drank some beer, thinking of Hatherleigh's books.

'But sadly,' Jane said, 'not all of what we do, or study, is respected by modern opinion or the more tedious political fads.'

'And, I suppose that is why you call it "Art History B".' I sat back. Everyone smiled as if a little secret had now been lain bare.

Alex emptied his glass and offered to get another round. Francis and Jane, who seemed to prefer sipping red wine to drinking beer, declined the gesture. And so, while Alex was getting more for himself and for me, Jane described how Hatherleigh liked to run the tutorials, and Francis recalled their studies from earlier terms. Subjects such as Pythagoras, harmonics and astrology. They'd argued over free will and destiny. Memory and the nature of time. Other worlds. And even the essence of God.

'And that, Richard, is why we'll all burn at the stake.' Alex placed two beers on the table, as if readying me to douse the flames.

'But Alex,' I said, 'surely we have a right to study these things? If you want to understand the basis for modern ideas and scientific progress, don't we have to go back over Renaissance thinking? Even if some of it sounds a bit odd at times.'

'I didn't say it was odd.' Alex sipped his beer, leaving me scrambling for my words.

'Okay. So, we have to consider it on its own terms. I should have said that.' And I had to say it louder as the pub had got busier. We shuffled closer while Jane did her best with the clothes.

'And just when you think it's safe to pop your head out, down comes the hatchet.'

'Hatchet?'

'You can't bloody well study anything, Richard. Eventually, you'll upset someone. Politicians. Scientists. Fanatics. They all have precious rules to keep the rest of us in the dark, mate.' Alex took a defiant draught of beer. 'At least they weren't laughing when I ripped up one of their stupid posters today.'

'Alex, you didn't.' Jane spoke sharply.

'I did. Well, half of it. I wanted to annoy that fucking group of clowns who charge around the piazza as if they own it. They chased a bunch of actors from the front of the church this afternoon. You know who I mean.'

Jane looked at Francis. She wasn't smiling.

'You were in the piazza?' I asked.

Alex drew attention to a small cut high on his forehead. 'They have this demented thing about anyone who disagrees with them. They can't be normal.' Alex was ready to resume the fight but surprised us instead with a more mocking gesture: '"Thou shalt not suffer a witch to live", he said, intoning the words in a sinister sounding voice, and adding a reference to Exodus as an aside.

But Francis was unconvinced. 'Alex, it didn't say witches now, did it?'

'And mathematicians,' he added, looking po-faced at his friend.

'And art historians too, I suppose,' said Jane, still annoyed.

Alex shrugged. He reached for a crisp packet, spilling the last of the crumbs on to the table. He blew the crumbs towards Francis.

Alex's sudden humour dismayed both Francis and Jane, and I wondered if his behaviour was a deliberate tease. Jane tried to explain. 'Alex got himself into trouble with the university last year, so we are both a little annoyed, Richard.'

'I was banned for a term, Richard. Banned from lectures—even ones I never attended. All because I challenged an arrogant tutor to a public debate. Of course, he wasn't interested. "Presumptuous young man," he sneered.' Alex gestured with his hand as if taunting an away-team at a football game until stares from the adjacent table quietened him down. 'And then they came up with this stupid "ico" thing. I'd made them very sore.'

'Iconoclastic,' explained Francis wearily. 'It wasn't only favourite notions that you'd smashed, if you remember.'

'Yeah, there was that. A window, someone's ego, so what? I must have just dodged the flames, Richard.' Alex drew a slow, delicious mouthful of beer, still relishing the memory.

'Please.' Francis lifted his hands. 'Can we have an end to talk about burnings? We know how things will turn out. And what we have to do about it.'

It seemed a curious thing to say, and I had no idea what they were talking about, but it brought Alex's restlessness to a sudden halt. He leant towards me and suggested another drink. The rest of us hadn't yet finished our own, but I took it as a hint. He'd asked too for a different beer.

The frivolity had dissolved with Francis's rebuke. Yet for all the friendly chatter, I hardly knew the people I was buying drinks for. Some of the evening had been quite high brow and laced with allusions to things I wasn't privy to but allowed to overhear. Some secrets would have to wait, it appeared.

I glanced around. Their conversation was muted. And Alex was shaking his head. I heard Jane mention my name, and she looked anxious, but I lost the drift amidst competing calls for the barman's attention. I rattled off the order, though my quickly timed move triggered an angry stare from a guy at the other end of the bar. A little subdued, I headed back with Alex's drink to a heavy silence. Jane made the first move.

'Oh, we haven't asked Richard about his other studies. You must know lots of Elizabethan authors, Richard.' But Jane's curiosity sounded flat. Their minds, I could see, were on other things, and I wasn't sure that they had settled the disagreement between them. No matter, I played along with the pretence as we discussed the rise of the theatre, the bunch of writers called the University Wits, Shakespeare's contemporaries, the Metaphysicals, John Donne. They listened attentively, nodding even when I threw a feeble comment across their brows. And they must have known as they tossed classics and out-of-the way authors at me without pausing much to remember.

I was perplexed by this. And uncertain how I might prove my own credibility amidst their knowledge and learning. But then, they were older than me, with one or two years more study under their belts, even if Francis looked as fresh-faced as me with a near adolescent chin. He also had an occasional twitch that seemed to disrupt his concentration and cause him to drop his head forward, as if caught between thoughts. Jane, though, hardly noticed. And I wondered if they were together, even though she didn't pay Francis any more attention than Alex or me.

But then I felt a nudge. Alex had a question.

'Richard. Have you read a poem called "The Road Not Taken"? By Robert Frost.'

'You mean the American poet?'

'Yes. He spent over two years in England.' Alex stretched once more, leaning back in the chair. 'Before returning to the States, I believe.'

I shook my head. 'I don't really know much about American poems. But I remember reading "Hiawatha" once, when I was young. By Longfellow, I think. But not sure that helps. And we read "The Raven" in a class at school. And the "Masque of the Red Death". Now they're scary,' I quipped, glancing at Francis and Jane but losing Alex. He was in a more plaintive mood. I chose to be less frivolous. 'No, I'm sorry, Alex. Why do you ask?'

'Well, it isn't scary. At least not like Poe. The setting's autumnal: yellowed leaves, intimations of regret.' Alex indulged me with a smile. 'Readers find it oddly inspirational. Yet I'm inclined to think more of impulse and doubt.' His eyes fell back on his beer. 'I just wondered. That's all.'

'He's only teasing you, Richard.' Francis folded his arms.

'I'm not. Frost is a fine poet. And the poem's most striking metaphor is the fork in the road ...'

'The classic dilemma,' I said.

'Perhaps. I've often thought about it.'

'Maybe I should do the American module next year, Alex. You can guide me on the authors.'

Francis sniffed. 'I know more American authors than *he* does.'

Alex grinned. He clicked his fingers. 'You're really such a cool guy, Francis.'

'Alex. Please.' Jane slapped a twenty-pound note on to the table and told him to go to the bar. He rose without speaking; and as he ordered more drinks, I slipped off to the gents.

I'd heard so much this evening. Literature, art, philosophy even. And everyone so willing to help me. And how clever of Jane the way she'd handled the conversation, moving us from one topic to the next but not too pushily. She was clearly used to Alex and Francis and whatever else was going on. Francis, though, was less patient, and ready to draw the line. And nor was he shy of the sweeping statement, at least between mouthfuls of food. And Alex? Alex was different. One moment he'd have a laugh full of gestures and tease, but then he'd suddenly go quiet. Except for his trouble at uni and his confrontation in the square. Alex and Francis, I thought. There was obviously something needling them both. I wondered because, right now, in a warm, congenial haze, draining a pressing, but accommodating bladder, I wanted us all to be friends. And for a few unguarded moments, I relished a long, soothing yawn.

I zipped up and headed out of the gents for a last, inebriating pint. Suddenly, I fell back as I re-entered the bar. My shirt ripped as a hand gripped the collar around my neck. An angry face taunted me. 'Next time you want a drink, pisshead, just go to another fucking pub.' He turned to a mate, as if to alert him to the impact of a fist in my face. But it was Alex's hand that got there first. My assailant fell back, stunned by the swiftness of the blow.

Alex pushed between us. People shifted, afraid there'd be a fight. A shrill voice shouted from behind the bar, and our opponents retreated. 'Not this guy,' said his friend, pulling his partner, bloodied, through the door.

I'd frozen, feeling more shocked than angry or upset. Alex put his arm around my shoulder and led me to the table. 'They won't be back,' he said.

'What on earth happened, Richard?' asked Jane, looking alarmed by the commotion.

'I'm sorry. I must have upset someone at the bar when I got the drinks. But I'm okay.' I sat down, holding the front of my shirt in the absence of a couple of buttons.

'Well, there's no need to apologise. The bar is always chaotic at this time of night.' She looked at Alex. 'I think you'd better go next time,' she added, before a smile in my direction softened an edge to her words.

Francis nodded to Alex, pleased by what he'd seen.

We talked more, but fitfully and in lowered tones. The next tutorial, the department noticeboard, Ms Lopez and my reading card at the British Library, even my room in Drury Lane. It wasn't as lively as our earlier conversation, but it helped dissipate an awkward frustration. We didn't hurry the drinks, but after twenty minutes our glasses were clear.

It was after ten as we prepared to leave. Jane and Francis wanted to window shop in one of the arcades, and Alex and I agreed to catch up in the meantime. I put on my jacket, checked that my book and phone were still there, and waited for Alex as he made one last trip to the bar—the adrenalin, he explained, still teased his thirst. We left together, turning into an alley that had once witnessed a more celebrated fight. It had sounded like a good story when I'd first read it on the pub's website. John Dryden's satirical blows in a line of verse. The Earl of Rochester's paid thugs in reply. And an unseemly brawl that almost killed the Poet Laureate. Something for tutorials, I'd fancied. Now, I wasn't so sure.

We wandered along Floral Street, before turning right and then into Covent Garden's piazza. Shops in the old market building were winding down. Cafés ringing the last bills of the night. There'd been a brief shower of rain, and it was much cooler than earlier in the day. Alex had reclaimed his sweater, throwing it over his shoulders, the sleeves falling like floppy straw arms across his chest. We meandered around, sharing a beer, and for no particular reason, stalled in front of St Paul's Church, which brooded alone in the lamp-tinted light that suffused the square. I stared at its solid portico.

And what now of the day's drama? The upheaval. The dispersal. And Alex somehow mixed up in it. I looked around before fixing my eyes on the balustrade that overlooked the open space below. I turned to my friend, remembering my encounter with the old man. 'Alex, do you believe in somewhere like Arcadia? Somewhere … where everyone's happy.'

'And no one fights anymore?'

'Suppose so,' I added ruefully.

'Like a paradise on Earth. Ruled by the rustic Pan and his fun-loving friends.' He held out the can in a mischievous salutation. An elongated shadow fell on the cobbles beneath our feet.

'Well,' I said, not sure if he was taking the piss, 'that's the classical myth. At least, how the poets describe it.'

He returned the beer to his lips but hesitated whether to drink. 'If you ask Francis, my friend, he will tell you of infinite worlds. Each with its own destiny. So,'—he screwed his eyes, scanning the clouds above our heads—'one of them must be Arcadia.' He drank before turning to me. 'And beds of roses, and fragrant posies.'

Alex drifted towards the portico as I puzzled over his words. 'But we have only one world, Alex. This world. Where *we* make its future.'

'And do the poets say that too, Richard?' Alex scanned the church's wooden pediment perched thirty feet above the ground. 'I thought they were always railing against the stars, cursing their lot.'

'Sometimes.' I caught up alongside him. 'And sometimes they wonder if things can change. Through a word or a good example.'

'And is that what *you* believe?' Alex studied my face. I wondered if I had said something silly.

'You know, earlier today, an old guy told me a strange fact about the church.'

'You're going to tell me about the door. The forbidden door.'

'Yes,' I said, open-mouthed.

Alex drank again before offering me the can. I sipped, handing it back to him. 'Interesting, isn't it?' he added.

'But why? The old man said it was in the west. Where they traditionally are. So you can look east. To Jerusalem or something.'

'Well, someone forgot to tell Inigo. Or maybe he had another idea. That everyone should look west.'

'You mean St James' Park,' I mocked, 'or the setting sun?'

'Or Arcadia.' Alex was teasing me now as he grinned at the cleverness of the idea. 'The church is like a temple, Richard. A gateway to Arcadia.'

'A gateway? Hang on, that's what the old guy said to me, today. At least before he disappeared.'

'Well, there you are. Though the landscape doesn't look so verdant today.'

No. The piazza lay draped in a blank, urban grey under the ghostly veneer of electric street lighting. More rain threatened to chill its damp surface. 'I think you are right. Pan would be disappointed.'

We headed under the portico for cover and leant, slovenly, against a column that supported the pediment above. Alex handed the can back to me before a new impulse grabbed him. He jumped forward, landing his fists on the blocked-up doorway.

'Let us out of this mad world,' he cried. 'We demand conference with the gods. Francis has sent us.' I nearly choked on the dregs of beer. Alex turned to me. 'Richard, stand up. We'll argue our case with Pan. Let him judge if we are worthy to enter his domain.'

I couldn't resist. And in a fit, we beat the walled-up entrance oblivious to the noise that we were making or the spectacle we invoked, before sliding, like two intoxicated fauns, to a stone-slab floor and our own earthly dominion. We huddled closer.

Alex dropped his head. 'They say Pan is dead.'

'Who, Alex? Who says that?'

'The Christians, of course.'

'Oh Christ …' I crunched the beer can. 'The pagan god of music and drama?'

He nodded. 'Dead. Milton proclaimed it.'

Then we both looked up. Wide-eyed, with hands on her hips, Jane reared over us. She snatched the twisted can from my hand. 'This is a church,' she insisted. 'And it happens to be a public place.'

Alex stared at the ground, avoiding eye contact with Jane.

But Jane was not really angry, and her rebuke was more a show of irritation. Standing back, she shook her head and with a glum smile seemed to excuse my complicity. She headed back across the piazza, holding the empty can by her side. I wondered if she and Alex had been much closer in the past, such that each little hurt threatened to revive older wounds and check their carefree moods.

'Are you still fond of Jane?' I asked.

Alex stirred. He paused before answering. 'Yes. But it's been over for three months now.'

'And Francis?'

'No. Just friends. They share a flat near the British Museum. I used to stay there until we split. I've got my own pad now. A few stops on the Tube.' He stretched his legs along the ground. 'We still meet there, though. For our work.'

A trickle of blood rolled down the side of his face. He had thrown himself at the stone wall with abandon and had reopened the cut above his eyes. He wiped a thin smear of red on to his fingers. 'One of those … those morons in the square. It's why I'm feeling hyper this evening. I still want to get back at them.'

The portico shielded us from the gentle rain, and our slumped, adjacent bodies from the cooling, night air. I thought about the next few weeks. The rush of studies that would chase me. The assignments. My first English seminar in the middle of next week. I knew I could handle the literature. But this art history thing? Where should I begin? They'd wrapped up their lives in it. I looked at Alex. Still pensive. Staring out as if the world was no longer there. He turned his head and, looking at me with sad eyes, uttered a solitary line.

'"Will in us is overruled by fate…"'

I tried to break the spell. 'Alex, come on now. Who said that?'

'A poet. But I can't remember. Didn't I say they were an unhappy lot?' He fiddled with the strands of his hair.

I stood up and helped Alex to his feet. And like two chastened boys, we drifted back across the square. We joined Francis and Jane close to the last of the square's solo acts: a figure, frozen still, braving the elements in a stark, inanimate pose. It seemed a lonely and ironic way to make a living.

Francis and Jane said they'd walk back to their flat. They reminded me of the tutorial notices before slipping away. 'We don't use mobile phones, remember.' I grinned and looked at Alex. He had a final yawn, held his arm aloft in a friendly farewell, and turned towards the Tube. He'd slipped out of sight before my own hand had dropped to my side.

I headed home. What a day, I thought. And *what* a night.

9

Larry kept the kid waiting.

He'd warned him about reckless contact. And hell, at two thirty in the morning, the punk had a nerve.

It was his fourth bar of the evening, but he'd lost count of the Scotch. Nine or ten, maybe more. He drank again, but he'd need another before heading out. 'Make it double, Carlo, something American. Got to tramp these friggin' London streets.' He checked the time. 2.38 a.m. What the fuck, he'd hung round bars till four or five in the morning back home with the guys, soaking up beers and chasing pussy. He shifted his weight on the stool. His left foot slipped to the floor. Jeez, the kid has a nerve. A fuckin' nerve. Larry slapped a twenty-pound note on the bar and reached for his phone.

Carlo poured the drink and turned aside.

Three texts from the kid. One-liners. Larry sent a return. *Same place, asshole.* He threw the whiskey down his throat. 'Adios, Carlo.' He headed out of the basement bar.

A staircase led him up to the damp Soho milieu and a red neon sign that drew strangers. He adjusted his eyes and headed east, the drink propelling the extra pounds. What the fuck? He thought. The kid had made him mad. Just like those jerks he despised at high school. He listened to the sound of his own footsteps. Steady. And straight. But he could sprint too, he remembered. Like in college, when he outran them all. He threw a punch into the air and hollered out.

Larry crossed an empty road and then a narrow, twisting lane. He slipped into a side alley and its twilight embrace. He unzipped his jacket and slowed his pace. Not far now.

Larry's approach stirred the young man. But the kid's craving gave way to alarm as Larry, in one final stride, loomed over him. He muffled a cry and shut his eyes.

'Stop that fuckin' whining.' Larry pinned the kid to a garage door. 'You're a jerk. A whining, baby, baby jerk.' The whimpering ceased. 'I told you never to use my cell phone number.'

'But you said if it was important—'

'I said *never*. Don't you understand never, jerk?'

Larry gripped the young man's hair. He drew his head closer.

'I saw him. The agent … the guy I should watch out for.'

'Where?' Larry's grip tightened.

'You're hurting me … In the square, in Covent Garden.'

'When? When, jerk?'

'Today. At the demo. About the Gods.'

Larry froze, still holding the kid's head. 'Describe him.'

'Old … please. You're …'

'How old?'

'Sixty. Sounded foreign.'

'He spoke?'

Panting, the young man eased back and nodded. He spat. 'To a student called Richard … you're hurting me, please. In the café. They were looking around. They were talking. About books. And the church.'

'Screw the church.' Larry released the kid's hair. The kid stood up. He cried.

'Stop whimpering, fuck you. Stop it or I'll hit you.' The kid fell back against the garage door, pressed by Larry's weight.

'No. I followed him. The old man.'

'Where?'

'To his home. I can show you.'

'Just tell me, now jerk, if you want to breathe again.'

'Wait. I wrote it. Here.'

Larry eased back before snatching a crumpled sheet of paper from the kid's sweaty palm. A narrow beam of light shot from Larry's phone. He could see some lines. And the sketch of a temple. 'It's a fuckin' church, you creep.' Their bodies crashed against the shutter door.

'No. There's an address.'

Larry flipped the page. There were words. And an address. He relaxed his weight. The kid slithered to the ground. If the kid was telling the truth, he thought, he'd soon stuff them all. The boss. The lying Brits. The good old CIA. Adrenalin teased his veins. He crouched down. He needed more.

'This Richard. Find out about him, you hear? Everything you can. Where he studies. His friends. Where he lives.' Larry hauled the dishevelled young man to his feet and, for the first time, smiled at his pale, scrawny frame, his eyes piercing those of the kid. 'Just don't get cute with me,' he warned. 'This is business.' Larry took out his wallet and flashed a wad of notes in front of the young man's face. 'There's more. Much more. If you find out.'

The kid snatched it and stuffed an empty pocket.

'You always promise me.'

'Just deliver. You have to work for your dirty pleasures.'

The young man looked away. He leant, unaided, against the coarse, undulating shutter, trembling as it rattled in the night air. He wiped his eyes.

'Pull yourself together, for fuck's sake. Stay here for twenty minutes. Don't follow me. Use the cash to get some food.'

Larry turned. He hurried away. He'd shower once home. And change his clothes. He felt clammy. And soaked in rye. But better. Like renewed. And kind of free. But it was okay. It was business. And only the kid knew. Only the kid.

Larry made his way through quiet streets. Holborn. The City. Barbican. London Wall. He turned south towards the river. Soon the final clues, he figured, would come his way. The foreign agent. The agent's associates. Richard … and a link to his friends. All he needed was one unguarded call. The team would do the rest. He walked faster, sketching the outcome in his head. A smarter job. More dough. Real chicks. He smiled. A citation. Prestige. The rye sweetened his lips.

His mind switched back to the task. He'd have to work the kid a little harder. Like his hair. His skin … his body. The stakes were high, and our *Mister* Dudley had given orders. And the rules … yeah. A smirk slid across his face. A little more forgiving.

10

J osh's text surprised me.

He'd told me he was studying engineering, so we at least had mathematics in common. But that wasn't all. I read it again, just as surprised.

Hi, he said, *I've joined your English module. No kidding.*

English literature? I screwed my eyes. In that case, I think I'll do fluid mechanics for a laugh. But no, he was serious.

My girlfriend says I have to read poetry. I'll be less of a brute. Ho, ho, ho.

Well, why not?

BTW. Got an email from the tutor. She wants us to read an elegy for class tomorrow. It's by John Donne, he added. *He's a poet. Number 19. The one with XIX in the title.*

I checked for the email. It was sitting in a stack of six. She'd also mentioned 'Twickenham Garden', which seemed to follow me around after its impromptu reading in the piazza, and 'Satire 1'. I guessed Josh gambled that one might be enough, at least for starters.

You know it's called 'Going to Bed', I replied. And your girlfriend might not be so amused when you read it to her. Oh, and you're right about the number. See you tomorrow.

I knew the elegy from school. And our tutor was throwing us straight in at the deep end. She'd suggested a theme as well: ego and the brazen conceit. I rather liked it. Donne's verse wasn't for the softheaded, and the poetic conceits could sometimes look weird or just downright provocative. I wondered how Josh might handle it. Maybe syntax and metaphor had a wider appeal, after all.

It took over an hour to trawl through the poems, the accompanying notes and commentary from a few online critiques. And that was it. My first real bit of prep for my first class at uni. And so, a little bleary-eyed, I checked the alarm on my phone and put the laptop aside. 'Away thou fondling motley humourist,' I mused, still thinking of Donne, and with a delicious yawn slipped off to bed.

* * *

I was one of many converging on the Front Lodges as students streamed into the quad on their way to the first week of classes.

No one but Donne, a baffled Dr Johnson had once declared, would have compared a good man to a telescope. Or lovers to the points of a compass, I thought, sweeping past the two small observatories just beyond the university gatehouse. Ahead lay Shakespeare and his contemporaries. It had taken years of study to get this far, and the Metaphysical poets were now my first port of call. I followed the instructions to find the classroom.

Josh was sitting on his own in a bright, naturally lit room that was quietly filling around him. His eyes bulged as I approached him.

'Thank god you've got here, Rick. Have you read the poem?'

'Yeah. Quite a tease, isn't it?'

'Tease? It's downright horny. She won't ask me to read it, will she?'

'Only if you keep your head down or try to look dumb.'

Josh scanned the room. He was sipping water from a plastic bottle, hoping it might act as a kind of shield. I sat next to him, halving the odds.

I remembered him looking so cool the first day we met. Headphones around his neck as he paraded snapshots of his pretty girlfriend. He was dark-haired and had an athletic build that looked quite natural rather than one beefed-up in the gym. But now he looked rather sheepish. Maybe he wasn't such a brute after all whatever Sophie had said to chide him.

Dr Fisher, our tutor, sat at a control desk facing us. And the class in one of three continuous desk rows arranged like the crescent of the moon. Each row was a step higher as the desks banked away towards the plate-glass window at the back of the room. At full capacity, the room accommodated forty students. We were just short of half that. But sitting alone, in a swing leather chair set apart from the rest of us, was a guy four or five years older than a typical first-year undergraduate. He looked quietly aloof, brandishing the occasional smug grin that wasn't out of place with his buttoned-up blazer and dark-blue tie. I watched as he tried to draw the tutor's attention. But she parried the looks. Just a polite smile. Tempered, I thought, with a little anxiety at his gesturing.

I turned to Josh. I knew about the engineering and now the poetry but beyond that, nothing else about my new friend. 'So, what exactly is your degree?' I asked as he clung to his bottle of water.

'Civil engineering. It's a four-year course. But I have to do something from the humanities department in my first and second terms. It's meant to expand my horizons.'

I thought of telescopes for a moment. Three latecomers slipped into class. Josh adjusted the chances on staying hidden.

'Hmm, civil engineering. I did maths to A-level but no sciences. Though I can draw.'

'Didn't you say you were doing something with art?'

'Yeah. Art history. But not to draw. I'm doing it to get a better grip on the poems. It's supposed to expand my horizons as well.'

'OK, then. You tackle the poetry. And I'll explain bridge spans and load distribution. Agreed?'

'Agreed. But over a pint or two.'

'You're on. Right after class, Rick.'

The tutor closed the classroom door and returned to her chair.

'Welcome to your first tutorial on the Metaphysical poets. Just a few introductory comments before we begin. I know I have spoken to each one of you in the last few days, so I have an idea where your interests and strengths lie. Those of you already familiar with Renaissance literature may need only a quick refresh of the background reading, while those who are new to this period should work through the recommended texts. I trust your enthusiasm for the poetry will make up for any shortcomings in your sixth-form studies.'

'If I might interject …' Our eyes turned to the guy in the jacket and tie. 'Jonathan Saunders,' he announced. 'I'm undertaking research as part of a new MA programme.' He glanced back at the tutor as though hinting at something unsaid. 'I'll be joining you from time to time. I have a particular interest in these writers and their connections.' An odd grin concluded his intervention, but it appeared to perplex the rest of us. Dr Fisher included.

'Well …' continued the tutor, 'just a little reminder to switch off your mobile phones. We have only one hour a week on this module, so please come prepared for the readings and discussion. And remember the guidance on feedback when responding to others' comments. Evidence and not just opinions.' She cast a wary glance towards Jonathan. 'Shall we begin?'

I opened a new, unblemished notepad and wrote the date. It wouldn't be long before I'd saturated the page, making lots of notes. Not always elegant, but fresh and more helpful than the carefully written phrase, while Josh, arms crossed and with a hint of sweat on his brow, stared at his phone. Jonathan, I noticed, had powered up a tablet-sized laptop and was already scrolling through his notes.

We turned to Dr Fisher.

'The Metaphysical poets,' she said, 'developed an ingenious and radical talent for versification. The subject range of their poetry is wide and amenable to further subgenre classification. Early critical opinion progressed from an appreciation by a group of sympathetic male admirers to one of bewilderment and neglect. The twentieth century saw a complete reversal of this trend, driven by a sense of angst about the modern world and, more recently, an interest by feminists and post-structuralists in seeking new perspectives.'

She paused. By now, we were all writing furiously.

'At the heart of the Metaphysical School is John Donne. And we shall see from today's readings that he is a poet not shy of controversy or outlandish statements.'

Josh gave me a nudge. He'd been fiddling with the mobile phone and had found another holiday snap when the class, once more, turned to Jonathan.

'We should not be misled by the term *metaphysical*. It had no otherworldly implications.' He nodded towards the tutor. She frowned at the intervention.

Dr Fisher continued. 'The elegies present a different, and in some ways a more dramatic thrust to the better-known songs and sonnets. You should have detected this contrast when you read the elegy and "Twickenham Garden".' She glanced sharply at Jonathan to pre-empt any remarks. 'I'd like you to read down to line twenty in the text. "Elegy 19", everybody.'

There is a lot of undressing in this poem. And an impatience for action. Even Donne's fiercest admirers tread delicately around this one, my teacher advised, while the critics attack its frivolity, squirming at the brazenness of the sexual metaphors that link a seductive striptease with a relish for how it will all end. No wonder the authorities banned it in the seventeenth-century. It seemed a long way from Donne's career in the pulpit of St Paul's Cathedral.

The first two lines set the scene: 'Come, Madam, come, all rest my powers defy, | Until I labour, I in labour lie.' But my thoughts were rudely interrupted.

'This is a shocking poem,' said Jonathan, seizing our attention once more. 'At one level, it is horrible smut. Dirty Elizabethan smut. A thrill for the lads during drinking sessions at the Inns of Court. At another, a shameless apology for colonial expansion and adventurism of the worst sort.'

Josh looked at me as if he'd read the wrong poem. I whispered, 'Metaphorically,' and he re-scanned the lines afresh, not entirely convinced of the connections. I read a few more myself amidst an echo of fierce accusation: 'Off with that girdle … unpin that spangled breastplate … a far fairer world encompassing'.

The poem's detractors have a point. And I wondered if ravishing the land was akin to a sexual experience. Like a body violated and exhausted. A world corrupted. Perhaps this is what Jonathan meant? I was sure that Josh was puzzling over it, too.

A silence encouraged Jonathan to develop his theme. Women, sex, land, empire, even religious impiety. The poem was a catalogue of abuse, he declared, flipping between screens on his laptop, flaunting one angry authority and then another. He might be impressing the tutor, but did he really believe what he was saying? But then literary analysis is often like that: strident interpretations marshalled towards a fiery, ringing indictment. He mentioned the Virginia Company and early English settlement as proof. Clever, I thought. And yet there was an interesting connection since Donne, around 1609, had applied to be its secretary. I made a note to follow it up, although, unlike Jonathan, I never cared to shake my fist at history. Anyway, I felt a yawn coming on. Perhaps the poem was just a mischievous flight of fancy. Not all the critics seethe with indignation.

The tutor stalled Jonathan and asked for other appraisals. I couldn't bear the awkward silence, so I ventured a contrast to the more shadowy lovers in the poem 'Twickenham Garden'. And the lines, mocked by my tormentor in the Covent Garden café, came back to me. I struck out, quoting them from memory. '"But oh, self-traitor, I do bring the spider love."' I mentioned my name after a pause.

'And what does John Donne mean, Richard, by "spider love" and "self-traitor"?' the tutor asked.

'Well, he's afraid that his love will prove to be a poison, and I suppose destroy the thing he really wants. Whereas with his mistress, it's just, you know, like physical. And he doesn't care.' The girls in the room stared back at me.

Jonathan intervened. 'But "Twickenham Garden" is also about ambition. It's still about ego. That's the dynamic impulse in these poems. Surely that's clear from even a simple reading.' I could see Josh and others hopping between the poems and the textual notes. Jonathan flipped to a new screen and started calling out lines and metaphors before anyone else could speak. And in this surreal drama, my thoughts shifted to the underlying sentiments of the poem.

'Twickenham Garden' seems to distil Donne's fears about the loss of innocence and the eviction from paradise. His poetry often dwells on the threat of rejection amidst the heightened bliss of physical contact and desire. And a yearning, and yet a self-doubt, for a promised salvation. Or a partner's sweet love. But why self-traitor? As though we must, in the end, let ourselves down. The cause of our own misery.

A silence checked my thoughts. Everyone had turned to Josh. He was staring ahead, looking pensive and unemotional. The tutor rephrased the question that had put him in the spotlight. Nodding gently, he spoke in what sounded like a considered reply: 'Hi everybody, Josh. "Going to Bed"? Yeah, it's a fine poem. What is it about? It's about two people having a shag.'

It was like being back in sixth form.

The tutor drew back. 'Well, I don't think the class will disagree with your initial assessment, but I was hoping you might have something further to say beyond the superficial. Perhaps on the imagery.'

I sensed Josh was sinking into quicksand. The tittering hadn't died down when Jonathan held up his arms in disbelief. I threw in a diversion. 'What if the poem is just a fantasy? Like coming to terms with things. A sort of surrogate experience. It doesn't have to be real.'

Jonathan now spoke as if appealing for a sending-off. 'The previous speaker should have better prepared for this tutorial.'

Josh hit back. 'Don't call me the "previous speaker". I told you my name. It's Josh. And what else do you think they're doing?'

'Then you should try to appreciate the political premises behind this poem.' Jonathan spoke airily, punctuating his words with a condescending grin. 'It's clearly a manifesto for domination and speaks to the misogynist trait that hides behind the poet's sensational conceits ...'

For a minute or two, Jonathan held the class in thrall, citing more authorities and more quotes free of any mitigating context, determined not to give way. I listened as Josh pondered what was being thrown at him. He seemed perplexed and turned to me. 'Misogynist?' he whispered. 'Means woman hater, doesn't it?' I nodded. He looked down at the poem. 'But my girlfriend—she's going to love this.'

A commotion outside the door allowed the tutor to cut Jonathan short, and as the class prepared to vacate the room, she reminded us of our essay topic on Donne and the impact of Renaissance ideas on his verse. The class stood up to leave, but she hadn't finished with me.

'So, Richard. Which modules did you sign up to?'

I winced. I would have to own up. And better not sound too wimpish, I decided. 'I've joined a different course, Dr Fisher. Outside the English department. It's part of the complementary-study programme.'

'Who teaches it?'

'Dr Hatherleigh. It's the Art History B module.'

Jonathan rose to his feet. 'But that course has been withdrawn. It is no longer permitted.'

If the tutor hadn't overheard his comments, I wouldn't have replied. 'Well, it's got three students already,' I said.

'Who?' he demanded.

'Alex Rowdesley, Francis Eggar and Jane Shere. We're good friends. We've got a tutorial later this week.'

'Alex Rowdesley? You should be very careful who you mix with. I suggest you check the validity of this course. The university's enrolment office will be very interested to learn of this.'

'Well, they … OK'd it last week,' I said, turning to the tutor for support. But she was unwilling to intervene.

'Is it any of your business what my friend studies?' Josh pushed forward.

Jonathan retreated to his puny laptop. A few moments later, he swept out of the room, leaving me puzzled at the encounter. I looked at Josh. He looked ready for combat. But then we both laughed. Josh still had the crunched-up plastic bottle in his hand, even if all it could do was squeak like a toddler's toy.

'So, Metaphysical poetry,' I said. 'What do you make of it?'

'Interesting. Difficult at times. But there's something in it.'

'I agree. And now, my friend, "Good morrow to our waking souls."'

'Sorry?'

I'd mystified him. 'Oh, nothing. Just another line.' I laughed again. 'Come on, I'll take you up on that pint.'

11

A group of young East Asian guys, brandishing the Word like a sword, hurried towards us. Cropped heads and eager smiles. Animated pubescent faces. They threw open their arms, and in bright, high-pitched voices, declared we were both saved.

Josh dodged sideways, and with an apologetic glance, I followed his lead. We had less exalted desires on our mind. 'Don't worry. It isn't far,' he claimed. 'I promised to meet a friend at his favourite pub.'

The walk was adding more vigour to our thirst. A few beers would be our salvation.

We found the pub, hidden snugly, in the City's legal quarter close to Chancery Lane. It looked like the custodian of a lost age.

'Who's your friend?'

'His name's Martin. Helps run the uni boathouse by the river in Chiswick. He's a post-grad. Twenty-two or twenty-three.' Josh stalled at the entrance. He gritted his teeth as he turned to me. 'Have you got any ID? Just in case.'

'Leave off, Josh. I'm nineteen.'

'Sorry, mate.'

His stubble was darker than mine.

Josh swung open the door, and we eased our way through a swish bunch of lawyers and clerks. We must have caught a slack spell in legal affairs judging by the lively bonhomie.

We approached a young man at a table, a few inches taller than me, wearing a short-sleeved shirt that looked as if it might burst at the seams. His face lit up. 'Possession is nine-tenths …' he declared, as we dropped bags and jackets within the occupied space. 'I'm Martin,' he added as Josh headed to the bar.

'Hi,' I said. 'I'm Richard.'

'So, you two both friends, then?'

'Yeah, I met Josh on my first day. At enrolment. And he's taken up the same class as me now.'

'Engineering?'

'Nope. Renaissance literature.' Martin screwed a face at me. I shook my head in sympathy. 'Not sure why he's doing it, to be honest. Something to do with his girlfriend. What about you?'

'Masters. Political science. I did my first degree at the London School of Economics. I'm down the road at Kings now. Two-year course.'

'So how do you know Josh?'

'Student rowing. I'm on the committee. I gave him a trial on the river. Fancy a go?'

'Might … but still finding my feet on land, Martin. Rivers are wet, aren't they?'

'Yep. All that water. But we always head upriver. The regular boatrace course. The stream's safer. It's a bloody nightmare in the middle of London.' He narrowed his eyes, sizing me up for a boat.

I'd never even thought of rowing. My interest in sports had never gone beyond a social kickabout with a ball or the odd humbling visit to the crease in some old cricket gear. Anyway, I preferred long-distance running to the usual team games. And I had done two half-marathons to prove that. But who knows, one day?

'Get this inside you, Rick.' Josh had returned, holding three pints together. Carefully, we extricated them from his two-handed grip. Team-effort, we agreed, not spilling a drop.

'A few slow pints, lads, and you're ready to face the world and all its mediocrities.' Martin eased back with a kindly air. 'I take it, that you and your tutors have finished up for the day?'

Josh shrugged and reached for his mobile.

'It so happens, that I might do some prep work in the library.' Donne and art history, I remembered over a consoling gulp of beer. 'If I get away, that is.'

Martin grinned, mocking my lame intentions.

Josh was reacting too, though not to the banter but a text message on his phone that had just caught his attention. He pounded out a hurried reply.

'What about your first degree?' I asked.

'Economics and law. But I also did a separate thing in art history. Some cultural swanning around for the mind … or something like that.'

'Really? I'm doing that. At UCL.'

'Art history? So, who's your tutor? It's not old Arbetta, is it?'

'No. He's called Hatherleigh. But I know who you mean. Arbetta runs the A option. I'm on the B.'

Martin looked at me with a drawn-out curiosity. 'You're doing B?'

I nodded, catching a change in his voice.

'But I'd heard they'd shut that down. All witchcraft and black magic were the rumours. Even the students' union wouldn't go near it.'

Ha, ha. Here we go, I thought. I put my glass down, and with a weary sigh, offered a defence. 'Why do people get so uptight about these studies? It seems okay to quote this stuff in a poem or a play, but not to study the background to it. You don't have to believe in it, for heaven's sake.' A mischievous smirk greeted my words. 'Yet all I hear are people rubbishing what they don't understand.' I resorted to my beer.

'Oh, there's a lot of that. We thrive on it in political science. You have to tiptoe around a bloody minefield today.'

I shrugged. He wasn't going to fight me, I decided.

Josh interrupted our exchange. 'Sorry guys, my girl's freaking out over tonight. Got to make a call. Keep my place.' He slipped away for some quiet.

Martin rolled his eyes. 'You first-years. He's supposed to be in the gym this evening. I've got him down for rowing machine training and weights. What am I going to do with him?'

I couldn't help. But Martin's offhand reply about political science intrigued me. I dug deeper. 'How can you study politics if you can't be open-minded about what you read and say?'

'Oh, such innocence …' But Martin wasn't completely having fun. 'Well, first you follow the rules. Get the layout of things. Like what's okay and what's a complete no-no. You can still tease the old dears, especially if you quote their own views back to them.'

He sipped his beer, eyeing me above the rim of the glass.

I wasn't sure that I was ready for such casual cynicism, even in the pub. I had another look for Josh, but with all the commotion between us, he was out of sight. A sudden laugh greeted a disclosure by one of the nearby silks. Nothing subtle or whispered in that little tale, I fancied. They raised their drinks. But still no sign of Josh. I turned to Martin. 'So *why* are you still studying? Why be a post-grad and end up spending a fortune?'

'Not sure. Probably the boathouse. And the pubs around here. I'll join the rat race in my own good time. Before, if they figure me out. But I'm too smart for that.' He enjoyed another slug of beer.

So that's how it is in political science. But literature wasn't exactly unfettered by outraged opinion. 'All right, so what about art history? Surely you can make—'

'Just as bad, friend.' Martin seized on my words like a mistimed stroke. 'I reckoned Arbetta was a real fraud. Breezing through galleries with his gaggle of admiring young things.' I smirked, pretty sure what I'd hear next. 'We were always looking at Greek vases. The charmingly lascivious ones. And it wasn't just the ceramic technique that he marvelled at. The posing was meticulously described as well.'

I sat back, leaving Martin to enjoy an even slyer mouthful of beer. Alongside the artful whiff of innuendo, of course. Yet I couldn't imagine Hatherleigh in the same vein. More mind than body. And too academic to be cavorting around. I tried to tempt my new friend's thoughts elsewhere as he drained his beer. 'You'd think they come up with something grander than options A and B.'

'Yeah.' A sordid grin slid across Martin's face, but he resisted anything smutty. 'You couldn't magic up another pint, could you? Same again. Don't worry about Josh.'

I didn't have to. He hadn't touched a drop. I could see him now on the other side of the bar, but couldn't quite make eye contact as he shrivelled around his phone. Sophie must have given him an earful. I headed back to the table with two pints, court sessions having cleared the way after lunch. Martin was already primed with a new line of attack.

'Hatherleigh, you say. Isn't his place off campus?'

'In one of the local streets. Much more relaxed.'

'Oh, they love all that.' He was still musing on Greek vases. 'I went there once. Noisy lift, I remember.'

'They're very fond of it,' I replied.

'Likes books too. Latin and Greek. All very erudite. And a bit dirty, I shouldn't be surprised,' he added, nodding his head. 'We even had afternoon tea to loosen up a little, I recall.'

'Come on. It's not like that.'

'There was a girl. Jane, I think. Is she still around?'

'Yeah, Jane Shere. Did you meet her?'

'I did. She was always with a guy called Francis.'

'They're good friends. And we're all studying together.'

'Art History B. Sounds as if you're up to your neck in it.' He raised a hand to his chin. 'Remind me, isn't Francis something of a whiz at geometry?'

'The renaissance mind,' I boasted.

'I remember Arbetta getting miffed at his digressions on perspective. And Jane. She's a real classicist.'

'The tenth Muse,' I suggested.

'You may be right. Knew her Homer. And always impeccably turned out.'

Martin's more serious recollections didn't seem that amiss. And they prompted a question on my part. 'You know, there's another student in the group. His name's Alex. Alex Rowdesley. Did you ever meet him?'

'Alex. Oh yes, I know of Alex. Everyone knows of Alex. You really are in distinguished company.' He smiled as if I had joined an exclusive lodge or something. 'So, Art History B rises again. Well, well, well.'

So much for it being a secret.

Josh was still fighting his corner. And still a pint behind. But at this rate, I wouldn't even get started on my essay. Less than two weeks to the deadline, I fretted, and the tutorial with Hatherleigh before then. And Plato's 'Timaeus'. Socrates and his friend Critias. And eighty pages of Attic Greek. I could see a faint ghost of myself in the beer. But at least I had a good translation. Though if Martin was right, the others would breeze through the original, leaving me adrift. I let go of my pint and drew a short breath. All this extravagant praise wasn't helping me to settle down. I just wanted my art history friends to be regular guys, not renegade celebrities. Why are they so good? I wondered. Okay, so they've studied classics and maths as if they were training for the medieval quadrivium. But there was more. They were friendly and protective. And they didn't seem to have any problems with money. Except Alex. Though he'd told me he didn't care about it. I reached for my glass. Art History B. And for some reason, it's come my way.

Josh returned, looking triumphant. He would stay and he'd make it up later. We raised a salute. Josh grabbed his beer and turned to his coach. 'Sorry about the gym. Have to go to the cinema instead. Can we do tomorrow evening, by any chance?'

'No, we can't. We're on the river tomorrow. If you're not fit, you'll just have to be sick in the boat.'

Josh took the blows. The real boss had won.

'I've got him in a scratch eight, Richard. With all the other charlies. You should see them. Technique like a Mississippi paddleboat.' Josh whirled his arms in a guilty, self-mocking pose. Martin tried to make the best of it. 'I'll just have to lash these blokes to the rowing machines or find another bleeding crew.' He leant back, tensing his muscles. 'I dunno. We're racing Imperial at the end of the month.'

Josh fiddled with a beer mat as Martin homed in on his woeful technique, threatening further twists in the training. But he paused long enough for Josh to change the subject. 'Oh, I told my girlfriend about a line in the poem we read. The one with "Atalanta's balls". But I couldn't explain it.'

Martin's jaw dropped. I sat up, enjoying our friend's sudden bewilderment. 'You didn't. Not "Atalanta's balls"?'

'Yeah. In the elegy, "Going to Bed". What does it mean?'

I grinned back at him. At least he'd got us away from rowing machines and food supplements. 'It's a classical allusion, Josh. About women. What the poet's suggesting is that they are a distraction. And the men are dupes for being lured into their arms.'

'That's it. That's what I've been telling him.' Martin raised his hands as if suddenly vindicated by my remarks. But Josh shook his head. Can't. Not tonight, old pal.

'So, what's this film you're off to see then, Josh?' I asked.

'Something soppy. She's already seen it with her friends but wants me to watch it now.' He shuffled uneasily before a taut grin discouraged any further probing. I sipped my beer.

The hours slipped by. We talked about home, school, interests, and what we hoped to do in five years' time. Josh had done the

Tolkien films. Hobbits. Dragons. War games. Computer games. The same adolescent diversions as me. He'd also worked at a few pocket-money jobs. Dated his girl. Taken her to Mykonos. And had started to drive, though he was nearly eight months younger than me. I was more books, I admitted. Keen to impress. Wanting the top grades. But now … maybe I should row.

Martin checked the time on his phone. 'High tide,' he announced, as he stretched his arms towards the ceiling, his thirst satiated and his glass empty. He wiped his lips and stood up. 'Got to talk to a man about a boat,' he added, explaining his departure.

We staggered out later than planned, but feeling invigorated by the carefree rapport. Josh had slipped one more deadline. We teased him, but he stayed aloof. He'd catch most of the film, he scoffed. And probably a thick ear.

It was just gone six. I hurried off to the library at UCL and the essay on Donne that I'd already meant to have started. A deep, nagging voice whispered the way.

12

I'd heard that there was a statue of Satan somewhere in UCL's main library. I couldn't find him, but Jeremy Bentham, one of the founders of UCL, was still kept in a wooden box on the ground floor of the uni from where, as a prank in 1975, some students ran off with his skull. So maybe the jokers had taken the devil as well—just for a laugh.

Besides books on Renaissance stuff, the tutor had listed a few well-known critics on Donne: Carey, Gardner and Leishman. They were always safe ground, she'd advised, and could usually be found lurking somewhere on the shelves or in the online catalogue if all the physical editions were out on loan. And for sure, I found great tomes by each of them, but nothing by another she'd mentioned, a poet called Empson. But they'd do, I decided, and looked around for an empty desk.

Donne and all this 'new philosophy', I mused. Sun and Earth. Circles and ellipses. I brain-dumped a few inter-connecting ideas. Religion. Astronomy. New lands. New freedoms, perhaps? There were lots of allusions in the poems to lend support, even where Donne was driven more by doubt than by any hard-headed conviction. But I'd have to tie it up with death and love, somehow. And good old consciousness. And a sense of detachment from the world in which he lived. It was always the case with Donne. It would take a lot of reading. And not all the critics would agree. I swapped the books around, not sure if they were in the right order. What

I needed was a snappy quote to start the essay. And a copy of the poems. I yawned, stood up and tried to figure out which shelves to go back to.

Josh had sounded funny this morning. 'Going To Bed', I thought. I recalled his words: 'What else do you think they're doing?' I found the incriminating poem and read a few more lines. It wasn't just magic that got people wound up and excited, I could see. I held on to the rack as Josh's other half came to mind. 'Licence my roving hands, and let them go ...' And then ... consorting with books. Rows and rows of them. My thoughts drifted. I couldn't believe that Hatherleigh's books were dirty. Greek, Latin. Surely not? I read on, my eyes falling on random lines. 'Full nakedness, all joys are due to thee ...' Christ. I gave myself a mental nudge. This wasn't exactly helping my theme. I let go of the rack. 'Twickenham Garden' came back to me with a vengeance. I returned to my desk and turned to the relevant page.

Jonathan had dismissed this as much as he had the more notorious elegy. Ego and ambition, he'd protested. I reread the lines, convinced that he must be wrong. I checked a critique. There was a short note on sixteenth-century gardens, and a reference to a plan of Twickenham Park, near the Thames to the west of London. This was Lady Bedford's rural retreat, and Donne often wrote letters and poems to her. I found a more detailed description of her estate that described how the garden comprised concentric circles of trees that symbolised the medieval cosmos before its overhaul by Copernicus. Copernicus? I wondered. Of course. That was it. The astronomy-angle. With the Earth pushed aside. And the sun at the centre. A new cosmos. A whole new philosophy. Wow, this should work. I looked around for my pen, before finding it on the floor. And I could laugh now at those clowns who'd mocked me in Covent Garden. Do you understand this stuff? they'd sneered. Yeah, actually, I do. I'm studying poetry, you know, and its double meanings. Except … except they might have a point about the serpent, I conceded. I felt a panic coming on and read the lines again. '… that this place may be thought | True paradise, I have the serpent brought'. I flipped through the critics. And that wasn't all. What about the 'spider love'? Spoiling everything it touched, corrupting the very world of perfection? Wasn't that how the clown in the café explained it to me? Or was it the tutor? I yawned, wondering if Josh's film had ended.

When I was at sixth form, I remembered how my lessons were such a struggle. Look, our English teacher would say, conflicting accounts of the *same poem*. How can this be? I wasn't sure. But Anna would make her case even if she turned out to be wrong. And then Simon and Becky would take the same side, leaving me adrift. Anna. And Simon and Becky. And still I haven't heard from any of them. Not since early summer. But maybe I'd give it a few more days to let them settle in. Durham is quite a long haul north, I know. But then Oxford isn't so far away. My thoughts drifted.

'And so, what do you think? The poem, Richard, the one in front of you. What do you think?' The teacher's words came back to me, challenging me on a slippery metaphor that I'd stumbled over while quoting the text. 'It's not enough to mention it in line seventeen or line eighteen, Richard. Try to explain it. Tell us what the poet means.'

'He's distraught,' I cried. 'He's feeling excluded, sir. Lost. Expelled from his former happiness. His love. His mistress.' A nod from the teacher betokened his hard-won approval.

The poem came back to me as if dictated in a dream. 'Blasted with sighs, and surrounded with tears, | Hither I come to seek the spring.' This was Fallen Man, my teacher explained, driven out of Eden yet still pining to return. And then the drama in Covent Garden's piazza playing on a similar theme muscled in. With Saturn and Zeus fighting for supremacy. And the Golden Age … yielding to the hard edge of Iron's testing ways. And a world soured by regret and tortured by illusions. Maybe Donne understood that too. Repent, Man, and you can come whimpering back. Everything is forgiven. And safekeeping assured. Just obey. So, Fallen Man, then. Wanting to hurry back. Waiting for redemption.

And yet I wasn't sure … and it didn't sound like 'new philosophy'. I thought again. 'But, sir, what if he was seeking new knowledge the whole time? No longer happy in contented ignorance, he was going to do something with his life.'

'And the expulsion from Eden?' my teacher asked.

The ideas swirled in my head. The first reluctant steps in self-awareness, I figured. The Fall is an escape, I realised. A duty, even. I ran through the lines. 'And that this place may be thought | True paradise, I have the serpent brought'. He can't go back because of what he now knows. The serpent is his knowledge. He knows he's barred. And that he has outgrown his innocence. The clash of old and new. The Ptolemaic skies. The Copernican revolution. It's a psychological transformation. The struggle to come to terms with a new existence even while … a pre-conscious longing draws us back to the past.

Yes! I could make something of it. Two thousand words. Eight or nine pages with quotes. And all those circles of trees. And I remembered that Josh had said something helpful too about hobbits. But surely they're not in it?

'Hello. Richard. Richard, wake up. I notice that you have several of the course text books.'

I opened my eyes. A girl on my course was glaring at me, talking in a loud but edgy whisper. 'I'm sorry, I must have dozed off.'

'You were fast asleep, Richard.'

'Sorry. I don't need them all.' She was still staring. 'Just trying to get my bearings,' I whispered.

'You had the last copy of Carey.' She helped herself, lifting the book from under my arms.

'I didn't realise.' I grinned, as if to acknowledge my helpless state. But then I remembered her face. 'You were in the class this morning. Sorry, I didn't catch your name?'

'Jenny.'

'Hi, I'm Richard, but you already knew that.'

'And I wanted to ask you a question … but you and the other guy kept talking.'

'Did you? I'm sorry.' I tried to sound contrite. 'This morning's a bit of a blur, I'm afraid. Josh and I went to the bar … for the afternoon.' I glanced down, stifling another yawn.

'I can tell. You know it's nearly ten o'clock.'

'Ten!' I gasped. I needed to read something on art history for the Friday tutorial. Oh shit, the next couple of days would have to be flat out study. Suddenly, I was a lot more sober.

Jenny looked at me, frowning as she spoke. 'The humanities school is running a social for freshers at the end of next week. If you can …' she paused, 'are interested, I could include you in a text. It's at the Kings College Strand campus.'

I nodded.

'We've got a few guys from some other subjects coming. They seem pretty cool.'

'I can be cool too,' I countered.

She stared at me before grabbing another book she fancied and, with a grin, headed off to the library checkout. She'd already got hold of the Empson. Well, at least I now knew her name. And next Tuesday, I would meet a few of her friends as well.

13

I took the stairs without hesitation. Red-faced or not, I was determined to make it to Hatherleigh's tutorial.

Above me, I could hear a voice, Jane's voice, winding its way down the stairs, recounting a rash summer experience. Francis was there too, I reckoned, chuckling quietly in the background. And then another flight of steps and I was up on the top floor. I took a deep breath before slipping into the room. I nodded to Hatherleigh and sneaked a quick smile towards my friends. Pleased to be here, I thought. And by the look of things, ahead of Alex, as well. I gently closed the door.

Dr Hatherleigh gestured to one of two unoccupied chairs around a low glass-topped table positioned close to his desk. Francis and Jane sat opposite me. 'We feared you might have acquired a cold, young man,' he said, before returning his attention to Jane's story.

Francis looked up as I settled in the chair. 'If only Richard had been with us, he would have answered all our prayers.'

I smiled back, unsure what I'd have done to save the day. I placed a copy of Plato's 'Timaeus' on the table next to a much grander version of the same dialogue.

'You don't mean that you would have sacrificed Richard to the demon as well?' asked Hatherleigh.

Jane recoiled. 'Oh, Richard, you mustn't think that!'

I didn't. I thought I was being flattered. At least by the prospect of a shared adventure. As for the demon … I pushed back my hair and left it at that. We were still waiting for Alex.

Dr Hatherleigh turned to me. He quietly lamented how his own duties made it impossible to pursue such adventures—Aegean or otherwise. I listened respectfully as he referred to life-long projects, and to many hours of research, often in the face of obstruction and ridicule. But he sounded less aggrieved now than when he had first broached these anxieties with me in my interview at the start of term. I got the feeling too, that his commitment to these studies was more than just academic interest, however wearisome and frustrating the workload had become. And I noticed too, how his comments encompassed both Francis and Jane in these endeavours, blurring the usual lines between student and tutor.

I studied my new friends as they turned the pages of the large, heavy volume that overshadowed my own prim, little paperback. And it really was fifth-century Attic Greek. Something from Hatherleigh's shelves, I assumed. Francis pointed to passages while Jane turned the pages back and forth. I glanced at the tutor, but he, too, was contemplative. Pouring over his notes. I looked idly around the room, hearing an echo of Martin's little tease. 'So … Art History B rises again,' he'd said. Yes, I thought. Here, amidst all this elegance and studied reflection. He was right too about Jane. Fastidiously attired. Small pearls in her ears. A soft-leather bag. She must have had her hair done. And even Francis's hair was cut. My eyes wandered. There was a painting. Or a large faithful print that I'd seen somewhere before. A fresco. By Raphael, I guessed. Probably in a textbook. And then the old French clock renewed its acquaintance. The rhythmic beat slicing away at a never-ending silence. Jane turned another page. I crossed my legs. Oh, Alex, where are you, mate? The tutorial has already started. I picked up my copy of 'Timaeus' and removed a piece of paper that I'd slipped inside the day before. I wanted to say something. Something to lighten the mood.

'The note,' I said. 'It was really helpful.' I held it in my hand while trying not to appear anxious or forward. 'I found it on the refectory noticeboard earlier in the week. I'd been looking out for it, guys.'

'You must thank Francis for that,' Dr Hatherleigh explained, still focusing on his notes.

'I could do the reading. Ahead of class.' Francis nodded, as if to acknowledge what I'd said. But Jane barely glanced. 'It's quite stimulating … "Timaeus" I mean. One of Plato's great dialogues, wouldn't you say?' I looked at the others, nervous for their reaction.

'Oh, I do hope,' replied the tutor, 'that Francis didn't tell you to read all of it. The Greek idiom can be very obscure in places. It would be so easy to be controversial.'

'Oh no, not at all. I read a translation. And the standard commentaries …' My words trickled away. I pointed half-heartedly to the book. But no one responded. I realised their attention was elsewhere, on a long, whining scream from outside the tutor's door.

Dr Hatherleigh's eyes widened. 'Ah! The cage, I believe.'

Puzzled, I glanced at Francis. He smiled. 'The lift,' he explained.

The door swung open. And, like a breeze, Alex swept in, clad in washed-out jeans and a bright rugby shirt with the sleeves pulled up to his elbows. He clutched his books to his chest before letting them fall to the table in an uneven pile, flashed a disarming smile at the rest of us, and finally settled down as if to watch TV. He nudged me gently. I returned the grin, stretching my legs in a gesture of relief.

'Alex,' said Dr Hatherleigh, his face animated, 'you have missed a wonderful story. Jane and Francis were telling us of their visit to Greece. And their discoveries on the island of Delos …'

But Francis cut Hatherleigh short, explaining how helpful my presence would have been if we had met earlier.

I started to blush.

'I would have joined you too but, as you know, I stayed in London.' Alex leant closer to me. 'They are right. We always have a good time. I'm fond of them both.'

'Maybe we should all go next summer,' I suggested. 'But I'm not sure about the demon thing though, Francis.'

He gently shook his head. It didn't seem to matter.

'Jane,' said Dr Hatherleigh, launching us in a new direction. 'Was scepticism towards the Olympian deities a theme central to the intellectual life of ancient Athens or merely indulgent posturing by a few conceited posers?'

I gulped at the tutor's challenge.

Jane cleared her voice. 'Socrates paid a terrible price once accused of it,' she observed, reaching for her notes. 'But Plato is unwavering in his respect for the gods—recall our tutorials on "The Laws" and "The Republic"—even if the nature of Socratic inquiry posed a challenge to the conventional beliefs of the time.' Jane smiled at me. 'Exacerbated, I fear, by the mischief the playwright Aristophanes had at Socrates' expense.'

'"The Clouds",' I said. 'You know, his satirical drama. The one that mocks the sophists.'

Jane paused.

'You are well informed,' Dr Hatherleigh remarked. 'Jane, would you continue, please?'

As Jane developed her thoughts, our tutor rose from his chair and moved to an adjacent bureau. He poured coffee from a silver pot while keeping an ear to Jane's exposition. Subtle gestures acknowledged the offer of refreshment. I raised my hand while being quietly amused by the ceremony.

Jane finished with some observations on Homer and the 'Iliad', recalling Achilles' disagreement with Agamemnon and its debilitating consequences during the Trojan War. It, too, she explained, was rooted in an act of impiety that offended the gods, not to mention the squalid bargaining over captive women by a bunch of petulant male egos. She looked away before flitting a glance across the table.

Alex shrugged. I kept my head down.

'And "Timaeus", Hatherleigh enthused. 'Isn't it a wonderful and curious account of the conception of the cosmos?' The tutor placed the tray of coffee and biscuits before us, edging Alex's books to the side. 'And the story of Atlantis—an instructive counterpoint, would you not agree?' Hatherleigh looked at me warmly as he returned to his chair. A little self-conscious, I lifted my cup and drank.

Jane continued. 'And a precautionary tale. It demonstrates the law of hubris—the most provocative form of irreverence towards the gods.'

More posturing egos, I imagined.

Hatherleigh's eyes focused on me once more. 'Atlantis, young man. A society once lauded for its humility, yet, forsaking virtue and peace, lusted instead after a worldwide hegemony.' He sipped from his cup, holding the saucer in reserve. 'Am I not right, Francis?'

Francis nodded in agreement.

Dr Hatherleigh continued. 'And Jane, does Zeus tell us *why* Atlantis sought conflict with Europe and Asia as our sources describe?'

I knew the myth. And the story told by Timaeus to his friends, Socrates, Critias and Hermocrates, of the Egyptian priests' own account of the destruction of Atlantis. Disasters were not new, the priests had said. The Earth had been overwhelmed many times. Deluges such as Deucalion's—a flood myth known to the Greeks that came complete with ark and intrepid birds just as much as the more familiar accounts in Genesis and Babylonia. And there would be others, too, they averred, set to destroy us. Conflagration. Inundation. Of course, there was a simple lesson in this: stern, jealous gods driving the people up into the mountains or down on to the plains in a bad-tempered rebuke at humanity's wilful and irreverent behaviour. Innocent and guilty, judged and condemned alike.

But most readers of Plato dismiss the story as invention. It's extraneous to the real preoccupations of 'Timaeus' and the more elaborate attention that is given to the creation of the universe, populating the heavens with gods, developing templates for the world, and somehow underpinning it with numbers, ratios and geometric figures. These revelations, which form the backbone of the dialogue, were of an altogether subtler nature than the swashbuckling drama of Atlantis and the exploits of Athens and their patron gods Poseidon and Pallas Athena, which, rather oddly, forms a flimsy preamble to Plato's work. And so Jane intrigued me with her opening remarks.

'We always consider Plato's "Timaeus", Richard, alongside its companion dialogue. The one by Critias that Socrates also came to hear. Especially the extended text that has now come into our hands.'

'Zeus, gentlemen!' Hatherleigh was keen for more. 'Jane, the full story of Atlantis, please.'

Alex and I opened our notebooks.

'"Critias". Lines seven hundred to seven hundred and fifty...' Jane's finger followed the lines of text, translating freely as she made sense of the gender and case. 'At first, it was not difficult for Zeus to rally support against Poseidon,' she declared. 'Athena and her allies were fearful that the entire world might be enslaved.'

'Indeed,' Hatherleigh concurred. 'It was a most dangerous time.'

Jane switched to another section of the text. 'And here, Europa expresses particular outrage at the encroachment on her lands. And then, a few lines on, Libya complains of seduction by Poseidon before Athena and Poseidon finally go to war.'

I nudged Alex, puzzled by Jane's account.

'Poseidon was worshipped in Atlantis,' he whispered. 'And he'd already had a bust-up with Athena over the lordship of Athens.'

I whispered back. 'They're a fratricidal lot, Alex. The gods, I mean.'

He nodded before throwing a glance towards Francis. 'Zeus, remember, was the big, bossy brother.'

Jane continued, hopping between sections in the text. Conferences. Lists of crimes. Vengeance and retribution. But I wondered if someone in antiquity had fabricated the myths for a gullible audience, eager for mysteries and fabulous stories. My eyes slipped along the bookshelves. And then to Alex's untidy pile. And I still hadn't written anything down. Art History B, I pondered.

'I think we might be losing Richard.' Alex gave me another nudge.

'Sorry, Jane. You said Zeus called a conference ...'

'Yes, Richard. And a second and a third. The issues were quite complex.'

'Sorry.' I sat up, holding my pen to the page.

'But the crux of the argument lies elsewhere. And once the gods had cast their lots, Poseidon's offspring in Atlantis were doomed forever, and the best that Athena could hope for, for her own people, was the cycle of rebirth, as time began again with another round of brutal experiences.'

She paused and smiled at Dr Hatherleigh.

'And so, Atlantis was destroyed in one terrible catastrophe that swallowed the Athenians as well.' The tutor looked at us with consternation. 'But Jane, this hardly seems fair. Had not the Athenians fought their adversaries to a standstill? Were they not dismayed by their feckless allies? And then we find that they too are obliterated with their enemies. What sort of justice is this, may we ask?' Hatherleigh's eyes seem to fall on me accusingly.

It was an odd outcome, I thought. 'But what if the Athenians had annoyed the gods as well?' I proposed.

'I fear you are right, Richard.' Francis placed the text in his lap. 'If you look at the indictment drawn up at the final conference of the gods, where Zeus dismisses the mortals' appeals, you'll see that the detailed charges and the constant lust for revenge are far more encompassing. Everyone … everyone was implicated.' He checked a phrase with Jane. She nodded. 'Athens and Atlantis. That's why Athena's allies quit. Mad at—'

'Despairing,' Jane whispered.

'—at the unending cycle of violence. Critias in his dialogue makes this point immediately after the second … decisive sea battle.' Francis returned the book to the table, leaving it open at Critias's account.

I stared back. Wondering at what I'd just heard.

'And a convenient point for more coffee.' Dr Hatherleigh refilled our cups. But I was still at a loss. And Alex was in a world of his own, doodling characters in Greek, not interested in notes. 'Do finish the biscuits,' Hatherleigh suggested.

'And so, to return to your original question, Dr Hatherleigh. The irreverence abhorred by the gods was a deep anxiety at the reckless potential of mankind's knowledge and behaviour that went beyond any assessment of the Atlantis incursions,' Jane explained.

'And an anxiety that surely begs a grounding in ethics. Would we not agree?' Dr Hatherleigh sat back, letting his words hang in the air before returning to Jane. 'Thank you. As always, I find your insights into these texts quite refreshing and, if I might say, illuminating.'

Jane smiled. I tried to make eye contact, but her attention switched to items in her bag.

'Francis,' continued Hatherleigh. 'We can only guess at Zeus's mind in this predicament, yet should we not shudder at the inevitability of the outcome?'

Francis stayed quiet.

Zeus's decision did seem harsh. At least, if you believed in the story. Total wipe out. No appeal. But was it inevitable? What the tale needs is a real hero, I thought. Not fancy, pontificating gods.

After a pause, Francis placed his fingers together. 'No, Dr Hatherleigh. The seeds of destruction were sown from the outset.

There was no other decision. Apocalypse was inevitable. A collapse underpinned by the grim humour we find in Socrates' account, mindful of his own conflict with the Athenian assembly.'

'A humour misplaced?' said the tutor.

'The assembly made him drink poison,' added Alex, quietly and incidentally, for me. He was still doodling, though.

'Or maybe not,' Francis ventured. 'Perhaps the glass of hemlock was welcomed. An antidote to his weariness. And bewilderment with the world.'

The mood slipped into a more reflective phase while the ancients' strange dialogues stared back at us. I was unsure about this embellished account of Atlantis. But with 'Timaeus' being about the creation of the world and time, and 'Critias' with their undoing, it nicely satisfied the Greek fondness for balance. Thesis and antithesis, as Hatherleigh might propose. And no one all that curious about the finality of it all, as I listened to them sharing a few words amongst themselves. Socrates and Plato, I thought. Dialogues. Myths. Symbols. What do they mean? And I still had an English essay to do for the following week. And then, after that, I might pop home for my little sister's birthday. The clock ticked amiably.

Alex stretched and yawned, drawing me back into the fold. 'Well, I'm not surprised the gods pulled the plug on the whole bloody lot of them. Just think what we might do today,' he said.

'But Alex,' I queried, 'who'd want to be a judge of our own state of affairs?'

Alex shrugged. Francis and Jane stayed quiet.

'Well, Richard,' said Dr Hatherleigh. 'An intriguing question. But suppose *you* were to make that judgement. On what grounds might you proceed?'

'You mean … against the world?'

'Indeed. Like Zeus, Richard, we call upon you to dissolve the world and give birth to another.' His words raised a smile.

'Well, actually, I'm not sure, Dr Hatherleigh, that I'd want to dissolve the world, anyway.'

No one stirred.

Dr Hatherleigh removed his glasses and pondered my response. 'Very well … what if we consider some undesirable aspects of our society?' He rubbed his eyes. 'There must be something that troubles you. Something you might wish to change in our public affairs?' He replaced his glasses and placed his hands together on his desk.

'Such as squalid behaviour,' said Jane, turning to me.

'Or anxiety about the past,' proposed Francis.

Or like this little spotlight, I thought, starting to feel awkward. 'Well, I suppose if we could change things, like things that affect us, then unfairness could be grounds. Yeah. Unfairness. In lots of ways. Past and present,' I said, hoping to relax their stares.

Alex returned a smile. I eased back in my chair.

'Unfairness!' repeated Hatherleigh, seizing the stage. 'I agree with you completely. Humans are justly condemned, everybody.' He lifted his cup in a tribute to the ruling. 'And, Jane, what might your grounds be if you were similarly instructed?'

'Oh, I'd charge them with selfishness, Dr Hatherleigh.'

'An appalling condition. Rooted in so many around us. To oblivion, we say!'

Alex didn't wait to be asked. 'I'd condemn everyone for arrogance.' He stretched his arms once again, smiling playfully at Francis. 'Just hand over the formula from Otto's book of spells. We can decide on the outcome as we crunch up the rest of Hatherleigh's biscuits.'

'Ha, ha, ha. Alex. Otto doesn't have a book of spells. It's much more scientific than that.'

'He's winding you up, Francis.' Jane removed her bag from the table, placing it beside her chair. She barely looked at Alex.

'I know,' said Francis. And not for the first time. But to dispose of a world, you must know when and where it was created.'

Francis folded his arms. He whispered something to Jane before checking his wristwatch. I heard the name Otto mentioned again.

'Francis, forgive me for sounding naïve, but what do you mean when you say a world is disposed of?' I asked.

'I mean, it's gone. Zapped. That particular universe is dissolved. From the point of its inception. Like the fate of Atlantis.'

'Zapped? As if it had never existed …?'

'Exactly. The history is unwritten. And so you start again.'

'The history is unwritten?' I queried.

'That's what the dialogue of Critias means, Richard,' Jane countered. Her eyes focused on me once more.

'Okay.' I spoke, sensing the spotlight again. 'And just how does everything start again?'

'Well, you could begin with "Timaeus",' replied Francis. 'And Plato's eighty-page explanation.'

I smarted. Of course, we could, that's what I'd bloody well read for half the night! I could feel the adrenalin simmering in my veins. '"Timaeus", guys. But didn't we get kind of sidetracked on this matter, with all this Atlantis stuff?'

Everyone stayed silent. I was feeling more than bewildered.

Our tutor clapped his hands. 'And so … the complete doctrine of the ancients. That man is forever on the edge of destruction and forever in need of renewal in his search for perfection. A doctrine, I remind you, that subtly informs his art and his architecture, as we have seen in other tutorials.'

And not just his art, I fancied. It haunts his imagination, too. Some stray lines from Donne added to my unease: 'He ruined me, and I am re-begot, | Of absence, darkness, death: things which are not.' Is this what they were driving at? Even the poem 'Twickenham Garden' seemed to shed some of its irritating obscurity. I bit into the last chocolate biscuit, barely lamenting its destruction.

A short chime from the old clock brought the session to a close.

'We shall pick up where we have left off at our next tutorial,' said Hatherleigh, retrieving a small desk calendar. 'I'll post a notice for it in due course … but sometime next month.'

And then a new chaos. The transition from class to hurried departure took me by surprise. I tugged Alex by his arm and suggested a bite to eat. He shook his head. How about a quick coffee? But no, he had to go. Something to do with Otto and the museum, he added, grabbing books from the shelves and calling out reminders to Francis and Jane before, pack-like, the three of them scrambled down the stairs, slamming the front door as they left the building behind them.

Had they forgotten I was still here?

'Richard. You studied drawing, Jane tells me.' I nodded, conscious of the tutor's solitary gaze. He turned to the celebrated fresco. '"The School of Athens"', he remarked.

'Yes. Raphael, I believe.' I gestured to leave, but his stare resisted my intention.

'A very precise demonstration of perspective, wouldn't you say?'

I studied the print and the well-known gathering of ancient philosophers.

'See how our eye is drawn to the *point de fuite* in the distant background?'

'The vanishing point?'

'Indeed. The vanishing point. And the origin of all causes.'

Dr Hatherleigh stared wistfully into the frame. He barely noticed my departure. I closed the door behind me, and ignoring the lift, or whatever Hatherleigh liked to call it, took a few puzzled steps to the top of the stairs. And as I made my way down, my mood hardened. I've got a hundred fucking questions, Alex, and all you do is clear off to the museum. My pace picked up. Art History B, I wondered. What the hell is going on here?

14

'We all wish the world was a different place, James.' Alison Farring, Secretary of State for Foreign and Commonwealth Affairs in the United Kingdom government, looked quizzically at her department head. 'But this paper of yours … it doesn't give us much choice in the matter.'

'I regret, ma'am, that the situation with our American friends has taken an unforeseen turn.'

Alison Faring shifted uneasily in her chair. 'This William chap. We appear to have lost a sympathetic partner. Did I ever meet him?'

'Yes, you did. The reception—downstairs in the history department, if you recall. William joined me in the library with Professor Littlejohn.'

'Hmm. A tall gentleman, I remember. East Coast, wasn't he?'

'Boston. His family were amongst the earliest settlers in North America, he claimed.'

Alison returned her attention to James's slim but baffling report. 'And this new team on the case … this Warren fellow?'

'Warren Dudley, State Department. A religious revivalist, I understand. And a friend, too, of the president. I rather fear he means business, ma'am.'

'Really?' A hint of belligerence unsettled James. 'So, what am I going to tell the prime minister? That a bunch of academics and undergraduates are plotting to destroy the world? That the Americans have linked them to a satanic cult in the middle of

London? And we're the Johnny-come-lately still twiddling our thumbs?'

'I'm not sure you should be so candid, Alison … if I may say.'

'Candid? If any of your report reaches the public, we'll be a complete laughingstock.'

'I could redraft my paper if you so wish.'

'No. But frankly, I'm in two minds on this. If I'm to present to the Cabinet, I need a proper grasp of this threat. Perpetrators. Motives. Timelines. Means. I can't waffle on about obscurities. Just how on earth do these people plan to blow everything up?'

A gentle cough helped James to clear his throat. 'My paper may appear extraordinary, foreign secretary. Hence my caution. And, if you would allow, some obliqueness in the matter.'

'Well, I'm not sure I do allow. I want you to be direct, James. I have twenty-five minutes before the Cabinet secretary wants me to make a statement. COBRA meets this evening.'

'Very well. The American fear, ma'am, is that the students have made a critical discovery in their studies.'

'Their *occult* studies?' The foreign secretary's finger tapped noisily on the first page of the report. 'Well, your account is not shy of saying that.' She turned the pages. 'Astrology … alchemy … and here a table of coordinates in time and space.' She leant forwards, affecting a sudden curiosity. 'Now, tell me, James, what's all *that* about?'

'It concerns an ancient doctrine concerning the origin of the cosmos.'

'Well, you'd better explain it. I never had much time for that sort of nonsense at Oxford, and I suspect the PM will want something a little more prosaic … if you wouldn't mind.'

James swallowed. 'It's a recurrent feature of ancient cultures, I am told. The world over, there are many enduring accounts of violent cataclysms and lost golden ages.'

'Golden ages? You're not making this easy, James.'

'Forgive me.' James paused as he rephrased his thoughts. 'In a more practical sense, the information we have received suggests the students are exploiting concepts that are known to cosmologists as parallel universes and encapsulated time, albeit, ma'am, behind a cloak of deliberate and misleading obfuscation. The more exotic references you mentioned.'

The foreign secretary scribbled a short note.

'Modern speculation about the origin of the cosmos is covered in quantum physics, I believe, and even explored using artificial intelligence.'

'And why does that alarm our allies?'

'Well, it would appear that the intention of the students is to substitute this world with a new one altogether.'

'You mean to get rid of ours and start their own?'

'In effect, ma'am. And with a global order somewhat on their own terms is our understanding.' James sat upright in his chair. A faint smile leant a delicate touch to his demeanour.

'In that case, I can see the Americans' point.' The foreign secretary added to her notes. 'At least I can tell the prime minister that we are up to date with their intentions.'

'Indeed. And I think it would be helpful to let the PM know that the United Kingdom would not remain unscathed in such a *denouement*.'

'Yes. James. I'm sure we can all draw that conclusion.' Alison Faring rose from her desk and stepped towards the window that looked out on St James's Park. 'Quantum physics', she sighed, catching the soft colours of the park. 'And mythic ages.' She turned back to her department head. 'The immediate priority, James, is to support our allies. I'm sure, that with the usual cooperation, these outcomes you describe can be avoided.' She smiled sternly at James before returning to her desk.

'And you can assure the PM that my team will work closely with Warren Dudley.'

'Good. I propose to tell Downing Street that we've uncovered a little mischief at the university, and we've asked the vice-chancellor to handle it internally.'

'Very well. And the Americans?'

'The Americans. Yes. I shall say that we are sharing our intelligence.' She flipped to the report's concluding remarks before reaching for a pen. 'Good. But I need answers to a few simple questions.'

James moved forward in his chair.

'How long has this group been on our radar?'

'For more than two years, but there is a much longer history ...'

'Let's keep it focused. I take it that more recent developments have upset our American friends.'

'Yes, although William was rather nonchalant about the whole business. Hence his ...'

'His replacement, James.' Alison Faring looked sharply across the table. 'Now, do we know why the university is the centre of activity?'

'London is the hub of their interests and research. And a reference point for determining the coordinates. But their network is shadowy, and they're disinclined to use any technology that would leave a trail on social media.'

'Hmm. So other places, names and institutions could be involved?'

'Yes. But if we had more resources ... and better access.'

'Well, we'll see. If COBRA thinks that this is a credible threat, there will be more. In the meantime, James, you must keep our allies sweet, please. And don't forget the usual jollies for them. Like the diplomatic circuit. And the arts committee.' Alison Faring glanced back at the report. 'Now this date and time business. I need an angle on this. I can't just talk about starry coordinates to the cabinet secretary. What on earth do they mean?'

'This is the key, so to speak, to the students' plans.'

'Well, unlock them for me, James. The clock's ticking.'

'Their belief in new worlds, ma'am, is based on a fundamental premise: that every world and age was configured and launched at a particular place and on a particular day. And that any new world may be invoked using these coordinates with the right instruments and calculations.'

'Invoked. Out of thin air?'

'Through a process controlled by a cosmic blueprint. A specific permutation, if the PM might allow, with events uniquely determined and inevitable thereafter.' James paused. 'I'm sorry if it sounds far-fetched, foreign secretary, but remember when the Committee on Historical Matters was launched in 1912, it was staffed predominantly by Cambridge physicists, as well as military intelligence.'

'Maybe. But the beginning of time for the prime minister was the last election, James. If we look as if we're not taking a threat like this seriously, then the next election just might be its termination. I'll make a note of "cosmic permutation" as the answer to my question.'

Alison Farring shuffled the pages of the report, satisfied that she could at least provide a preliminary assessment for the cabinet meeting. She checked the time again, before placing her hands down on the table.

A throaty cough disturbed her concentration.

'The bookshelf, if I may, foreign secretary?'

'Of course. Anything, if it lends more clarity to this bizarre subject.'

James retrieved a magisterial-looking atlas and placed it on the desk in front of his boss. Benjamin Franklin, according to anecdotal tradition, had consulted the work in the reign of George III when the Foreign Office was close to Franklyn's own residence in London. James turned the pages with care before settling on a large cartographic plate of the western hemisphere. The atlas was over three hundred years old.

The foreign secretary stared at the vast empty spaces, the spidery contours of barely discovered lands, the strange, fanciful names. And the silent, fading colours.

James coughed again. 'Somewhere. Somewhere on this map of

the New World, foreign secretary, lies the complete answer to your question on starry coordinates.'

Alison Farring looked up. 'And this is what the students have worked out for themselves?'

'Date. Time. And the place, we suspect. The point at which, they believe, our modern world was sprung from a pre-existing trajectory.'

'No wonder the Americans are curious.' Alison Faring shook her head. 'It's right in their own backyard.'

'Indeed, foreign secretary. And I fear they do appear to be the centre of the universe, after all.'

A gentle buzz diverted the foreign secretary's attention. A message flashed across her computer screen. She composed herself. 'I'm sorry. The cabinet secretary.'

James Ellison rose from his chair and turned towards the oak-panelled door that led to the safer corridors of diplomacy.

'Before you leave, James, there is something I should tell you. Two years ago, I had intended to remove you from this committee.'

James paused as his hand reached for the brass handle of the door. 'Yes. I believe there was such a discussion.'

'Professor Littlejohn interceded on your behalf.'

'Yes. He has always been supportive of our work, foreign secretary.' James smiled weakly.

'What you should understand, is that Her Majesty's Government has its own stake in this matter. If the students have this secret, then we need to know it too.'

'But of course, foreign secretary.'

'And you will ensure that the Americans' *anxiety* about these people gets the appropriate attention?'

James nodded before slipping aside from Alison Farring's long, equivocal stare. He stepped outside, closing the heavy door behind him. Above his head, and with a finger to her lips, the ghostly mural of the ancient Sybil bid him silence.

15

I paired up with Jenny on the dance floor. It was nearly ten o'clock and the humanities social that she had told me about was in full swing.

'So, where's your friend, Richard?' she said, shooting the words between screeching, chaotic chords from the band.

'You mean Josh?'

'Yeah. The one who gets off on poetry.' Jenny veered to the left. We closed up again before the space filled with arms and heads that thrust out of nowhere.

'Don't be cruel,' I said, not sure if she was serious. 'He was only saying the obvious.'

'Yeah. For a bloke.' Jenny crashed into me, but bounced away before I could offer support. More guys rushed to the floor like a galloping herd. I tried to get closer. 'So where is he, then?' she asked, shouting the words.

'He's been held up. Something going on. By the river.'

'He's gone home. He's ditched you.'

She veered off to the side again, eclipsed by the glitzy, flamboyant lights. Icy, metallic blues and demonic reds swept the air, landing fast and furious on all the head bobbing faces around me as I tried to stay alongside. 'He's with his girlfriend,' I said as she edged further away. 'They do everything together. Like dancing.'

But Jenny was uninterested. I spun around with my own show of defiance, losing any sense of her bearings. The music blasted a familiar tune, while a chorus of raw, rasping voices strained to keep up with the beat. It was uninhibited. Testeronic. Clothing seemed a burden in the sweaty heat, and my short-sleeved shirt clung to my skin like a tight-fitting sheathe. Pairing didn't matter any more.

But the tempo was too much. And the bass pounded my ears. I needed a break, and a gentle buzz in my jeans gave me cause to slip away from the floor. Sapped-out, I unbuttoned my shirt and drew a long, resuscitating breath. I wanted to shower in ice-cold beer.

Jenny had headed back to the girls' table to deliver her report. I'd turned up an hour before and splashed out on a few drinks, hoping to improve my ranking. But while a few guys still fancied their chances, others were now sinking pints. I wavered between the two camps before crashing at an empty table nearby. I'd get another drink for sure. But first, I needed to check out whatever had happened to my mate and his girlfriend.

Josh had said something odd in his flurry of texts. I read them again. *Will be late*, he'd said. *Near the river. Embankment Gardens.* And then, *Trouble.* And his last one. *Helping police.* Helping police? What the hell's going on? I thought. Would they even make it? I couldn't say, but I'd stick around. And he'd mentioned that his rowing pal, Martin, was somewhere at the bar. I lifted my head, but couldn't see much as I screwed my eyes at the constantly flashing lights.

'That guy sounded a bit pompous the other day.'

Surprised, I swung to my left. A girl my own age had pulled up the chair next to me.

'Who?' I asked, no longer having to shout.

'The guy in the tutorial. The one who upset your friend. Wasn't he called Jonathan?'

'Oh, yeah.' I tucked the phone back into my jeans. 'But he's just a show-off. Spouting his own kind of crap.' I did up the buttons of my shirt. 'You're doing English?'

'Yeah. I think the poems are really interesting.'

'I agree.' And as I studied her face, Josh's predicament slipped from my mind. I noticed she wasn't wearing makeup. And she'd tied her hair behind her neck. She smiled at me.

'The real genius is in the language. And the way Donne intensifies quite ordinary experiences. I mean, with deeper meanings and conflicts of desire.'

I nodded, still looking at her face. 'Did you study Donne in sixth form?' I asked.

'Songs and Sonnets. Elegies. We also did the other metaphysical poets: Herbert, Vaughan, Cowley, Carew, Traherne.'

'Wow. So, you know them all?'

'Nearly.' She smiled again. '"Had we but world enough and time …"'

Andrew Marvell, I remembered. 'To His Coy Mistress'. A bashful glance by me completed the line.

The band shifted to a slower number.

Maybe I should buy her a drink, I thought. Or have a dance. But I wondered about my shirt. And the beads of sweat still crawling down my skin. But then another buzz in my jeans alerted me. 'It's Josh,' I explained. 'You remember, my friend in class? He's been helping the police with something.' I pulled the phone from my pocket. 'I'm sorry, I forgot your name.'

'Fiona. I can send you a text, Richard.'

'Sure.' I was about to exchange numbers when Josh's own words leapt out at me.

Call me. Urgent.

I mumbled my number to Fiona. 'Sorry, got to make a call.' I flashed the mobile. 'He might be in trouble. Back soon.'

I skirted the dance floor and headed for a space near the bar. As I approached, I spotted Martin lurking alone with a pint. He called me over, looking keen for some company.

'Well, how did it go, Richard?'

'Oh, Jenny. So-so. Just bouncing around on the dance floor. Didn't really get close.' I checked the signal on my phone.

'I meant your tutorial. With Francis and Jane.'

'Oh that.' I was still fiddling with the phone. 'Well, it was okay. Very civilised. We even had tea. As you said.' The signal faded. 'I'm trying to get Josh.'

'Doesn't surprise me. It'll be supper next.'

I still couldn't connect. I turned back to Martin. 'But there were things I didn't understand. They seem to be desperately serious about something.'

'I told you.' Martin had a sip of beer.

'Did you ever do anything on Atlantis?'

'Sorry, friend. Don't do weird.' He rolled his eyes.

'That's what I'm thinking.' Martin took a larger swig of beer. 'I thought I'd come over and check out the new intake. Post-grads are a miserable bunch at the start of term. Might even find a crew for the boathouse if the bleeders would stand still for a moment. By the way, who is the band?'

'They're called Fornax. Fornax,' I repeated. 'It means furnace in Latin, I think.'

'Well, they've come to the right place. Like a bloody oven in here.' Another gulp and his glass was empty. 'I'll get them. My round after our last little outing.'

While Martin got the beers, I read the rest of Josh's last text.

Sophie upset. Wants to go home.

Fuck. I grit my teeth. Oh, well. Another time. He'd sent his first text at nine. And it was well after ten now. So, something was up. I watched Martin count out his cash as I figured how long I might stay. But I had hoped to meet Josh's girlfriend. And … oh Christ, I'd promised to get back to Fiona. I glanced across the dance floor. The table I'd just left was now full of guys. Close by were the girls. But no Fiona. Nor Jenny, for that matter. I slipped my phone back into my pocket.

Martin handed me the beer. 'Never really got into all that philosophy stuff. Now the art history …' He clinked my glass.

'Cheers.'

'Well, at least you can see something on a wall. We did a lot on … who was it now? Those early Dutch chaps.'

'Bosch,' I suggested.

'Yeah, Bosch. Now, he was a bit of a joker. Oh, and Van Eyck. I liked him.' Martin eased back and, posing for a moment, held a finger to his cheek. 'Yes. Oil mainly, I believe.'

I nodded.

'And old Arbetta going on about the Pre-Raphaelites. You know …'

But I didn't. I just wasn't tuned in. Girls. Mates. Lectures. They were all out of control. I reached for Martin's arm. 'Listen, how well did you know Francis and Jane?'

'Well, not like having-a-few-beers sort of friendly. Or the other guy, Alex. But I remember Alex bragging about the trouble he'd got into. And the windows he'd smashed.'

'The windows?'

'Yeah. Politics came off worst. I don't blame him, mind.'

'And the police. Were they involved?' I was still worrying about Josh and his girlfriend.

'No. That was the strange thing. One moment uproar. Next, everything hushed up. They're a funny bunch, your friends.' Martin sipped his beer.

I started to wonder if Alex was the real outsider in all this, whatever his art history affiliations.

'You're not having second thoughts, are you?'

'Not sure. I'm confused about everything to do with them. I'll give it another tutorial. See how it goes. There's always the other art course instead.' I stared into my glass. And the one I'm kind of signed-up to, I remembered. I drank, wondering how much it might matter.

'Well, before you change your mind. You see that guy with the admiring throng of groupies?'

I looked up, sensing one of Martin's more juicy asides.

'That's Lionel Arbetta.'

'You are kidding.'

Martin shook his head. He looked as old as Hatherleigh and was partying like a fresher. Martin nudged me with his elbow. 'Won't be many innocents on his watch once they've done the Grand Tour.' We both laughed, helplessly spilling our beers. 'You're safer on the B option, Richard.' He winked again. 'Reminds me of that painting by ...'

But he never said. Another text buzzed in my jeans. I retrieved the phone.

Look up now. I'm free.

Josh appeared in the flickering light. 'Made it, guys. But Sophie's gone home. She's upset.'

'So, what happened?'

'You won't believe it. But someone got shot.'

'And you were there?'

'Yeah. Some guy was being chased around the gardens' We closed up as Josh shared the news. 'He ran right past us. And then these other guys, they like, threatened us, as if we'd helped him escape.'

'And did you see him get shot?'

'No. I was helping Sophie after they had pushed her to the ground. We'd been walking in the gardens when they came running out of nowhere.'

'So how do you know he was shot?'

'Because we heard it. Like bang!' Josh shook his head. 'And then the police grilled us and called the uni to check out our story. And now we've got to make a formal statement in the morning.'

'Statement?'

'Yeah. And I said she's upset. That she's crying. So they said we could go, but we'd have to come back tomorrow. They were still searching the gardens for something when we left. I had to sneak the texts to you.'

I nodded. But felt unsettled by his account.

'So why were you hanging around Embankment Gardens in the first place?'

'Leave off, Martin. We just went for a walk. Sophie wanted to talk things over before we came here. That's all.'

'Is that what you told the police?'

'Listen. Just get me a beer. I need a drink.'

Martin went to the bar. I grinned at Josh. At least they were safe, if a little shaken-up by the experience. But that poor guy who got shot. 'Did anyone say who he was?'

Josh shook his head. We'd find out eventually, he reckoned. Martin returned with a beer and a double Scotch.

'Better get this inside you.'

Josh threw back the whisky while I held his pint.

'Thanks, guys, needed that.' He wiped his brow. 'We're going to Charing Cross Police Station tomorrow. For the statement. Do you know where it is?'

'It's near Trafalgar Square.' I gave him his beer. A few generous gulps, and he'd downed most of it.

The band segued into its closing routine. Most guys had finally flagged and staggered off the floor. And not all of them would make it home, I reckoned. Josh's misfortunes had dampened our mood, and his own thoughts were on Sophie, anyway. He checked his phone for messages, shaking his head. There wasn't much for it except to drink up and go home. But first, I needed to catch up with the girls. I asked Martin and Josh to hang on while I slipped across the empty dance floor. I approached one of Jenny's friends. She saw me coming.

'Looking for Jenny, are you, Richard?'

'No. Another girl. Her name's Fiona.'

'She's not with us.'

I looked around. Maybe they weren't hanging out. 'So where's Jenny, then?'

'She left with her boyfriend. He's a second-year.'

I turned back to the guys. It was time to leave. I had some serious thinking to do.

16

I stared at the Thames, wondering how much Josh enjoyed his new exertions on its ever-shifting waters. Martin had told him that rowing unshackles the mind and liberates the spirit. That he would see the world in a different light. Well, perhaps. But he'd see the twilight dawn for sure. And the steady break of a dull autumnal day.

I'd gone to Victoria Embankment Gardens and the river's hard, protective wall, hoping to meet Jane. I'd finally freaked out over the art history. No one was telling me anything. And since we'd last met at our tutorial, I'd been to three more classes in English. I'd finished that essay on Donne, seen off Jonathan and his sneers, and did a good job on Donne's poetic friends as well. Even Fiona was pleased.

Josh, too, had sorted things out with the police. Three pages of testimony. Who he'd seen, what he'd heard, and why he was there. But he didn't say any more. A shot, that's all. And Sophie pushed to the ground and in tears. So, I left it alone. And then he disappeared for a while, skipping the last two classes that we shared. But he sent me a few texts on weights, rowing machines, and boats. And the river. He'd even won a few plaudits from his coach. Well, Martin had dropped some of the lip, he'd said. Good for him.

And I'd read a few more books. Popped home for my sister's birthday. And talked to Dad about him losing one job and then getting another. Mum was pleased.

I rested my arms on the river's granite wall. The water was swollen now. A steady mass held by the great blocks of stone that lined its meandering shores—poised, as if stealing itself to turn. I stared, waiting for that uncertain moment in its journey back and forth, to and fro. I wondered, whimsically, if it might ever stall. As if time itself might linger between opposing goals. Or whether … whether it might just continue from beginning to end without rest or pause. But no, just an idle thought. The tide always turns. This way, that way. Set in obedience to the silent, toiling moon—its distant tasking companion. I raised my eyes. 'With how sad steps, O Moon thou climb'st the sky'. Sad steps … now who wrote that? Some poet. And some forgotten tutorial, I supposed, stretching my arms and yawning at the memory.

And now, now it was I who was idling. Stalled like the fully loaded Thames, swamped by my own heavy currents. I should have grabbed Jenny by the hand when I had the chance. And kept on dancing. Instead, a pushy second-year pulls rank. Someone cool. So, I screwed up. Had a chance. And blew it. 'Fear death by water'. More telltale, taunting lines. And tell me, stricken brain, who's that? Eliot, of course. T. S. Eliot. And shall I dare? Shall I dare disturb … the universe? I dunno.

I looked downstream towards the bridges and piers of the City of London. And I hope that Josh can swim. The boats are so flat and flimsy. Skimming the water with lashing, beating oars. Like dealing with life, I mused. And hanging on and braving random, hostile waves. Like a sea of troubles. Or a friendly surge. A tide in the affairs of men. I smiled. Yes, brain, I know who said that.

I checked the time. It was almost twelve. And the sky—blank and grey. No sun. No moon. No nothing. I looked again. A leaf stirred. Between the impulse and the motion … falls the shadow. I smiled. The river had turned. Like a whisper nurturing an infant's breath.

I wondered about my art history friends. How they'd met and what kept them together. And why they seemed to hide things. To talk discreetly. Obliquely, the tutor had said. It wasn't as if I was fooling anyone. Or even wanted to. I was happy with the course. The

Renaissance insights. The perspectives. This was my erudite guide to those hungry, literary cravings that drove me on. At least it's what I'd said to Hatherleigh. At my interview. So, okay, I knew already that the moon was the goddess Diana. Silvery and fickle. And that poets worship her melancholy face. But now, they're saying there's much more. Things unseen. Under the surface. And that, too, I'd heard before. Old boring teachers at school. Look deeper, they'd moan. Deeper. But I didn't. I just didn't. The river flowed. Building its strength, setting its stride at an increasing pace. And still no sign of Jane. I scratched the letters *RA* on the harsh granite wall. Slowly and jaggedly with a coin. Would anyone see? Would anyone care? I wasn't sure. Even my school friends had ditched me. Four weeks now and not a word or call. No texts. Just silence. And slow-dissolving stares.

I messed up at Oxford, too. Something in Latin on the tutor's door. I'd felt alarm. And so why me? Why are they so keen that I should be in their precious group and share their plans? Why Jane? Francis? And Alex? Why all that pally embrace and open-heartedness? 'Don't worry,' Alex had said, 'we'll look after you.'

But why? I looked away.

'"Sweet Thames, run softly ..."' The words coasted on the breeze.

I turned. It was Jane, looking contrite but standing apart from me.

'"Till I end my song",' I added, completing the line. She smiled back, but stayed motionless. 'The poem celebrates a marriage, I believe. By the poet, Edmund Spenser ... You're ten minutes late.'

'I'm very sorry, Richard. We realise that we've let you down. Francis insisted that I go and meet you. We were very sad when we saw your message.'

'And Alex. Is he sad too?'

Jane stepped closer. 'Richard. You know he likes you. He speaks of you often. And he will be in touch. But he is stressed. We all are. By our work.'

I turned aside and traced a finger on the granite wall. My initials had hardly scratched the stone, and for a moment, I wondered if she and Francis saw me as some simple adolescent forced to linger in their busy, eclipsing shadows. *They* had invited *me* into their world and their strange preoccupations, for heaven's sake. And now I just wanted to be friends. I wasn't even sure that Jane would turn up today after her hastily scribbled reply. Like that first day, when I'd got back from Hatherleigh, bursting to share the good news. I turned, but waited for her to speak first.

'I realise it must seem rude. But we can't discuss everything yet. We want you to know, Richard. And Alex *will* tell you.' She lowered her head. 'But we don't want to place you in any difficulties.'

'Well, if you can't say what's going on, can we at least have a means of communicating? None of you have any phones. I can't keep running up to noticeboards looking for odd messages. I don't even know when the next tutorial is.' I swung back to the river in frustration.

Jane touched my arm. 'Let's go for a coffee. It's a little too open here. And we should talk. We can walk through the gardens.' I turned my head. Her eyes lent a fleeting sparkle to her face. 'I always think of them as special, Richard. And they're so full of history.'

Coffee, then. And a chance to breathe. We crossed the road, leaving the river behind us. I slipped the coin back into my pocket.

We found a café at the western end of the gardens, near a squat, stone arch that had once marked the boundary of a much wider Thames. Jane mentioned its history. An improbable survivor from turbulent times, it is known today as York Watergate. Once part of York House, the home of Tudor earls, it looked quite humble now. And solitary. We settled at a table nearby sheltered by a large, towering tree resplendent in autumnal golds.

'Alex, Francis and I, have known each other for over three years, now, Richard. Young, curious spirits'—her face brightened—'alive to the same ideals and quiet passions from the moment we met.' She lifted her leather bag to the table and offered to pay. I noticed the logo of a fashionable brand.

'So, were you at school together?' I asked.

'No, not at all.' Jane retrieved her purse. 'Although I was born in London, my schooling was mostly overseas. My father was in the army, so lessons followed postings. Cyprus. Brunei. Only in Germany did it ever get cold. We were always dabbling in languages and cultures, I remember.' She paused as a breeze ruffled the leaves above our heads. I gestured to the waiter. 'Francis is from Oxfordshire and was educated privately, including some years at an academy in the States. He's not very athletic though, and is not at all fond of water. Alex … he's from Kent. He won a scholarship at eighteen.'

'Really? Seems hard to believe.'

'Yes. Everyone says that. But we first met at a residential sixth-form conference more than a year before we arrived here at the university. We then went on holiday in Greece. And across the Aegean.'

Swanning around the islands, I thought. 'Must have been fun.'

'Yes, over two years ago, now. We'd ventured to the heart of the Cyclades. Everything gleaming white and blue. The noisy harbours bustling as you arrive. Feeling carefree, I remember. And that's when we first visited Delos and its temples.'

It was not difficult for me to conjure the scene. The lazy days. The fierce sunlight. The silent ruins. And all those elusive gods and heroes to marvel at. And I used to in class, lingering over my textbook's glossy plates, trying to lend substance to impossible myths and obscure, brutal tales. I smiled. Forlornly. Maybe next year, then. Island hopping. And swimming …

The waiter joined us. We ordered coffee.

'Francis is the deep thinker, though he can be obstinate in his view of the world. And he will tease Alex too much, Richard. And then Alex just explodes, insisting on his own right to decide.'

'Is that why he didn't travel with you over the summer?'

'No, not really.' Jane looked away, her face drawn. 'We'd already made several trips. But last summer was different. Alex stayed in London. Something had happened between us and he was very upset.' She clutched the handle of her bag as if to protect it. 'So Francis and I went alone. We had a specific investigation in mind while Alex worked with Dr Hatherleigh and a friend, Otto, at the British Museum.'

Jane's comment intrigued me. 'So Hatherleigh is part of this … research, too?'

'Yes. It started, Richard, at the conference. I mentioned this strange affinity. It was as if destiny had thrown us together.' She paused, relaxing the grip on her bag. 'Do you believe in such things? In destiny?'

I shrugged. 'Sometimes odd things happen. Why we make one decision and not another.'

Jane smiled. 'It wasn't easy for us at first, hearing these obscure tales of ancient times, learning from texts that whole worlds and epochs were predetermined in their course of history. That every one of us follows a fated path.'

'Sounds like "Timaeus",' I replied.

'Yes. Plato.' A sudden breeze diverted our thoughts. We both looked up. 'Francis grasped the maths. Lots of exotic equations and ratios. New insights. And our field excursions helped to answer questions and fears that lurked within our own minds. The things the ancient sources mention in their tracts and mysteries.'

'Delos,' I interrupted. 'Wasn't it the birthplace of Apollo? And some sort of oracle?'

'Yes. And of his sister, Artemis. Sun and moon, remember.' Jane retrieved a brochure from her bag. I could see upright columns and paved, rocky walkways set under a rampant sky. 'Look. The Sanctuary of Apollo. To the Greeks, Delos was once the navel of the Earth. They even marked it with a stone.' She pointed to a black-and-white photographic image. 'An omphalos. Perhaps you know the meaning?'

I shrugged. 'No. I've never been there. And I don't think Aristophanes made any jokes about it, either.'

The sound of a few sliding chairs drew our attention. A couple and their child readied themselves to leave while hesitating over the tip. Jane placed the brochure on the table.

'You are right, Richard. We can be so intense that we forget how to behave.' She forced a smile.

'You gave me a hard time, Jane. At the tutorial. And I had pre-pared. I'd ploughed through the whole of Plato's bloody text. And instead, we talked about Atlantis. You and Francis. And all those stupid legends. And then everyone just cleared off at the end.'

I still felt the hurt.

The waiter reappeared with our drinks before turning to the vacated table and its token gratuity. Jane returned the brochure and placed her bag by her feet. Our eyes met. I still hoped I could be part of their group. That we could sort things out between us. I glanced down, caressing the coffee cup with my hands. Glad for its warmth and a soft heat that tempered my pride. Another breeze swept through the branches overhead, swelling the leaves with a soft percussive roar. We looked up as a leaf fell towards us, dawdling in the air, before a gust snatched it away. Jane reached for my hand.

'Richard. We want to invite you to dinner. At our place. We have a little celebration we want to share.'

'You mean, near the British Museum?'

'Yes. In Bloomsbury. And Alex will be there.' She let go of my hand. 'He's even promised to play for us and sing a few songs.'

'Alex?' I drew back.

'Yes, it is rather funny, Richard. But he studied music.' We lost eye contact as she reached for her cup. 'Of course, there's a very ordinary side to Alex. As we know.'

And a more settled one too, I reckoned. 'I'd love to come. But I haven't much of a voice, I'm afraid.'

'Oh, don't worry. Francis is unmusical too. And anyway, Alex knows how to entertain us when he has a mind. We always had a wonderful time in Greece. Singing and dancing late into the night at the tavernas.'

We finished our coffee, and as we relaxed, I noticed a gull stamping the ground towards us, eyeing the table for food. We shared a laugh at its boldness.

Jane opened a small pocket diary. She tabbed the pages until landing on a date. 'Shall we say Friday evening, two weeks from now? At seven thirty?' I nodded, checking the calendar on my phone. 'I'll order some fresh food,' she added. 'Francis does a lovely fish pie. But you'll have to remember the address, I'm afraid.'

'Hold on.' I glanced mischievously to my left and right before handing Jane the phone. 'Add the post code as numbers for me. I can always work it out if you prefer to keep it secret.'

She took the phone and entered the address. And as she returned it to me, I heard a chair crash to the ground. I looked around and saw Francis running towards us. 'Jane. Jane,' he called, his voice heavy with emotion. She turned and rose to her feet. By the time that I had risen, he was standing beside us. He was shaking.

'Jane … Paulo is dead.'

Jane sat precipitously. 'How?'

'Shot. Murdered.' His jaw fell as he drew breath.

'Oh, Paulo,' she cried.

Jane snatched her bag and stood up again. She fumbled with her purse, slapping money on the table for our drinks. We left without ceremony and hurried up the steps to a street that lay behind the rough-looking arch from long ago. And old iron railings that almost barred the way. And the sudden shock of death.

They fell into each other's arms. Braving their grief in a tight, bitter-sweet embrace. I stepped back, conscious of my own helplessness and solitude.

Jane turned to me as they separated. A sigh softened her composure. 'He was a wonderful man, Richard. A wonderful friend.' She wiped her eyes.

'I'm sorry,' I mumbled, unsure what to say. Or do.

Francis led us up the terraced street. It sloped gently towards the Strand. Once, it too was foreshore and mud, but graced now by solid, eighteenth-century facades. Quietly and decently minding our tears. And as we trudged away, leaving the gardens and their innocence behind, you could still hear the busy gulls. Swooping keenly. Squabbling for scraps of food. And cars driving beside the Thames. And people going about. And the chill, flitting wind.

Unreal city.

We crossed the Strand and walked up Bedford Street before turning into the small public garden that lies at the rear of the church, at the western end of Covent Garden's piazza. An old gateway led us into the square alongside the portico of St Paul's where, a few weeks before, Alex and I had played the noisy fools. And where Jane, I recalled, had rebuked us. We paused once through the gate.

Francis raised his hand and pointed towards the balustrade of the building ahead of us. His eyes moistened. 'Just there, Richard. That's where we first met Paulo. A few days after we had enrolled at the uni.'

I stepped back, though my eyes remained fixed on the balustrade.

'Richard, is there something wrong?' asked Jane.

'I'm not sure.'

She moved closer. 'You've gone quite pale. And you are shaking.'

'Sorry, Jane.' I felt my heart pound. 'You mean the small café, Francis?'

'Yes, Richard. Paulo used to manage it. He had a lovely old print of the piazza, I remember. By Wenceslaus Hollar. Just above the till.'

My legs weakened. I wanted to run.

17

The ceiling of the Locarno room in the British Foreign Office was easily thirty feet high. Constructed in the 1860s, its bright, gaudy plaster was emblazoned with stark, pagan motifs.

Warren Dudley dismissed the symbols from his mind. He turned to his phone and rechecked the date and time of his appointment with James Ellison. November seventh. 9.00a.m. He flipped to his mail file and to an update from an associate in Washington, DC. There were still issues that troubled him. Issues of loyalty, faith, and history. Shying the content from his subordinate, Larry Antony, he eased back in his chair, anxious for answers.

Committee on Historical Matters

First talked about in the forties, after Pearl Harbour, but didn't really get going until 1950 and the White House reconstruction under Truman. The British agreed to share their stuff, and we offered to support.

Warren scrolled through the email, noting provisions to intelligence agreements and conditions attached to American financial packages in the post-war years. Nothing was free, he observed with a smile.

<blockquote>

An office was set up on Pennsylvania Avenue. The Brits had theirs at the Foreign Office in Whitehall. The US side was led by Colonel Dearing. In 1953, the CIA became involved at the request of President Eisenhower. (Footnote: Dearing, I've discovered, was on Walter Fairbright's team in Europe. Interested in art theft and weird occult sects at the end of WW2.)

</blockquote>

Warren reflected on the dates. 1950 was the year that his father returned from Europe following military service. It was two years before his parents had married and joined their local church community. The Foundation had followed in 1960. And after that, the mission overseas to the UK. And his days as a young man preaching to the fallen in London's Soho in the early eighties. He warmed to the memories before refocusing his thoughts.

<blockquote>

Committee reports: They're signed by Col. Dearing. File references ARC1950.164-1, -2 and -3. The first one is about history. The Virginia Company. The East Coast settlements. There are some early maps and copies of freehold plans, trading agreements with native tribes, land surveys, and missionary accounts. But many records were lost in the destruction of Congress by the Brits in 1814 and more when the old Patent Office burnt down in 1836. There are sections on Canada and Newfoundland but don't know why.

</blockquote>

Warren paused. He recalled the invasion planning under President Hoover. It might be relevant, he decided.

A second report covers a bunch of things like
architecture, buildings in the US and England,
and has a list of landscape paintings. Could
be something visual. I can follow this up if it
means anything to you. Kind of reminded me
of my art classes in high school.

Warren looked again at the décor. He still felt uneasy at the extravagant display around him. The gold and red that blazed everywhere. The panels, quadrants and columns that indulged the wicked, lurid scheme. And a ceiling that arched above his head boasting a palette of shameless lies. He shuddered. Perhaps even here, amidst this vile, blatant deceit, there was a clue. In the arrogant planets. And the phony, lounging gods. Irritated, he returned to his email.

The third report includes a lot of math and some ancient
Greek texts, but doesn't say why. But nothing about dates.
Or locations. And that's it. I'll send copies of what I've got.
If there were any more meetings, I can't trace the reports.

He scrolled again.

CIA Assessment Briefings: Hit a problem. Langley
doesn't want to know. Can your people assist in any way?

Warren thrust the phone into his lap. If the CIA won't help, then it'll have to be the military. Like the 82nd. Or maybe nuclear. He recalled the name of an old friend in the Defense Department before turning to the last few lines of the mail.

Postscript: Col. Dearing transferred to US Occupation
forces, Austria in September '52. Brigadier-General

*Harry E. Peters succeeded him. (Peters had worked on
Operation X-roads in Bikini back in '46 on the atomic test
program). Peters retired in 1957 and died in Honolulu in
1975. Dearing in Virginia in 1998. See reports in local
newspapers via the link.*

Yes. He remembered. His dear late wife had been Abe Dearing's daughter. He logged out of his email.

The information confirmed what the Foundation knew already. Family histories, newspaper cuttings, Revolutionary testimonies. Draft treaties with the British. All carefully catalogued by his team at home, including the huge collection of documents his father had discovered in Prague and Berlin right under the noses of Soviet forces. But nothing new regarding a date. Nor a place. And still the whole darn East Coast to figure out. His mood paled at the prospect. If only the records of 1814 had survived. He sighed. And without some lead States-side, he depended on the Brits. Or the students. And their only confidant was Satan.

Warren turned to Larry, but the sound of a door opening diverted his attention. He watched as Felix entered the room and approached. They both stood up.

'Mr Ellison has just left a briefing with intelligence. He should be with you shortly.' Felix offered his hand.

Warren reached out. 'We were a few minutes early. But we've been looked after. By the young lady.' He glanced towards the large mahogany table at the other end of the room where a woman typed at a keyboard. 'She was kind enough to offer us coffee, but we declined.' He looked around. 'It's a very fine room, if I may say. And strangely decorated.'

Felix smiled at the observation.

'And those stairs back there,' added Larry. 'They were just awesome.'

'Yes. It is rather grand. It's part of the Locarno Suite. There's a dining room and a separate conference area, too. But, to be honest, I find the décor a little bewildering.' Felix paused as his guests looked around. 'The design was commissioned in the nineteenth century. And the motifs, I've heard, are inspired by patterns found in Athens. The Acropolis, they say.'

Warren adjusted his glasses.

'You can get a better view of the ceiling and its designs over there.' Felix pointed to a table mirror placed near the centre of the room. 'The room's had a chequered history, though. At one time, it housed a government cypher team. And then a contraband department.' Felix glanced towards the mirror before turning back to Warren. 'In the sixties, there was a plan to demolish it, I believe. And rebuild in a more contemporary style.'

'Seems a shame. Such a big room.' Larry gestured with his hand. 'Must be a great place for you guys and all those socials.'

Felix nodded politely. 'Oh, I'm forgetting. James asked me to let you know that he has an additional item for the agenda. If that's … okay with you, gentlemen?'

Warren nodded cautiously.

'Nothing controversial. But James has organised some invitations.' He stepped back. 'Quite exciting, I believe.'

'We are curious to hear, Felix.'

'Well, I won't steal James's thunder.' Felix rubbed his hands before motioning to leave.

An indulgent smile from Warren allowed him to slip away.

The Americans returned to their chairs and the omniscient chatter from the young lady's keyboard.

High above their heads, pentagons, and squares spread out like a tessellated sky. The planets and stars shone in a sea of pastel blue. Jupiter gazed down at them. And amongst the constellations and astrological signs, they could see Leo and Taurus. And a shape like a dragon. Another like a serpent that was held aloft by an outstretched arm. And the claws and tail of Scorpio. And the Scales.

Warren turned to Larry and spoke in a low voice. 'The pagans knew no true God, Larry. Nor the Son of God. Comfort in the Lord. And your devotions. Your work with the Foundation will soon be complete.'

Larry lowered his eyes. 'Kind of draws you in, though, sir. I mean the pretty colours. And the clever shapes and signs. And their crazy meanings.'

Warren remained still.

At the far end of the room, the keyboard ceased its soft, repetitive slog. The young lady rose from her desk, checked the security pass that hung around her neck, and left the room by an adjacent door.

Warren turned to Larry. 'The information that Ellison promised? The Karlstad ring?'

Larry nodded. 'Got it. The whole caboodle.'

'And the code keys?'

'In another week. From their GCHQ. We should be able to review everything before Thanksgiving.'

'Good.' Warren glanced back towards the mahogany table. 'You know my priorities.'

Larry nodded once more.

'Repeat them to me.'

'Maps, sir. Diaries. Temple drawings ...'

'And anything that could be a date or a place, Larry. Anything ...' He paused, hearing an echo of his voice. 'Or a latitude or longitude. The numbers have deep meaning for our country, Larry. And the work of the Foundation.'

Warren closed his eyes. The final battle would soon begin, he averred. And nothing could or should forestall it. Satan had corrupted this world, and now his ignorant servants dared to seal his tenure for all time. With their false alchemy, their ungodly delusions, and secret knowledge. He placed his hands together and recalled a prayer. They must be opposed. And they must be defeated. Soon, he yearned … soon the Day of Judgement will be upon us. And the sins of Adam will be washed away. The faithful restored to paradise. And all the enemies of truth and grace, he prayed, swallowed by the ground beneath their feet. Praise be to God. Praise be to God.

He turned back to his subordinate, renewed by his conviction. 'The instructions, Larry? The Italian courier?'

'Neutralised.'

'Neutralised.' Warren smiled. 'How?'

'Two bullets, sir. One in the throat … and one in the chest.'

Warren tightened his fists. 'Where?'

'Embankment Gardens, sir. By the river … the River Thames.'

Warren drew a breath that filled his lungs. His voice hardened. 'The river of *hell*, sir. The filthy, burning lake. The godless stench of pandemonium.'

* * *

To Larry's eye, the mirror, set lower and some ten feet away, cast the world in oblique colours that were lifeless and stale. Yet if he walked towards it, the image, he thought, would surely sharpen and flatter the crisp, pagan sky.

He glanced around. It was a big, pretentious room. Like one of those fancy *salons* you see in foreign movies. Full of whispers and prying eyes. And a cold, creepy silence.

His mind drifted. There was nothing like this back home. Not his home. Not on the ceilings and walls. There was a photo. In an old book. Like when they did plates. And there were junk shops. For things you throw away or dump in the yard. Or sell for a dime when you're broke. Or things you mustn't touch. Like when you break something as a kid. Or sing a dirty rhyme and get your ass beaten by your angry folks.

The silence intensified.

He stared at the wall. A strange figure teased his eye. Decorative and stencilled in gold against the panel's lascivious red, it spiralled round and round like a wheel. A strange shape. An alien shape with bulging hypnotic eyes, and dead-hung stems of weeping bulbs that called to him … beckoning from the opposing wall. He raised his arms, blanking the morbid image with his hands. But it flared anew. Red and gold, red and gold. Brighter. Hotter. Coiling round and round. With lines like serpent tails and owl-faced creatures swirling at its base. And horns turned down. And eyes bloated, that loomed towards him. Laughing and laughing. Louder and louder. Screaming. Threatening. Larry gasped. He gripped the chair. His flesh rose to flee … But the demon goblin fell away. Sinking. Drowning. Choking. Its demented eyes uncoiling. Its breath suddenly stilled.

Larry shivered. Night's dark and wayward path, he feared. Sweat ran down his neck. And his back. Making his shirt cling. But a sharp sound launched him to his feet.

James Ellison swept towards him. Beaming with smiles and selfless bonhomie.

18

'Alex, stay still. Where are we going?'

'The British Museum. Francis is there. In the wilds of Archaic Greece.'

We swung around the old block of flats in Drury Lane and headed north. The British Museum was fifteen minutes away. Alex moved quickly, and I hurried to keep pace. There was something on his mind. It was seven-thirty on a cold and wet November morning, and it wasn't just the rain now falling on our heads. Half an hour before, I was fast asleep in bed.

He darted across the road and headed towards a shop entrance for cover. I slipped alongside.

'The museum isn't open yet, Alex.'

'Don't worry. Francis has sorted it. I just give our names.'

'Can he sort out breakfast, as well?'

'Yep. No problem.'

We made another dash. I caught up and latched on to his arm, trying to stall him as we shifted, dripping, along the empty street. 'So what's the deal with Archaic Greece?'

'Ceramic pots. And myths. And it's close to where we'll eat.'

The thought of pots sounded promising. But so did breakfast. 'And then what?'

'That's when you help me out. At the lecture. But don't worry, I'll explain. Promise.'

He rushed off.

I followed Alex, dodging cars and puddles, unperturbed by the rain that slithered down my neck or by the clingy, warm damp of my obliging jeans. He was up to something, and it felt kind of cool to join in and be part of it.

* * *

Our names seem to open gates and doors like a magical spell.

We shook ourselves dry inside the entrance lobby and then slipped through the galleries to our left, skirting fabulous beasts from the Assyrian Empire and plump little figurines from late Minoan Crete. Archaic Greece was not far away, Alex said. Slotted between the Greek Dark Ages and the more familiar posing of the classical world. In a few brisk strides, we'd swept through a thousand years of history. And a swathe of broken, vanished times.

Francis seemed oblivious to our arrival. A red-on-black ceramic pot held his attention, blanking the steady beat of our steps. He stepped back as we halted alongside. Alex shook himself once more.

'You're like a dog shedding water, Alex.'

'Well, you wanted us here by eight. Didn't you?'

Francis brushed a few drops from his jacket, using a pocket-sized guidebook as an aid. 'Then you're early. And you both look as if you've showered together. And one of you forgot to shave.'

Alex slipped away for some paper towels, leaving me bemused at the exchange. With a more modest gesture, I pushed back my hair and shook the moisture from my hands. Francis resumed his previous pose.

'It's an interesting depiction of the myth, Richard, don't you think?' I glanced at the exhibit and then at the curator's note. *Early fifth century BCE*, it advised. *Orpheus and Eurydice. On loan.* I could see the pining figure of a disconsolate young man, his iconic lyre discarded at his side and his back turned on a gaping chasm in the Earth. Francis explained the drama.

'He's lamenting the awful fate of his beloved. And his pride. Did you ever study them at school?'

'We did. The tragic lovers of ancient Greece. Poetry and music.' I moved closer. 'Didn't Orpheus get torn to shreds, though?'

'By the maenads. And his head ended up in the sea.' Francis pointed to a group of wild-eyed figures on the side of the pot. Above them, the god Dionysus symbolised their fury. 'Misfortune and a trampled snake had cast Eurydice into the shadowy world of Hades. And Orpheus had pursued her. But in the end, as we learn, he left empty-handed.'

And so a heartbroken Orpheus sat alone on a rock. Even the trees seem to weep. 'He should have tried again, Francis.'

'Oh, he did, Richard. But he was rebuffed by the growling, three-headed beast that forbids mortals the right of way.' Francis leant upright. We turned aside from the pot. 'You know, there's an intriguing observation by Plato that Orpheus was a fraud. That he'd somehow sneaked into the underworld and planned to charm his way out.' Francis slipped his hands into his pockets. 'Secure, of course, with his prize, Eurydice.'

'Really? I didn't know.'

Poor old Orpheus, I thought. One moment, the darling of all nature. The next, a recluse, spurning the world around him. And those mad, ecstatic women. Revved up on drink and bent on revenge. I wondered how such tales were ever spun.

I stepped back. Alex had placed his hands against the cabinet. He'd caught part of our conversation and was grinning mischievously through the glass. He raised a finger. 'Just remember, young lad … Next time, don't sodding look back, mate.' We all laughed. 'Come on. Breakfast's on me.'

We followed Alex. The myths slipped out of our minds.

* * *

Alex had already marked out our space with a jacket thrown across a chair. Two other chairs stood back from the table, as if inviting us to sit. Francis and I moved them closer as Alex went off to get the food that he'd offered to buy us.

'I'm sorry about the early start, Richard.'

'Don't worry, there was a note a few days ago from Alex. And a reminder about dinner tomorrow.'

'Yes, he said to me.'

I glanced over to Alex as he ordered the food. 'Is Jane going to join us?'

'Later. When we attend the lecture.' Francis checked his wrist-watch. 'She wanted to see some prints by Dürer before the museum opens to everyone else.'

'You know, Francis, it's strange walking around here. I mean, when it's almost empty. Creepy even.' I was still feeling a little embarrassed at the way Alex and I had breezed in earlier. And a little puzzled.

'It's the best time, really.' Francis paused as he opened his guide-book and retrieved a loose sheet of paper on which he had scribbled a few notes. He yawned. 'But it's never empty. Security, of course. But some researchers prefer to work through the night. I think the quiet and the darkness helps concentration. We sometimes meet here late when we study together. There's an early breakfast too if you make it through the night.'

Night school, I imagined. Hardly a paradox. And while Francis looked as if he was flagging a little, Alex was all go. Stacking cups and plates on a tray. Making sure of a good breakfast for all of us. And maybe the right time to mention something that was still nagging away at me. It would need a quiet word with Hatherleigh at our next tutorial, and I hoped Francis could suggest a way. As he lifted his eyes from the piece of paper, I caught his attention. 'Francis. There's something I wanted to run by you. Regarding the course module. And the course code ...'

The rest of my words were lost in the noise of descending cutlery and plates. Alex had arrived like a wave crashing ashore. And, like the sea, he went back for more. Eggs, bacon, mushrooms, toast. Bags of sugar. Milk. Finally, he joined us. 'Thirty quid for this lot, guys. But today...' He snapped his fingers. 'It's all on me.'

We gave Alex the thumbs up and tucked in before he changed his mind.

'So what are you roping Richard into, Alex?'

'I'm going to get back at that ... that Vivien guy.'

'Who?' I asked, heaping food on to a fork.

'He's called Vivien Weekes. He's in the medieval history department.' Alex reached for his cup. 'He rubbished one of my essays during last term. Six months ago.'

Francis didn't disagree. But I wondered about the name. It sounded familiar.

'What really gets me is the way he slags you off in class for saying something, but uses the same arguments in his own precious articles.' Alex's knife and fork reinforced the assertion. Francis and I retreated.

'So, what did he say, then?' I asked.

'It's about astrology, Richard. Every time you mention it, they run a mile. Except in their own clever-clogs little clubs. I saw the article a few weeks after my essay. Of course, he'd missed the whole point.'

Alex finished his breakfast, wiping the last of it from his plate. I wasn't far behind myself, happy that it was worth the bleary-eyed start and the mad dash through the rain. At least I felt ready for the day.

Francis yawned. 'I don't understand why you bothered to take Medieval Church History last year. It only winds you up. I told you that you'd get into trouble.'

'Trouble? It's Weekes who's in trouble.'

Alex smiled. He looked like a cat poised, I fancied, with a plan running through his head, ready to pounce at any moment. He tossed me a friendly glance before giving Francis more studied deliberation. And he, too, was thinking. Or maybe just flagging from the night before. But as I drank the last of my tea, Francis perked up.

'Are you still planning to see Otto this morning, Alex?'

'Yes. If he's upstairs in his office.' Alex picked up a paper towel and wiped his mouth. He grinned at me. 'I'll explain later, Richard. He has a room above the Enlightenment gallery.'

I stayed silent.

Francis leant forward. 'In that case, shouldn't you wait rather than stir things up with Weekes?'

'Francis, your trouble is that you don't hit back when you have a chance. You're too careful.' Alex turned to me. 'Weekes gave me the lowest grade for the course, Richard. He even wanted me failed.'

'Alex, you will draw attention to yourself. Again. And, this time, to Richard.' Francis's words were more insistent.

'Richard, ignore Francis for a moment. Just tell me what *you* think?'

'Well, if you explain to me what you want me to do, Alex.'

'All right. It's like this. Weekes is giving the annual lecture on one of his favourite subjects. The one we're going to.'

Francis interrupted. 'Weekes specialises in medieval debates on philosophy. And he maintains that the accepted position on occult matters …'

'Yes. But this is astrology, Francis.'

'Same thing,' countered Francis.

'No, it isn't. Well … a bit.' Alex paused, puzzling over his own words. 'Okay. So everyone knows that the stars don't tell you who you're going to'—he rolled his eyes—'to meet … or when to make a bet.'

Francis frowned.

'What I was pointing out, Richard, is that the ancient world has always known that certain star groups tell a story that parallels the human condition.'

'Okay. You mean symbolically,' I said.

'Yeah. But also crossing thresholds. And things,' he added.

'Or life and death,' Francis suggested, holding his cup close to his lips.

'Exactly,' agreed Alex. 'Just look at Homer and even the New Testament. They're bloody well full of star signs.'

'Alex, discreetly please.'

A member of the museum staff walked by. Alex shook his head. He folded his arms. 'Now. As I was saying ...'

'Alex was arguing about free will, Richard, in his essay.'

'I was not arguing about free will.' His eyes rolled, careering left and right. 'I know fucking well what I was arguing about.'

Francis raised his hands as Alex leant forward. He was ready to listen. Before the whole cafeteria joined in.

'What it comes down to is this: if God can foresee everything, then everything must already be decided. Which is like saying that everything is fated. So the church, Francis, is no different to ...'

'To modern-day determinists?' suggested Francis.

'Yeah. Cause and effect. But you can still do whatever you want, anyway. And that's why the constellations don't actually mean any-thing. Except like a story.' Alex flashed a grin. And scanned our plates.

I ran his thoughts through my mind, trying to make the con-nections.

'So what do you reckon, Richard?' Alex asked. 'Are we free to make our own decisions? Or are our actions predetermined for us whatever we think we do?'

I looked at my plate. It was bare. 'We decide for ourselves. Especially where there's a choice.'

'But what if you are forced to do something? Something you don't want to do?'

'Okay, Alex. But we still decide.'

'So why are you going to die, then?' he asked, as if I'd drawn up a plan. 'Is that a choice?'

'Sometimes,' I said. Not sure if he was being serious. 'But we can't go on forever, can we?'

The sound of cutlery from the kitchens distracted us. Alex lifted the guidebook on the table. He flipped through a few pages before letting it slip from his hands. I stayed still.

'You know Weekes hates Hatherleigh and wants to shut down our course. Am I not right, Francis?'

'Alex …'

Alex was not giving ground. 'The two of them had a blazing row in the street once. Jane saw it. Just ask her.'

Francis retrieved his book. I noticed a food stain on the front cover. He tried to remove it with a paper towel. 'So what happens next, Alex? Richard must be a little anxious about your plans for Weekes.'

I braved a smile.

'There's nothing to worry about, Richard. We'll pin the bastard down, that's all. In front of everyone.'

I looked at Francis.

'There'll be at least two hundred people in the hall, Alex.'

'So?' Alex was undeterred. 'Are you with me, Richard?'

I shut my eyes. 'Is there a Q and A after Weekes's talk?'

'Yep. In the afternoon. And I've got your arguments worked out.'

'Arguments? You will be there as well, won't you?'

'Yeah. And once he gives you his usual bullshit, I will read his own article back to him so everyone can judge who is right.'

'You'd better write it down for me. If there are hundreds of people, I'm going to have to get it right.'

Francis stared at his empty plate. Alex had helped himself to the unfinished toast. I caught a weary glance as he stretched back his arms and yawned. He'd given in, I reckoned. But Alex didn't crow. He searched his pockets, hoping to find something on which to write. He gestured to Francis for help before scribbling on the inside cover of his guidebook.

'Here you are. That's what you need to say.'

'What is it?'

'It's a quote from the New Testament. You'll really trip him up once you read that out.'

Alex stood up. Pushed back his hair and ran his hand over a stubbled chin. He grabbed his jacket from the chair and slung it over his shoulder. 'Why don't you take Richard around the Marbles while I see Otto, Francis? Tell him your theories.'

Alex left. I wasn't sure what I was letting myself in for, but I was helpless in the face of his badgering charm. I reread the note from Alex and then passed the book back to Francis. He, too, was smiling. We rose, stacked the plates and cups on a tray before making our way to the glories of classical Greece. It was only a short walk to the collection and, Francis maintained, the most intriguing sculptures in the western hemisphere.

19

Otto stretched out his arms and yawned. 'I'm sorry, Alex. We didn't finish until after two this morning.' He gestured towards the coffee pot on his desk. 'There are still details of the plan to complete, but it's not possible for us to proceed until we have a clear answer to our question. It's too risky otherwise.' Otto rose and stepped towards the large Georgian window that overlooked the street below. A dreary light veiled the break of day. 'Where are the others?' he asked.

'Francis is with Richard. He's explaining the sculptures.'

'And Jane?'

'Chasing prints. Francis mentioned the Dürer collection.'

'Yes, that's right. Paulo was fond of them. Francis and Jane talked about him last night when I met them at their flat. You should have joined us.'

'I wanted to think. And sleep on my decision.'

'Yes. Francis did say.'

Alex glanced around the room. Nothing had changed since his last visit, he noted. The same vases. The same colourless blooms. And a silver coffee pot that seemed like a permanent feature on the desk. He shifted his attention. 'Are we sticking with the same time-line, Otto?'

'Yes, Alex. No changes there. Sometime around the winter sol-stice. Mid to late December is the plan. Once the existing world dissolves, the reconstruction of its space-time will follow.' Otto returned to his chair. 'Kalinsky has the date and the location of the world's origin. He's wrapped it up in a line of verse for safety.' He paused, stifling a yawn. 'He'll be here later today. So, young man, we need your decision. You can't do this on your own, you know. Not on your own.' He yawned again.

Alex nodded, still fresh from the morning's rain.

'So, what is it, Alex?' Otto rubbed his eyes. 'Is Richard the man for the job? Yes or no?'

'Yes. Richard is the man.' Alex shifted in his chair. 'There may be things about him that we still have to work at. But I'm ready to trust him.'

Otto rose. He leant forward on his hands and stared across the desk. 'You trust him, Alex, with our plans to rebuild our world? And you trust him with your life?'

'Yes. And yes.' The words darted back. 'Of course, I trust him with my life. He's my friend. So let's get on with it. Let's have an end to this world, and god knows, bloody well everything we've screwed up in it.' Alex stared back, drawing a defiant breath.

'Francis agrees with you,' said Otto, slumping back into his chair. 'But Jane, last night … was still unsure.'

'Why?'

'She's afraid that Richard will let you down, Alex. Leaving you adrift, and the world unchanged … its future blighted.'

Alex shook his head. 'Jane frets too much. Anyway, I've made my decision. I trust Richard. Completely.' He pulled his chair up to the desk. 'Now explain exactly what we have to do.'

Otto reached for a blank sheet of paper and drew several circles and lines. 'This is what will happen. This is how Richard will, and must, play his part.' He pushed the drawing closer to Alex. 'You and Richard will both enter what we call the indeterminate zone, or the IZ for short.' Otto pointed to a cloud-like entity at the centre of the page. 'It is devoid of dimensional aspect and permits access to the start of any past or parallel reality.' He added groups of boxes at the edge of the cloud. 'You see how space-time is clustered.' Alex nodded. 'Within this cluster here,'—Otto marked heavy crosses over several others—'lies our own space-time configuration, our own "box". A box that began in North America hundreds of years ago. And when Kalinsky arrives, we will learn the date and location of its genesis precisely.' He reached for his coffee.

Alex studied the sketch. 'Why are there so many boxes within our own cluster, Otto?'

'Because each box has its own configuration, though as a set it has a common base.' Otto flipped the sheet. 'Imagine space-time branching out like a species.' He added more lines and figures to develop the analogy across the page. 'You see. Adjacent lines linking adjacent worlds with their own histories and their own delicious fates. Many of these worlds sprang-up thousands of years ago, others during the dimly recollected past. The Flood, the inter-dynastic gaps of the Egyptians, Dark Age Greece. One in the sixth century of our own time and another in the eighth. And of course, the current cosmic arrangements devised not so long ago.' Alex followed the lines, noting one that had passed through the medieval age and beyond but had then divided itself into two, triggering a new space-time continuum as its parallel sibling diverged alongside. 'The concept of clustered and bifurcated space-time is a wonderful after-dinner conversation, but back to our plan.' Otto returned to the drawing. 'Now, let me explain why we need Richard. By leaving the indeterminate zone and re-entering our world at its start point, when it branched off from its parent base, you, but not Richard, will lose your link with the present world and time.' Otto drew another box that overlapped the one marked as Alex's destination. He drew dotted lines between them to show a temporal association between a world past and a world present within the same space-time configuration.

'So Richard will stay behind.' Alex pointed to the cloud. 'I suppose here, in the IZ.'

'Yes. He will. While you reconfigure the fate of our world, he will stay in the indeterminate zone. His link will stay secure. And once you have played your part, Richard will lead you back. So long as he stays strong.'

Alex closed his eyes. 'Like Ariadne's thread.'

'Indeed. And once you both return, the world, our existing world, will be reconfigured, courtesy of your adjustments. This will set us on a new path since much of our recent history will have been discarded. Jane ran through a long list of changes last night—the conflicts in Europe, the settlement of North America, the exploitation of the East.' Alex opened his eyes. 'The cosmos is a dreadful labyrinth, Alex. This is where we have gone wrong before when attempting the things that you and Richard will soon undertake. And where brave souls before us were lost for ever.'

'And this is why I trust Richard, Otto.'

'Good. Because every choice requires sacrifice.'

Otto let go of his pen. He rose from his chair and moved towards a large, sturdy bookcase that stood on the other side of his room. Using a small key, he unlocked the glass-panelled doors. 'The techniques we use to slip in and out of the past are explained in this manual. Francis gave it to me last night. It is the final revision that our cosmology experts have prepared for us.' He handed it to Alex. 'There's an introduction covering the information that we've deduced from Plato's dialogues. Various speculations in books not known to the modern world. And the work of generations in solving the mathematical-philosophical riddles that underpin our existence.'

Alex placed the manual on his lap. 'I will have that coffee,' he said, turning the pages. 'Actually, Francis mentioned something to me about how they will activate a route through the void. Like a bridge across eternity.'

'Yes, with a high-intensity bombardment. They need to disturb a whole range of sub-atomic particles around the globe at specific times of the year when external cosmic forces are in our favour.' Otto poured the coffee. 'This is why the planets and stars matter. And why the ancients were so keen to study them.'

Alex reached for his cup. 'Did you know that Richard was born on the equinox?'

'Yes. Hatherleigh told me. It is why he is so suited to his task.' Otto looked at his sketches. 'You will need to explain this to him before you both embark. Otherwise, you may find yourself marooned in the past if Richard cannot meet our expectations.'

'I agree. But I think it's better to take it step by step, Otto. Build his awareness. Test his nerve. We've taken care of him so far. But he's still fragile. If I tell him everything now, it'll overwhelm him. Francis and I are still drawing him in. Building his confidence … and pushing him into tight spots to see how he reacts.'

'Very well. So does that mean you have something more in mind, then?'

'Yes, we do. I'm planning to have a little fun with Weekes this afternoon. At the lecture.'

'Weekes? That pompous fraud in the history department?'

Alex grinned. 'Richard will stick his neck out and fire a few awkward questions on free will in the Q and A. I expect Weekes to get annoyed. But we've fed Richard enough for him to stand his ground and argue on some points. Francis and Jane will come to the rescue if he gets into trouble.'

'Good. We need to be sure he's got backbone.' Otto paused. 'What do you know of his other studies? I have been following his course texts to help my assessment.'

'Pretty good feedback. He can be incisive. At any rate, the poems seem to gel at a deeper level than you'd find with most of his peer group. As though he's haunted by something.'

'The Oxford business.' Otto grinned. 'Does he talk about it at all, Alex?'

'No. But I suspect he just wants to forget it.'

'Yes. I'm sure you are right.' Otto placed his hands together. 'It must have seemed strange.' He glanced away. 'Very strange.' Otto drained the last of his coffee.

'Perhaps you should meet Richard.'

'Yes. I think I should.' He lowered his eyes, pausing before he continued. 'Alex, there is one other matter that you should be aware of. It involves another party. In fact, another person.'

Alex watched as Otto removed a small artefact from his desk drawer. A figurine made from gypsum that Francis had discovered on the Greek island of Delos. A gift to Apollo, Francis had told him, but destined nevertheless for the trowel. Jane thought of it as her lucky charm. A talisman. And Alex didn't disagree, still curious at the strange, ethereal glow that emanated from its white surface at night. He watched as Otto placed the artefact on the desk.

'I have set it just outside of the cloud. On the space-time box that you will visit. It's your counterpart. Your cosmic twin.'

'My counterpart?'

'Yes. A lady of your own age. A native of the past.'

Alex lifted the diminutive figure in his hand. 'Will I meet her?'

'No. But we think Richard will. Perhaps fleetingly.' Alex replaced the figurine on the desk. 'Our experts have advised us that once you leave the IZ and enter the past, a counter body from that world and time will be projected into our own present. This preserves a necessary harmony across the time-dependent worlds.'

'So what happens when I return, then?'

'She will go back. To restore the balance.' Otto drew an arrow across his chart. 'We can move freely around the IZ. It is a neutral zone. It's when we commit to a hard world that we trigger a reciprocal response. We've proved it several times now with small exhibits that we keep in the museum.'

Alex smiled as he glanced around once more before settling again on the object of their attention. 'I wondered why Francis and Jane were always so smug about it.'

Otto reached for the figurine and returned it the drawer. 'You'll find an account of our work in the manual.'

'Lucky Richard.' Alex placed the manual on to the desk.

Otto stretched his arms once more. 'We all have a role to play. Without you and Richard, nothing will happen. The world will continue along its miserable path, stumbling blindly. Francis was very gloomy last night. Mean lives. Shrunken spirits. Wasted endowments. A crippling legacy. And the future?' He shook his head. 'What should be a feast will be but a thin gruel, my friend, shrouded in atomic dust. Ravaged by the god of chaos.' A weary breath dissolved into a sigh. 'And it's our own fault.' Otto lifted his pen. His hand circled the sketchy cosmos that straggled the page, but his inclination appeared to falter. He put the pen down and turned back to Alex. 'What I most regret is the world's obsessions. Its persistent conceits. Its intellectual arrogance. That those who came before were always helpless fools and selfish cheats.' He paused. 'And you, Alex? What troubles you?'

'Its haste, Otto.'

'Yes, its haste. Time should be our friend.'

Alex nodded.

Otto leant back in his chair. 'I wish Paulo had survived. I looked for an old photo. After he was shot and killed. I still remember teaching him at our summer semesters.' Otto smiled affectionately. 'He was like you, Alex. Full of spirit. And turns.' He paused. 'It's nearly thirty years since we last had a go at these things. Kalinsky had discovered the dialogues. We had a clue about the origin of our world.' He checked his wristwatch. His eyes scanned the door. 'And we were hunted down even then, I remember. Back and forth across the Baltic. So we slipped out of sight. And developed a new cover.'

'The friendly occult.'

'Yes. Hatherleigh's colleagues have been wonderful, though we've done his library a few favours along the way. And the other paraphernalia he keeps in his rooms.' Otto rested his elbows on the desk. He slouched his head between supporting hands. 'People laugh at us. But only for so long, Alex.' He paused, yawning again. 'Soon their squabbles will be no more. Their world will have gone. And not all will survive … no, not all. But I think renewal should be our theme. I said that to Francis, you know … a regeneration.' A smile drifted across Otto's face. 'The museum will be larger. Much larger.' He yawned. 'A new spirit, Alex. A new public spirit, a new destiny.' He paused. 'The Americas restored …' His eyelids closed. And then again.

'You'd better get your sleep, old man.' Alex rose and turned towards the door, but before departing slipped behind Otto's desk. He retrieved a slender book of poems from his jacket pocket and placed it on the shelf amidst others.

Alex left, closing the door gently behind him.

20

'They were complete drunkards, Richard.' Francis pointed to a stone-carved relief fixed to the gallery wall. A headless centaur was assaulting a young man holding a shield. It was a desperate-looking struggle.

'Who won the battle?'

'Oh, the Lapiths, of course,' replied Francis, grinning. 'It all started when the centaurs went to a wedding and took a fancy to the Lapiths' wives. That and a few jars of wine really got them going.'

'Sounds like a rave.'

'Oh, but this was fatal. That poor old fellow was bludgeoned to death.' Francis stepped closer. A small metal plate explained that the slab was one of the metopes from the Parthenon temple above the city of Athens. The metopes, it continued, told a story of conflict and triumph depicting four separate myths: the gods against the giants, Greeks against Amazons, the battle of Troy, and as I could see, the contest between these improbable-looking creatures and their distant cousins, the human tribe of Lapiths.

'But Francis, did the Greeks ever believe that centaurs existed? Like in a mythical past.'

'What their writers say, Richard, is that the centaur symbolised our dual nature. The struggle between the noble and the base. Our centaur may have lost his head on this slab, but their king, Chiron, was a renowned and gifted teacher and mentor to the Greek pantheon of heroes. It was only the lower parts that got them into trouble.'

I looked again at the elegantly carved beast. Half man and half horse, poised in a fierce act of violence that seemed to epitomise something more. I stepped back. 'You're thinking about order and chaos now, aren't you?'

He smiled. 'Yes. I am. And the human ego. At least in its confrontational aspect.' Francis slipped his hands into his pockets.

'Reminds me of school,' I joked. And maybe Alex.

We turned away. The remnants of Athene and Poseidon posed for our attention. Francis explained as we stalled in front of it. 'All that's left, I'm afraid. It used to be the west pediment.'

'They both look as if they've been chain-sawed.'

'Probably the explosion. A shell from a Venetian ship did the damage. That, and the Ottoman's ill-fated store of gunpowder. But the early Christians had attacked them with hammers long before then.' Francis wiped his lips.

A museum account explained the events of 1687. Alongside it was a drawing that predated their demise. Athene and Poseidon. Their chariots and their entourage. They would have once been a splendid sight to an awe-struck Athenian. Now they could only despair.

'Alex said they fought over the lordship of Athens.'

'That's right. Athene won the dispute with her olive tree. All Poseidon could offer was a salt-water stream. No use to anyone.'

'And then Atlantis, Francis. When we did "Timaeus" in the tutorial, they were on different sides again, I remember.'

'Yes, they were.'

'Maybe that's why they stare out from the west pediment.' Francis smiled at the thought.

'Ah, the west. You are very perceptive this morning, Richard.'

'I rose early. And Alex paid for the food, remember?'

We skirted by another centaur.

'Francis, why was Alex given such a rough ride over his work?'

Francis turned to me as I spoke. 'Didn't he say that the tutor wanted to fail him?'

'Well, the essay was one thing, Richard. Lots of research on different cultures—Babylonian, Assyrian, Hebrew. All over the place, and completely at odds with medieval teaching.' We continued towards the Parthenon frieze.

'But Alex said that the tutor had used his arguments. For an article or something.'

'Yes.' We both paused. 'It was an American publication, I remember. Tutors can be very jealous, you know. But that wasn't all.' Francis gestured back to the west pediment. We were no longer alone. A party of obedient-looking tourists and their guide were retracing our steps a few yards behind. 'Things got difficult after Weekes's office was broken into. Just before exam time.'

'It wasn't Alex, was it?'

'No, not at all. But someone had been there. Searching through papers and books. Weekes was furious, and since the culprit was never found, we think Alex was made to carry the blame through his grades.'

'No wonder he's pissed off. But why did he even choose the module in the first place? It sounds a bit out of character …'

'Because Alex likes to fight, Richard, and will never resist a provocation.'

We'd reached the first of the sculptures forming part of the frieze. A group of four older-looking figures comprised a single slab. Francis mentioned how their function was disputed: either civic dignitaries like magistrates or famous heroes linked to the history of the state. He preferred the heroes, though, reminding me how Athene loved to champion them in their adventures, or their homage. I didn't disagree. It was her temple, after all.

With a few brisker steps, the party trailing us caught up. They huddled close to their guide. Francis stayed my impulse to move on. 'Let's linger a little to hear what he says,' he whispered.

'Please. The narrative of the frieze is a procession in converging but unequal parts. There were two sequences that wound their way around the temple, just inside the colonnade that supported the roof. One started on the southern side of the Parthenon, the other on the west.' The guide pointed to the sculpture on the gallery walls.

The immediate impression is one of horses and their young male riders marshalled in a cavalcade. But other walks of life made their appearance too. Male and female. Musicians and artisans. Officials, even. And to our rear, a group of sullen, tethered beasts led to a grim and sacrificial slaughter. We just had to imagine that we were looking up at the external wall of the Parthenon's inner chamber rather than the inside of a purpose-built room.

'There were over three hundred and fifty figures originally, before the terrible explosion.' The guide checked his notes. 'Phidias sculpted the frieze. With his students. Sometimes, I think the figures are paired as if they are by the same sculptor's hands. And sometimes they are sad. And beautiful. But quite sad.' His eyes fell away.

We moved towards another section of the frieze.

'This is the famous peplos scene from the east side of the temple. You can see several individuals standing between the larger figures of the gods.' The guide stood to the side as we settled on the central panels of the frieze. Alongside a female figure, a man held what appeared to be a large folded cloth. He was being helped by a boy. The guide continued: 'The peplos was a special cloth that the people of Athens gave to Athene at the end of their celebration. Athene was the city's patron.' The guide smiled at us. 'Do you recall the name of the celebration that I mentioned to you when we entered the gallery?'

A voice responded: 'The Panathenaea.'

'Yes! The Panathenaea. Thank you.'

Whatever the significance of the peplos, Zeus and his brood were in no hurry to acknowledge its presence. Several large, god-like figures sat on stools to the left and right of a more diminutive group of mortals that attended to the cloth. It all seemed rather low-key and something of a yawn, I decided.

'Are there any questions before we continue?'

'Sir.' An American-sounding voice drew our attention. 'My pastor back home says that the sculpture shows the Prophets. And the cloth is a scroll with the laws of Moses. And that's why the pagan gods are looking away, because they are ashamed of their impotence.'

The guide frowned. 'I have not heard that interpretation. As I said, it is the cloth of the Panathenaea.'

I looked at Francis. He shrugged. After a few moments, the group slipped away. We both stepped closer. 'It's surely too big to be a scroll,' I said.

'Oh, far too big. But in a way, the American is right. It's what's drawn on it that counts, Richard.' Francis sealed his lips as if withholding a secret.

'Well, you must have x-ray eyes.' I could see folds for sure, but images or words? Francis ignored my puzzlement.

'Do you remember, Richard, how Athens led the city states against their foe, the Persian empire?'

'You mean the Delian League? Fifth century, wasn't it?'

'478 BC. Well, the Athenians built the Parthenon from its funds. Not the original intention though, since the reason the cities clubbed together and stored their gold on the island of Delos was to build up their military strength.'

'But with Athens overseeing the contributions?'

'Yes. And in 454BC, the Athenians shipped the whole lot to the Acropolis.'

'And couldn't resist the urge to spend it on themselves, I suppose.'

'Precisely. That's gold for you. But it wasn't the only thing that they transferred from Delos to Athens.'

'A cloth,' I suggested.

'No, not quite, but you're getting close.' Francis gave me a moment lest the answer might come to me. It didn't. 'Plato gives a hint. In one of his dialogues ...' I was still listening. 'It's where Socrates talks about a civil war amongst the gods before mentioning the designs woven into the robe made for Athene's festival.'

'A robe? I remember doing something on Plato's "Republic". But not a robe.'

'It's in one of the shorter dialogues.'

I stood back from the frieze. The same five figures. Two women with things on their heads. Another positioned towards them. And then a man with a boy hardly up to his shoulders. And then the cloth. Or maybe a robe. My mind played with the overlapping folds that added subtlety to the carving. 'So, you're saying the real mystery is what's drawn on it?'

Francis took hold of my arm. 'Think back to Hatherleigh's tutorial. Atlantis and the end of the world. "Timaeus" and the creation of new worlds.'—How could I forget?—'The missing clues in this, Richard, are the lost commentaries by the Neo-Platonists.'

I could sense a sudden keenness in his voice. He ushered me aside as he continued. 'If we could unfold it now. Here. On the floor. We would see a great plan. A plan of the cosmos, Richard. And the mathematical ratios and geometry that underpin its construction, we would find stitched into its borders.'

'And this is what these commentaries discuss?'

'Yes. The configuration of a specific world and its place in the universe. The gods, for instance, are projections from the cloth. They symbolise the forces of nature that give substance to the plan. They may be lounging around in the frieze, but in reality, they are disinterested participants, not uninterested spectators. But that's not all. Look at the horsemen—some riding, some preparing to mount, others in a settled trot. They represent time itself. And Athena, the cosmic principle, embodying both creation and destruction. Our sources declare this.

But they tell us more. They tell us how we can develop a new plan and engineer a new world altogether. Or even to revise or decommission an existing one, Richard.' Francis's face brightened. 'We even know how to change this world completely.' His voice softened as he relaxed his grip. 'Because we've discovered how to re-write its past. If we dare, that is.'

'The past? But how?'

'By altering the world's design, Richard. By modifying it at birth. Every age starts somewhere. Just think of all the creation myths in cultures around the world.'

'You mean something like the Garden of Eden?' The American's voice came back to me.

'Exactly. And like plucky Eve and the luckless Adam, we're going to do something about it. It's just a question of initiation.' He let go of my arm.

'You have some strange theories, Francis,' I said.

He shrugged. 'Space and time are just a distillation of chaos, my friend. It might all seem …'

'Bewildering, Francis?' I suggested.

'Exactly. But all you need is the formula. The ancients solved it long ago.' He glanced back at the peplos. 'But we still have things to resolve. And that's why Alex is with Otto. Shall we continue?' We were about to resume when Francis ran his hands over his jacket pockets and turned pale. He scanned the floor behind us. 'Did you see what I did with my little guidebook and Alex's notes?' I shook my head. 'Blast, I've left it on the table in the café.' He snapped the words as if scolding himself. 'I need to go back. Check out the sculptures while I look for it. I won't be long.'

Francis slipped through the double glass doors of the gallery, leaving me adrift. I was as curious about his exotic claims for the frieze as I was by his sudden temper with himself. Not quite the cool veneer I was used to. But no matter, I needed the notes we'd made earlier over breakfast. There was still the Q and A to deal with and my part in

Alex's plan. I looked around. There was an unoccupied chair in the middle of the room. I headed over to it, sat down, and then checked for messages on my phone. Josh, I could see, wanted to talk.

Where are you?

I replied: *BM Parthenon gallery.*

Why, Josh asked.

For a lecture. Later. On some medieval guys.

I waited for a response.

Who? Josh asked.

Aquinas and Albertus Magnus, I replied.

He rephrased his question. *Sorry, I mean, who are you with?*

Francis & Alex.

I was about to ask why when a sudden cry distracted me. Someone in the tourist group had slipped over and needed help. I watched people assist as Josh fired off several messages in the meantime. The last one had repeated. *Still there, mate?*

Yes, I replied before catching up with his earlier messages, including one on a grade the tutor had given him for his essay. I teased him. *She likes you*, I said.

Oh no, he replied.

And a real turnaround, I thought, since his first encounter with her in class. *How's your girlfriend?* I asked.

Sophie is OK. Enjoys the poems.

I smiled. *This is getting serious*, I said. *You are an engineer, not a poet.*

Got time for a pint, mate?

Okay. But local.

And since the Q&A wasn't until after two, and the first of the day's lectures would finish before one, I agreed. I was about to text again when a voice interrupted me.

'Please excuse us, young man.' An American lady stood a short distance from me. She smiled awkwardly. 'My husband is feeling unwell. Would you be kind and let us use your chair?'

Her husband stood alongside her. He was the guy who'd mentioned the Prophets, I realised, and right now looked quite glum. 'I'm sorry, I didn't realise. Of course.' I offered the chair and then volunteered to get a glass of water. But they declined. They always drank bottled water when away. His wife gestured to a small knapsack and medication. I smiled before edging away. I switched back to my phone.

Josh had mentioned a televised rugby game in a follow-up text. England and Samoa. At a pub across the road from the museum. I said I'd make it. And buy the beers.

Okay. See you later, he replied. I slipped the phone into my pocket.

I meandered towards the frieze and found myself amongst the small group of visitors still following the guide. They were fewer now than when Francis and I had first latched on to his words, but he still smiled. He addressed the group once more. 'The horsemen and their horses dominate half the total length of the frieze. Some are heavily draped. Others almost naked.' The guide pointed to an athletic-looking youth with an arm raised and his head turned. 'There are sixty riders on the north frieze,' he added as he checked his notes. 'And sixty also on the south frieze. Sometimes experts suggest there is a meaning in the numbers. For instance, there are ten chariots on the south side but eleven on the north.' The guide stared wistfully as we pondered these remarks. Sixty sounded promising and even ten. But I wasn't sure if eleven had any significance. Maybe Plato had an idea. Or Pythagoras. Who knows? The visitors slipped away. I lingered, looking at their finely crafted heads. Some tilted, some staring straight ahead. Others cast down. And their faces, fresh and animated. And though idealised by the art of the day, I wondered if the horsemen were sympathetically paired. Hiding a blush, perhaps. And sharing a single thought. A sudden impulse and a selfless desire? I drew a breath. Love and death, I thought.

I turned my head. Francis flashed the guidebook at me.

'I was about to nudge you, Richard, but you looked lost in a trance.'

I grinned. 'Just some words that came to mind. A poem. Or rather, a line or two from it.' I glanced again at the riders on the frieze. '"But at my back, I always hear, Time's winged chariot hurrying near."' I turned to Francis. 'Your fault, I reckon. There are twenty-one chariots, apparently.'

He nodded. 'The poem. It's Marvell, isn't it?'

'Yep,' I said, still thinking of the line.

Francis checked his wristwatch. 'The registration starts in another fifteen minutes. Downstairs in the conference suite. Jane said she'd wait for us at the door and Alex'll join once he's finished up with Otto. Whenever that is.' He shook his head.

These guys, I thought. 'Oh, there's just one other thing, Francis. I plan to pop out during lunch. To see a friend. In the pub across the road.'

'No problem. There's an hour and a half between Weekes's presentation and the QA. We can go over the questions once you get back.' He handed me the guidebook and grinned— still in two minds about our escapade, I suspected.

I watched Francis slip away before I turned back to the frieze. It was a procession, for sure. A hallowed ritual. A potent sacrifice. I glanced again at the horsemen, still feeling drawn to the youthful cavalcade. My pulse rose. 'Wish me luck, guys,' I whispered. With the lecture. The tutor. And Alex's Q and A.

21

eekes's lecture finished around twelve thirty. I had a quick chat with Francis and Jane before heading off to find Josh.

The pub was across the road from the museum, just beyond the iron railings and gates that secured the open space in front of the British Museum's grand facade. Josh had said the game would start at one, so I had enough time to catch him for a pint. And a quick drink, I fancied, would settle my nerves before I helped Alex at the Q and A. I headed up to the atrium from the lower-ground conference area, left the museum through the entrance lobby and down the flight of steps that descend to the forecourt. About halfway, I stalled. Ahead of me, just in front of the gates, there was some sort of commotion.

A small crowd had gathered and was blocking the exit. I could see a man struggling with at least two other people. I was about to give Josh a call when the guy being restrained broke free. He ran, charging towards me. A voice shouted, 'Get down! Get out of the way!' I heard a gunshot. And then another.

We crashed to the ground together. Blood streamed from his wounds. I screamed. Another shot ricocheted off the steps, splintering the stone beside me. I tried to shift his weight, but his arm held me secure. He lifted his head and stared into my eyes. 'Boy. Listen to me, boy … "At the next world, that is, at the next spring: For I am every dead thing—"'

He fell silent.

I pushed him aside before Alex, rushing to my side, hauled me to my feet.

'Run!' he pleaded. 'For Christ's sake, run!'

* * *

I leant over the bathroom sink as Alex and Francis stood beside me. My blood-stained jacket and shirt lay on the floor. Tears streamed from my eyes. And a sour vomit from my mouth.

'Why, Alex? Why?'

A swirl of water cleared the bowl.

'Richard,' said Alex. 'The old man. Did he say anything to you?'

'Maybe. Something.' I lurched again, splattering the sink. Francis stepped back. An acrid smell filled the air.

Alex placed an arm across my shoulders. 'Richard … his words … were they from a poem? Like some kind of verse?'

'I can't remember, Alex. Someone's just been shot, for Christ's sake.' More vomit invaded my mouth. My body tensed as I spat it out. Alex released his arm. I turned to Francis. 'The face. I think I know the face.' I spat again.

'You know him? But how?'

'He was … in the café. The one you said was Paulo's café. I went there before I met you in the pub. He talked to me. About my studies. And a sketch I did. Of the church.'

'You mean the first week of term?' Francis looked at Alex.

I nodded, splashing water on my face and around my lips and eyes. I leant upright and stared into the washroom mirror. Only the taps made any sound. 'I'm cold, guys. And I'm scared.'

Alex pulled off his sweater and handed it to me while Francis stuffed my shirt and jacket into a large plastic bag. I stood back as they tackled bloodstains on the floor, dragging hand towels with their feet.

176

'Where are we?' I asked.

'We're still in the museum, but below ground, Richard. Don't worry. We're okay.'

Underground? I started to shiver. The room darkened. Images flashed inside my head. The crowd. The shots. The screams. The old man's face. I felt my legs give way before Alex caught me in his arms. He lowered me to the floor. I held the sweater to my chest. Still shivering.

Alex knelt down beside me. 'The old man, Richard … He'd come to see Otto. He had important news for us. A date. And a place. For our plans.' I looked up. Alex leant closer. 'Richard. You have to remember what he said. Otherwise we're screwed.'

I shook my head.

Alex stood up and washed his hands.

My phone buzzed from inside the plastic bag.

Francis found it and cut it dead. 'They've withheld the number, Richard.' I tried to stand, but my ribs ached from my fall on the museum steps and the weight of the old man. There were tears in my eyes.

'We'd better not hang around, Alex. Whoever is trying to contact Richard might not be a friend.' Francis stared down at me.

I reached for the sink and pulled myself up from the floor. The tap water was still running. I wiped my face before Francis handed me my phone. 'What do you mean—not a friend?'

'Your phone, Richard. It can track your movements.'

'Track me? But who wants to track me?'

Francis ignored my question and spoke to Alex instead. 'I'll check with Otto and the museum's cameras. We'll cut anything showing Richard. Whoever was shooting from the gates might be captured amongst the crowd.'

I felt confused. 'But if someone's been shot, shouldn't we go to the police?'

'We'll see, Richard,' replied Francis. 'But remember Paulo. He, too, was in Covent Garden. And you've had the misfortune to meet them both. You could be next.'

My jaw dropped. I looked at Alex. And then around the room at its white, sterile walls. Two people, I thought. Both of them at the same café. I shut my eyes. I needed to get out. To get away. I slipped my phone into a trouser pocket and then reached for the plastic bag.

'You must trust us, Richard.'

'I do, but I don't understand what's going on.' I dropped the bag. My clothes were covered in blood and vomit.

'Listen. If we talk to the police, they won't help us.'

'Why? It's their job, Alex.'

'Sorry, Richard. But *our* world is a lot more complicated.' Alex put his arm around my shoulders. 'If you trust me, just listen for fuck's sake. We are all in danger now.'

'Why?'

'Because of what you've just learnt. From the old man. From Kalinsky.'

There was tension in his face. His embrace tightened.

'Alex. Take Richard home to his flat. Stay with him for a few days. See if he can remember the lines of verse.' Francis wheeled back against the row of sinks. 'You can take the black cab from the underground car park. Eddie can drive. There's a bottle of whisky under the back seat.' Francis opened his wallet and handed him a bundle of twenty-pound notes. 'Don't use any cards until we're sure. Cover your faces whenever you're outside. I'll see if there's any word on Kalinsky.'

Alex took the cash.

Francis turned to me. 'You'd better keep your head down, Richard. And keep your phone off for now. I'll get Hatherleigh to give you an alibi for this morning.'

'But I was planning to meet Josh.'

Francis paused. 'Okay. But you didn't. You had to leave earlier. We can make it urgent.'

'It still doesn't work. The uni might query it.'

'Why?'

'Because the enrolment got messed up. I'm registered on Arbetta's course, guys. Not on Hatherleigh's.'

'The A option?' Francis stepped back.

I nodded. 'I'm sorry. It was when the network crashed at the start of term. There was a mix-up, and I should have sorted it out. But I was too embarrassed.' Water still ran from a tap. Alex tightened it. I heard him swear.

'Then Arbetta will have to do the alibi.' Francis screwed his face as if the ground was falling beneath our feet. 'Does anyone else know of your studies with us?'

'Josh. The guy I was going to meet. And a friend of his called Martin. He used to study with Arbetta. Sometime last year.' Francis checked eyes with Alex. 'There's also another guy called Jonathan.'

'Jonathan? Who's he?'

'He's a post-grad or something. Turns up to the English classes. Got all agitated when I told him about you.'

Alex remained thoughtful. But Francis was going pale. He turned to me. 'Richard, if you are registered on one course and not attending the lectures, your study module will be cancelled. You might be suspended. Or even asked to leave if there's suspicion of fraud.' Francis folded his arms. 'I'm worried. You could be compromised. That's how the bastards work.' We lost eye contact.

'Hang on, Francis,' said Alex. 'Not if we keep cool. Arbetta owes us, remember? And we'll just have to help Richard with the assignments.'

Francis looked at me. 'Okay, I agree. It's better that everyone thinks you are doing what the records say. We'll just have to sort this out between Hatherleigh and Arbetta.' He covered his left eye for a moment as he leant back against the row of sinks.

'And Jonathan?' I asked.

'Tell him you met us at some … some social, that's all. If he talks to Enrolment, they'll tell him he's wrong. In the meantime, we'll get you up to speed on the other course.' He checked the time. 'I can still catch Otto and Jane, Alex. We need to re-plan our other operations. And dinner.'

Francis washed and dried his hands, unrolled his sleeves, and buttoned his cuffs. Grabbing his jacket, he headed to the door and left, still angry.

Alex and I stayed silent.

'The Q and A, Alex …'

He shrugged. 'It doesn't matter.'

'No. I suppose not.' I looked around. A thin moisture had settled on the washroom walls and lingered like a cold sweat. 'This Otto … You're both working for him, aren't you?'

Alex nodded.

'And Hatherleigh. And Arbetta as well.'

'Yeah.'

I stared back at the wall. 'Is there anyone else I don't know about?'

'There are other people. Outside London.'

'Where?'

'A place called Culham. Near Oxford.'

'And how long has this been going on for?'

'Years. Before me, if that's what you want to know.'

I wiped my lips with my hand. Vomit had dried around my mouth.

We picked up the last of the dirty towels and secured the plastic bag with a knot. I washed again and then pulled Alex's sweater over my head. My breathing steadied. As I studied my appearance in the mirror, I tried to smile. For the moment, I felt safe. But inside … unsure. I'd come to uni to study poetry. And now some fleeting line from a mystery poem threatened to be my undoing. I sensed another tear.

Alex reached for my arm and gestured to leave. He headed for the door. But as his hand touched the handle, he turned to me and looked into my eyes. 'You're one of us now, Richard.' He held his stare. 'One of us.'

He pushed open the door and made his way out. I followed, slipping through the exit before the door swung back behind me.

22

'I saw Eternity the other night'.

Felix Leighton reread the words of a poem by Henry Vaughan, enjoying a gentle smile. It wouldn't do much for Larry Antony, he fancied, but the old man might warm to the line and the poet's imagery of light and dark. He checked a web page commentary on the author. Vaughan, a seventeenth-century Welshman, it explained. A writer, linked to the school of Donne, who had a twin brother called Thomas, known for his interest in magic and alchemy. He scrolled through the page, quickly digesting a synopsis of the text: metaphysical, rich in mystic allusions, with a Platonic angle. A poem about the salvation of the soul or its damnation. He eased back from the screen. A vision of Warren to the sound of biblical thunder arose in his mind.

Felix closed the web page and reached for his pen. He wrote the word 'eternity' as the keyword for the cypher that would help unravel a clue within the poem. And maybe test the credibility of Larry Antony as a mathematician and cryptographer. He followed the instructions provided by his contact in GCHQ, creating a matrix of letters of three and a half rows and eight columns comprising the keyword along the top and the rest of the alphabet in the succeeding rows beneath. Below each letter, he left space where he assigned a number. So far, so good. But he wondered if such a simple construction would prove much of a challenge to his American counterpart. Or even to a child. He pondered the word 'eternity' as he re-opened a window on his laptop. A sequence of numerical data appeared on the screen. Using the correspondences with the table, he wrote down a solution. He looked at it carefully. It was gibberish. He reached for his phone and called a senior analyst in GCHQ.

'Malcolm, hi. I've followed your instructions.'

'Good man. What have you got?'

'A matrix of letters interleaved with another one of numbers.'

'Okay. First step completed.'

'But it doesn't help crack the encrypted text you sent me.'

'And it won't. Not until you use an additional key. You have to adjust the values of the encryption. Then you can read off the result from the matrix.'

Felix glanced back at his instructions. He'd missed the line about phoning his colleague. 'Sorry. I was in a hurry. Antony's still bugging me.' He looked back at the screen. 'What's the extra key, then?'

'It's another sequence of numbers. Magic numbers.'

'You're kidding me?'

'No. Francis Eggar is a mathematician, remember? He's like me. He likes puzzles and mind games.'

'And magic squares. Okay, I get it.'

'But I had to play around a bit. And for this key, let's say he's used two rows from a base-six square that starts from the number one and goes up to thirty-six. I found it in an old book by Cornelius Agrippa. He was some sort of Renaissance mystic or cabbalist. And a contemporary of Dürer. Anyway, here are the numbers from a row in the square: thirty-four, twenty-eight, fifteen, twenty-one, ten, and three. If you check the square, you'll see that all the rows add up to one hundred and eleven. And six hundred and sixty-six if you tot the lot.'

'Okay. What do I do now?' Felix cast his eyes around his room but took care to keep listening.

'Write them under the cypher text I sent to you and then take them away with no carry-over adjustment. It's the same method that the Russians used in the Venona files back in the thirties and forties.'

Felix copied the number-encrypted text from the screen and subtracted the additive line using the first three numbers of the magic square. The operation yielded '81', '96' and '1'. He reread the matrix, decoding the result as 'the'. The next section of cypher produced 'world'.

'Got anything?'

'Two words. It's clever. The title of Vaughan's poem.'

'That's right. Bang on. Now, let's use the method with another message.'

Malcolm read out the encrypted text. Felix used the magic square numbers to perform the subtraction and then checked the result against the table he had constructed.

'Make any sense?' asked Malcolm, chuckling in anticipation.

'I think so. It looks like a place.'

'It is. And it's up in the Arctic. Named after an English astronomer, apparently.'

'Hold on.' Felix flipped to a map on his laptop. He searched for the name and zoomed in on a place in northern Canada. It looked remote. A topographical view showed a bleak greyish-brown landscape of barren rock and summer snow. A small native settlement scratched a living nearby. If this was the origin of the cosmos, it was more like a frozen hell than the Garden of Eden. 'Are you sure about this?'

Malcolm was still chuckling. 'Yep. And I know it looks grim, Felix, but I checked out the history. Guess what, English explorers have been poking around here since Frobisher and John Davis.'

Felix dragged the map across the screen. The Earth's magnetic pole was not far away. And James, he recalled, had once talked of an electromagnetic realignment when explaining the students' plans.

'Felix? Still with me?'

'Yes, Malcolm. But I'm wondering if there is something else we can throw in. Something astrological. You know planets and stars.'

He thought again about the poem. '—a great ring of pure and endless light. | All calm, as it was bright; And round beneath it time in hours, days, years, | driv'n by the spheres'. The image of a clockwork universe occurred to him. And the spheres of the Middle Ages. He smiled. Francis would have thought the same.

'What are you going to do with it?'

'I'm going to send it to Antony. I'll tell him it's another intercepted communication from the Karlstad ring. They already have hundreds of others following the agreement by James.'

Felix looked back at the screen and a region of harshly shaped lands that once groaned and sharpened under layers of ice. Malcolm was right, map makers and explorers had hugged its tortuous shores looking for a route to India and its riches. He reached for a pen and wrote the coordinates of the location he had identified on the map. It had a plausibility that should keep the Americans busy, he thought. And the history department could have something to support Malcolm's ruse. He made a note to contact Professor Littlejohn.

'Felix?'

'Sorry, just wondering about the location. But, to tell you the truth, Malcolm, I'd rather we didn't provide too many clues on deciphering it.'

'Oh? Wound you up, has he?'

'Well, you could say that. Let's just put it down to differences in our approach.'

'Cryptology for you, Felix. Full of geniuses and eccentrics.' He chuckled again.

'Well, I'm a philologist, Malcolm. I used to study ancient texts. Such as Sanskrit. And Old Persian. It worked best when we collaborated. But Larry makes me anxious. He may be a loner, but is he a cryptologist?'

'I can always look him up for you.'

'No. At least not yet. But if he's for real, he should be able to pick his way through the data. He once boasted to me about his intelligence training on Soviet signals traffic.'

'Well, in that case, let's see how good your American friend is. What I'll do is tell him the source of the additive line, but not the specific sequence from the magic square. He'll get there if he knows his stuff.'

'But what about the date, Malcolm? The old man is having kittens over this. And they think we're hiding it from them.'

'Still working on it. I'm trying out some ideas from the AI mob. But I could knock something up with one of our history bots. Should keep them busy.'

'Maybe. But let me run it by James. We're not getting much from these guys in return, and it might look suspicious if we don't hold something back.'

'Okay, I'll call you when I get some data together. You can decide how much you want to give away.'

'Thanks, Malcolm.'

'Best of luck with the Yanks.'

Felix replaced the phone. The secure line signal to GCHQ faded as he leant back in his chair. He looked again at the poem. A reference to moles in the second stanza caught his eye. '—and lest his ways be found, work'd underground, | Where he did clutch his prey'. Poets and their sly metaphors, he mused. He closed down the synopsis and flipped to another screen.

Entering his password, Felix accessed a classified folder that held regular feedback on the student group at UCL. A tutor at the university had added the most recent entry. He made his own comments before logging out of the file. He clicked again on the Arctic wastes. Would Warren buy it? It was still North America. And historically possible. If James's plan was to win more time, it was worth a shot.

Especially if Larry blundered along the way. Felix rubbed his chin, wondering how he might handle any fallout. Suddenly, a message flashed in the corner of his screen. It was from James. *King William Street. Now*, it barked.

He grabbed his jacket and phone, snatched a last glance around his room and hurried to the security barrier by the entrance to the Foreign Office compound. A black cab, primed to leave, was idling in the street beyond the gates. 'Where are we going?' Felix asked, as he stumbled into the back seat alongside his boss.

'The Bank of England, Felix.' James looked at him gravely. 'One of their former employees has just been shot at the British Museum.'

23

'Josef Kalinsky? I hardly knew the man.' Tommy Godson reached for the salmon starter. 'HR had him down as Toby White. From Cambridge.' He poured a little wine into a glass, swirled it gently and took a sip. 'Started in the Notes Directorate. Late nineties. Left us last year, I believe.' He gestured towards a spread of salads, breads, cheese, and cold meats that he had ordered for the meeting.

'The Notes Directorate?' queried James.

'Forgeries, old man. Only reason the Bank of England would ever hire someone from the book trade.' Godson cast his eye over the plates of food. He lifted a slice of beef with a fork. 'Liked to sit in the Bank's garden. Reading poetry, I remember. By the mulberry trees.'

'We believe he was from the Baltics. With Russian connections.'

'Russian? Would explain all that bowing, then.'

Godson tucked a white linen napkin under his chin. He settled closer to the table. 'It's the best we can do. In the circumstances. But do get stuck in.'

James looked sharply at Felix. And then more favourably at the spring water. 'He studied forensics. And then a doctorate in art history. Prague. During the mid-eighties.'

Godson caught the words between sampling the food. 'I heard he switched to bullion in 2007.' He lifted his glass.

'Bullion?' Felix's surprise drew the others' attention.

'Gold bars. And banknotes. That's our business, you know.' He gestured once more to the lunch.

Felix reached for the bread.

'If memory serves,' said James, 'the issue in the original Kalinsky case involved a sequence of numbers.'

Godson eased back in his chair. 'Oh, the blessed date nonsense again.' He removed the napkin from his chin and placed it on the table. 'So that's what it's about.' He looked towards Felix. 'I suppose he's got you caught up in all this, as well?'

Felix nodded.

James turned to his colleague. 'There has long been a suspicion, Felix, that this blessed little number lies hidden somewhere in this building.'

'Hidden, James?' Godson frowned, pointing at the mixed-leaf salad. Felix moved the bowl closer. 'Old Montague, our pre-War governor, took the place apart in the twenties, remember? Brick by brick, chasing that infernal date business.'

'It was a terrible loss, was it not?' Felix asked.

'No, not at all. We kept the best rooms. And a few old originals.' Godson picked away at his plate as Felix and James looked across the room at the marble fireplace and a painting of Covent Garden that was fixed to the wall above. 'The government paid for the reconstruction. I'm sure a small profit was reported. In the long run, as they say.'

'I'm sorry, sir. I meant Soanes's great masterpiece. The halls, the vaulted ceilings, the gardens. Its wonderful symmetry and proportions.'

Godson reflected. 'Oh, the old buildings, you mean?' He looked at James. 'I think we can blame that one on Whitehall. "Examine every square inch," they said. Every slab of stone, looking for the ruddy thing. It was harder than the lottery.' He resumed eating.

'Pevsner described it as a loss greater than the damage done to London in the Blitz,' ventured Felix.

'Who?' asked Godson.

'Pevsner. The architectural historian, sir.'

'Wasn't he German?'

'Yes. I believe he was.'

'Well, he should know, then. They did bomb us, old boy.'

James reflected on this earlier episode. Every brick had been examined. Every vaulted arch dismantled. Even the graveyard of a medieval church that now formed the Bank's secret garden was dug up and the corpses dispersed to a cemetery in South London. Only the defiant walls of Soane's great citadel remained today, still adjoined by a small replica of the Sibyl's temple of Vesta in central Italy. He glanced again at the painting before his eyes fell on the silver cutlery beside his empty plate. The Bank's own hallmark reminded him of his purpose.

'Tommy, please. And Felix, thank you, but no more architecture. Or art. The PM has an interest in our deliberations. If we could return to the agenda, gentlemen?'

Felix placed his cutlery to the side of his plate.

'Three hours ago, Josef Kalinsky was shot in the grounds of the British Museum.' James removed a briefing stamped with the Foreign Office logo. 'His background, Tommy. By the security services.' Godson left it on the table. He patted his lips with the napkin as James continued. 'We believe that Kalinsky's intention was to meet his controller at the museum prior to implementing their plans for worldwide upheaval.'

'I see … Well, he was a bit of a rum chap, now that I think of it.'

James passed another document across the table. 'From the Treasury, Tommy. A request for cooperation with our inquiries.'

'Ah.' He placed it with the security briefing. 'And what sort of help are you wanting from us this time?'

'Assay numbers. The gold, Tommy.'

'Every bar, James?'

'I'm afraid so.'

Godson reached for his phone and opened the calculator. He scribbled some numbers on to the Treasury request and did some sums. 'What with central bank swaps and other silly disposals, there's been a lot of movement over the years.'

'You mean the fire sale, Tommy?'

Felix glanced at James.

'Late nineties,' recalled Tommy with a sigh. 'Half the gold out the door for a song. And then that *angst* at the Bundesbank.'

'The Bundesbank, sir?' asked Felix.

Godson nodded. 'We used to keep their stuff downstairs.'

'But they've got it back, haven't they?'

'Most of it. Blew up around the Millennium.' He slipped his napkin over the calculations. 'They too were keen on assay numbers, I remember.'

'Really?' James thought for a moment. 'And there was that Greek business during the War as well. I'll see if GCHQ can help us with anything on the matter.'

Felix nodded.

Tommy Godson stretched out his arms before looking at his wristwatch. 'Monetary Committee, four o'clock, I'm afraid,' he explained. 'You chaps will have to excuse me.' He gathered up his papers and rose from his chair. 'I'll send what we have through the usual channels, James.' He turned to Felix, casting a wearied grin. 'Best of luck with the numbers, old boy.'

James and Felix stood. Tommy Godson made his way to the internal door of the office and his monthly deliberations on monetary policy.

James led Felix out of the ground floor office and stepped into the garden of the Bank of England. A steady rain beat the ground ahead of them. The mulberries had long since shed their pretty leaves. And the old graveyard had forgotten its ruthless disembowelling.

James hunched his shoulders and pulled his jacket tighter at the lapels, but paused before making a dash. He turned to his colleague. 'Did you notice the obelisk at the centre of the painting, Felix? The painting of Covent Garden.'

'Yes. It was supporting a globe, I think.'

'That's right. And a sun-dial. I wonder why?'

24

Like a soft toy, Alex had lain bleary-eyed on the floor of my room, his head on a cushion, and the rest of him wrapped in a spare duvet that my mum had given me on my last trip home. We'd spent most of the money on letting go. I saw more of central London in just under a week than I'd seen in over six. He knew his way around, and it was the boost he reckoned I needed. A faster pace, Alex had decreed. And a new taste for adrenalin, whatever the outcome.

Jane had woken us at seven, knocking quietly but continuously on the door. There'd been no time to clear up, and empty bottles and cans littered my room. A DJ chatted tirelessly on the radio, long after we'd stopped listening to the tracks he'd been playing. Cups and empty takeaways cluttered the sink. While my laptop, battered in action during a crazy computer game that we'd both wanted to win, lay somewhere under my bed.

Jane had pretended not to see—clearing a space on my desk, opening the window, and silencing the DJ as we'd got ourselves dressed. She'd unpacked a heavy-looking shoulder bag that contained two large textbooks, a bunch of old DVDs, and a set of notes that she'd written herself. She'd glanced at them briefly as I'd fumbled with the buttons on my shirt. My crash-course in art history was about to begin, she'd gleefully announced.

We'd sat around the desk. And between occasional yawns and cups of tea, Jane had outlined my new round of studies. Just follow the suggestions, she'd said. And I'd nodded. Start with Giotto. And I'd nodded again. The 1300s. More nods. And then the Quattrocento. Which I think she had to repeat to me. And don't forget the 1500s, she'd added, as I'd slumped back in a heap, not sure if I wanted to cry. But then it got serious. There were three essay titles from which I would have to choose. Something on linear perspective or civic virtues and the city ideal; and if those didn't take my fancy, 'Visions of Arcadia in the late Renaissance'. I'd gulped twice, and glanced at Alex. He was scratching his head and rolling his eyes. More brain-juice, he'd joked, passing an empty can of beer to me. I hid my head. And no cheating, she'd said, wagging a finger at me like my mum. Arbetta would read whatever I'd come up with, she'd warned. But she'd smiled, too. Even affectionately. And in three or four weeks … who knows, I might run tours at the National Gallery. And I'd be off the hook with the uni.

Jane had given me a hug. She'd said I was brave. That I'd get through it. That we all suffer shocks and loss. Reminding me of the Embankment and the river. And then the old-fashioned notice board as she'd handed me a list of codes. Grinning, I'd glanced at them, but in a mood more of resignation than thanks before placing them alongside her textbooks. And would there ever be an end to it? I'd wondered. Or even an explanation. Then Alex and Jane had left together, leaving me to clean up the room on my own.

And that's how I remember it. Still in the dark.

For the next few days, I'd got stuck into books and the DVDs. My only moment of apprehension was late one evening. There were mystery footsteps on the stairs, followed by a gentle tap on my door. I'd waited. Not sure who it might be. But it was only Fiona, looking relieved but mad as well. 'Why haven't you answered my calls? Or my texts?' She'd asked. I'd looked away, sheepishly, before making up some excuse about losing my phone. 'Remember the agreement we made, Richard? On Donne's Satires?'

I'd missed our last tutorial as well. Though the next one, I'd fig-ured, was still five days away. Cringing, I'd asked her in … wonder-ing if she might stay.

There were five satires by John Donne, and we had agreed to compare notes. Fiona had already tackled the third and fourth. I should have done the first and second. We'd worked out a new plan before she'd made her way home, pretty miffed, I could see, by my feeble excuses and odd behaviour. I'd tried to say sorry. Then I'd tiptoed back to my bed. Another time, maybe.

* * *

Donne, I mused, holding a hot cup of tea. He makes everything so intense. If he were alive today, what would he be doing? Preaching, I bet. He'd have spent the whole morning at it. In the churchyard. Like one of his famous sermons that scared everyone with the spec-tre of death. I glanced up from my laptop and out of the window by my desk. St Paul's cathedral was a twenty-minute jog down the road. Donne had been its literary hero.

I put the cup down. 'Satyre 1' came back to me. I smiled, thinking of Alex. And 'Shall I leave all this constant company, | And follow headlong wild, uncertain thee?' The satire, I recalled, seemed torn between outcomes. Work or play, I wondered? And like Donne, I too was feeling wracked. I reached again for one of Jane's books on art. I turned the pages. A fresco by Masaccio, 'The Holy Trinity'. I shut my eyes and ran through what I knew. An all-seeing God in the background. Christ crucified on the cross. Another … bleed-ing arch. I opened my eyes. And a corpse. Of course. A reminder of death. I turned more pages. Donatello, Ghiberti, Fra Angelico. I yawned, tempted to give up. Maybe I could just bluff my way to the end. Or get Jane to finish the essay for me. I was mixing up the artists, anyway.

My thoughts wandered. I could wash-up instead. Or I could shave. I touched my chin. It was growing faster now, I reckoned. Or I could make the bed and hoover the floor. And that shouldn't be a problem. Nor for anyone else in the house who wasn't crashed-out already, after some Saturday-night out with his mates. Or still away—fixed up for the night with a partner. Even the guy who's supposed to live next door to me. I listened out. But nothing. Just silence. The silence to read lots of books. And to think. And maybe write. Or maybe to … I smiled and stretched my legs. Or maybe Alex'll drop by—wild, uncertain thee. I leant back, placing my hands behind my head. So … maybe that jog, after all.

The museum, though, was still a blur. As if everything had happened at once. But I remember we'd had breakfast, and that we'd got drenched on the way. And that Francis had talked about ceramic pots and marble sculptures. And things ending and somehow starting anew because of strange patterns in a cloth. I remember, too, a crowd and a struggle. And screams. I closed my eyes. Lots of screams. And Alex giving me his sweater. And Francis giving me my phone. And then a taxi and being helped up the stairs. Yeah. Here. To my flat. And I'd said … that I was okay. That I knew the way, guys. Like it's only the third floor. But I was glad that Alex had stayed. Eros was first born, he'd said, as he'd led the way. But the old man's words. Those whispered words on the steps of the museum forecourt. No. Those I don't recall.

I flicked around my laptop. Josh had sent me an email. *Meet me for a beer. Near the river.*

I felt a sudden rush of guilt for not explaining my absence ten days before. I checked the time. He would row till four or five, he'd said, so it was no good trying to phone. But what the hell? I'd just go. It would take me a little over an hour to find my way across London to a club he said was on the river at Putney. I could always workout if he was still on the water. I shut down my laptop. Grabbed my jacket and my wallet from my bed, slipped into some old trainers and then headed down the stairs, leaving my unfinished essay on the desk behind me.

I shrugged. I needed a break. And I still owed Josh a pint. And *that*, strangely, I did remember.

25

'Better mind out,' a voice declared.

I looked behind. 'Sorry?'

'The eight.' A young woman pointed at the river. A rowing crew steered towards us in the fading light. 'The guys are novices,' she explained, pulling up the zip on her brightly coloured gilet. 'You'll have to watch out when they swing the boat out of the water.'

'Okay.' I stepped back on to the road by the water's edge. 'Just waiting for a friend.'

The eight pulled up alongside me. I retreated further as the rowers launched themselves from their seats in a well-practised routine. An array of metal rigging flashed before my eyes, and with a heave, the young lads lifted their boat like a trophy into the air. They headed barefoot across the tarmac and into their boathouse. Two of the crew dashed back for the blades.

'Pretty slick,' I declared.

'Coordination. The first thing you learn once you are part of a well-trained crew. That and commitment.'

'I saw them go by earlier. They seemed to get it together.'

'Doesn't take much,' she said, brushing back her hair. 'But six weeks ago, they were trembling, bloated jellies. Where you're standing now.' I noticed how the river breeze had moistened her face and eyes. 'Do you row?' she asked, stepping forward.

'No.' I flicked a glance towards the river, shying at the thought. 'Must be pretty cold out there.'

'That's what Josh likes to say.' She reached down to pick up some clothing left by one of the lads.

'Josh?'

'Yeah. He's my boyfriend. We're at uni. UCL.'

I smiled. 'So, you must be Sophie,' I held out my hand. 'I'm Richard. Josh is in my class.'

'Hi.' She looked upriver. 'Josh is with Martin. In a pair, I hope.'

In the distance, I saw two small figures further upstream, silhouettes against a darkening sky. Sophie shook her head as we watched them zigzag towards us before Josh, grim-faced and pulling hard, swept the boat ashore.

'Remember how to lift it, Josh?'

'Yeah, yeah, yeah. I can do it, Sophie.'

He was looking sore from the session, but I gave him the thumbs up as he clambered from the stern. He turned back to the boat and, with a nod from Martin, they swung it above their heads. I grabbed the blades, before we made for the boathouse—now free of the amphibious eight.

'Did you go far?' I asked.

'Kew Bridge and back,' replied Josh.

'Looks nippy, though.'

'Bloody freezing.'

'Because we kept stopping,' blasted Martin. 'More a bleeding crab than a pair.' We stopped again as Sophie dislodged a small stone from Josh's right foot.

Martin and Josh placed the boat on to a boathouse rack. A quick inspection of the rigging proved that everything was secure and safe for another outing. Someone had christened it 'Hermes', I noticed, as Martin slapped the side like a faithful friend.

'You can put the blades over there, Richard.' Sophie pointed to another rack. I'd been balancing them flat in my arms like a temple priest. I made the offering.

Martin mumbled about untidy youth as he sealed some forgotten kit in a plastic bag. 'The changing room's free,' he declared. 'But wet. So, mind yourselves as you go in.'

Sophie threw Josh a towel before disappearing into the room with a kit bag. He wiped his face. Hard work on the water had puffed up his lungs and reddened his cheeks. 'You know, Fiona was looking for you, mate,' he said, talking through the towel.

'She came to see me. About the essays,' I replied, stepping forward. Josh waited for me to say more. I grimaced awkwardly. 'Look, I'm sorry about the pub. Something came up … I couldn't get away.'

He yawned back at me. 'You missed a good game. I tried to catch you at the end. But the call went dead.'

'You phoned me? At the museum?' My voice rose.

'Yeah.' He let go of the towel. 'But I had to use Sophie's phone instead of my own.'

I should have realised, I thought, instead of panicking in front of the others. I drew a breath, enjoying the fresh air. 'I'll try to explain over a beer. But something … strange is going on.' I slipped eye contact as I picked over my words. 'I'm kind of caught up in it. And I don't know why.'

'Can't make the beer, I'm afraid.' He stretched his arms.

It sounded like revenge. I glanced towards the changing room.

'No, Sophie's okay. But we're going to church. By Putney Bridge.'

'Church?' I wondered if I'd misheard.

'Her dad's reading the lesson,' he explained. 'At St Mary's. I promised Sophie I'd go.' He picked up the towel as I digested the news. 'You can come as well if you want,' he added, before slipping away to join Sophie and get changed.

I was wearing a dark-blue padded jacket I'd bought with Alex when we'd hit the town. A woollen hat that I'd found in a pocket to keep my ears warm. My old trainers scuffed around the sides, and baggy tracksuit bottoms in case I did have a go on the club's rowing machine. It wasn't exactly my Sunday best. I hadn't even shaved.

Martin re-emerged, already changed and showered. 'He was all over the water today. I hope he doesn't write essays like that.'

'I could see you zigzagging,' I recalled.

'Yeah. I'll have to put him back in a four.' Martin ran his hand once more over 'Hermes'. 'So, are you three off to the pub, then?'

'No. We're actually going to church.' I tried not to sound sarcastic. 'Sophie's dad is doing the reading.'

Martin rolled his eyes. He called to the others. 'Come on, you two. Hurry him up, Sophie.' He smirked before continuing. 'You haven't got time to rub him down. Not if you're going to church.' The lights flickered on and off as Martin made his point. 'I need to get away, Josh. I promised the club secretary I'd lock up before five.' He shook his head. 'I came here to try out one of their boats. And I still don't know if it'll go in a straight line.' He rolled his eyes again before looking back at me. 'There's always the bash in Covent Garden next month, Richard, if you're still missing a few pints.'

'Sorry?'

'The booze-up. The Saturnalia.' I winced, but Martin just shrugged. 'At least, that's what your arty types like to call it.' He checked the time.

'Don't know about it,' I said, shaking my head.

'Humanities organise it. Last year was a riot. Ask your chums Alex and Francis.'

As Martin played with the lights, I caught sight of a pair of rowing gloves under a bench. Must be Josh's, I thought. I picked them up and put them into my jacket pockets. Martin flicked the lights once more. It was way past five.

Josh and Sophie emerged dressed for church. Josh was wearing black shoes and pressed trousers. Only his hair and a steamy

complexion from the shower hinted otherwise. He lifted his foot
and pulled up a sock that had slipped around his heel.

It was the cue for Martin to usher us on our way before heading
off to his car.

'The service starts at six, Richard,' Sophie explained. 'And my dad
would love to meet you. Josh is always mentioning you.'

I caught Josh's eye, a little surprised by the remark. 'You don't
think I'll look out of place?' I said, rubbing my chin.

'No. Not at all.'

'Okay, then. But that beer. Can we make it another time, mate?'

'No problem.'

Sophie smiled at us both. 'It's the last Sunday before Advent, you
know.'

She reached for Josh's hand, happy to lead the way.

* * *

A bell pealed as we sat in the nave of St Mary's. Sophie described the
unfamiliar layout to me while the congregation took their seats. The
pews were removed, she said, following a fire many years before and
the seating rearranged in a semi-circle in front of the displaced altar.
It was a historic building, she added, mentioning its dramatic role in
the English Civil War. I nodded, aware of the history from a half-for-
gotten lesson at school. We sat still until the bell ceased to toll.

As the choir assembled in the corner of the nave, a group of
clergy approached from the left, led by the cross. We stood. I'd been
handed the order of service on entering the church. I glanced at
the details before turning to Josh. 'Have you heard about the street
party?' I asked, quietly. 'It's in Covent Garden. Martin reckons.'

'Yes. But Sophie and I are away. We're staying with her parents. In
the country,' he whispered. We resumed our seats.

'Sounds serious.'

He grinned and looked ahead.

I nudged him. 'Your gloves, Josh.'

Mounted candles burned steadily, lending a soft, contemplative glow to the ambient light. After a few preliminaries, we rose and sang the first hymn. We then sat again. I glanced around, studying the layout of the church as the service continued. Part medieval. And part rebuilt, I figured. But then I gazed up at a roof that looked quite modern. Nothing stays the same, I reflected. And then the War in Heaven came back to me. And the piazza. My thoughts drifted amidst a background of mumbled prayers. And that this place—I looked around again—may be called 'true paradise, I have the serpent brought'. John Donne. And that idiot … in the Covent Garden café. I shifted my feet, annoyed at the connections.

A member of the congregation approached the lectern and faced west. 'That's Sophie's dad, Ian,' said Josh. I listened as he read aloud something on sheep and goats.

After the reading, Sophie joined her father for communion. And as I puzzled over the rite, Josh leant towards me. He pointed at our place on the order page. 'I think there's another twenty minutes.'

'Thanks.' I'd already lost track of the responses, thinking of parties and pagan gods.

'We can join her dad for coffee,' he added. 'If you'd like to meet him.'

I nodded. We shook hands with each other at the request of the priest.

The service concluded with a hymn. 'The Day Thou Gavest Lord has Ended'. And, for sure, the darkness outside was now complete. But my final exercise of vocal cords helped dissipate a stiffness of mood, and build a thirst for a strong cup of tea or coffee.

Sophie's dad was pleased to see us as we joined him in the glass atrium that ran alongside the nave. I tried not to look too conspicuous in a casual, dressed-down sort of way.

'You look as if you've been out on the river, Richard. Were you rowing with Josh?'

'Er, no. I'd just come here for a beer,' I said, blushing and looking to Josh for support.

'We were going to have a pint, Ian. But we asked Richard along instead,' explained Josh.

'I was planning to have a go on the rowing machine … so I'm not quite kitted out … for the service, I mean.' I was still blushing. Sophie handed me my coffee.

'Oh, nothing to worry over. We're more than happy to share our celebration with anyone,' said Ian.

'Dad, you did the reading very well.'

'Thank you. I hope it made sense. It's a striking parable. And the postscript to Matthew twenty-four when the stones are thrown down in the temple.'

'You were fine, Dad. And no one will throw you down.' Sophie kissed him on the cheek.

'I enjoyed the final hymn,' I said, catching the more relaxed mood.

'Oh, definitely one of my favourites,' agreed Ian.

'It's funny,' I added, 'how you know them without sort of knowing them, if you see what I mean?'

Sophie smiled. 'You were singing louder than Josh, Richard. Everyone must have heard you.'

Or maybe my baggy trousers and scruffy chin had raised a few stares, I thought, colouring up again.

'Are you two lads studying together?' Ian asked.

'No. I'm a humble humanities guy,' I explained. 'He does the clever stuff. With maths and engineering.'

'No need to sound defensive.' Ian bit into a slice of cake. 'I'm a humanities man myself. History at Durham. The seventeenth century in particular.'

'So, you would know about the church?' I asked.

'Oh, yes. The Putney debates. We're very proud of that. Quite a radical time.' Ian pointed to an inscription on an arch inside the church comprising a quote by Colonel Thomas Rainsborough from the debates in 1647. 'He was an early advocate of a much wider suffrage, you know, one that implicitly acknowledged the sovereignty of the people over their chosen form of government.' I read the well-known quotation about the life of the poorest *he* as worthy as that of the greatest *he*. 'You must visit our exhibition. Are you doing history too?'

'Well, English literature, in fact.'

'Richard's an expert on John Donne,' Sophie added.

'A good choice. He was dean of St Paul's, you know.'

'He also studies art history. And magic,' said Josh, teasing me.

'Early science, guys.' I rolled my eyes. I was in a nice little church, not a Hatherleigh tutorial. But the debates intrigued me, and I wanted to learn more about them. I turned to Ian. 'This Thomas Rainsborough—' I said, before an outbreak of applause interrupted my words.

'You must excuse me for a moment, Richard. I want to say goodbye to a friend. He's heading home to the States after Christmas.' Ian turned to his daughter. 'We will lose a good tenor from the choir unless we can persuade this young man to step into his shoes.' He slipped away before I could ask my question.

I think he was joking about the choir, even if I'd grinned at the compliment. But he was right about the history. It seemed odd that a tranquil Putney church was host to one of the most radical debates in England. Parliament against the king. Oliver Cromwell. Diggers. Levellers. Petitions and cries for reform. And yet it had all gone wrong, I recalled. My old English teacher used to rage at it. 'Bloody oafs. Bloody fools,' he'd say. 'And why is this?' he'd blast, before glaring at me. I'm not sure, I'd reply, turning to my friends for support and an answer.

A queue edged towards the coffee and cakes. People chatting quietly. It wasn't as if they were going to the barricades. Okay, I thought. So, the Levellers never had a chance. And the Fifth Monarchists … well, they were just out of their minds. I flicked a glance towards the inscription and the exhibition in the church. And then I yelped. I'd spilt the coffee all over my hand.

'Richard. Are you okay?' Sophie took the coffee from me.

I nodded, holding my hand close to my chest.

'You're looking pale, Rick.' Josh handed me a tissue.

'I'm sorry. I've just remembered something. Just come to me. Like, out of nowhere.' I covered my hand.

'An essay deadline?'

'No.' I was sweating. 'No. Something else. That someone said to me. When I was at the museum. Over a week ago.' I swallowed.

'Do you need to sit down, Richard?' Sophie asked.

'No, I'm okay.' I looked around again. People still chatting. Suddenly, I felt a great burden weighing upon me. I looked back at Josh. 'Listen, we'll have to catch up another time, Josh … for that drink. There's something I need to do.' I smiled at Sophie. 'You must thank your dad. But I have to leave. Say sorry for me.'

I headed straight out of the building. A breeze freshened my face as I stood by the medieval tower. I drew the air deeply into my lungs. I could hear words. Alex's words. Tripping through my head. 'Come on,' his voice declared. 'You're one of us now, Richard. One of us.'

My jaw fell. *One of us?* What the hell did he mean by that?

<h1 style="text-align:center">26</h1>

Larry Antony entered the elevator and made his way to the executive suite of the Foundation—a dark, mirror-glass building, on the east side of London's financial district, just north of the Tower of London. At the fifteenth floor, he stepped on to the hard linoleum floor and made his way along a corridor to the locked door of the suite. He swiped his identity card through a reader before turning his face to a camera set in the wall. The door opened to the sound of a low, gravelly buzz. Ahead of him, in a large, brightly lit room, Warren Dudley sat upright in a high-back chair. A painting of the Crucifixion adorned the wall behind him.

'I have called you to my office as a matter of urgency,' said Warren.

'Sir.' Larry stepped forward, holding a bundle of intelligence briefings close to his chest. The door closed behind him, locking to the sound of a solitary click.

'As you know, the Foundation is eager for progress.' Warren gestured to a chair on the other side of his desk. Larry crossed the room and sat as directed. 'Your assignment is critical to our plans. We expected answers from you last week. Before Thanksgiving. It is now December fifth.' Warren placed his hands flat on the desk.

'It's like how I said. On the phone, sir. Good progress. But some difficulties here and there.'

'Difficulties?' Warren looked long and hard at his subordinate.

'A kind of mismatch. In the data.' Larry wiped the sweat from the palms of his hands before searching through the briefings. 'The guys have been on to the Brits about it. But we're making progress, sir. Like this.' He retrieved a page of binary numbers and set it on the table. 'It's a communication. By the students.'

Warren glanced at the document. 'Are the British holding back on us, Larry?'

'No. But I can't say for definite since they sent the decrypt, like we demanded. And I spoke to their junior … their Felix guy. He sent me a breakdown of the key construction so we can check their results and work on fresh material. Must be two weeks ago.' Larry nodded, as his eyes, struggling with the light, shifted around the desk. He lifted his head. 'And it's like I thought, sir. Just like the Soviets.'

'The Soviets?'

'Yeah. And hell, if the Brits are playing games. I mean, this isn't no kind of—'

'How far has the decryption progressed?' interrupted Warren, sharpening his voice.

Larry straightened up. 'I'd say … over eighty percent.'

'Over?'

'Yep. About eighty.' Larry nodded before looking away.

'And your team, Larry, are they hiding anything from us?'

'You mean the date, sir, and the place?'

'I mean the date and the place, sir!' The desk reverberated as Warren slammed his fists in frustration. 'We know already it's in North America, damn you. The Brits know that too. Because they invoked it.' Warren removed his glasses and rubbed his eyes.

Larry remained still until his boss settled. He glanced at his feet and some paperwork that had fallen from his lap. He looked up. 'I mean, the Brits think it could be Greenland. Or Northern Canada …' He shifted in his chair. 'But the guys think they're wrong. It's not so simple. Like I said, sir. On the phone.' He reached nervously to the floor and gathered loose pages.

Warren rose from his chair and moved to the other side of his suite. He paused in front of a photograph that had been framed and set against the bare office wall. 'Forty years ago, I joined my father in his work.' He glanced back at Larry. 'And two years later, I met my late wife, Ann-Marie, in Bible class. We courted. We made many dear friends.' His eyes lingered on the young, innocent smiles that stared back at him from the frozen scene. 'Fall, '81,' he muttered, touching the surface with his hand. 'Scripture tells us, Larry, that the Temple of Man will be thrown down. That the sun will be darkened. And that the stars will fall from the sky.'

'Holy scripture, sir.' Larry wiped the palms of his hands on his thighs, glancing anxiously around the room. 'We're working hard, sir. I mean, no distractions. For the team.' He swallowed. 'And only yesterday …'

'Yesterday?' asked Warren, turning his head.

'Yeah. A guy called Richard. We think he's a lead. He could have the data we need. Like on a phone call. Or a text, sir,' said Larry, searching the paperwork. He raised his head. 'The guys are checking. But they need … a little more time, sir. For rechecking. But it's looking good.'

'More time?'

'Another week,' added Larry, shuffling the notes. 'Like I said, progress is good. Decrypts. Profiles. We're getting there. Sure thing.' He slapped his knees with his hands.

'Without the date and place that the world was created, Larry, our plans cannot be fulfilled.' Warren spoke softly. 'Satan's empire grows every day. We will not be denied the Apocalypse. The Foundation has promised this to the faithful.'

'I'm with you, sir … I know we're close. Like it could be a week.' Larry flipped through more papers. Another page fell to the floor.

Warren reached once more for the photo and touched his wife's lips. He lingered as tears moistened his eyes. He smiled and returned to his desk.

'The Foundation has been kind to you, Larry.'

Larry bowed his head.

'Your scholarship gave you access to the skills you needed to perform our work. And your military training.' Warren leant forward, resting on his arms. 'And the Foundation has counselled you in personal matters. It has shown generosity and compassion.'

Larry clasped his hands in a show of contrition. 'I … I am deeply grateful.'

'Your parents' departure from the Church was the work of Satan, Larry.'

Larry nodded, staring fiercely at the floor. A spiral formed on a page at his feet, making eyes that bulged and pulsated. 'My mom and pa … they lied to me. They lied about Satan.'

'The Foundation forgives you. You have repaid their disobedience. But you must not fail now. Nor must you be tempted by what you learn of the secret. Your duty, Larry, is to us.' Warren turned to the painting behind his desk and contemplated the suffering of Christ. 'Giving is receiving. Only the chosen will be saved.' He breathed quietly before returning his stare to his subordinate. He reached across the desk.

Another buzz prompted Larry to rise. 'Sir,' he said, before making his way to the open door, holding the briefings to his chest.

* * *

South of the Thames, in an unlit space beneath a railway viaduct, Larry pulled his cell phone from his pocket and phoned a number. He waited, anxiously, until a screech above his head broke his concentration. Avoiding the sudden flight of a pigeon from its perch, he cut the call. His heart pounded as he rang again, but the sound of a heavy, clanking train drowned his thoughts. Unsettled, he looked around. A van moved towards him along the street. He turned aside to hide his face. He checked the time. Eight hours since he'd left the old man. Eight hours sweating the streets, the bars, the late-night delis. He leant back against the wall, hearing a trickle of water above his head. He phoned again, holding the handset against his ear. Another train pounded the track. 'Fuck you,' he snapped, hitting the wall with his fist.

Larry headed for the river and recrossed the Thames. Carlo's was not far, he remembered, retracing his steps through the streets until he stopped, unobserved, in a quiet alleyway near the Strand. He stared at a bin loaded with restaurant garbage. Soft drink cartons and unfinished takeaways lay strewn at its base. The smell of urine lingered in the air. He raised the lid, but hesitating, let it fall back again. Then, holding his nerve, he undid the cuff of his shirt and rolled his sleeve above his elbow. Closing his eyes, he thrust his arm deep into the bin and buried the useless pages of code into the contents. Relieved, he phoned again. The call connected.

'Listen. Don't hang up. There's lots of money. Double. No tricks. Like I've said.' He shifted along the alley. 'I've got to talk. I need everything. Everything you know. On Richard. Only this time, it's your place. Promise. Now.' The call ended. Larry clutched the handset to his chest.

The kid had agreed.

27

I'd looked-up the festival of Saturnalia before heading off to the piazza at six. Roman with a Greek counterpart, I'd learnt. And if Martin was right, the world, and Covent Garden, would turn upside down while some old Cronus fellow would rule a new golden age. That … or there'd be a lot of clowning around, I reckoned, and a few angry complaints from the locals. But as I headed into the north arcade, I noticed that not everyone was getting so carried away. Francis was sitting alone, wearing a winter jacket and a loose hanging scarf, quietly disdaining the antics around him. A large glass of red wine and what looked like a bowl of his favourite nut mix kept him company. Unobserved, I slipped alongside the see-through partition that marked out the café enclosure and then made my way to his table.

'So, Francis, man is the measure of all things.' I thrust my art history essay at him with a delicious grin. I was back on my feet and ready for the encounter.

He smiled. 'So you got the note?'

'Yep, usual place.' I pulled up a chair. 'But I wanted to arrive early, mate. I'd heard the social sciences mob were planning a riot or something.'

'Possible. But they'll want to eat and drink first.'

The arcade was decked out for a students' Christmas party. Several cafes and bars were hosting the bash, running backwards and forwards with beers and plates as guys hung around the tables, joking and chatting. Everyone was enjoying the last lap of term, even if an essay, and a few other things, were still on my mind.

Francis adjusted his reading glasses. He reached for the first page and read.

'It's all there,' I explained. 'Visual pyramid. Orthogonal lines. Transversals and vanishing point.' I'd spent the last three days slogging away on linear perspective. 'Should keep Arbetta happy,' I added, flashing a smile at the endeavour.

'So, you've started with Alberti.'

'Yep, 1430. Or thereabouts.' I leant back. Soon he'd get clinical.

Francis turned the page. He studied the diagrams, nodding as my explanation progressed. I'd copied them from a treatise on perspective by the Italian humanist Leon Alberti. And I'd followed this with a few iconic names from the Quattrocento: the Florentine painter Masaccio, whose mural, 'Expulsion from the Garden of Eden', had caught my eye, the Dominican friar Fra Angelico, and the geometer and mathematician Piero della Francesca—three of whose works I'd found in the National Gallery just up the road. I sat back. A few more pages, my friend, and it'd be mission accomplished. I stretched my arms as he deliberated over the finer points of my essay.

Francis took another sip of wine. 'It was quite innovative,' he said. 'I mean, in terms of space. And integrated subject-matter.' He paused, removed his glasses, and rubbed his eyes. 'As a technique, it makes the illusion of flat-surface painting appear almost 3D. And gives depth to meaning.'

I agreed. But a sudden noise and the flash of a camera close by caught our attention. Two more guys had joined a larger party sitting between us and the café's service counter. They'd painted their faces like circus clowns, prompting a flurry of texts and photos that soon went viral. Saturnalia, I remembered. And still the whole evening to enjoy. 'Sorry, Francis. Are they serving beers with the food or is it just wine?'

'Beer, if you ask. But the wine is an iffy house red.' He turned another page, helping himself to his nut mix.

'I'll stick to the beer, then.' I raised my hand, looking towards the bar.

'You know, the geometry behind this, Richard, can get complex.'

'Didn't I say something about Uccello as well ...' I broke off as a waiter unloaded beers at the adjacent table. I pointed at the bottles as he turned towards me, but he swung away without noticing.

'Yes. I saw that. Paolo Uccello. But what I had in mind was more extreme. Something on distortion.'

'Sorry?'

'Perspective anamorphosis,' he explained. 'It's where an image looks contorted when you view it. At least at first.' He lifted a page of the essay and twisted its shape. 'The National Gallery has a good example. An elongated skull. By Holbein. It reminds one of death,' he added.

'Thanks. But I thought the purpose was to make everything clear and lifelike,' I said, conscious that everyone else was sinking pints.

'It does. To those who understand the intention. But whenever an innovation appears in art, such as perspective, it's copied and even abused. Or like an argument, Richard, that seems at first to say one thing, but in reality means something else. Or nothing at all.'

Another group of guys parked themselves at a table next to ours. And while Francis enjoyed his wine and savoury nibbles, I unzipped my jacket and placed it on the chair beside me. Francis returned to the start of my essay. He picked up his glasses.

'What I am thinking of, Richard, are your opening remarks.' He ran his finger over the words I'd quoted at the top of the first page.

'About man, you mean? And the measure of things?'

Francis nodded.

'But didn't it help Alberti get his drawing right when he explained perspective?' I'd drawn a baseline and marked it off at intervals. And from each of these intervals, I'd drawn lines—the so-called tram-lines of perspective—that receded to a central point in the diagram. This was the vanishing point. 'These intervals here,' I explained, 'aren't they equal to one third of the height of your average man? Isn't that what Alberti means?' Francis didn't disagree. I looked again at the baseline. 'Have I left something out?'

'No. The geometry works fine.' We both cast a glance at the receding lines. 'What I was wondering was whether you think there's a contradiction in how Alberti quotes this claim about man and yet uses it to build a single perspective?'

Essays, I wondered. And the guys around me had ditched any notion of them. I pulled up the sleeves of my sweater. 'Okay, Francis. You are the tutor.'

'Well, if man is the measure, and the classical debate on this refers to his judgement and his tastes,' he recalled, lingering between thoughts, 'it could lead to conflicting opinions. Or even shaky arguments.' His face fell at the prospect. 'How, Richard, might we ever know the truth if everything is relative to everything else?' He folded his arms and leant closer. 'How will we be able to decide on anything?'

I shrugged. It was an odd place and time to get precious about philosophical contradictions, I thought. 'Sorry, Francis. But why shouldn't we have different views on something? Think of a land-scape. It might be harsh and rugged-looking. Or look like a roman-tic paradise. Yet we could easily disagree on which was the more beautiful.'

'But what is beauty? What is truth? And is there a yardstick for determining them?'

I shrugged again. 'Well, if we can't make up our own minds, we can seek advice. Go to the experts. They study it, don't they?' I tracked the waiter, still hoping to get that beer.

Francis held his wine glass by the stem. 'But the experts might be deluded, Richard, or just self-serving.'

'So we ask lots of them,' I added. 'Weigh it up. See what comes out best.'

'For whom?'

'Well … for the argument, of course.' My attention switched as a young lady rescued my thirst. I ordered a pint, a bag of crisps and another bowl of the nut mix for Francis; but while he was okay with his red, he was still unconvinced by my words. I tried to meet him halfway. 'All right, a yardstick,' I agreed. 'But isn't Alberti saying that about man, because it works in his drawing? Like that is his yardstick.' I suggested. 'Something that works. Something useful.' I pointed again to the diagram.

'So is that all it means, Richard?' He was still studying the wine.

'Look, Francis. You asked me to write an essay on linear perspective. And vanishing point. Not philosophy. Right?'

'I did. But perspective influences everything we do. And why we do it.' He put his glass of wine down and grinned back at me.

Francis wasn't giving in, and as my beer arrived, I scanned the inside of the building. If we could start with something visible and even tangible, we might settle the point. Like the high brick walls with cast-iron columns standing to the front of them. Or the sloping glass roof that peaked above our heads. Or its supporting metal frame with ribbed, skeletal arches, painted in a pastel blue, that stopped it from crashing down on to the flagstones of the floor. This was the 3D on the surrounding arcade. A Victorian gem or an over-designed engine shed with no trains? How about that for perspective, my friend? I turned back to Francis. 'All right. You see the columns and trusses supporting the roof of this hall? I would say, Francis, that they are functional but not beautiful. But someone else might disagree.' I mimicked the architecture above my head. 'They might think the framework was very elegant,' I proposed, 'or just a load of old iron holding up a roof.' I lowered my arms and readjusted my sleeves. 'And that means we have different perspectives. But both are true. I can't say that my view is better than someone else's when we both see the same thing. With our own eyes. And when everything around us is changing, anyway.' Grinning, I sipped Francis's wine as a tease. I wiped my lips. He was right about the iffy red.

'But if you have a standard, Richard, you can. Much like the base-line you drew in Alberti's diagram, a baseline that points us in one direction only, you'll notice. With one outcome. One truth, per-haps.' Francis retrieved his glass. He drank, not fancying my beer.

My mood sagged. The roof wasn't getting us anywhere. I changed tack. 'Maybe we should all read more poetry, Francis. Because not everything can be reduced to simple numbers or arguments. What if feelings were to count?'

'Ah, the madness of poets,' he mocked.

'It's not madness,' I retorted. 'Explaining contradictions is part of the challenge. That's what Donne does. Intellect and emotion. Somehow, both can come together. And then you make your choice. There's no need to be rigid. Same with landscapes. Or art. Or roofs, even.'

Francis had listened but, his eyes distant, seemed to work on something new. One of us will surely give ground, I thought, so we could just get on with the evening and have a laugh. Otherwise, he was going to be a real pain until Jane and Alex turned up. What I'd said made good sense to me. Okay, we may have to think things through, as Francis was saying, but we have to consider our feelings, too. I drank more beer, hoping to cool off. And then I opened the crisps and let the contents fall to the table. We could take whatever we wanted, rationale or not, I fancied. I gestured to the crisps.

'Thanks. But let's try a test, Richard.'

'Okay.' I nodded, placing my arms across the essay ... just in case.

Francis grinned at my gesture as he leant back. 'Why did you join the art history course, Richard?'

'Why? Because you and Jane suggested it.' My eyes narrowed. What was Francis getting at now?

'Well, we did. But that was our opinion. And we'd only just met you.'

'But you sounded convincing. You had good reasons.'

'Was that all?'

'No. It wasn't. I told Hatherleigh about my literature degree. And how it would help.' I leant forward. 'The poetry, remember?'

He shrugged. 'But you could have done Arbetta's course. Instead, you chose Hatherleigh's.'

And if I had chosen Arbetta, I wouldn't be sitting through this tedious business with you, Francis. Why won't he let go? I hadn't come here for a fight. I drank some beer. Maybe a fuller explanation would close him down. 'Okay, but you were both so knowledgeable. And Jane could explain Dürer. And you mentioned the myths. So, I thought … I could learn from you both. You are older. And then Alex helped me in the pub.'

'But you didn't meet Alex until later.'

'I didn't say that. What I meant was that you were great guys. Ready to help. And everything happened so quickly when I saw Hatherleigh.'

'And does that make it the right choice?'

'Oh for god's sake, Francis. We're supposed to be having a drink. Who knows why I chose it? Maybe it was fate.'

'Well, in that case, it certainly wasn't your choice.' Francis retired to his wine.

There was no escape. And in my mind, I could see Hatherleigh urging me to recollect the reasons for joining his class. I ran back over the meeting. First, there was that stuff on the occult. Second, the connections with art and the links with literature. And Dürer and his kind of nutty 'Triumphal Arch'. And then there was the challenge of just standing up and arguing my case until I got somewhere. This wasn't Oxford, I remembered. Or even the disagreements I'd had at school. That was for sure. But Francis just stared at me as I raked over the memories. So maybe it wasn't fate, I decided. Because if it was, I really didn't know where the hell this was going. And I'd just spent two weeks slogging away at a course that I have to pretend I'm studying. And now I am being quizzed as if I have done something wrong. I could see myself screaming in the witness box.

'Francis, where are the others?' I snapped. But before he could answer, a furious sound burst above our heads. A pigeon, bewildered by the lights, careered from side to side before fleeing towards the darkness and making its escape into the night.

'They're buying presents for us, Richard. It's a festival thing, remember, even if we're celebrating a little early.'

'Presents? I didn't know.' I glanced up at the roof. 'Should I have got something?'

Francis shrugged. 'Don't worry.'

'You should have told me. On the noticeboard.' I checked my wallet. Apart from three ten-pound notes, all I had was a two-pound coin tucked into a tight pocket alongside the notes. I'd have to use my card. Forty or fifty quid at least. I squeezed my fists and looked away. 'Someone should have said.'

'It's not a problem.'

'Look, I can pay for the food and drink instead.'

'No. I've already arranged things. Even your beers.'

I slipped the wallet back into my pocket.

Francis picked up my essay. 'What I was trying to say, Richard, is that we can make choices that are the wrong ones if we don't have a solid basis on which to assess them. We all struggle with this. Fleeing our own difficulties. Too ready sometimes to take the easy option and rely on old habits. To fall for the blandishments of others. When the best choice, Richard, the hard choice, is the one that might demand the greatest sacrifice.' Francis presented the essay to me. 'B. Or B-plus,' he chided, as if I were still at school.

So, man isn't the measure any longer, I fumed. Unless he gets it bloody well right. We lost eye contact as I smarted at his words. But at least that was it. A final say on the rigours of fifteenth-century perspective. But I wanted one last word before we'd finished playing student and teacher for the evening. I moved closer.

'Francis, I appreciate you want to help me. But there are some things that I just might have to figure out for myself.' I squared the pages, as if asserting my rights. 'Even when I make choices. And write essays, Francis.'

'Very well. There are still two more pieces of work to tackle, Richard.'

'More?' My voice rose.

'Yes. You now need to turn to the sixteenth century, but concentrate on Michelangelo rather than, say, Dürer or Da Vinci. And after that, I'd suggest something on Caravaggio.'

'Caravaggio.' I leant forward, my mood sharpening. 'I suppose you're talking about light and dark now?'

'Chiaroscuro, Richard.'

'Yes, I know the term, Francis. But the problem is, I still have other coursework to do. For English. That's my real degree. And it's suffering after missing two tutorials. Anyway, Jane has already suggested two other titles. So, talk to her first.' My chair screeched as I pushed away from the table.

'Richard, you are not doing this as a favour for us.' Francis's voice hardened. He was looking straight at me. 'If you appreciate our advice, then remember, we are trying to get *you* off the hook. *You* need an alibi. With Enrolment.'

'*I* need an alibi? Then maybe the mistake I've made was joining this bloody course in the first place. I'm getting pissed off with the whole thing.'

'There's no alternative. Two essays. Two thousand words each and we'll call it quits.'

I was ready to rip up the essay in front of us. I reached forward and grabbed Francis's hand, holding it fast to the table. 'Not so long ago, I was in a café, overlooking the church. I met two people, Francis. And I spoke to both of them, remember?' Francis eased back, his colour changing. 'And now … now one of them is dead, and the other has disappeared.' I stared hard at him. 'And you fucking well knew both of them. So instead of pratting on about essays, just tell me the truth. I want to know what's going on.' I released his hand, pushing it away. But my attention didn't falter. I wanted him to speak. And speak now.

Francis looked at his wine, unnerved by my rebuke. He lifted his head. 'Okay, Richard. The truth.'

We could both breathe at last, it seemed.

Francis removed his jacket and scarf and placed them against the glass panel running alongside the table. A gulp of wine helped his confidence, but the colour in his face was still drained. He glanced towards the guys sitting at the adjacent table, realising that our exchange had been overheard. He drank again.

'I need to explain something to you, Richard. Something of a dilemma, I fear.'

'I'm listening.' I folded my arms. 'But keep it simple, please. And to the point.'

'Okay. What if you know something that can help others?' Francis spoke in a more plaintive tone.

'You can share it,' I replied.

'What … if what you say puts that person in grave danger?'

'Then you'd better not tell them. Or anyone.' I wasn't in a mood to play games.

'But you, Richard … you have just asked *me* to tell *you*.'

My eyes shut for a moment. I was getting fed up with Francis's riddles. 'Okay, then. You'd better keep going.'

Francis edged closer, looking anxious as he spoke. 'The people you met, Richard … they were targeted because of what they knew.

These weren't random attacks.'

'Okay. Then tell me who attacked them.' I wasn't backing down.

'The security services.'

I frowned. Looking away.

'And others. Those who insist they know best, Richard. Until we change things.'

Great. So, the world is screwed up, I concluded. And a bunch of guys I know are going to solve it. 'You're still holding back, Francis.'

'So, let me finish.'

A brief disturbance deflected our attention. A young lad had stumbled close to the partition next to us in what appeared to be a scuffle between two strangers. Francis paused as a security guard intervened and brought it under control, barring a few angry shouts and the usual profanities. He turned back to me.

'Our world is locked on a path that cannot change. A worldwide disaster looms. And it doesn't have to be like this, Richard.'

'No, it doesn't, Francis. And if you want, you can start up your own political movement. Build a website or something. The uni's full of campaign groups. And hard-done-by causes.'

I swung around, not caring who heard. But Francis didn't budge. He continued. 'What we intend …' he paused, deliberating on his words, 'is much more fundamental than mere political movements. In fact, it is cosmic, Richard.'

'Cosmic? Francis, I'm sorry, but this sounds … like New Age stuff. The security services have got better things to do than shoot café owners and visitors to the British Museum.' I grabbed my pint. 'You're bullshitting me.'

Francis retreated. 'Okay. But I need you to listen a little longer.'

I yawned and put my beer aside. At this rate, it would take the rest of the bloody night, I feared.

'The reason things won't stay the same, is that *we* know how to change them.'

'We?' I thought of the others. And if they'd ever get here.

'But I need to sketch something for you.'

'Well, I suppose I asked for this. Whatever gets us to the truth. And then that's it. Okay?'

He nodded. Francis moved the drinks to the side of the table. He took the last, almost blank page of my essay, and taking a pen from his jacket, drew a fluffy cloud in the midst of it. Around this, he drew lines connecting boxes and circles before adding mathematical signs and formulae. I tried to make sense of it. 'By the way, has anyone ever done your horoscope?'

'No. Nor do I read tarot cards or go to seances,' I added. 'Anyway, is it relevant?'

'Don't worry. I'll explain later.' He leant forward, as if shielding the page from prying eyes. 'What we've learnt, and what we've discovered in London and in Greece, is breathtaking and revolutionary.' His eyes shifted left and right. 'And we have a wide network of friends ready to help us at the appointed time.'

I glanced back at the drawing. There were two stick figures enclosed within the cloud. And there was an arrow showing direction along a dotted path. And even if I wasn't connecting, Francis had drawn without hesitation. He placed the pen by his glass. The colour had returned to his cheeks, I noticed.

'We can make things better, Richard. And because we understand our world's space-time configuration, we can alter both its past and its future.'

My eyes flitted between his drawing and whatever I could glean from his face. 'So far, I know that two people have been attacked, one of whom you are sure is dead.' Francis nodded. 'And, okay, you're telling me who you think did it and why they did it.' He nodded again. 'And now you're telling me about a plan that's just … bizarre.' I leant back, covering my face with my hands as if to hide from the lunacy before me.

'Richard, even if you don't yet understand, you must take this seriously. This is for real.'

'Oh, come on, Francis, what are you getting at now?'

'I am saying that until we secure our changes, this world is fated to end.' Francis looked around again. 'But we can reset its course,' he whispered. 'With different outcomes for everyone.'

'Francis, even if I were to swallow this, the lessons of the past shriek, "No way!" at me.'

'No way? Why?'

'Because everyone who has ever wanted to change things radically has screwed up. Jacobins. Bolsheviks. Anarchists. You can't just idealise the world and expect it to fall into place.' I shook my head, wondering how I might escape this madness. 'Even the Family of Love and the Brotherhood of Man, for heaven's sake. History's full of horror stories and delusions.'

'And why?'

'Well, because of human nature. We're not perfect. And we never will be.' The adjacent table went quiet. I shrugged as if it was nothing while Francis managed a tepid smile. The waiters were too busy to care.

'You are right,' he whispered, edging closer. 'So, human nature must be reformed, Richard. Rather than society. That'll follow. Like Plato's 'Republic'. The perfect man. And the ideal city.' Francis glanced over his shoulder. 'But we need your help.'

'Francis. Please.' I tried to smile but ended up shaking my head. We both eased back. We weren't getting anywhere. Not with this. He seemed driven by a mission, and I just wasn't in the mood. We needed to snap out of it. Alex, Jane. Where are you? I reached once more for Francis's hand, but he pulled away unsure of my gesture. My arm recoiled and swept over his glass, knocking the wine all over the table.

'I'm sorry, Richard. I thought you were going to get angry again.'

'No, *I'm* sorry, because I want to be friends. I'm not angry,

Francis, just confused.' I righted the glass, as I watched the wine seep into my essay.

'You can't present it to Arbetta like that.'

I demurred at the thought. 'No. I'll send an electronic copy. Red wine is indelible.'

Francis checked the time. We'd been talking for over an hour and hadn't agreed on anything. We needed to wipe the table, so I suggested more drinks and something to clean up the mess. He nodded and slipped away, giving us both a break. I finished my pint. Around me people were having fun, and I wanted to share their laughs instead of a plot eked out in whispers. It can't be a dream. Not when someone is shot and collapses at your feet. I folded the essay and placed it inside my jacket, feeling dried out and no wiser by our exchange. I reached for the nut mix, cupped the dregs in my hand and threw it back in my mouth.

'Jane said she'd be here before eight.' Francis returned holding another chair and a roll of absorbent tissue. 'Alex will turn up whenever he wants. But we're now okay for seats.'

I wiped the surface dry of the residue of wine and dropped the paper to the floor. Nobody was watching, even though there were now more people in the café. And more pints going back and forth. And not much hope for a flapping, deluded pigeon, I fancied.

'We should start eating around nine,' said Francis, satisfied with the arrangement of chairs.

I checked my phone. 'Another hour. If the others can find us.'

'Don't worry, once the food is ready, this lot will settle down.'

A cheer from outside the arcade distracted our attention. Francis shrugged. 'It is either the band … or the Christmas tree's alight.'

'Sorry?' I asked, thinking of flames rather than illuminations. But a screech from a PA system resolved the matter. 'Francis … you drew two human figures in your drawing.'

'Yes, in the cloud. In no-man's-land.'

'No-man's-land?'

'Yes. It's to do with space-time.' Francis looked around.

'The essay. It's in my jacket. In case I forget.'

He glanced at the chair alongside me. 'Probably best.'

But I was still feeling uneasy. Something was gnawing away at me. I rested on my elbows and placed my hands together. 'You said you wanted my help.'

'Yes. To help Alex.'

'Alex?'

'We want you to work together. To make the changes. Hence the figures in the drawing.'

'And Alex is on board with this?'

Francis nodded. 'And Jane. We've been working for three years, now. The conferences. Delos. The museum. Some old monastic texts.'

I stared at Francis. My heart beat faster. I covered my face with my hands and slid my fingers through my hair. There was a thin sweat on my brow that like a dew sensed the nascent dawn. And a long, silent scream in my head. A whole chain of events weighed on me. The exhibition. The 'Triumphal Arch'. Art History B. They've known from the start, I realised. From my very first day at UCL. I lifted my eyes. 'The interview with Hatherleigh was just a set-up, wasn't it?'

'Yes.' He lowered his eyes.

'But why?'

'Why? Because we need you. And you asked for the truth, remember.'

I wanted to cry. I felt as if I'd been cheated. 'Look, whatever this is about, I didn't start it. I thought you were being friendly. And now I'm not sure what to do.' I pushed back, wondering whether I should stay. I was confused, hurt, and feeling scared.

Francis checked his wristwatch. 'I think Jane will be here soon. And Alex shouldn't be too long.' I looked down at the table. 'You know how he always makes us laugh, Richard.'

'Yeah, laughs.' I was still shunning any eye contact.

A waiter brought us the drinks that Francis had ordered. I watched as he placed them down before removing the empty glasses. Still upset, I shifted closer. 'We're just going to have to talk about this, Francis. Whatever you're asking me to do. All of you.'

We reached for our drinks.

'Hatherleigh has been involved for most of his life, Richard. And when he first confronted us, we were as puzzled as you. And we too wondered why.'

'So why are you going along with it?'

'As individuals, we each have our reasons. But once together, things kind of fell into place. Things in our own past. And terrible things that have happened since.' He looked away. 'Incidents. Sadness.' Francis edged back. He stared wistfully at the deep tone of his wine before the glass touched his lips. I waited until he'd drunk.

'Do you remember our first tutorial?' I asked. He nodded, still in thought. 'Well, at the end, after you'd left together, Hatherleigh pointed to his Raphael print.'

'"The School of Athens", Richard.'

'Yes, "The School of Athens". And he mentioned the vanishing point. The *point de fuite.* That was the hint, wasn't it?'

Francis smiled. He gestured towards my beer. But I was disinclined to drink. 'Do you remember the two central figures in the painting?' he asked.

I nodded. 'Plato and Aristotle.'

'Did you notice Plato was holding a scroll?'

'If you say so.'

'Well, he was. And the scroll was a copy of "Timaeus", Richard. His dialogue on the creation of the gods, the universe, and humankind.'

'Yeah. And all that stuff on Atlantis.'

'Yes. That stuff. The worldwide destruction.' Francis leant forward. 'Richard, when we study perspective, we draw lines towards a centric point. As if everything disappears into a ravenous black hole.'

I grinned. My essay had said *that*, for sure.

'But imagine, for a moment, the process in reverse. That from an infinitesimal point, a new world explodes. On to its own canvas. Full of colour. As if alive, Richard.' His face brightened. 'This is what we shall do once we renew this world and steer it in a new direction.'

'You are acting like God, Francis. And yet you say you need my help?'

'Because of what you know.'

'What I know?'

'Yes. None of us can do anything until we learn one thing for sure. The time and the place where this world began. Its astral-mathematical inception. That is the fundamental secret of the cosmos, and we must have it if we want to alter its future path or fiddle with its existing past.' He leant closer. 'The old man at the museum, Richard. He whispered something to you. On the steps, remember?'

'Yes. A few words. Before I pushed him away.'

'Lines from a poem, Richard.'

'Maybe.'

Francis reached across the table. He placed his hands on my forearms. I could feel the raw beat of his pulse as his grip tightened. 'These words, Richard, are our clue. The clue that will tell us the day, the month, and the year our modern world began. And from which we will deduce the coordinates of its initial location.'

He released my arms, but his eyes remained fixed.

I eased back, parrying his stare. 'Some lines of poetry, then.'

'Whatever he said. Before he passed out.'

'Okay.' I raised my hands and placed them behind my head. Something that Francis had said to me earlier slipped back into my mind. 'It would seem then, my friend, that the madness of poets is not so empty-headed, after all.'

28

A sudden roar filled the air.

Francis and I stood up. Another roar followed. We looked towards the far end of the arcade. Someone had been lifted into the air. 'What's happening?' I asked.

'Saturnalia, Richard. And the Lord of Misrule,' explained Jane, appearing suddenly alongside me.

She planted a quick kiss on my cheek before sitting at the table. She'd been buying presents and, judging by the name-dropping bag she was holding, had gone to some expense.

'Was Alex with you?'

'I left him in the Strand, Richard. He's on his way.' She turned to Francis as I sat. 'Be a darling and get me a drink. I'm worn out with all this shopping.'

Jane wore a slim tailored jacket and a white blouse. A delicate scent countered the smell of beer around us as I watched her slip a silk scarf from around her neck. A small brooch caught the light as it glinted on her lapel. It was the first time she'd ever kissed me, I realised.

Another loud roar diverted our attention. 'It's like this every year,' she said. 'Last time, Alex tried to get elected. He was so funny. But we voted him down.' She opened a leather purse and gave Francis two twenty-pound notes for the bar.

'Maybe he would have been good.'

'Too good, Richard. Anyway, it was only attention-seeking.'

Jane removed the presents from the bag. Each item was labelled, and their ribbons twirled and trimmed. She knew what to do, I thought, as she returned all but one of them to the bag.

'You've been very generous,' I said.

'Family. And friends.'

'I've done nothing yet. There's Mum and Dad. And my younger sister.' I glanced at the present she'd left unpacked. 'She turned fourteen a few weeks ago.' I added. 'And is already telling me what to do.'

'A young lady, then. She'll want something grown-up, you know.'

'I know. And I'll try to think of something.'

Jane retrieved the item on the table. She placed it inside her handbag. I glanced towards the bar. My earlier exchange with Francis still weighed on my mind. I turned back to Jane, wanting to talk, but another roar distracted me. I waited for the commotion to subside. 'By the way, I could treat everyone. Say tonight.'

'Oh goodness, no, Richard.'

'Then I'll look out for something. At least a gesture.'

Jane stayed silent, greeting my offers with a smile.

Francis returned. In one hand, he held a fresh glass and a loosely corked bottle of red, and in the other, a pack of beer cans strung together by a flimsy, plastic band. He placed the drinks down. Thirty pounds, he said, before producing a ten-pound note from his pocket and handing it to Jane. There were more shouts from the square as the music and tempo ramped up a gear. I removed a can, snapped off the ring, and poured the contents into my glass. I was still unsure what to say or how I should say it.

'More antics.' Francis nodded towards the piazza before sitting down next to Jane. He flashed a tepid smile.

'Did you talk to Richard about the Saturnalia, Francis?' asked Jane, sounding politely curious.

'No.' He paused before lowering his voice. 'We spoke about our plans, Jane.'

Jane's attention switched to me. 'Alex will need your help, Richard. We can't do this alone.'

'So, I gather. Origins. And destinies.' I broke eye contact and reached for my beer.

Francis poured the wine without speaking.

An angry shout turned our heads. And then a thud against the café's glass partition caused us all to start. A guy, about twenty, shifted back and forth as security tried to detain him. He looked destitute and protested loudly as they led him away. His predicament sharpened my resolve.

'"The School of Athens", Jane. It was a clue, wasn't it? When Hatherleigh showed it to me. After you'd all … disappeared.'

Jane nodded. 'Julian is a friend, Richard. A family friend.'

'Oh, for god's sake.' I looked away, squeezing the beer can with my hand. I could still hear the young guy arguing with his minders.

'My father … worked in intelligence, Richard. At the embassy in Berlin.' She paused as my attention shifted back. 'Julian was researching a book. There was a cultural agreement. Protocols. Exchanges. Something involving museums and academics in East Germany. Just as the Cold War was fizzling out.'

I closed my eyes. It's a labyrinth, and I'm in the middle of it. 'And what about the monasteries and those texts you discovered?'

'Monasteries?'

'Francis said. Before you were here.'

Jane glanced at Francis. 'Yes. But that was later. When we met in Greece.'

I was getting deeper, but no nearer. 'And Delos, Jane. When I joined you for the first tutorial, you were discussing it. And you'd linked me to whatever it was you'd been talking about. You were even laughing.'

I looked back at Francis. But the vagrant had returned, stumbling alongside the café's divide. We paused as he righted himself before watching him slip away.

Jane reached for my hand. 'Delos, Richard. And its ancient shrines. There are so many temples there. Temples to Greek gods. Egyptian gods. Phoenician gods. Heroes, too.' Her touch was warm and gentle. And her eyes sparkled like her brooch.

'Even an ancient synagogue,' added Francis.

'We'd been to the House of the Dolphins, Richard. It has a wonderful mosaic, you know. A central rosette surrounded by floral patterns and griffin heads.' Jane smiled, still holding my hand. 'And the gods Hermes and Dionysus. And Poseidon, lord of the sea,' she said, drawing my eye, entwining her fingers with mine and tingling my skin. 'And the winged youths, Richard, the playful Erotes, clinging to the backs of the dolphins. Agile. Sleek. Cavorting in the waves.' She smiled again. 'Erotic, even.' She withdrew her hand. A soft blush slipped across her face.

I closed my eyes, letting the tension fade.

'We climbed the rocky path of Mount Cynthus. Overlooking the ancient harbour. It isn't high,' Francis explained. 'More a gentle peak with a rugged, sloping plateau.'

'But the views are wonderful, Richard. The islands. The Aegean spread out like a dark, polished gem. And even at night,' Jane added, 'the sea, still alive, still radiating the day's savage heat.' She smiled fondly at Francis. 'And above our heads, the stars drifting by. The great Orion. Perseus. The mythical Argo. Steadfast and serene. Pensive. In a vast ocean of sky.'

I edged back. 'Sounds Homeric, Jane.'

'But it was more than myth. We felt at one with the world. Its fabric. Its delicate harmony. And yet the myths were also a clue. To a violent start. An explosive beginning.'

Another roar made us pause. An earlier drama came back to me and players declaiming their lines. And Chaos. Night. Earth and Darkness. I held on to my glass, unsure if I should drink.

Francis leant closer. 'But it wasn't all cataclysm, Richard. It was also about impregnation. The seed. The celestial egg. The sky and earth conjoined.'

'Impregnation?' I swilled my beer. A light danced along the side of the glass.

'The myths of creativity are proto-sexual, Richard. To create and destroy is to show compassion,' said Jane.

'But I thought the pre-Socratics talked of hot and cold, Jane. I thought they'd ditched the gods. And all their myths.' I watched the beer settle.

'They did, Richard. And they enjoyed a dig at Homer's gods. But the source of creation still preoccupied them. And the outbreak of time. And the division of number.'

Jane's fingers strayed over mine. I studied her face. 'We've trodden a lonely path, Richard, with little time to fulfil our dreams.' She smiled, letting my eyes linger. 'This will be a redemptive act, Richard. Our world will be renewed. Like the tale of Demeter and her daughter.'

I stayed still, enchanted by her charm, until our hands parted.

'Once the realignments are complete,' explained Francis, 'the present order will be overthrown. The Age of Iron will fall.'

I had no time to react to his words when a face, pressing against the glass divide, startled us. The young man had crept back. He rose and slid his tongue across the pane, smearing the glass with a glutinous trail.

Francis and Jane recoiled in horror.

And as the adjacent tables erupted in laughter, I found a reason to slip away. I pointed towards the shopping bags as Jane fumbled with her hair and Francis stared sulkily at his wine. 'Look, I need to get you guys something. Some presents. It's only fair.'

'But Alex will be here soon, Richard,' said Jane, still fidgeting.

'Don't worry. I'll think of him as well.' I reached for my jacket. And as I rose to leave, conscious that a spell had been broken, I remembered something else. I stood back from the table and looked at Francis. 'Just one more thing. Hatherleigh's print,' I queried.

'"The School of Athens?"'

'Yes. Wasn't Aristotle also carrying something in his hands? Alongside Plato and his scroll.'

Francis glanced at Jane. 'He was. Another scroll. A copy of his 'Ethics', Richard.'

'That's right. His treatise on morals. And what's right and wrong, I believe.'

Francis stared back at me. I turned and set off for the shops. The night air had just got a little cooler.

* * *

The Magi, I reflected, must have had an easy time of it. Whereas my guiding star, lost in a blaze of glitzy street lighting in London's West End, didn't seem much of a steer at all. Jane would disdain anything tasteless whatever her oneness with the world. I'd disappoint Francis if I chose a tacky fashion of the day. Yet what would intrigue him might annoy Alex. Giving was full of risk, I lamented. So Francis was right. I needed a yardstick. Something to help me choose beyond the whims of bullying, guilt-driven emotions, and a panic over how much I could spend.

A busy Strand beckoned, and turning west, I passed several narrow alleys, boasting grand historical names. They all looked dark and unalluring, but hinted at the great houses that once lined its route. Like Durham. York. The Savoy. Homes to proud, angry lives annulled in vengeance and blood. The Earl of Essex. Walter Raleigh. The Lady Jane Grey. I crossed the road and paused beside a dimly lit passage that once led down to the Thames. History is like that, I reflected. A journey to the block. A short, disjointed melancholy.

Bedford Street drew me back towards Covent Garden. It is the gesture that counts, I resolved. Goodwill to all. And don't mind the fee. I paused again. The Three Kings had given me an idea. My pace quickened as I headed to a small bookshop close by. I scanned the shelves. Alchemy. Arcana. And astrology. Kind of promising, I thought. I reached for a hardback book devoted to the sun sign Pisces and the springtime equinox. Francis would understand, I reckoned. New beginnings. And new epochs. Just like our biblical friends, of course—the Magi of old.

The shop owner popped it into a bag. That left Jane and Alex. Incense and myrrh, I mused. For Jane, I bought a scented candle with a round metal base. But before committing, a strange pack of cards caught my eye. I asked the owner. 'The mystical tarot,' he explained. And this card, I asked, holding the last one in the pack. 'The Hanged Man,' he said.

I let go of the card. 'The candle's just fine. But I need something else.' He led me to the back of the shop.

'Myrrh was a sticky gum or resin,' he explained. 'Once used for the embalming of dead bodies in Egypt.' So maybe not, I thought. I continued looking. I wanted something whacky or satirical, I said. He stayed silent, but opening a drawer at the bottom of a desk, he retrieved a paperback that looked long out of print with its cover only just attached to its spine. 'An old cult classic,' he said. I read the title and agreed. But he called me back as I left the shop. He held out his hand. 'You dropped this, young man.' I smiled. The two-pound coin had fallen from my wallet. I caught it as he flipped it towards the bag. It was the nearest thing to gold I had on me.

* * *

I was close to the piazza when a hand pulled me to a halt. 'Jenny!' I blurted, taken by surprise.

'So, where have *you* been hiding, Mr Richard?'

'Hiding?' Jenny moved closer before wobbling on her heel. She held on to me for support.

'Yeah, hiding. You've been missing lectures, naughty boy.' Her other hand probed the bag that I was carrying.

'Gifts,' I said.

'Are they for me?' she asked.

'No. A few friends.'

She bent down and adjusted her shoe. I tried to steady her.

'Thank you.' She stood upright. 'I want you to meet *my* friends now.'

Jenny led me back to the lower-ground café enclosure that was once the basement of the south arcade. I steadied her on the stairs as we avoided a potted plant that had spilt mud on the steps. We joined a group of other students seated around two tables that were pushed together. They looked as if they'd run out of things to say as they scrolled through their phones. I said hello, but there wasn't much response. I didn't know any of them.

'He's still around, girls. I found him outside the shops. He's bought us lots of presents.' She sat between two of the guys.

'They're for friends. You know, the festival. The Saturnalia.'

'Oh, the Saturnalia.' Jenny turned and winked at her companions. 'We've seen videos on that, haven't we, boys?'

There was no reply. Someone yawned.

'It was actually a pagan celebration,' I explained. 'To do with the light around the mid-winter sun …' My words faltered. No one was listening.

'So, let's give Richard a drink. He's too serious. He needs to get … to get …' Jenny coughed several times. I thought of giving up, but she seemed to revive. 'I'm okay, I'm okay, everyone,' she said, before waving her hand.

One of the guys retrieved an old lemonade bottle from under his chair. I unscrewed the top and sniffed at the contents. 'Pretty strong,' I said, before tasting the mouth of the bottle.

'It's not poison, if that's what you think.' Jenny put her arms around the guy on her left, pulling him towards her chest.

'What's it made of?'

'Whisky. And vodka. And rum. The boys made it in a lab.'

I handed the bottle back ready to leave, but Jenny persisted. 'So, what mark did you get? In your last essay.' She pointed at a friend. 'Siss got a 2.1.' There was a desultory cheer.

'I got a 2.2.'

'Not so clever, then.'

'I was not very well.'

'Ah …' Jenny looked around the table, but the chorus failed. The guys wanted me to leave. 'So where are your arty friends?'

'Who.'

'Those third-years you mix with?'

'Francis and Alex?'

'Oh, Francis.' Jenny made a face. I was feeling awkward.

'We're going to eat. In the other arcade.'

'So why do you always hang around with blokes, Richard?' She laughed. But the guys were uninterested.

'There is another friend.'

'Fiona?'

'No. She's called Jane. Fiona's gone home for Christmas.'

'Is she your girlfriend?'

'No. Just a friend.'

'So why don't you have a girlfriend?'

I smiled. 'She's at Oxford.'

'I bet she's really …' Jenny coughed again. She freed herself from her partner's embrace and stared ahead. Another hand removed her drink.

'Look guys, I have to get back.'

'No wait, Richard,' snapped Jenny.

I turned, but really wanted to say goodbye.

'We want you to join our game.'

'He has to go, Jenny. Let him go,' said a voice.

Jenny looked sharply at the guy. 'He doesn't. He wants to join in. Give him the fucking bag.'

The guy passed a cloth bag to me. It was sticky and damp from beer and other drinks that had spilt on the table. 'You have to write your name out and put it into the bag,' he said, handing me a pen and a piece of paper. 'If you're that interested.'

'It's a dare, Richard. Siss … she suggested it.' I looked at the girl called Siss. She was enmeshed in another guy's arms.

'And then what?' I asked.

'We choose a name.' Jenny eyed her friends, making another face. 'And the loser,' she added, her head swaying, 'the loser has to run. Around the square. Starkers.' She tried to reach for her drink.

I opened the bag. There were several names there already.

'So, who's making the draw?' I asked.

'Steff. He's over there, getting more drinks.'

I wrote on a scrap of paper and placed it into the dirty bag. I didn't care. 'Sounds a laugh,' I said, trying to make fun of the outcome.

'Yeah. We've all done it,' said Siss.

The guys smiled. Someone snapped a photo. Before and after, I reckoned. I handed the bag to the guys. And with my presents, headed for the stairs. As I reached the potted plant, I looked back and wondered for a few moments about Jenny, but then continued on my way.

29

I could hear Alex's voice as I returned to the north arcade. He was singing. And we all knew the tune. Then Francis rose, pitching low. And Jane too, with a soaring note that bounced above our heads. 'What do I do?' I pleaded, as eyes from around the tables fixed on me.

'Sing, Richard, sing.'

I gulped and bawled out the words of an old football chant. The Anacreon drinking song spun with an irreverent verse. I sat to a chorus of cheers, placing the presents by my feet. The next table took up the challenge.

'So, what's happening?' I asked.

'The rugby guys started it,' said Jane. 'And then the DJ supplied the tunes. Including that well-known anthem.'

'And if you falter,' said Alex, reaching for his drink, 'you pay a penalty. In beer.' He wagged a mocking finger at Francis's red wine.

I looked around. More laughs. More cheers. Only this time for someone who'd lost his way. And as the music stalled, I gave Alex a friendly nudge as I sat beside him. 'Glad you made it.'

Alex handed me a can of beer. 'Did they tell you what happened last year, Richard?'

'Yeah. Weren't you supposed to be Lord of Misrule, or something?'

'Don't wind him up,' said Francis, rolling his eyes.

'I led a riot.'

'Alex, you didn't lead a riot.'

'I did. Because you voted me down. So, I started a coup.' Alex stuck his tongue out.

'And it wasn't a coup. It was a lot of posturing around. Even Hatherleigh was annoyed with you.' Francis sipped his wine, sharing a quick glance with Jane.

'Are the tutors here, Alex?' I asked.

'Dunno. Some join in. They like to dress up in disguise. Makes them feel young again.'

I stood up and scanned the tables. 'You're making that up, mate.' He shrugged but was still pulling faces. I sat down and grabbed my beer.

Alex stretched and yawned. 'You know, I've got an essay to write ... for the old goat.'

'Well, if you don't send it to him on Monday, it won't get a grade,' said Francis, grinning gratuitously from the other side of the table.

'Really? So, we're sticking to deadlines now, are we, Francis?'

'Could help, Alex,' countered Jane. 'He's off to New York for Christmas.'

Alex lowered his arms. 'Anyway, I didn't say I would finish it.' He sat upright. Francis wasn't playing.

Jane too shook her head. 'What about you, Richard?' she asked, turning to me.

'Oh, I've got something on early drama. It's a new module for next term.'

'No, I meant Christmas. Are you staying home or going away?'

'Oh, just home. Might see my old sixth-form friends. If they are around, that is.' The singing picked up again. 'But ... why don't we meet up? Say at New Year.'

Alex glanced at Jane before turning to me. 'She's off to Switzerland,' he explained.

'Family, Richard. We try to catch up on the slopes. My mother remarried a few years ago.'

'Oh.' I forced a smile.

'But you're not doing anything, Alex, are you?' said Francis, letting go of his glass.

'No, I'm up for it.' Alex finished his beer. 'There are some good country pubs nearby. And you can stay over at my place if you want to.'

I smiled. 'Don't mind. But I'll need your address.' I ran my fingers through my hair and back behind my ears. It was almost as long as Alex's now, but not as straight.

Plates of food slowed the tempo of the arcade, and for a few minutes the waiters were back in charge. We made our choices without too much deliberation. Alex opened another beer and Jane wiped the plates with a tissue. So if Saturnalia was about turning the world upside down amidst fanciful games of role-reversal, it didn't look very different to the one I was enjoying. We were still eating, drinking, and chatting. So maybe changing things is never real. Like nothing changes under the sun, as they say. Just faces and chairs. I nudged Alex. 'Not much happening,' I said, taking a bite of food.

'Don't kid yourself, Richard.' Alex dug into his plate. 'The Lord of Misrule prances up and down later. There'll be uproar. In the old days, they used to chop him up and eat him.'

Francis stopped eating. 'Who told you that?'

'A little bird.' Alex swallowed.

I cast back. Any bird that ventured by now would struggle to stay clear of the kitchens. Or Alex's fork.

'Don't humour him, Richard. He's garbling the myth,' said Jane, enjoying more modest portions of food.

'I'm not,' insisted Alex. 'Saturn ate his own kids. And the Titans ate Dionysus. That's what the myths say,' he added, munching between words as if dismembering the syllables. 'We're all cursed, guys.'

'Oh, Alex, Saturnalia is a celebration of rebirth, not human sacrifice,' pleaded Jane.

Alex wiped his mouth with the back of his hand. 'I was talking, like, figuratively.' He took another bite. 'Anyway, it's what I have to write about.' He leant towards Francis, still holding a knife. 'And one of those creepy Black Paintings by Goya.'

'Alex, let's talk about something else, please,' said Francis.

'If you say so. But time devours us all.'

Alex carried on eating, aloof to the glares. And it seemed the right moment to change the mood, if not quite the world. I stood up. 'Rebirth, everybody,' I declared, holding my bag of presents in the air to a modest cheer.

'Oh, Richard,' said Jane, her voice softening. 'How very considerate of you.'

'I got them earlier. When I slipped away. But I wasn't sure if I should do Christmas or the mid-winter festival,' I said. 'But then I settled for the Three Kings—well, astrologers at least.' Everyone laughed as we forgot about Saturn, and a morbid appetite for his own offspring.

Alex put his fork aside and shifted the plates. 'So, who's got the shiny gold?' he asked.

'No one. Twenty pounds was all I spent.'

'Alex, behave. Remember, it's the gesture.'

'In that case, Jane, you can be first.' I handed her my gift.

She removed the wrapping. 'How nice. An incense candle.'

'Look at the base. There are lots of symbols. Like a strange language.' She passed it to Francis after he reached for his glasses. 'It could be an incantation,' I suggested, 'but I was really thinking about darkness and light.'

Francis smiled before returning the candle to Jane. An art essay flashed through my mind before I reached for his gift. 'What do you know about the so-called Great Year, Francis?'

'It's when Hatherleigh gets my essays on time,' said Alex, lowering his arms and head to the table. A whine added a touch of drama to the antics.

Francis ignored the tease 'You mean the Earth's precession through the zodiac, Richard?' said Francis, as Alex continued to moan.

'Yep. I did say the theme was astrological.' I handed him the book I'd bought.

'Interesting.' He turned the pages. 'Well, the Greek mathematician Hipparchus gets the credit for its discovery. Late second century BCE, I think.' He looked up. 'The cycle is around twenty-six thousand years, Richard, and is divided into twelve ages to align with the zodiac.' He found a drawing that detailed the movements of the Earth through the various star signs.

'So, which age are we in now?' I asked, before Alex lifted his head, opening and closing his mouth in a slow-motion gesture.

Jane looked away.

'The Age of Pisces,' said Francis, presenting a dustcover swarming with fish.

'You know the fish symbol,' said Jane, 'was always important to the early Christians. Hatherleigh used to say that Pisces was the house of secrets and other kinds of reality.'

'And the demise of one age and the start of another,' added Francis. 'Like the Stoics, with their cycles of rebirth and destruction.' Francis raised his glass to his lips and cast a long glance at Alex, now looking quite saintly, and uncharacteristically still.

'Hold on, guys,' I said, raising my hand, 'there's still one more present to go.' Alex turned his head. 'Something to look at over Christmas, mate. Or a beer.' I handed him his gift, and with a nod to the table, I sat down. Gesture made, I thought. And just the right balance for the evening.

Alex unwrapped his present. 'Another book,' he exclaimed.

'Well, it's not any old book, Alex. Just open it,' I said.

He flipped through some pages. 'Hey, the "Apple of Discord". And shaggy old Eris.' His face brightened.

'Show me,' said Francis, reaching forward and trying to wrestle it from Alex's hands.

'It's a second edition. I know it's a bit of a piss-take, but it's for Saturnalia,' I said, as my eyes settled on Jane. 'Eris was the daughter of Night, I think. In the myths.'

'And the mother of hardship and ruin, Richard,' said Jane, sourly. 'She messed up Thetis's marriage, remember, before the Trojan War.'

Jane wasn't smiling as Alex jumped from page to page to the sound of witless giggles. And as I shrank from Jane's glare, I thought of the two-pound coin still in the bag. I slipped my hand in to retrieve it as Alex kept the others entertained.

'You should read it, Francis. It's really, really … droll.'

'Thank you, Alex. But on second thoughts … it sounds rather tedious.'

Alex shrugged. He grabbed a chip from his plate and, like Saturn, swallowed it whole. I drank some beer, wondering if I should divert their attention.

Jane came to the rescue.

She unzipped her bag and handed me the small present she had placed there for safety. 'It's something we brought back from Delos, Richard. An alabaster figurine. Early Cycladic in date.'

The gesture re-orientated the mood. I felt the packaging. It had large breasts like a fertility symbol. Or proto-sexual, I mused, recalling an earlier conversation. I looked back at Jane, half-conscious of a youthful smirk.

'You don't have to open it now,' she said, glancing at the others.

'Okay then, I'll keep it for later.' I placed it alongside my plate.

'But there's one more item, Richard.' We turned to Francis as he removed a buff-coloured envelope from his jacket. Holding it between the fingers of both hands, he waited as Alex cleared our plates, stacking them at the side of the table. The envelope had my name on it. 'It's your horoscope, Richard. I drew it up a few days ago.'

'My horoscope?' I removed a sheet of paper. Unfolding it, I placed it in the space that Alex had cleared.

'Hatherleigh told us your date of birth.'

'I'm supposed to be a Libra, Francis.' I glanced down at the drawing.

'Yes. That's right. The Scales. But I didn't know where you were born. So, I used Covent Garden as the natal point in your chart. There used to be a large obelisk in the piazza before the old market hall was built.'

'Well, you're not far off. I was born in University College Hospital just to the north of here. In Gower Street. Must be why I ended up across the road at UCL, even though I grew up on the outskirts of London.'

Francis raised his hands. 'So, it was fate, Richard.'

'Or just genetic,' I joked, but Alex, I noticed, frowned.

Jane drew me closer, pointing to the segments that divided the birth chart. These, she explained, were the houses that fell under the sway of planets. And the sun. And the moon. She talked about oppositions and conjunctions. And the significance of angles. I tried to follow, but the details seemed strange and opaque. I asked her what it really meant.

'It means your character, Richard. Your resolve. And your future.'

I felt uneasy. I looked at their faces. Drawn and sad. And Jane's brooch, lifeless and pale as her words tripped around in my head. I swallowed. 'I'm not sure, guys, what you want me to do? Or whether I can.' My pulse rose as they leant closer.

Jane reached for my hand. 'Richard, we need you. We need you to play your part in our enterprise.' She looked into my eyes with a conviction that they all seemed to share. Her grip tightened. 'To help ...' But the word 'Alex' barely crossed her lips when, with a start, she pulled away. Dr Hatherleigh, in a mask covering his eyes like a Hollywood bandit, had thrust out of nowhere between us. He was shaking with fear.

'Francis, Jane,' said Hatherleigh, 'Ms Lopez has gone missing. Otto is alarmed. We've got to act. None of us are safe.'

Francis and Jane stood up. And as I followed, Hatherleigh crashed to the table, scattering the glasses and plates. I lunged sideways, dodging a blow aimed at my head before the panel shattered around the table.

I caught sight of a face amidst the tumult and screamed, 'Jonathan! You bastard, Jonathan.' I launched at him in a rage, striking blows that sent him to the ground as panic and shouts cleared a space around us, and then at a guy pinning Francis to the floor as Alex, fighting alongside me, freed Jane from an arm held around her neck. Jumping up, reeking of beer and an animal-like odour, I was ready to strike again. I was alive. And anger and outrage raced through my veins.

Bloodied and thwarted, our opponents fled.

We grabbed whatever we could. Jackets. Scarves. Bags. Things from the floor. There was no time to choose as we made our escape: Francis, Jane and Hatherleigh to the flat in Bloomsbury—Alex and I … the streets of London.

30

We ran … because we were free.

Darting like the wind. Skirting cars and dodging strangers. One moment in the Strand, the next Embankment—the dark, brooding river, always near. Alex led the way, setting the pace and our feet, a steady rhythm. We drew breath like kerosene. Fuelling our dash, our daring. Firing our resolve. We ran one mile, and then another. Past one bridge, before the next. Until at last, our legs wearied, our lungs raw, I cried out. 'Alex. Look at the City. Look at the Globe.'

We were alone on the Millennium Footbridge, midway between the granite banks of the Thames. To the north of us, the vast dome of St Paul's Cathedral. To the southeast, the angular Shard. And ahead … a squat, patchy white blur. The crucible of time. The wooden O.

'This Jonathan guy,' said Alex, crouching and snatching air, 'you've mentioned him … somewhere … before.'

I nodded, still panting, still looking around. 'He turns up at my class, Alex. He tries to … to tell us what to do.' I laughed, catching my breath. 'What of him? He's a joke.' I turned my head into the breeze, relishing the air against my face and its chill on my brow.

'But I recognised him. Two months ago. In Covent Garden.'

I staggered over. 'Two months ago … when you were hit?'

'Yeah,' he said, spitting. 'He broke things up. With some other guys wielding sticks.'

Alex ran his fingers through his hair, letting his head drop back. The old wound had gone. But there were new bruises. Around his eyes. And blood fresh on his shirt. We laughed. 'He grabbed Hatherleigh,' I said.

'I saw. And you punched him. In his face.'

'And I'd do it again, Alex,' I said, still angry. Still smelling of beer.

But Alex didn't respond. He settled down on to the metal walk-way, drawing a long, consoling breath, cooling the rawness of his cheeks. I slipped alongside—the night's adrenaline sapped-out in both of us.

'Alex, what do you think will happen? I mean to you and me.'

'There'll be loads of questions. Like when I got into trouble with Weekes.' He lowered his head.

'Questions? But we were attacked, Alex. We were defending our-selves.' I punched the air. But lamely.

'I know. But it doesn't always turn out like that, Richard. Not if Jonathan has connections.'

I drew my legs towards my chest. A lingering sweat caught the coldness of the wind. And the wind, the moistness of my breath. 'But there'll be cameras,' I said.

'Were there?'

'Maybe. But there *were* witnesses, Alex. Right next to us. Lots of them.'

'Yeah. Witnesses. If they're brave.'

'And Hatherleigh. He was there. And he's a tutor. Isn't he?'

'Julian Hatherleigh. Art History B.' He smiled glumly.

'And Renaissance art, Alex. And myths,' I said, unsure of his mood.

'Yes, Richard. He is a tutor. And we are his students.' He rubbed his eyes and looked up at the moon.

I rose to my feet and, leaning against the footbridge, cast a glance along the City side of the Thames towards a nightscape honeycombed with lights and shadows uneasy in their glare. And sounds that unsettled the night. My thoughts wandered. 'Alex …'

'What?'

'My present. I left it behind. The one from Delos that Jane gave me.'

'Oh,' he said, joining me at the rail. We closed up against the cold, looking downriver towards the Isle of Dogs. 'But she was grabbing things. So, maybe … at the end.'

'Yeah, maybe,' I replied, sensing loss.

'Or Francis. He was looking for things. His jacket. And glasses.' Alex checked the bloodstains on the cuff of his sleeve.

I swung around, careless of the breeze as the evening filtered through my mind. The fight. The fury. The painted faces. My drunken classmate. The vagrant. And things said to me in snatches and in passing. I locked my arms, trapping the heat within my jacket. 'You know … Jane told me about Hatherleigh. Earlier. That he's an old friend.' A gentle nod acknowledged my claim. 'And there was something else, Alex … something on embassies. Something her mother must have said to her.'

Alex raised his foot and placed it on the strip lighting that illuminated the walkway at night. 'Her parents divorced when she was fifteen, Richard. Hatherleigh had known the family for a long time. Then her mother remarried. After a year, Jane returned to London where she started sixth form.' He toyed with a section of the lighting with his foot. 'She would talk to me about it. When she was low.'

'When you were together?'

Alex nodded.

A gust of wind swept a carton along the bridge. I turned back to the river.

'Hatherleigh was researching books and making contacts. Prague. Budapest. Castles and libraries. Secrets. And that … that's when Kalinsky comes into the picture.'

'Kalinsky? The old man at the British Museum?'

'The old man, Richard.'

I gripped the rail and stared ahead. 'There's so much … so much you haven't told me. About you and your tutor. Leaving me to figure things out, Alex. To ask these questions. To hurt. Inside.' I edged away.

'I'm sorry. It's how the world works. It isn't a game any longer.'

'And now …' I shook my head. 'Now you want my help.'

'We *need* your help, Richard.' His voice hardened as he stepped closer. 'We need you to play your part. Like Jane said, damn it.'

I turned. 'But why, Alex? Why?'

'Because … you are one of us. Understand? One of us.'

'One of us? Because of a fucking poem?'

'Yes.' Alex grabbed my arm. 'Listen, Richard … if you want to quit, mate, you can. Right?' He pushed me back.

'Quit? Like step aside?'

'No. For real,' he snapped. 'We could split up. Okay? Go home for Christmas. And *stay* there.' Alex thrust out his hand in a brazen farewell.

'And drop our classes?'

'Drop us, Richard. Me. Francis. Jane. We could all say goodbye. Adieu. You'll be safer. You're only screwing up.' He swung away, clenching his fists in an angry stare at the water.

'And pretend that the last two months have never happened, Alex?'

'I mean, forget everything. Forget Hatherleigh. Forget Kalinsky. Forget we ever met. In the pub. In your flat.' He stepped back and thrust his hands into tight denim pockets as if threatening to leave for good.

'You don't mean that, Alex. Not after what we've been through.' I reached out. But my hand wavered. Afraid. Unsure to touch.

'I mean …' He turned aside. 'I mean, you need to get out of your tent, mate. And *do* something.'

I stared at the river and the empty darkness that lay before me. A blank space trapped within the contours of the Thames. A no-man's-land, I thought. A drowned land. The abode of bodies surrendered to the sea. I tensed, biting my lip, hearing the cries of the wind. Troubled, I turned to my friend.

'I … I saw one of my classmates. Earlier. In the square.'

'So?'

I looked down. There was mud on my shoes. 'She was partying. With friends. Some second-years.'

Alex flicked a glance. 'Have I met her?'

'No.'

'So, what's her name?'

'Jenny.'

'No. Don't know her.' He stared ahead, still distant.

'She does English with me. Playwrights. And poets.'

He shrugged. 'Read her a poem, then.'

'Alex …' I edged closer. 'They were getting pissed. Like smashed. At least Jenny was.'

'So why are you talking about her?'

'Because … because she asked me to play a game. Where you do a dare.'

'And did you?'

'I suppose I did. Sort of.'

'Sort of?'

'I mean like one of those games, where if you lose, you do something stupid.' An eddy swirled beneath the bridge, moving with the flow of water as I watched.

'And did you?'

'No. Anyway, it was the last thing in the evening. If you lost, that is.'

Alex turned away from the river. 'And now we'll never know.'

'No. I suppose not. Except …'

'Except what?'

'I wrote *her* name down on a scrap of paper. And dropped it into their draw.' Jenny, I thought. Poor, drunken Jenny. I could still smell their concoction in my nose.

'Sounds like a stitch-up.'

'Yeah. But of *me*, Alex. I was meant to lose. It was my name they would have pulled from their bag.' I looked down at the Thames. Watching the flow. 'They took photos. Before I left.'

'Are you worried?'

'No, not now. But I was wondering …'

'Wondering what?'

'If it was right. What I did to her. To Jenny.'

'That she might do something stupid?'

'No, Alex. To have tricked her. And then…'

'What?'

'To have left her. When she was drunk. With all those guys.'

I looked ahead, counting the low arches of Southwark Bridge. And would she? Would she have stripped off for real because of me? And run through the crowd and around the square, starkers, until someone covered her up and got her home … to be sick, or worse. I wondered. And would I? Shirt off. Pants off. Naked to all the world. Braving the dare. Their laughs. Playing the fool at my expense. I wasn't sure.

The river flowed, darkening in the distance.

'If we split, Alex … what would happen?'

'Nothing. Everything would stay the same. The world, that is.'

'But you'd still … do your studies? You'd still be at uni?'

'Maybe. Or I might travel. Europe. North America.'

I looked towards the sea. 'On your own?'

He nodded. 'Take my chances. Do something else.'

'And Hatherleigh's course? Art history?'

'Cover its tracks. Call in a few favours. There'll be another chance. Another partner. Another day.' He turned his head. 'Maybe we're just not cut out to be heroes.'

'For what?' I threw my arms across my chest.

'To give us a break, Richard, so we can rebuild our world. So we can start again and rethink the things we do. The way that … that Francis has been going on about, for God's sake.' He swung around. 'You've heard him. And Jane. If you were bloody well listening, that is.'

I looked down. A stretch of thread dangled from the pocket of my jeans, hinting at our flight and our struggle. And I'd try to forget. And do my best. Taunted by strange, ambiguous lines. And legends. Myths. And fears. I pulled the thread, tugging at its slender length. Drawing it from the seam. So easily cut, I thought, and wondering how, and if, it might still be repaired. And yet … I was listening. And remembering … and thinking. I let go of the thread. 'Alex, who was Demeter's daughter?'

'Her daughter? Why do you ask?'

'Oh. Just something Jane said. When we were talking. About the world. And your plans to change it.'

'Her name was Persephone, Richard. Dürer did a drawing of her on a horse.'

'Was she a goddess?'

'So they say.'

'Tell me what happened to her.'

Alex stepped away from the rail. 'She was seized. And seduced, Richard, by her uncle.'

'Her uncle?' My jaw dropped.

'Yeah. Hades, king of the dead. He was Zeus's brother.'

'But why?'

'Because he fancied her. And he found her picking flowers one day. So he whisked her off to hell. A load of pigs covered his tracks, they say.'

'And what did she do? In hell?'

'She was made a queen. By Hades.'

'Of the dead?'

'Suppose so.'

'Seems a rotten price to pay. I mean, for just picking flowers.'

Alex leant against the rail. He raised his elbows and yawned. 'But that wasn't all.' I stepped closer. 'Her mother freaked out, searching everywhere until at last, she gave up in despair.'

I glanced at the river. 'Because her daughter was lost, then?'

Alex smiled. 'No, not quite. An old hag took pity on Demeter, her mum.'

'An old hag?' I smiled back.

He stretched his arms, catching the breeze. 'Yeah. Her name was Hecate. Goddess of the cross-roads.'

I copied his gesture. The wind freshened.

'Well, Hecate told Demeter to talk to the Sun because he saw what had happened. And what he said made her mad. So, being the goddess of the Earth, as well as the wife of Zeus, she stopped everything from growing. Until she got her daughter home again.'

'And did she? Stop everything?'

'In a deeper, mythological way.'

'And what does that mean?'

'Well, old Zeus had to sort things out. His world was like a waste-land. There were no trees. No crops. No pretty flowers. Everything was dying off. His world of humans was going bust.'

Going bust, I thought. I fiddled with the thread. 'And so what happened next?'

'Zeus came up with a solution. But there was still one problem, Richard.'

'I'm listening.'

'The problem was that Persephone should not have eaten during her stay underground.' He shrugged. 'It's a decree of the Fates, they say.'

I smiled, guessing the outcome. 'Okay. So, what did she eat?'

'Seven seeds of a pomegranate. She'd wandered into an orchard, found the pomegranate, and picked the seeds out of its skin.' Alex looked at me. 'Some accounts say that Hades tricked her.'

Frowning, I crossed my arms. 'Does any of this make sense?'

'It might do.'

'But how?'

'Well, Zeus, the story goes, brokered a new deal between his wife and his brother, after Hermes, the emissary of the gods, got everyone together.'

'You mean a compromise?'

'More a fact of life and death, I'd say.'

'Oh?'

'Hades, Richard, could keep his queen for four months of the year. But once winter was up, at the start of spring, Persephone would go home to Demeter. And the world could grow again. Trees, crops. Pretty flowers. Blossom.'

'But was that fair? I mean, she had been abducted.'

'Well, if you enjoy the fruits of hell, maybe you have to return for its harvest.'

Poor old Persephone, I thought, hustled back and forth like the river. Madness without end. Like Sisyphus's boulder. And Ixion's wheel. I looked at my friend. 'Tell me something. What is it that Francis hates about the world?'

'Does he?'

'Alex, he does. Don't you remember?'

'What?'

'Our first tutorial. Well, my first tutorial. When Hatherleigh asked us what we'd change in the world. I mean, if we could.'

Alex yawned. 'It's a while ago, Richard. I can't really remember.'

'No, that's the point. Hatherleigh didn't ask him after you'd jumped in. And so he said nothing.'

Alex grinned at me. 'There you go, then.'

'But there must be something. Something that bugs him.'

'He's pissed off with me. We always argue.'

'I know. All the time.' The breeze slackened. 'But it's not that. Jane said she hated selfishness. Right?'

'And anything petty, Richard.'

'Yeah, okay. And you said arrogance.'

'Did I?'

'Yes, Alex,' I insisted. 'And I talked about unfairness. In the world. Don't you remember?'

'Sounds like a reason. If you care.'

'Yes, a reason. But if you'd asked me two years ago, I wouldn't have said anything.'

'Really?'

'Well, the obvious things. Like war and famine, I suppose. But what can I do about those?'

Alex didn't answer. He dropped to the walkway of the bridge once more and slid his hands into warmer pockets. Another yawn beckoned sleep, stealing him away. I started to shiver. And fear.

'And my old friends at school, you know, they used to go on about the world too. We'd talk in class. Argue even. With the teachers. Politics. Visions. Declarations. But I reckoned they were just posing, Alex. I mean, they weren't going to rebel or take anyone on. Like in a fight. Like us. So what's the point? What's the point of whining and preaching? I'd say … as we drifted apart. Disagreeing. And they'd say that I was a fool and laugh at me. That I didn't understand. And just accepted things. And that I was naïve.'

I stared ahead.

'And were you?'

'Was I what?'

'Naïve.'

'Maybe,' I said. 'I'm not sure. Some things don't work out, do they? Or friends. And … are too hard to admit.' I swallowed, sensing a tear. 'But we're not supposed to look back, are we?' I wiped my eyes. 'Just soldier on. Or break up. And go our separate ways.'

The wind picked up around us.

'You know, Richard, the Persephone myth has an Orphic connection.'

'Yeah. Orpheus. Francis mentioned him. Remember? In the museum.' I laughed, feeling the tears roll down my cheek. 'A loser, wasn't he?'

'Well, sometimes looking back might be the wrong decision.'

'Don't look back,' I repeated, shaking my head. Aching inside.

'But regret, Richard, is something else.'

'Regret.' I cried, leaning against the rail. 'And then what?'

'And then … we go forward. Free of burden. And guilt.'

The river hurried towards the sea. A patchy light stretched wide across its thin, diaphanous skin. And eddies circled here and there like little worlds or systems churning amidst the constant flow, forming and reforming. And bubbles strung out like beads along a spiral trapping air. With specks of life. And memories. And light that measured time till all the suns were spent. Their days numbered and run. I lifted my head and slipped my hands into my pockets. Tearful, I turned, and leant against the bridge. 'Nothing stays the same,' I said. 'And all … all must change, Alex. Or be changed,' I sighed. 'Changed. And re-begot.'

My heart raced.

'Alex, stand up.'

'You're shaking, Richard. What is it?'

'Persephone.' I reached for his arm. 'Her return. In the spring. At the next world, Alex. "At the next world, that is, at the next spring; For I am every dead thing." The old man's words. On the steps of the museum.'

'It's by Donne. It's about renewal.'

'And resurrection, Alex. "He ruined me. And I am re-begot of absence, darkness, death; things which are not."'

I was still shaking. I wiped my eyes.

Alex threw off his jacket and thrust it into my arms. He unzipped a pocket and removed a mobile phone.

'What are you doing?' I said, stunned by its appearance.

'I'm texting Otto. At the museum.' He pushed closer hiding the phone between us. 'We can still save Lopez. And change the world.'

'But the phone, Alex. Whose is it?'

'Francis's. It's got an encryption app we use for texts.'

'Like secrets?'

'No, mate. *The* secret.'

And as Alex typed, enciphering the enigmatic words of a meta-physical poem, I noticed two figures on the north side of the bridge. One raised a hand to his ear as if to catch instructions. A third hurried to join them before slipping away.

'Alex. I think we're being watched.'

'I know. They followed us, earlier.' Alex stepped back and with a gleeful cry hurled the phone into the Thames.

'What have I done?'

'You've given us the info we need.'

'The clue? To the start of the universe?'

'Time and place, Richard. They're in the poem.'

Alex grabbed his jacket. We turned towards the Southbank and the Globe theatre. 'I've just remembered …' he said, taking me by the arm, his face and mood alive.

'Remembered what?'

'What Francis hates … about the world.'

'What is it?' I asked, doubling up to keep pace.

'It's hypocrisy,' he replied, freeing my arm. 'Now let's get the hell out of here. I've got some explaining to do.'

END OF PART ONE

PART TWO

31

'Gold, silver or bronze?' A steady voice beat out the words above the dull, guttural drone of a Rolls-Royce engine.

James Ellison, standing alone in an annexe to the much grander Durbar Court, at the heart of the old India Office in London's Whitehall, stared at a digital display screen in the corner of the room. A PR video, running on a continuous loop, caught his attention. He watched as a Hercules transport rumbled high above a rusty-looking landscape criss-crossed with desert tracks and dry, waterless gullies. 'Gold, silver or bronze?' the voice repeated, as the plane, a silhouette against the setting sun, flew steadily towards a light-scarred horizon.

The sound of footsteps disturbed his concentration. He turned to the glass partition that separated the annexe from the Court.

A young man, wearing a dark blue, unbuttoned blazer, beige chinos and a white, open-necked shirt that bared a raw, sturdy throat, leant against the glass door with his weight. He held a box of sparkling wine against his chest. A nod and an impish smile excused his incursion as the door closed behind him.

'The white, sir. From hospitality. A full case.'

'Thank you,' said James, stepping back before the box was released into his care. He gestured to a table, already prepared with canapés, coffee cups and glasses ahead of the lunch-time reception he had arranged for his two American guests.

The assistant swung away and placed the case of wine on the table. He removed two bottles from the case, inspected the labels, and then placed them alongside the glasses. Returning to the rest of the wine, he lifted the box, dropped to his knees, and in one movement slid the contents behind a white linen cloth that draped to the floor. He sprung effortlessly to his feet, clasped his hands, and turned back to James.

'I chilled the wine earlier, sir. Do you want it served here or in the big atrium?'

'Er, the Court, please,' said James, unsettled by the young man's brisk and confident manner. 'The annexe is a little intimidating.'

The young man glanced around. Four full-length portraits set in carved gilded frames hung near each corner of the room. He puckered his lips as if to whistle, but spoke instead. 'I think you're right about that, mister.'

'Oh, I'm glad you agree,' said James, taken aback by the flippant response.

The young man smiled and folded his arms. 'You know the video, sir. I was watching it earlier. When I set up the table for the reception.'

'Oh?'

'It looks like somewhere in Africa. Where the plane's flying.'

James reverted to the screen. New footage had overtaken the sunset. 'Yes. Eritrea, perhaps. Although the Arabian peninsula is also a possibility.'

'But I was wondering, sir … the references to gold and silver in the voice-over.'

'Yes, gold and silver. They're code words.' James paused for a moment as his attention switched to the young man's fresh complexion. He turned back to the screen. 'Words we use in a crisis. They help us galvanise our response during emergencies.' He glanced again, wondering if the assistant was an intern or an apprentice on a training scheme. 'You seem interested in our work.'

The young man nodded before relaxing his arms. 'I'm thinking about what I should do. I mean, in the future. When I leave my college and start work.'

'So, you don't work for us already?'

'No, I'm on a secondment. Twelve weeks.'

'And what, if I may ask, are you studying?'

'Marketing. With event management.' The growl of diesel engines drew their attention back to the screen as a group of vehicles were driven on to a waiting plane. 'But my brother, he's in the army.'

Not entirely dissimilar, thought James.

'He says he likes the postings. And the patrols.'

'Your brother is a brave young man.'

'Yeah. But he's not as good as me at sports.' He shifted on his feet as if primed for a match or the start of a race.

James edged back. 'Of course, we are never short of events at the Foreign Office.'

'I know. And you don't always get them right, either.' He threw a playful punch.

'Oh?' said James, looking concerned.

'Like last month. My first big event and we served the wrong wine.'

'And did that upset someone?'

'No, nothing like that.' A look of surprise pierced his jaunty demeanour. 'Just that my boss ... she said I should have served it last.'

'Really?'

As the credits drew the video to a close, the young man reached for one of the wine bottles he had placed on the table. He took a white napkin and wrapped it around the neck of the bottle before drawing the cork slowly. James eased back as the fizz rushed to the top before the overflow was stifled with the cloth. The young man returned the wine to the table and then repeated the procedure a second time. Holding his breath, he drew the cork. 'Have you worked here a long time, sir?'

'I suppose I have.' James tugged the sleeve of his shirt, feeling flattered by the inquiry. 'I think it was 1984 when I joined. As a graduate following Cambridge.'

'I think even my mum and dad were only little in 1984.'

'Yes. It is a while ago, now.' James pressed his lips as he glanced around the room, his eyes lingering on the glass chandelier above their heads. 'The Foreign Office has been a generous home to me. Over the years.'

'I think it's more like a palace.'

The cork popped suddenly from the bottle, forcing the young man to press his palm against the mouth until the gas subsided. He wiped his hands with the napkin before returning the bottle to the table. Turning around, he looked at James. 'I mean, with all those paintings and statues on the walls and stairs. Are they famous?'

'Well, let's see what I can remember.' James took the young man by the arm to the glass door of the partition and looked out across the atrium. 'The Court was designed by Mathew Wyatt in the mid-nineteenth century. It was once an open courtyard but now has a glass panelled roof. They glanced up before James re-directed the young man's attention to the atrium. As you can see, each corner has two statues.'

'On different levels. One above the other.'

'Yes,' said James. 'And at the far end, you will find Warren Hastings, the Earl Minto, and Baron Teignmouth.'

'Wow.'

'And to your left, Robert Clive, and the Earl Cornwallis.'

The young man looked to his left and right. 'I bet they're all dead.'

'Oh, very much so. And sourly remembered.'

'But weren't they important?'

'Well, Clive laid the foundations of British rule in India in the eighteenth century. Later, he was offered the command of British forces in North America but declined, dying not long after in tragic circumstances. Cornwallis's career was less successful.' The young man frowned. 'He fought the last major engagement in the American War of Independence. At Yorktown.'

'The Americans won that, didn't they?'

'Oh, decisively.' James gestured towards the Court. He pointed to the statue of the Earl of Minto, wavy-haired, with thick sideburns, clad in a tight military jacket sporting wide lapels. A classical toga added an air of authority to his stature. 'Now, he was the nephew of the last British governor of New York.'

'You mean we owned it?'

'Until the Treaty of Paris, I believe.'

James stepped back from the atrium, intrigued by his own observations. Hastings too, he recalled, had faced the French in their alliance with the rebellious Americans, half a world away on the battlefields of Bengal. He shrugged. Bedfellows of necessity, he chided.

'It's not always right, is it, sir? I mean, taking over other people's countries all the time.'

'Perhaps not,' James paused as he noticed a small blemish on the young man's neck. 'But I fear there is a destiny we cannot avoid … even if the memory haunts us.' James looked away, turning once more to the atrium as the foreign secretary and a small party of her officials stepped into the Court. COBRA flashed across his mind. And Kalinsky. He turned back to the young man. 'You said your brother is in the army?'

'Yeah. He was even in Afghanistan. But he reckoned the yanks weren't as smart as the Afghans.'

'Did he?'

'I think he was only showing off, though.'

'Oh, why?'

'Because he likes fighting.'

'Well … but you are fond of sport.'

'Football. Every weekend. Scored twice on Saturday. One a volley clean off my right foot.' He shook his head, playing the game back in his mind. 'Their goalie had no chance,' he added, before reaching for his phone and checking for messages. He looked up. 'I think your guests are coming soon, sir.'

'Thank you.'

The young man cast a glance along the table, satisfying himself that everything looked in order. He turned back to James. 'I'd better leave now. My colleague wants me in the atrium.'

'Well, before you go …' James removed an invitation card and a pen from his pocket. He wrote *Conference Room* on the card and handed it to the young man. 'Would you pass this to the foreign secretary for me?'

'To Alison Farring?' His eyes widened.

'Yes. Let her know I wish to speak to her before the Americans arrive. I shall stay here in the annexe.'

The young man studied the card. 'You haven't said your own name, though.'

'Oh, James Ellison. And you are … if I may ask?'

'Chris,' he said, buttoning his dark blue jacket with a smile. 'My manager's Melinda Bennett. In hospitality.'

'Well, Christopher, good luck with your secondment and choice of career.' James led him to the steps of the atrium. 'Try to catch her now. While she's in a good mood.'

James returned to the annexe as another video sequence repeated on the screen. Gold, silver or bronze, he recalled, as covered trucks dashed across a red-scorched terrain. Yes, young man … before the Americans arrive.

* * *

'So there you are, James. I've been looking for you the whole morning.'

James turned his head, alerted to the foreign secretary's icy vowels.

'The PM, James … he wants to know what's going on.'

'I'm sorry, Alison?'

'The Middle East, James. Russia, China.' She waved her Downing Street briefing in her hand. 'Your assessment …' she paused as her eyes fell on the uncorked bottles of wine, 'your assessment said that these endless crises were predictable.'

'Predictable, foreign secretary? I thought I said inevitable.' James gestured to the coffee and canapés. He smiled weakly at his boss.

'Well, that's what I told the prime minister, James … predictable.' Alison Farring placed the briefing alongside the cups and from an ornate silver pot poured herself a coffee. 'And he wasn't best pleased when I told him.'

James reached for a small jug of milk and topped up her cup.

'By the way, who's that messenger boy you sent to me?'

'Government hospitality. A bright young man from the north of England. Interested in art and nineteenth century portraiture,' said James, raising an eyebrow in a gesture of approval.

'Well, he asked me if Earl Minto had been governor of New York or something.' She lifted a bottle of wine and studied the label.

'English, Alison. A sparkling wine from the vineyards of Kent.'

Alison replaced the bottle and reached for a canapé. 'I've discussed your paper with the PM. If there's a pattern underlying world events, he wants to know more about it.' She flicked her fingers free of flakes. 'Before everything runs out of control, James.'

'In that case, we must get closer to the students.'

'I agree.' She turned to the display screen. 'COBRA are ready to run with it,' she added, sipping her coffee to the sound of distant drums and a convoy of land rovers sweeping across an empty plain. 'Oxford and Cambridge have agreed to join the investigations— something about futures that intrigues them.' She stepped closer to the screen. 'Remind me, who was in charge in Helmand last year?'

'Special Operations, I believe.'

The foreign secretary continued to watch the screen. 'It came up in Cabinet this morning. The PM's still furious.' She placed her cup on the table before examining the spread of food. 'How many people are coming to this party of yours?'

'Warren Dudley and Larry Antony, of course. The arts committee. And Professor Littlejohn and his staff.'

'Littlejohn?'

'Yes. He's agreed to cover the cost from the history budget.' James gestured to the atrium and to a painting concealed behind a sheet of drapery.

'You have seen the picture, James? I hope you're not handing out Old Masters again.'

'Not at all. And the Pre-Raphaelites are quite safe, ma'am. We've settled on a reproduction of an early nineteenth century work.' He paused, still mindful of a quizzical stare. 'Something dear to Warren's heart, I believe.' James poured himself a coffee. 'Littlejohn proposed it, and I agreed.'

'Well, if we can achieve our objectives, I'm sure this little jolly will pay for itself.' She chose another canapé.

'Thank you, foreign secretary.' James stirred his coffee. 'I'm planning ...'

But a fierce noise interrupted their exchange. They watched as a new action sequence unfolded on the screen. Flares and ground clearings gave way to low altitude drops, followed by bursts of gunfire. Then explosions ... before an unnatural quiet focused their thoughts.

Alison Farring broke the silence. 'These space-time co-ordinates you mentioned are a new field of physics, according to the government's chief scientist.' The foreign secretary reached for a tissue and wiped her fingers. 'The least we must do is assess the defence possibilities.'

'But what should I tell the Americans?'

'Nothing. COBRA has earmarked the New Year for a decision and the PM wants us to take control of developments.'

James nodded. 'Three weeks, Alison. It's not long, but as I was about to say, I am already preparing the ground in our favour.' He raised his cup and saucer to his face. 'I intend to put one of my team on the ground. We have a cell in Gower Street, next to the university. History, mostly. And friends of Littlejohn.'

'Who?'

'Felix Leighton. Felix is one of MI5's protégés. He joined me two years ago, and is ready for something a little more challenging, I believe.'

'Good. But send me his profile. I need more visibility on your people.'

'Of course.' James stepped closer and speaking in a quieter voice said: 'Felix is familiar with the Karlstad operation. As well as the Kalinsky incident at the British Museum.' He paused again as an official walked past the glass divide. 'On a related matter, I've arranged for the detention of a Ms Lopez at the British Library. Her records identify another member of the students' group. An undergraduate studying literature and art history. He may be important to their plans.'

Alison glanced towards the atrium. 'Is there a risk that Warren's team could move first?'

'Unlikely. They're still digesting the material that GCHQ sent them.'

'Hmm.' She checked her wristwatch and retrieved the Downing Street paper from the table. 'This presentation of yours. I can give it fifteen minutes, James, and no more. I'm being chased by the Cabinet Office on another matter concerning the Ukraine.'

An usher approached the doorway of the glass divide. 'Excuse me, ma'am. I have a message for James Ellison.'

'The Americans?' said James.

The usher nodded before slipping away.

'In that case, Alison, we had better join our guests.'

James led the foreign secretary into the atrium. The young man, he noticed, was cheerfully serving drinks.

32

Shut away from an inquiring sun, the balconied tiers of Mathew Wyatt's imperial Court look down on an inner, sheltered domain. Columns and arches cathedralise the space as the illustrious Court, guardian of a-once world, a re-membered world, rises, grandly, like an opera first heard or an epic tale unspun.

James slipped down the grey marble steps to the sunken floor of the atrium, and with brisk, confident strides crossed the Court. He thrust out his arm, catching his guest unawares. 'Warren, how absolutely wonderful to see you again.'

'James,' said Warren, disengaging from his phone.

'May I introduce the foreign secretary?' James turned as Alison Farring approached, still a step behind her radiant colleague.

'My pleasure, ma'am,' said Warren, looking bemused by the attention. He slipped his phone into a pocket and presented his hand. 'I am honoured. This is a very fine venue.'

'And the perfect setting for this afternoon's presentation,' said James, moving closer. 'I was just telling the foreign secretary about the excellent co-operation we have at all levels.' He clapped his hands in a gesture of appreciation. 'And my goodness, the contri-bution by Mr Antony's team has been vital to our progress.'

Warren acknowledged the compliment. 'And your prime minister, foreign secretary ... he is aware of our work and our goals?'

'The PM? Yes, very much so. The prime minister takes this threat seriously.'

'My president shares the concern, ma'am.'

Alison Farring glanced at her briefing papers. 'In fact, only this morning, it came up in Cabinet. I was telling James. Just earlier.'

'This very morning?'

'Yes. And he wants it solved.' The foreign secretary held her papers to her chest. She nodded at James.

'Would you agree, in that case, that our investigations should be more consistent when sharing data and intelligence assessments? Just recently, ma'am, we have become aware of a link to the British Museum …'

'I'm sorry,' said James, interrupting. 'Is Larry not with us?' James glanced around, unsure if Warren's colleague was absent or lost somewhere in the building.

Warren paused before replying. 'Unfortunately, there has been a difficult, last-minute issue that has detained him.' He stepped back as his face coloured. 'I regret, ma'am, that we could not inform you in advance. I hope you will forgive this small breach of protocol.'

'Well, nothing too serious?' said Alison, glancing towards James.

'A matter of personal conduct.' Warren cleared his throat. 'I have asked William Carter of the CIA to continue in his post until the end of January.'

'William?' said James with a hint of curiosity.

'Until matters are properly resolved.' Warren swallowed, slipping eye contact with James.

A little laughter trickled around the Court as attendees enjoyed the canapés and a glass of wine. The diversion allowed James a few moments to digest the unexpected news about William. Looking unperturbed, he turned back to his guest. 'I don't believe you have visited the Court before, Warren.' James gestured with his hand, inviting a perusal of the building around them.

'That is correct,' said Warren, glancing at the cloistered setting before lingering on the glass panelled roof. 'The architect, if I might say, had a generous vision.' He fixed on the differently styled columns and arches built one level above another. 'Like choirs of angels,' he said, 'bathed in a soft empyrean light.' He turned back to his hosts. 'I am reminded, foreign secretary, of the great cathedrals and abbeys of Europe. And God's abiding grace.'

Alison reached for the arm of James. 'We must ask Warren to contribute to our website blog. I've never thought of the Court like that before.'

'What a brilliant idea, foreign secretary!'

An attendant approached with drinks. Warren chose a lime cordial. Alison and James, the sparkling wine before gesturing a modest toast. James leant forward, keen to catch the mood before it slipped. 'The Court was designed by Mathew Wyatt in 1861.' James turned to the foreign secretary. 'Of course, his work with Brunel on a west London terminus was well known before he partnered with Gilbert Scott, in the design of the India Office.' James sipped from his glass as he eyed his companions discreetly.

Alison Farring remained still, looking unsure about the railway connections. She raised her glass and drank, anyway.

'I believe, sir,' said Warren, casting his eyes around the venue, 'that the Byzantines, in both their architecture and their politics, also favoured an eclectic approach.'

'Indeed,' replied James, musing for a moment on the clash of aesthetics with the fury of nineteenth century steam.

Alison nodded, still looking uneasily at James.

'But I remember young Felix telling me there had been a plan to demolish the whole building and start again.'

'Yes,' snapped Alison. 'In the Sixties. Philistines, if you ask me.' She looked sternly at James. 'But I'm not one for wholesale destruction or childish gestures. Am I James?'

'No, not at all, foreign secretary. It would have been a terrible loss to the country's prestige.'

'I just wish the more radical elements in our world could understand that.'

Warren acknowledged her comments with a smile. 'There is a natural hierarchy in society, ma'am. One sanctioned by God that mirrors his dispensation to the angels.' He looked again at the balconied tiers, each boasting a hard-edged plinth and a colourful frieze. 'It is through their intercession that we do God's work and confront heresy.'

'Heresy?' Alison Farring glanced obliquely at James

'The church must remain vigilant, ma'am. And warn those who will otherwise perish in the lawful apocalypse ... as Revelation informs us.'

James sipped from his glass as he watched the attendants serve the wine. If Larry was under a cloud, he reasoned, William must know the details about his demise. He wondered, too, if this was connected with the data sets released by GCHQ. He would talk to Felix. A diplomatic storm, just when COBRA was ready to act, would not help the PM's plans. Or his own. Vigilance, indeed, he agreed, before his thoughts returned to the young man's curiosity about paintings. His face brightened as he reached for Warren's arm. 'I understand you have connections with the art world, Warren.'

'Yes, that is correct. My late wife took a master's program in art history. Her thesis was on the expulsion from Eden and its artistic legacy.' Alison and James nodded politely. 'We spent many happy hours touring Italy and its fine collections.' He lowered his glass. 'The arts are a faithful window on the soul.'

'How very true,' said James, placing a hand to his chin. 'And of course ... that wonderful fresco by Masaccio. Isn't it in one of the Florentine churches, Warren?'

'That is so. The church of Santa Maria.'

'And the figures … so disconsolate. So heart broken, I remember.'

'God's punishment. For the sin of Eve,' explained Warren.

'And the complicity of Adam, I fear.' James shook his head. He glanced towards his colleague, but an official in the cloister had caught her attention. He shrugged. The complicity of Adam, he assumed.

'And your plans for Christmas?' asked Alison, returning to the conversation.

'I shall, of course, stay in London, ma'am. The Foundation will celebrate the holy day, and then the feast of St Stephen.'

'And you, James? Is it Cambridge again?'

'Yes, Alison. Until the New Year. My alma mater is Corpus Christi, Warren. We're a small college. Mid-fourteenth century. I expect to meet a few old friends. And share the usual memories.'

Still holding their glasses, James led Warren and Alison along the periphery of the Court, their eyes lingering on pink granite columns and ochre coloured balustrades before pausing beside the statue of General Cornwallis.

'I did my MA in theology. Patristic studies and New Testament Greek.' Warren studied the statue without comment. 'It was at bible classes I met my wife, Anne-Marie.'

'Alison is an Oxford protégé,' said James, as they resumed their perambulation.

'Politics and Economics,' said the foreign secretary before another loud whisper drew her attention. 'Cabinet Office, James.' She checked her wristwatch again. 'Please start without me. I'll catch up once I'm free of distractions.'

The foreign secretary handed James her unfinished wine and joined an anxious-looking colleague in a corridor alongside the atrium.

James gestured to a Court attendant. The young man he'd talked to earlier returned to collect the glasses.

* * *

Standing shorter than the drape covered easel, a plump Professor Littlejohn invited the assembly to draw closer. 'The Committee on Historical Matters has a long and distinguished record and has been at the forefront of historical research in seeking a definitive understanding of past events and their impact on modern affairs. The study of origins allows us to ask if a single event determined subsequent developments, or whether the stresses of any individual case generate their own outcomes.' James nodded as Professor Littlejohn moved closer to the easel. 'The History Department has researched many contemporary and historical dilemmas to determine root causes, and proposals on how they might evolve in the future.' He paused, giving space to his thoughts. 'We are, of course, blessed with an abundance of records in the UK from official State papers to correspondence, cartographic surveys and personal memoirs of those closest to events.' He glanced again at James. 'Such records are often a cause for reflection and regret, but we should also celebrate the contribution our country has made in promoting welfare and stability in uncertain times and dangerous places.' Murmurs of approval greeted the professor's words. 'It gives me great pleasure to welcome a senior representative of the US State Department who has supported the committee's work on a question of mutual interest.' A round of applause greeted Warren Dudley as he stepped forward. 'As well as having a long-standing association with members of the current American administration, Warren is a collector and admirer of religious art.'

'For many years now, friends.'

'And so with the help of the best minds of the arts committee, we have chosen something suitable to mark today's occasion.' Professor Littlejohn paused as further applause punctuated his remarks. 'I will now ask our guest to unveil a token of our gratitude and a thank you for his country's enduring support.'

Warren removed a piece of paper from his jacket pocket. 'Thank you, Professor Littlejohn. And thank you to your foreign secretary,' he said, noting her return to the atrium. 'I would like to convey a message from my president thanking your committee for their diligent work on issues of great interest to the American public.' James nodded supportively. 'And today, James Ellison has kindly shown me the splendours of this extraordinary building and its many works of art ... though he seemed a little tongue-tied as we paused beside your General Cornwallis.'

James stayed aloof to the titters as Warren Dudley feigned a look of surprise.

Warren moved to the side of the easel, and taking his cue from Professor Littlejohn, uncovered the hidden canvas. A panoramic view of a flat desert landscape greeted the eyes of the attendees. Warren adjusted his glasses and leant closer. He read the title and the attribution aloud. 'The Fall of Babylon. An Old Testament drama in the style of Mr John Martin, 1789-1854.'

Warren stepped back, gripped by the epic scene. Dark swirling plumes of smoke rose above the wasted landscape. Fires issued from underground wells. A mighty, alien horde swarmed at the walls of a city condemned. Warren breathed deeply as the words of the prophet Isaiah came to him. 'O Lucifer,' he whispered, 'how thou art fallen.'

33

'Hi. I'm Richard. I live upstairs.' A guy in stark red underpants opened his door to me as I waited outside his room. He was sweating and his hair fell in strands across his forehead. 'I'm … a first year,' I said. 'English Literature …' My voice dropped as I stared back at him.

'Jesus, man, I'm with my girlfriend. Know what I mean?'

I stepped back. 'I'm sorry, but I think the internet is down.'

'So?'

The door wavered in his grip. My eyes shifted. 'Look, I need to contact a friend. We've kind of fallen out, and I want to tell her how I feel … Like sorry.' This is bloody embarrassing, I thought.

'Well, phone her.'

A voice from within the room called softly to him.

'She won't answer,' I said, catching sight of his face as he pushed back his hair. 'You know how it is when they're mad at you.'

'Which flat is yours?' he snapped.

'Six. The other one on my floor is empty.'

'Stay there,' he said, shutting the door in my face.

I leant against the adjacent wall as my heart pounded. The trouble at Covent Garden was catching up with me, and in an email from the uni, my classmate Fiona and I were blamed for the disturbances in the square. If I didn't get some answers back to them, I'd be in deep shit by Christmas. I closed my eyes, but all I could see were red underpants. How was I to know he was with his girlfriend?

I heard whispers as he reappeared at the doorway.

'I've reset it, mate. If it doesn't work—tough.'

'Thanks. And sorry to have … woken you.'

He shrugged. Some of his ardour had wilted. 'And the flat next to you isn't empty. There were two guys there Friday night.'

'Guys?'

'Yeah. They were arguing before one of them stormed out.' He glanced over his shoulder. Another whisper drew him back to bed.

I headed upstairs, closed my door, and went to the window. The courtyard below was dark except for the eerie sheen of the sodium streetlamps that fell on its surface. Staying still, I listened for sounds against the beat of a racing pulse. A car caught my attention as it moved slowly towards the piazza until it changed gear. I drifted back to my bed. History, I thought. And I'm with my girlfriend.

I lay down, placed my hand between my thighs and yielded to the urge of a restless moment.

* * *

A key turned in my door. I jumped up, thinking of strangers.

'It's okay, Richard, it's me.' Alex flashed my key in his hand. 'I found it outside. Just now.'

I checked my pockets, before zipping up. Alex entered with a sports bag. He dropped it at his feet and looked around.

'But downstairs?' I said. 'How'd you get in? The entrance should have been locked.'

'It was. But Eddie has a key card.' He closed the door.

'Eddie?' I glanced towards the window.

'He's driving around. Keeping an eye on things.'

Alex threw me my room key. I guessed he was staying the night as he removed his jacket and woolly hat, lodging them in a space still free on the bookshelf. No problem, I thought. The spare duvet was still under the bed from his last visit.

As my friend settled in, I retrieved my laptop and refreshed the screen. 'Alex, there's an email that I have to show you.'

'What does it say?'

'That I'm under caution.'

'Why?' He opened the bag and removed a clean shirt and a pair of jeans.

'Because of the fight, last week. The university is accusing me and a girl in my tutorial group of rioting.'

He read the email. 'Who's Fiona, for Christ's sake?'

'She's on my English course and she knows Jonathan.' I closed the screen and sat next to him as he searched his bag. A belt landed on the bed. 'What can I tell her when she was at home with her parents and nowhere near the party?'

'Just tell her what happened. Then everyone else,' he added, removing a shoe from his bag before shaking it. An object, wrapped in tissue paper, fell into his hand. His face brightened as he turned to me. 'Remember? Jane spotted it before we dashed from the cafe.'

'You mean my present for Saturnalia?'

'From the three of us.' He removed the paper and handed it to me.

The figurine was four inches high and stood upright with the legs together. Both arms were half-raised in a symbolic salutation. The abdomen was distended, and the breasts were firm. 'Like I said ... a fertility thing.'

'Like Persephone,' he said, holding out his hand. 'It's supposed to glow in the dark when the light is off.'

'Well ...' I said, keeping the object out of his reach. 'The uni expects me to respond to their email.'

'Forget them.'

'But Alex, there's going to be an inquiry next term.'

Alex stood up, but his attention was on the fertility symbol as he moved closer to the switch by the door. My grip tightened. 'Uni first.'

He shrugged before plunging us into darkness. A warm glow radiated from the object as I relaxed my hand.

'Told you,' he said, only a silhouette himself.

The light came on, and as I examined the slender neck and delicate mouth of the carving, Alex sauntered towards me. Jane had said it was Early Cycladic. An adornment from a long vanished culture of a pre-literate age. But was it once a charm? I wondered. With a mystery at its heart that stirred a subtle mind … until Alex fell on me with a triumphant cry. We landed together on the floor. Prostrate, and with my arms pinned down, I opted to lie still.

'Now I've won,' he said, his face hovering over mine.

I released the innocent artifact. 'But if we don't sort this out, mate, we'll both be losers.' I wriggled free as he lifted his weight and we both got to our feet.

Alex returned the gift to me, and as I set it down, I noticed he'd stopped smiling—the sudden vigour of his gesture having drained his humour, I assumed. Distracted, he shuffled to the bed, looking pensive. After a moment, he spoke. 'The figurine, Richard. It's a token of renewal. A harbinger of spring. Remember our talk by the Thames?'

'I remember you charging ahead of me before we raced through Bankside, not sure if we were being followed.' I stretched my arms. 'We got away, though. Didn't we?'

'Yeah. But whoever was following us let us escape.'

'Oh? And is that why Eddie is playing boy scout?' Alex looked away as he clenched his fists. If it was another ruse, I now had the advantage. I stepped closer.

'The figurine's about changing things, Richard. Things that have gone wrong. And will deteriorate if nothing is done about them.'

'Let's leave the myths alone, Alex. This is for real. There's a risk I might be expelled. Along with Fiona, and then the rest of you, once everything comes out.'

'Francis and Jane?'

'Yes. They're in it up to the necks as well, mate.'

'I know,' he said. 'They'll be here in the morning. To explain what happens next.'

Good, I thought. At least we can get our story straight, whatever else they have in mind. Fiona might even get an explanation, if everyone talks sense for a change. Yet I still felt uneasy as my brain picked away at the evening's events … and our conversation on the bridge. But then a memory of flashing cameras lifted my spirits. 'Alex, I bet someone has a photo or even a video of us fighting. We can use it as evidence in any inquiry.'

Alex rubbed his chin. 'Don't worry, Richard. Jonathan got what he deserved, and the damage wasn't much. A few glasses, a screen. West End cafes are used to that. The uni have to go through the motions, but I reckon they'll drop your case.'

'No, they won't. Especially when the investigation learns about my course code and the fraudulent essays that Arbetta has sanctioned. And Hatherleigh strolling around in a face mask as if attending a fancy dress ball.'

I slipped into the kitchen and switched on the kettle. I leant against the metal sink, waiting for the kettle to boil. After a minute, Alex joined me. I punched him playfully on the arm, torn between an irritation at his passivity and a gut belief that our behaviour was justified, anyway. But Alex was right about Jonathan: he'd learnt a lesson the hard way before retreating with his friends.

The kettle boiled. I made two cups of tea. 'The sugar's there, mate. Take more if it helps.' I went to my desk and waited for Alex to join me. He stirred his tea as I considered my predicament and the uni's unambiguous threats. I stirred mine. It was the last day of the autumn term, I reflected, and after three months of lectures and tutorials, I was on the wrong art history option, even if the enrolment office thought otherwise. A demented post-grad was harassing me in my English class, and I was mixed up with a bunch of friends who want to dissolve the world because they're fretting about its future. Only the silent artifact looked composed. 'We've got to talk, Alex. And we've got to get serious.'

He nodded and let go of his spoon.

'Alex, tell me why you've come here this evening. I mean, staying overnight before Francis and Jane join us.' We glanced down at his bag. Clothes and the contents of his shaving kit were scattered around the floor. 'Are you dropping out of uni?' He shook his head. 'Then you agree we have to come clean about what has happened.'

'Maybe,' he said.

I still wasn't sure if I'd won him over, and yet I needed his support if I was to confront Francis and Jane whenever they arrived. Standing up, I scanned my room. My laptop was under his clothes. After checking the Wi-Fi, I returned to the desk and launched a new email. 'Why don't we write something together before the others arrive?'

His hands caressed the figurine. 'It might be better to wait, Richard.'

'Alex … listen to me. You know, when I came to uni, I made a promise to my parents that I would study hard.' A nod acknowledged my words. 'Because nine months before I arrived here, I went through hell at my interview in Oxford, quizzed by a panel of tutors who asked me lots of stupid questions I couldn't answer.'

'Really?'

'Yes. But there were other things, too. Strange things that I didn't expect or understand.'

'You were younger, Richard.'

'Twelve months younger, that's all.' I let go of the keyboard. 'You know, I've not discussed the interview with anyone. Not even my mum and dad.' Alex lifted his head. 'I just let everyone think, well … whatever they liked. Because I wasn't … and because I couldn't tell them without causing a fuss.' I tapped the desk with my finger. 'So I settled for English literature at UCL instead.'

'And art history B.'

'Yes. And I'm not screwing up a second time.' I snatched the cult object and threw it across the room on to my bed. 'And I don't want you to screw up, either, mate.' My fingers fell on the keypad in a frenzy, and in one continuous paragraph, I listed all the reasons I could think of to steer us out of trouble. Yes, I'd be thrilled to stay on Arbetta's course or Hatherleigh's, I typed. Yes, everything's a joke. No, I'm not mad and yes, I'm ready to be tested. And Jonathan won't exist once the world has been destroyed. I checked the uni's own pompous words, looking for weaknesses in their accusations. I scratched my head. Is it possible, I asked, that you've emailed the wrong Richard Addings? Because, I don't recall singing and dancing in the piazza that evening. Or rioting. Though I did consume a lot of alcohol, I admit. I stopped typing and looked po-faced at my pal. 'I'm going to tell everyone I was at home with Fiona.'

My antics raised a smile.

'Who was at your interview, Richard?'

'Who?'

'Yes. At Oxford.'

'Two men and a woman. One guy was much older. There might have been someone else.'

'What did they ask you?'

'Nothing that made sense. It was just weird.'

Alex ran his hands through his hair. 'Were they all from the UK?'

'Not sure.' I re-read my email. Total gibberish. 'The tall one sounded American.'

'Can you remember what he asked you?'

'No. The memory's been cancelled. Anyway, it's got nothing to do with what happened a week ago.'

'Try, Richard.'

'I think he mentioned missile sites.'

'How about the others?'

'Sex. And poetry. Modern poets are keen on it. So were they.'

'Was that all you discussed?'

'No. We talked about myths and I was shown two paintings by pre-Raphaelite artists. But they asked me questions that weren't remotely rational and wanted me to play strange games. Listen, Alex, it's last Friday that we need to focus on, not bloody Oxford and a pantomime that tripped me up once they'd invited me in behind their creepy walls. There was even ...' Alex darted to the door and cut the light. As we listened, heavy footsteps descended the stairs. 'Don't worry,' I said. 'It's the guy on the second floor and his girlfriend.' The front door of the apartment block slammed behind them, telling the rest of the building they'd left for the Christmas hols.

'Is anyone else in the building?'

'Don't know. All the courses have finished now that it's the end of term. But ... maybe next door.'

'Next door? Who?'

'Not sure. The guy downstairs told me he heard two people arguing.'

'When?'

'Friday. While we were in Covent Garden.'

Alex stepped on to the landing. A dull light from the floor below eked its way up the stairs as he crept towards the adjacent door. He listened before quietly retreating. Once back inside, he flicked the light off and on in what I assumed was some kind of signal. Eddie was patrolling outside, I remembered.

'There's something I must tell you, Richard. Before it's too late.'

'Okay.' I said, sensing a change in his mood.

'It's why I've come here tonight. To talk things over before we get serious tomorrow.'

I nodded, ready to calm down myself.

'I want to say sorry for what happened after the party in Covent Garden.'

'For what?'

'For hurting you. When we were on the bridge together. And I talked about quitting.'

I smiled and nudged him gently. 'Only real friends can say sorry, Alex. And mean it.'

He stayed still, unmoved by my words or gesture.

'There's something else, Richard. Something that troubles me. And for which only Francis has a solution.' He lowered his head as his face paled.

'What?' I asked, feeling alarmed.

'Something happened. Something terrible for which I'm to blame.'

'What Alex?' I stepped forward.

'An incident. In which someone died. Someone I knew.'

I held him as tears moistened his eyes

'And only Francis knows how we can undo it … and restart our lives again.'

34

'In the beginning,' declared Francis, 'there was total confusion. It wasn't until the stars and planets had crystallised that we find order and destiny in the sky around us.' He shared a glance with Jane as he unrolled a large, poster-sized sheet of paper on to my desk. Drawn on it was a map of the heavens and the promised solution to Alex's woes.

It was seven in the morning. I hadn't slept well, and I was unsure of my friend's mind or his emotional stability. His confession, though sounding sincere when I heard it, now seemed free of remorse, while his faith in Francis, and Francis's schemes just foolish and naïve. Yet, as he sat alongside Jane looking subdued, I knew that my own predicament was increasingly mixed up with his.

Francis gestured to his handiwork.

I examined the chart. Amidst a dark, and infinite void, clusters of planets spread out across time and space. Many had end dates pencilled alongside them, but some only a start. A few, like exhausted stars, had already expired and were crossed out with heavy red lines.

At the centre of this cosmic landscape was the chaotic impulse that had given it energy and form. The vanishing point of creation, I presumed. And towards the edge, I found a new world that had broken free from its parental predecessor—the planet earth. Francis waited as I pondered the implications of this unusual cosmography where worlds lived and died, while others spawned offspring in moments of turmoil or despair. 'This drawing, Francis … it's different to what you drew before, when we talked in Covent Garden. The one showing two figures in a cloud.'

'That's right, and it wasn't all we discussed, either.'

'No. Human nature as well, if I remember.' I glanced at Alex.

'We'll come back to that, Richard.' He pulled the sleeves of his sweater higher as if to reinforce his intention. I sipped from a cup of tea, ready to pick holes in his thesis.

Alex left the table. Jane watched as he slipped beyond the kitchen doorway before returning her attention to the chart.

'I'm listening, Francis,' I said, stifling a yawn as my eyes switched to the figurine, alone on my bookshelf.

'So, right from the outset, space-time was underpinned by fundamental laws. These laws are known to modern cosmologists as a group of mathematical formulae.'

'You mean the things that explain its structure and control its expansion?'

'Correct. But not its purpose or how it can be fine-tuned to avoid disasters.'

I frowned. 'Purpose, Francis?'

'Is anything devoid of purpose?' he said, raising his eyes to counter mine.

I looked again at his map of the cosmos. Francis was taking me somewhere, so I'd have to stay alert. But then a smile from Jane hinted at an explanation.

'The purpose is to achieve harmony, Richard.'

I nodded, remembering a more seductive approach at our party. 'Okay. But this model speaks of decay and termination. How can that achieve harmony?'

'Through renewal,' she said.

'The cycle of birth and death, Richard,' added Francis.

'And this applies to planets, as well?' I rested my arms on the desk.

'Unfailingly, Richard.' Francis placed a finger on a discarded world where he'd scribbled the word Troy. 'The ancients knew this and understood the forces that would lead societies to their destruction. Such as fate or necessity.'

'Moira and anankē,' said Jane, resorting to ancient Greek to identify the forces, and reminding me of a Hatherleigh class for a moment. 'As worlds lose their potential, a new world springs into being. Like after the Trojan War, or the biblical flood. Or when one social order ruthlessly supersedes another.'

'And what about justice and compassion?' I asked, uncertain of the classical terms.

Jane remained silent.

I left the desk and joined Alex. He was leaning against the sink with his arms folded. 'I think you should join us,' I said, handing him my empty cup.

'Francis can explain it better, Richard.'

'Damn it, Alex, this involves you.'

'We are the figures in the drawing, Richard. And the agents of renewal.' He dropped eye contact.

I was on my own, I realised, and if I'd misjudged Alex and his moods, then I was no less determined to probe the others' intentions. I took the cup from him and placed it in the sink. 'If you think so,' I said, leaving him to his thoughts.

Francis and Jane were on their feet when I returned to the room. The figurine, I noticed, was now in the middle of the desk.

Jane drew closer. 'Richard, we want you to play your part, and rebirth the world through a redemptive act.'

My jaw dropped. 'Oh, don't be so bloody stupid, Jane. You want Alex off the hook when what's happened has happened and can't be undone or changed by anyone. Your own model should tell you that.' I shut my eyes, but the feint glow of white alabaster unsettled me.

'Richard, please. Alex needs your help.' Jane reached for my arm.

'How can I help him, Jane? Look: worlds split. They go off in different directions. I can't explain how. But they don't go into reverse. Deeds, failures, and crimes go with them whatever happens thereafter.' I shook my head. 'I want to help Alex, but playing God with the universe isn't an option … if it was ever real, anyway.'

'Let's calm down.' Francis called Alex from the kitchen, and as I settled at the desk, his voice sharpened. 'Listen to me, Richard, before you mock. You are being emotional.'

Alex rejoined us. He mentioned Eddie as he returned to his chair next to Jane. I flicked a glance towards the window, but a more indulgent yawn overtook my curiosity.

'It's not only about Alex,' said Jane, taking his hand. 'There are other things that will happen. This is what I meant when I used the term anankē.'

'Necessity.'

'Yes, necessity,' said Francis. 'So let's consider what this means.'

I shrugged.

'To ancient Greece, everything was driven by cause and effect. Whether it was the mind of Zeus or the early science of their philosophers, everything was locked in a chain of events. Democritus explained this to Fifth Century Athens.'

'You've forgotten Leucippus, Francis.' I wanted to be pedantic.

'Yes. They were the first atomists.' Francis paused, distancing himself from my quibble. 'The goal, as Jane said earlier, is harmony. That's the ultimate purpose. To reconcile contraries and resolve division. This is what renewal means.'

'And you believe this involves a succession of worlds?'

'I do,' said Francis, 'as separate space-time constructs.'

'Then why poke around in Alex's misfortune? Let the cosmos get on with it.'

'Because we want to forestall the consequences of Alex's past actions in the future.' He pushed back in his chair.

I leant closer.

'Recall,' said Jane, 'how Apollo punished the Greek army at Troy with a deadly pandemic because of the impiety of King Agamemnon towards a local priest.'

'It's a myth, Jane. Like the sacrifice of his own daughter to raise a jolly good breeze for his ships,' I said.

Alex wasn't smiling. Nor was his silence helping, either. Sitting pensively. Contrite, maybe, though I wasn't sure. Why doesn't he challenge Francis, I wondered, instead of leaving me to argue alone? Nor did I believe the world would turn on Alex's past, like the wings of a helpless butterfly provoking the proverbial storm. But if this was their argument, that one thing leads inexorably to another … I leant back and eyed Francis quizzically. 'Okay, then. If undoing events means identifying a specific cause, then you must find the cause of the cause right back to the start of time.'

'No, not so, Richard. If we return to the origin of any space-time construct, we can revise its configuration and clean-up whatever we don't like about its development.' Our eyes fell on the earth.

'But it isn't only Alex's actions that alter in that scenario.'

'That's right. Other things will change as well.'

'Okay … so you fiddle around with history, and Alex is freed up from his fate. Without regrets, I suppose.'

'There's nothing to be sorry for, Richard,' said Alex, perking up. 'What I did will be undone by removing the cause that provoked it.' Jane gripped his hand, although his voice sounded fragile.

'This … new world, Francis?'

'Well, a better and improved one, Richard.' Francis rose and moved to the window, still talking as he scanned the street. 'We want a world scrubbed of its past, not another burdened with famil-iar debts when it is re-conceived.' He waved his hand as a dull light struggled to free the day.

'And did the ancient Greeks, Francis, propose a means to achieve that?' I thought of the Parthenon gallery and the cloth presented to Athena.

'It wasn't obvious at first,' he said, returning to the desk. 'Several old texts provided clues and then trips to the Aegean strengthened our insights. The rest was hard mathematics. More quantum physics than philosophical speculation, to be honest. A team, at Culham, near Oxford, are building the de-accelerators that give access to any slice of a space-time's profile—in this case, our own and its chequered history.'

'And where do matchstick figures belong in these equations?'

Francis stretched his arms before his attention returned to me.

'You and Alex will leave our current space-time together. The timing will depend on physical alignments in the sky and how dark matter is distributed throughout the cosmos.'

'And then what? A trip back in time?'

'Not quite, but you will enter a timeless dimension. The philosopher Epicurus called this region the inter mundia, describing it as a zone where worlds are formed in sudden outbursts of creation.'

'The Roman writer Lucretius outlined these concepts in a poem,' added Jane.

I nodded, not sure what they were talking about.

'The purpose of this zone,' said Francis, 'is to provide access to the past of any cosmic entity. But once you've committed, you'll need a guide to bring you home again.'

I eased back in my chair. 'Great,' I said, clasping my hands as if everything had been solved. Even Alex, I noticed, braved a ragged smile.

'Well, Richard, be prepared for a surprise: you are the guide.'

'You're kidding?'

'No,' said Jane, dislodging any doubt.

'Alex will continue his journey alone to the start point of the modern age.' Francis placed his finger at the edge of the poster.

'You, Richard, will stay in the intermediate zone and wait for him to return.'

I was trying to find fault with a proposal that sounded logical, but irrational, while my less than serious scepticism wasn't making headway, either. But I was still looking for flaws.

'Alex will re-configure the modern world at its point of inception. The outcome, once he returns, is that many chapters of history will no longer trouble us … not least, Alex's fateful encounter nor the upheaval that threatens to ensue. Otto has the list of our revisions in the British Museum.'

'So how do I coax Alex back into this cosmic tunnel when he's due to return?'

'No, Francis. Let me explain.' Alex lifted the alabaster figure from the table. 'When I enter the past, another person will travel in an opposite direction as a substitute for me.'

'This obeys the law of harmony,' said Jane. 'And means that space-time configurations which are in contact are also in balance.' An uncertain smile trailed her words.

'Who?' I asked, conscious of the object in Alex's hands.

'A girl,' said Alex. 'Someone my age who is native to the place I shall visit. You might meet her as she passes through the inter mundia.'

'A native girl?'

'Yes.' Francis took charge of the figurine before passing it to Jane. 'Your focus should be on Alex, and when the lab guys reverse the transfer, you will lead him back to us and a radically new future for everyone. Meanwhile, the native girl will return to her own people as if nothing had happened.'

'Can't your lab geeks do this without me, Francis?'

'No. We must step out of space-time altogether before entering a different dimension.'

'You're the visceral thread, Richard, leading Alex back to our shores.'

And through the labyrinth of the Minotaur, I recalled. 'When is this supposed to happen? I might need to set expectations once I pop home. Perhaps a hint over Christmas lunch before we set the pudding on fire.'

'There won't be time for that.' Francis pulled the map from in front of me. 'We launch next Tuesday. Around 10 pm.'

'In four days?'

'Yes. When the planetary alignments are at their strongest.'

Eight days before Christmas, I thought, before remembering an email and my laptop. 'By the way, you haven't mentioned your friends, Paulo or Kalinsky, Francis?'

'No longer required,' he said, rolling up the cosmos like an ancient scroll.

'And old conflicts or famines?' I asked.

'Some of them shape us, of course.' He got to his feet and thrust the map at Alex, catching him on the chin. 'Part of the grim learning curve of life. We don't want to change everything.'

'Not even families or friends?'

'Depends on their bonding and resilience. You know, Richard, if you'd shown more patience the other night, I could have shown you how everything turns out.'

'That's why we did your horoscope, Richard. So you wouldn't be afraid,' said Jane.

I ran my fingers through my hair. 'And what then, Francis? A new Golden Age?'

'Not at first. But there'll be changes in many of its socio-political aspects, of course. Different seats of power. Different goals. There's enough material in the social sciences to give us a firm direction on that. In fact, when we were studying Karl Marx, we were impressed with many ideas that we found in his PhD.'

'Karl Marx? PhD?'

'Yes. On Democritus and Epicurus. He started out as a classicist, you know.'

I looked at Jane. 'What kind of utopia are you building? What are you asking me to do, Francis?'

'Richard. On Tuesday evening, at the Globe theatre, Bankside, there is a late-night performance of Christopher Marlowe's play Doctor Faustus. I want you and Alex to attend. We will give you further instructions based around entrances and exits in the play. The main action will follow Faustus's invocation of satanic forces.'

'Satan?' I laughed.

'Yes. In the first act.' He smiled at Jane. 'In the meantime, Alex has something he wants to discuss with you. Stick together and remember your lines.'

'So you're not giving me any choice in the matter, then?'

'There is no choice. That's how Democritus built his atomic model, and it's how Marx interpreted history. Everything is inevitable. Your presence at the Globe is one of them, whatever else you think.'

'Just like your presence in Senate House, Richard, when we found you gazing at the "Triumphal Arch".'

'I was gazing at Durer's drawing, Jane, because the uni's IT systems had crashed and I couldn't enrol on my studies.'

'The machinations of fate, I'm afraid.' Francis checked his wristwatch. He gestured to Jane before she returned the figurine to the bookshelf. Alex sat still, reconciled, I assumed, to what was coming his way.

'Looks like we've got to see a play, Alex.'

'And don't doubt it,' said Francis. 'You may think you are free to decide, but the fact is, your choice was pre-ordained when the world was created.'

'No, the fact is, it wasn't. And if you'd read your Epicurus better, you'd realise that he doesn't buy it either. The swerve, remember, and atoms doing their own thing. On their own. Without compulsion.'

He scoffed. 'There's no such thing as freewill. Marx ridiculed it. So do modern philosophers.' Francis grabbed his coat from my bed before searching the pockets. 'Just one more thing.' He handed both me and Alex a small tracking device to keep with us in the theatre. 'Set them on when you arrive. Our technical team will use them to pinpoint your co-ordinates.' He turned to Jane as she knotted her scarf. 'We need to catch Otto at the museum. He wants more details from me about the specification.'

Jane gave Alex a hug and joined Francis by the door.

Standing up, I pushed my chair aside. 'Don't take me for granted, Francis. I can throw the spanner in this if I choose.' But my words went unheeded as they hurried down the stairs.

I crossed my room and gently closed the door. My head was full of nonsense and mangled worlds, and now a play featuring devils and a trapdoor to hell. I drew a deep breath before turning to my friend. 'This person for whose death you feel responsible, Alex ...'

He stared back at me.

'It must have happened either earlier this year or the autumn of last. Right?'

'Yes. More than a year ago. Did someone say?'

'No. But it was the reason you couldn't go to Delos last summer.'

Alex nodded. 'Because of the temple of Apollo, Richard.'

'That's right. Anyone accused of blood crimes is forbidden access to the precincts of a temple.' I moved closer. 'So you stayed at home. While Francis dug for artifacts on the island.'

'I was ashamed.'

'Who was it, Alex ... who died?'

'Someone I knew.'

'You said. But who?'

He looked down before speaking. 'It was Francis's brother ... his younger brother. And I let him drown.'

I went into the bathroom and threw up.

35

'Of man's first disobedience and the fruit … thereof.'

James lingered on the words, hearing the soft echo of his late tutor's voice. He stepped towards the window of his fourth-floor study and the dull light of a bleak December day. A steady rain sealed the glass, drowning the empty courtyard below. Like the winter fens of Cambridge, he remembered. Vague and indefinite. A sea of land and sky that drifted in the mind … evoking long ago. And distant heady days. Corpus Christi, he recalled, touching the pane of glass, and the memory of his tutor calling to him in his youth. He had been a Party man since '45, recalled James. A young Marxist radical, his tutor had claimed. Fierce and rebellious, but alone. Drawn, as were others, by a hungry, piercing eye and the steady beat of a shy, restless passion. James raised a glass of scotch to his lips, catching his tutor's face. Remembering gestures and small gifts. The stiff etiquette of Master's Lawn. He sipped. Tasting once more those awkward, collegiate smiles. Those last words and final handshakes. Those still, yearning eyes.

A photograph, signed and framed, stared from the wall. June '84 and graduation. He sipped again as his thoughts, like whispers, stirred a troubled soul.

* * *

'James?' A voice came to life, straining beside a modest, open fire. 'Tutor?'

'Yes … Marcus. You do remember, James?'

James stepped closer. His eyes narrowed as he searched the low-ceilinged room in a fading light. 'Marcus? Is it you? Here? In my office?'

His tutor nodded.

James froze, unsure if he'd woken in a dream or had been struck by a hypnotic spell. He stepped forward. Surely not?

Marcus beckoned towards the old wooden desk. 'Here. In your favourite place near the fire. There's always a small draught by the college windows.' He pulled the sleeves of his cardigan higher and settled back with a smile.

James hurried to the desk. He sat and faced his tutor, clutching a handwritten essay in his lap.

'It's been so long,' said Marcus, wiping a tear.

'Thirty-five years, tutor.'

'And you've done so well, I see.'

'Oh, the Foreign Office.' He shied his face, sensing a sudden blush.

'Intelligence too, I believe.'

'Yes. Director.' He shied again. 'Various operations. It keeps me busy.'

Marcus wet his lips. A query crept into his voice. 'Some sort of committee, I hear … with the Americans, isn't it?' He reached for a fountain pen that was a parting gift from James on his last day as a student at Cambridge.

'Yes. Briefings mainly, tutor. But other things too.' He looked away. An old gramophone player from the nineteen forties caught his eye.

Marcus leant forward. 'Well, well, well. MI5.' He scribbled a few words on a sheaf of paper as a reminder. Pausing, he examined the pen, and the initials inscribed along the case. 'And your young lady, if I remember. Did you ever…?'

'No, we never did. There was someone else, I believe.'

'Like so many of us. The past is a hell of our own making, James.'

Marcus rose and moved towards the fire as its heat drew moisture to his eyes. He crouched low and landed on a knee. From a battered, metal bucket, he threw small lumps of coal to the rear of the fire's dwindling stack. 'All there is, I'm afraid. Until old porter does his rounds.' He went back to his chair. 'What was it they called me? The eighth man? Or was it the ninth in our Soviet entanglement?' He placed his hands together. 'Traitor, they sneered. And enemy of the state. But I didn't care. There were many of us, you know. We wanted to change things, damn it. For the better.' He sat upright, pursing his lips in angry defiance.

James watched the innocent flames. There was nothing left to hide. The fleeting loyalties. The snares and ploys of an endless game of spies amidst the fussy ceremonies of college protocol. His eyes shifted. A solitary book lay on the tutor's desk. And near, a strew of angry pamphlets from England's revolutionary age. The voice of radicals, he recalled. Of Levellers and regicides. Dog-eared and tobacco-stained from his tutor's constant study.

A sulphurous flame cast shadows against the walls.

Marcus reached for the book, lifting it with both hands. 'So … Paradise Lost,' he declared, looking into James's eyes. 'Where were we?'

'Book 6, tutor. The War in Heaven.'

'I remember. And the angel Raphael's account to Adam.' Marcus opened his cigarette case and selected a cigarette from behind a protective band. He coughed. 'So what is Milton telling us? What is he driving at?'

'Obedience. God was angry, tutor.'

'Obedience, James.' He held the cigarette in his mouth and reached for a box of matches. 'And why was your God angry?'

'Because Satan had rebelled.'

'Because Satan hated the system.' Marcus's voice hardened. 'Satan demanded justice. Not privilege for the Son. Or endless praise by God's fawning angels.' He drew heavily on the cigarette before coughing again.

'But Milton was not siding with Satan, tutor. Adam had earlier comforted Eve after her evil dream when the Serpent tempted her.' He turned the pages of his essay. 'Here, Book 4. And Satan's torment at the godly perfection of Adam and Eve.'

'Milton was of the devil's party but didn't know it.' Marcus stared at James. 'William Blake, man.' A flame in the fireplace danced higher, shifting light and shadows along the wall. Marcus placed the cigarette on a saucer. The ash fell away. 'Politics, James … politics was never far from Milton's mind. Or Cromwell. Or the obstinate Stuart king. Whose side do you think he was on?'

'He was standing by his principles, tutor.'

'He was standing in Whitehall when the King was executed.' Marcus snapped the case shut. 'He was Cromwell's secretary. He was a rebel. Like us, James. Like Satan.'

'But Satan was no democrat. He exalted himself, tutor. He declared himself above his own angels.'

'Satan needed to impose authority,' said Marcus, his voice sharpening. 'Without discipline, the system defeats everyone. His followers understood that. That's why they made sacrifices for their leader.'

'His followers understood nothing, tutor. They butchered themselves and others. He was a fraud. His chief officers were Sin and Death. He led his followers to the grave. Millions of them.'

Marcus left his desk and crossed to the window. Drops of rain seeped through the ill-fitting metal frames, leaving a puddle on the painted sill. He turned and faced James with folded arms—his tobacco raised sentinel at his elbow.

'So, these students. What do you make of them?'

'Committed, I would say.'

'We all were.' Marcus searched a trouser pocket for his matches. He re-lit the cigarette, glancing obliquely as he steadied the flame. 'Marxists, by any chance?'

'I don't think so. But radical.'

'And their tutors?'

'London based, but at least one in Oxford.'

'Good. We had cells in both. Do they have a plan?'

'Yes. To re-order the world according to their beliefs and objectives.'

'So was ours. But their chances, James?'

'Their chances, tutor?' James glanced at his essay. 'Somewhat greater than your own, I believe.'

'Really? Who are they?'

James crossed his legs. 'There are four students. Three males and a female. University College London.'

'And their backgrounds?'

'Jane is from a military family though a classicist by training.'

'Military. I always found them quite loyal.' He rubbed his chin. 'At least the chaps. Athletic, of course. The hearty sort. They cared little for our politics.' He drew on his cigarette. 'But a classicist, you say?'

'Yes. But her friend Francis is the real thinker within the group.'

'The group's ideologue. A Leninist, maybe?'

'A mathematician. Not easily deflected. Has the final say.'

'Like me.' Marcus rested his hands on the sill of the window. A tower of ash fell to the floor.

'Perhaps. Though he's often in conflict with one other member of their group.'

'Who?'

'Alex Rowdesley. A turbulent young man.'

'It'll be their downfall. Like Trotsky.' He drew again. 'You said there were four.'

'Yes, Richard. Richard Addings. He's a recent recruit and not sure if he belongs.' James shifted in his chair. 'Studies literature, but art history too.'

'And his background?'

'Oh, unexceptional.' James wiped a little perspiration from his forehead. 'Suburban upbringing and package holidays. His father's a salesman.'

'Lower middle class, then.' Marcus returned to the desk before stubbing out the cigarette in the yellow-stained saucer. 'We saw a few, of course. They'd come up through the grammar schools. Over-studious, I always said. Prudish, too.' He yawned, stretching the lines that scarred his face. 'But is he committed?'

'Conflicted, I'd say.'

'Doubt nurtures rebellion, you know.' Marcus locked his hands behind his head, fixing his eyes on his undergraduate friend. 'Peel-back the covers of any young man and you'll discover more.' He lowered his arms. 'But art history, you say?' James nodded. 'I was nineteen, I remember. Just after the war ended. Punting on the Cam. Worried about the world and its destructive potential.' He adjusted his sleeves as an acrid smell drifted from the saucer. 'I'd attended lots of debates and the usual society balls. Party meetings too, sometimes here, but sometimes in London. The things you and I did almost forty years later. There were trysts, of course. It wasn't just politics that seduced us.' A coal fell from the fire, flaring as it rolled from the iron grate. They watched it burn until the flame flickered and died. 'But their controller, James? You haven't said.'

'No. But based in the British Museum. There are other academics at the university. But we have our own people there.' James exam-ined his fingernails, slipping eye contact with his tutor.

'I remember.' Marcus left his chair and knelt beside the fire. He returned the coal to the flames with a pair of blackened tongs, star-ing as the heat warmed his face. 'It was six in the morning when I was arrested. Bundled out. Humiliated in front of the college staff. I was sixty-four. The past was forgotten. The Wall had fallen.' He got to his feet. 'I thought you were one of us. A Party man. Against the missiles and the bases. We marched together, remember?' Marcus wiped a tear as he heard the flames splutter. 'But the talent spotters of MI5 had already found you. Even at twenty, you'd sold out … before you cheated on me.' He clutched his chest with his left arm and coughed again. He spat phlegm into the fire.

James placed his essay on the desk. 'There were still loose ends, tutor. Your case was never closed. Eighth man or ninth? We wanted to know.'

'I was taken to a hotel in Bloomsbury. It was October '92. Eight years after you'd left the college. Clinton was heading for the White House. The old Soviet Guard had gone. China had changed course.' He clenched his fists. 'Five days, I suffered. Interrogation. No sleep. I told them everything, damn it.' He gripped the chair before sitting down. 'The hardest part was your betrayal.'

Marcus cried.

'We made different choices. Different loyalties, tutor.'

'To your class, James.'

'No! To fundamental freedoms,' said James. 'The right to make our own decisions. To build our own future. Not one imposed through the suppression of revolts. Like Budapest. Or Prague. Or Gdansk.'

Marcus slammed the desk. 'There is no free choice. Freewill is a delusion. Historical necessity drives us forward.' He lifted Milton's heavy text, thrusting it at James as his face hardened. 'Your God lied. He knew perfectly well what would happen in Eden. The Temptation was his own fabrication, a false flag to fool his priests and cover-up his own mistakes. The Expulsion was inevitable.' He placed the book on his desk and turned to the fire. 'Only the Party understands. Only the Party can save us.'

'But Adam chose of his own freewill. God gave him this right. Milton makes this clear. Even if he foresaw the consequences.' James found the page. 'Here, tutor. Book 5 Raphael to Adam "thy will, by nature free, not over-ruled by fate … or strict necessity".'

'Raphael was sent to Adam to get God off the hook, man.' Marcus waved his hand. 'Eve broke away. She knew intuitively. Look at her account of their useless work in the Garden of Eden. She'd even figured out the division of labour to earn her keep. Satan promised her equality and freedom from suffocating constraints. Book 9, James, where the Serpent opens her eyes.' Marcus rose and stepped quietly towards the door of his room. He turned the key before moving back to his desk. He stood alongside his student. 'Remember how we read the plot together? The forbidden fruit.' James trembled. 'Eve was ready to experiment. She wanted knowledge of the real world. The Serpent was only doing his job, James. Raising her consciousness. Of the class struggle.' He returned to his chair. 'While gullible, starry-eyed, Adam was busy pruning his master's plants. Like you. And the rest of society.'

James stared at Milton's text. Maybe his tutor was right, he thought. At least this was no rehash of Genesis, propounded in blank, lilting verse. Milton was making a point. Eve had struck out. On this, they'd both agreed. She'd argued with Adam, questioning their happy state, and the confines of their Maker. And she'd proposed a separation. And a trial. A test of resolve in the face of authority and temptation. He closed the text. But freewill or destiny, he wondered.

Marcus re-opened the cigarette case. 'If Adam chose, then he chose out of disgust at his servitude. And his ignorance.' He lit another cigarette and drew on its harsh breath. 'Even Michelangelo shows him storming out of Eden with his arms thrown back.' He flicked the dead match into the fire.

'Then, like Adam, tutor, perhaps young Richard and his rebellious friends will storm out of this world and hurl us into the next.'

'Rebels?' Marcus sneered. 'Bourgeois decadents. Angst-ridden aesthetes. Their only privilege is their delusion.' He pushed back in his chair. 'We had no time for pastoral conceits. Or blue remembered hills. We were the rebels, man. We fought in Spain on the Ebro. And in the suburbs of Barcelona.' Marcus dropped his head. 'They'll be rounded up. As we were, James. Laughed at and disowned … even by their own comrades.' His voice trailed, dwindling like the wispy smoke that staled the passive air.

A clock ticked. James looked up, noting the time. 'Tutor. Is there anything else before I slip away for supper in the refectory?'

'Yes, er … Book 9. I think you know the passage.' He removed a handkerchief from a drawer and wiped his eyes.

'Where Eve confesses to Adam?'

'Where they both sin, man.'

James swallowed. He read the text. '"Adam has tasted the fruit".'

'"At Eve's behest." Read Milton's words, exactly, please.'

'"Fairer now than ever. Bounty of this virtuous tree". James paused as his eyes skipped ahead. '"Her hand … he seized, and to a shady bank, thick overhead with verdant roof … he led her".'

'"Nothing loath", said Marcus, closing his eyes, filling his lungs with sweet draughts of air.

'"Flowers were the couch", tutor. "Violets and asphodel. And there". Blushing, James lingered as a heartbeat stole his breath. '"And there, their fill of love … and love's disport … their mutual guilt the seal". He let go of the book.

They shared the cigarette. And their languor. But the sound of footsteps outside the door caused them to start. James snatched his clothes from a chair.

'It's okay.' Marcus placed a finger to his lips. 'Its only porter. He'll knock first.'

They remained still, their eyes drawn to the fire. And the wild ecstatic flames of desire.

* * *

'They say Kalinsky was shot.'

'Yes,' said James, turning his head. He reached for his scotch.

'They say it happened in London. Near the museum.'

James shifted uneasily. 'So I heard.'

'Recently, I believe.' Marcus laughed as James, unsettled by the disclosure, rose to his feet and stepped back from the table. 'You know, he worked for us, James. And that I was his controller in the UK.'

'Yes. A KGB operation in the eighties, I gather. We have the details, tutor. Including his later career as a freelancer and Bank of England employee.'

'He fooled you, James. We all fooled you. You and your American cronies.'

'No, tutor. You fooled yourselves.'

'We offered hope to an oppressed world. We were the future.'

'You dealt in death. You silenced your critics.'

Marcus stood. 'We all did.' He thrust his finger at James. 'You had Kalinsky shot. You tried to kill him. To get your revenge on me, damn it.'

'You took advantage of me, tutor. When I was weak and alone.'

'I gave you what you wanted, remember? Nothing loathe. And then you cheated on me. Groomed by your minders in MI5.'

'You seduced me, Marcus.'

'Yes. Here. On the floor. Because you were willing and ready.'

'You lie, tutor. You lie.'

'Arrest the students. It is your duty. These are my orders from the Party. Or the struggle will fail.'

'No, curse you. No. The students are free. Free to choose. Free to make their own lives and carve their own destiny.'

James leapt across his study, and seizing the old photograph from the wall, threw it to the floor. Smashing the rigid frame. Shattering the glass. Stamping the memory beneath angry, frenzied feet.

36

A small, tender voice cried out.

Caught amidst the sharp spikes that protruded from a wooden beam, a sparrow, startled and afraid, struggled above my head. I reached up and took the small creature into my hand, its delicate feathers barely matting a soft, skeletal frame, or dampening the beat of its frantic heart. I rested the bird against my chest, watching as its dark, glassy eyes fixed on mine until its head drooped, gently and quietly, on to its breast.

Its pulse ceased. I looked away, feeling humbled. Being and non-being, I recalled, as I slipped the dead bird into my pocket not sure what to do with it. But it was not alone. The alabaster figurine offered silent company as I settled back in my seat.

Francis had chosen the line about existence—being and non-being—from the opening speech of Marlowe's play, 'Doctor Faustus'. I was in the upper gallery of the Globe theatre, near the river Thames in London's Bankside, sitting on a rustic-style bench that overlooked the yard thirty feet below me. Above the yard, the thatched roof was open to the sky. The walls were made of English oak and an ochre-coloured plaster that formed a twenty-sided polygon which, according to a note in the programme, was modelled on the original construction of the year 1600. It was 10pm, and still another week to Christmas Eve. The air was damp, and the temperature was dropping. I fixed my eyes on the stage as the lighting faded. A thick pullover and a padded jacket kept me warm.

Faustus stepped forward holding a heavy, symbol-encrusted book. A skull cap covering a shaven head gave him the air of a medieval scholastic. He was deep in thought and looked gravely sinister.

Francis's instructions were to sit still until the world was successfully re-engineered. It wouldn't take long: scene three, he'd declared, and a flash that would trigger a cosmic overhaul and restore whatever Alex had fatefully disturbed by his reckless actions. I glanced around. Both Francis and Jane were in the Globe's lower gallery, one tier below mine. Alex was somewhere in the yard amongst the groundlings, standing in front of the stage. We all had our parts to play, said Francis as we'd entered the Globe together. I'd grinned at his remark, checked my own lines and then switched on the tracking device. I was playing along for Alex, of course. The alignments and planetary coordinates, I was assured, for everyone else.

I watched Faustus raise his arm, drawing the attention of the crowd. They moved closer. A tremor ran through the oak beams, as if shivering with the night's cold.

I'd spent the last two hours arguing with the others. If the death of Francis's brother was an accident—I'd said to Alex—then maybe you weren't to blame. Or maybe you were just out of your mind, mate. Even the ancient Greeks blamed the irrational, I shouted, as we'd wandered, disconnected and emotional, around the backstreets of Bankside before the start of the Globe's late-night performance. You mean, just forget it and walk away, he'd countered? And then what? And then … you accept it. Like what's happened. Like what you've done. Even to a friend. You mean, to Francis's own brother, he retorted? Yes, Alex. Yes! But he was resistant to my pleas. Steadfast with his friends. The same binding loyalty I'd always known for all his bravado and willingness to stand up or stand out. And helpless, too, as Francis lectured on fate and how

Alex, like a debt compounded, was the turbulence damning time and place to come. Then Jane reminded me of my horoscope. My own actions and future. But we couldn't agree. And I'd mocked their plans and her intentions, telling her how she wanted Alex back, back in her arms, whatever the consequences or their high-minded goals or their brotherly love … until she'd slapped my face as we'd stood under the road bridge by the old Rose theatre, close to the Globe, tearful and exhausted before Alex led us away, head bowed. And we'd followed. And Francis gave me my instructions, and we took our seats. If this was destiny, I was still kicking at it like a cornered child.

I looked up, hearing a groan from the rafters. A ray of light alerted me to a figure crouching on the roof. I listened for sounds before turning back to the performance. 'All things that move between the quiet poles shall be at my command', said Faustus, entrancing the audience. I checked my own lines as Faustus summoned his servant.

O little bird, I thought. Would Francis insist that your sad demise was fated, too?

I'd told Francis when he and Jane came to my flat that I would make my own decision. I wasn't heading for the inter mundia or Alex for the birthplace of the modern world, if I chose otherwise. But the dilemma wasn't real, anyway. Like the tale of Atlantis. So Alex won't be lost or saved. The world won't be changed. The future will look after itself even if it chides us for our vanities along the way. That was destiny. I slipped the tracker into the empty pocket at my side. The good and bad angels entered the stage. 'O Faustus, lay that damned book aside,' said one. Before the other, full of pride, whispered slyly: 'Be thou on earth as Jove is in the sky.'

Faustus smiled.

I was not unmoved by Alex's confession. And still perplexed by events in London and the behaviour of the tutors at Oxford when I went for my interview towards the end of 2018. So if a magician's spell changed a million hearts, and saved a younger brother drowned … well, who would not pause and make a wish? Except the cosmos wasn't mine to rearrange, or the fate of others to dissolve. I shook my head before reaching again for the tracker. There is providence in the fall of a sparrow, I mused, remembering a line from a tragic Shakespeare play … oh, sod you, Hamlet. I'd shoved my hand into the wrong pocket. I let go of the bird.

Above me, there was more noise from the roof. And maybe whispers. Was it a disturbance, I wondered, to unsettle the audience and set their nerves on edge? Much like the wide-eyed toad that stared at us from Faustus's bookshelf, threatening to leap across the stage. But the intrusion was brief, and the toad wasn't real, so I settled into scene two of Marlowe's notorious drama. A boy, conveying wine, teased two scholars with his wit, and then made a mischievous show of not answering their question. They both looked puzzled by his cheek; the audience, by his flashy display of Latin as he answered back. I didn't care. Francis had written a translation for me in case I was caught out.

I'd boasted about my acquaintance with the University Wits on my first day at uni. The Wits, a group of Cambridge-based dramatists and writers, heralded the onset of Elizabethan drama in the 1590s. The best of them, Christopher Marlowe, or Kit as he was fondly known, was also a spy. He liked travel too and wasn't averse to clipping the coinage if it suited him. His first play made him a star, alongside his pal Thomas Kyd, but an underlying instability in his temperament sealed his fate. Play writing and epic verses soon lost out to the anxieties of murderous politics, and in May 1593, the darling of the muses met his end. A great, if final, reckoning as Shakespeare intriguingly recalled in act three of 'As You Like It'. Even if you didn't.

The lights dimmed as the smell of incense wafted around the Globe.

Faustus, dressed heavily in black, knelt alone in the centre of the stage where he drew a circle in chalk and then another within its circumference. He divided the circles into twenty-two segments before writing the symbols of the zodiac, the four elements—water, fire, earth, and air—as well as the planets, in each successive segment. He scribbled the names of saints backwards and forwards, cursing them with his lips as he wrote. Rising to his feet, he turned to the groundlings. Another tremor struck the building and the planks under my feet. I glanced towards the sky and an open roof that spared the galleries but not the yard from rain. Or the heavens. The audience hushed as Faustus drew closer. He opened his book of spells and read aloud. 'Sint mihi dei Acherontis propitii' May the gods of Hell be propitious to me, I echoed. The trigger. Faustus threw water around the stage. His boy, ashen faced, fled the stage, toppling the candelabra and its seven candles. I checked the roof. Another figure and more noise, like scrambling. And as the lights flickered wildly, I saw Alex stare back at me, his face pale and drawn. This must be it, I realised. The countdown and the end. Faustus cried out: 'Prince of the east. Monarch of burning Hell. Mephistopheles. Rise to us on our command.' The ground trembled. The building swayed. I shot up from my seat as Lucifer's servant burst upon the stage, writhing in slime and excrement. The audience froze. 'Now, Faustus,' the demon asked, 'what wouldst thou have me do?'

The theatre shook violently, and in a flash of lightning, I glimpsed a young man descend towards the stage as others lowered him by a rope. People screamed. They shifted, unsure whether to stay or flee. I left the gallery, but the staircase moved and the walls heaved around me. I scrambled back, ready to leap to the ground. But the crowd had turned violent and become delirious. An army, like a phalanx of the slain, marched into the yard. Persephone, the queen of the dead, rose from a rat-infested grave. There were shouts of Agincourt and Elsinore. Severed heads and limbs floated through the air. Stunned, I watched as Helen of Troy was ritually strangled while cadavers, with gloating eyes, devoured her flesh. This isn't Marlowe or Bankside, I thought. This is hell and damnation.

'Alex,' I screamed, as the building burned around me and I struggled to breathe. But amidst the darkening abyss and to the sound of a tolling bell, I saw a female face. I opened my arms, desperate for her help and her embrace.

But with a roar, the earth swallowed us. And then the raging sea.

37

Otto ended the call to Culham.

Two hours of anguished discussion had left him exhausted, but still convinced he was poised to rescue an ungrateful world. He re-examined the array of numbers that filled his computer screen, reflecting on a genetic code that would reconfigure the past and alter the path of human destiny before catastrophe overwhelmed it. He rose from his desk and stood by the window of his second-floor office in the British Museum. Fallen masonry and wrecked cars showed the chaos his team had unleashed the evening before. And yet the operation had failed to complete as planned and expected. The labours of renewal, he realised, were proving more protracted.

Otto slipped out of the museum by an unmarked exit. An unusual cold gripped the city, and an icy, blustery wind kept his head down as he hurried to the apartment of Francis and Jane, avoiding debris and shoals of tiles scattered across the empty streets. The front door of a terraced house opened as he approached. After shaking snow from his shoes, he went inside without speaking.

'They're both upstairs,' said Francis, closing the door against a sudden gust of air. 'We found them by the river, early this morning, as the weather turned violent and unpredictable.'

Otto wiped his feet. 'Eddie briefed me before I phoned the team in Culham.' He loosened his scarf and unbuttoned his coat. 'And Jane?'

'She's upset.'

'And you?'

'Confused. Not everything has worked, Otto.'

'I know. But the shortfall lay in the execution, not the overall plan.'

Francis led the way to the third floor of an early Victorian building in the heart of London's Bloomsbury, a district once known for its radicals and trendy intellectuals in the first half of the twentieth century.

Jane waited at the top of the stairs. 'They're sleeping, now,' she said. 'When we arrived, I gave them tranquilisers.'

Otto hugged her. 'There will be another chance, Jane. The upheaval isn't over yet.'

'Alex is lost,' said Jane, her voice wavering as she returned his embrace. 'We don't know where he is, or in which year he has landed.'

They followed Francis into the apartment.

Otto glanced around as he settled into a leather armchair. The dining table, he noticed, was pushed against the limestone fireplace. A drawing-room lamp threw half its light against the pale damask wallpaper while the smell of incense lingered in the air. On a makeshift bed alongside the sofa, the alabaster figurine lay discarded. Otto turned to his younger companions. 'Where is the native girl?' he asked.

'In my room,' said Jane, sitting down on the sofa. 'Richard is in Francis's.'

'We slept here on the floor,' explained Francis as he joined Jane.

'We must get Richard into the inter mundia.' Otto glanced down before continuing. 'I've told Culham to fix new coordinates for our next attempt. But they want details of Richard's movements during the performance to confirm their equations.'

'The play started at 10.00 pm, Otto. Fifteen minutes after we arrived.' Francis shared a smile with Jane. 'I gave Alex and Richard their devices and a list of prompts and explanations before we entered the theatre.'

'To the seating places we had identified beforehand?'

'Yes. We checked the geo-coordinates with an app. I showed Richard to his seat in the upper gallery, while Jane followed Alex into the yard where the groundlings were congregating around the projecting stage. She then joined me in the lower gallery where we had a box to ourselves.'

'Could you see them from where you were sitting?'

Jane nodded. 'At one point, Richard stood up and grabbed something above his head. But he returned to his seat as the scene started and Faustus spoke his lines.'

'Where in the script did you alert Culham to your arrival?'

'Being and non-being,' said Francis. 'Once Faustus had uttered the words in Greek, I sent a pre-arranged signal.' He reached for Jane's hand, blushing as she squeezed it. 'And then we followed our own instructions.'

Otto remained pensive. He recalled a sequence of numbers in his head. The quantum physics team would have opened the portal on the IZ, as they called it, once they had received the message from Francis. This would allow the subsequent transfer of Alex and Richard to their destinations later in the evening.

'Then the good and bad angels entered the stage,' said Jane.

'Faustus's conscience,' said Francis, rubbing his eyes as he settled back in the sofa.

'Yes. The oppositional polarity of the angels helped fix Alex to his target space-time and his counterpart to ours.'

'Just before he vanished from the Globe,' said Francis.

'But not Richard,' said Jane. 'I could see him in the gallery before he fled from his seat.' She rose to her feet and stepped towards Otto. 'We did everything that you asked. Everything.' Her face fell as she glanced back at Francis. 'Richard has abandoned us, Otto. I think he lost his nerve.'

Otto pressed his hands together as he considered their situation. Alex had departed this world while the native girl had appeared from hers and was asleep in the adjacent bedroom. The transfer of the parties and Alex's rewriting of the past should have occurred instantly. Instead, the execution had become protracted and left incomplete. 'What happened before Mephistopheles emerged from the pit?'

'Alex was looking up,' replied Jane, 'trying to attract Richard's attention from the yard.'

'The earth tremors became stronger,' said Francis. 'Gentle at first, before they felt like seismic waves.' He yawned. 'The audience assumed the vibration was part of the performance and was unconcerned.'

'The play was our cover, of course,' said Otto. 'The reputation of Marlowe's drama has always been satanic.'

'Then Alex disappeared in the confusion,' said Jane. 'And we can't say what has become of him or whether he's alive.'

Francis joined Jane. Taking her hands, he looked into her eyes. 'We have the young lady. So long as she is safe, Alex is safe. If Richard lost his way or his confidence, we must help him … to help Alex.'

'But the friendship with Alex has failed. Nothing is going to change. No one is coming back.' Jane turned away. 'This always was our fate and we have to accept it.'

'No,' snapped Francis. 'The outcome is destined. It will happen. And my brother will live again once Alex rejoins us.'

'Your brother is dead, Francis,' said Jane.

'I know that. There's no need to remind me. It's why history must change to save him.'

Otto stood. 'Francis. Did Richard lose his nerve?'

'I can't be sure. It could be inevitable. Maybe that's how he's supposed to decide as part of his fate.' He shut his eyes, quelling a sudden flicker. 'And ours until we try again.'

Jane folded her arms. 'Tell Otto what happened outside the theatre.'

'There was an argument,' said Francis. 'I think Richard was confused and emotional.'

'He was adamant,' insisted Jane. 'He wanted us to back off, Otto, and accused me of being selfish and wanting …' Jane's voice faltered. 'We were in tears. And then Alex headed for the Globe. And Richard followed.' She bent down and retrieved the figurine from the floor. 'But his heart wasn't in it.'

'And Alex?' asked Otto, sharply.

'Alex wouldn't budge,' said Francis. 'He was determined to go ahead. Whatever arguments Richard made, he still felt he was to blame for my brother's drowning and the consequences that will follow.' Francis turned to Jane. 'Look, we saw Richard sitting in his seat. He was in the right position when it mattered, Jane. The location ID on his tracker was enough to keep him in the action.'

'Well, he didn't disable it. Culham picked up the signal from the device.' Otto returned to his chair. 'Describe the moment Faustus appealed to the darkness.'

'He drew a circle in chalk. Stepped into the centre and called on Mephistopheles to join him from the depths. "Sint mihi dei Acherontis … propitii."' said Francis, repeating the line from the play.

'May the gods of hell be propitious to me.'

Francis shrugged. 'And then, amidst flashes of lightning, I sent the confirmation code on my phone.'

'Which was the cue for Richard to transfer with Alex to the inter mundia before Alex continued his journey alone.'

'But Richard stayed in the theatre,' said Jane.

'What was he doing, Francis?'

'We couldn't see, Otto. Everything was in chaos. The place was alight. People were fighting and screaming. There was total confusion on stage … one play merging into another. No beginning or end.'

'There was something else,' said Jane. 'I heard scrambling above our heads and saw a rope dangle from the roof to the stage as we lay together. Before the vortex swept us away.'

'I didn't notice. We then found ourselves in the street outside, but on our feet.'

'Before you searched for the others?' asked Otto.

'Yes,' replied Jane. 'We just assumed they were together nearby.'

'A crowd gathered in front of the theatre,' added Francis. 'And as they dealt with the fire, running a hose from the Thames at low tide, we discovered Richard and the young lady on the beach, the flames of the Globe throwing light on the water. They were in each other's arms, and barely conscious. The river lapped gently against their limbs.'

'The girl uttered a few native words,' said Jane. 'Eddie helped us get them into his cab, and we arrived here before the bridges and streets were blocked by the police.'

Francis nodded.

'Eddie phoned me afterwards. I let Culham know straight away.' Otto rose from his chair. 'Our next opportunity is the 24th when the planetary alignments will again be favourable.'

'We can't use the Globe theatre,' said Francis.

'Of course not. But we can use the underground chamber accessed from the museum. It hasn't been used since the war, but it is ideal for a communal gathering. I shall inform the Thirteen Elders of my plan.' Otto glanced at the figurine in Jane's hand. 'If our fragmenting cosmos doesn't frighten Richard into helping us, we'll need a dedicated ritual to persuade him and his bride.' He buttoned-up his coat and adjusted his scarf. 'Is there anything else I should tell our friends in Culham?'

Francis shook his head.

'Yes,' said Jane, as she moved to the dining table where she placed the figurine next to a padded envelope. 'I found this in the mud next to the statuette.' She emptied the envelope and stood aside.

'A bird,' said Otto.

'Yes. A sparrow. A small, dead sparrow.'

38

Warren Dudley stepped forward, and with the sweep of his hand, slapped his cowering subordinate hard across the face. He turned to William Carter. 'Tell this idiot the truth about these lying, phony numbers.'

'The Karlstad material is bullshit,' said William. 'It's a set-up by Britain's GCHQ. Felix Leighton runs the operation from Whitehall.' William handed Warren a two-sided report headed with the logo of the CIA. 'The specifics are listed here, including an assessment of the data's quality by my colleagues in Langley.'

'I trusted you and your team to analyse data,' said Warren, staring angrily at Larry Antony. 'I chose you for your expertise in IT and cryptography and yet I read this by our friends in the Agency: "Item: the works of art and lines of poetry used as covert communications show no underlying unity in their selection. Item: the encryption methods used to conceal information vary from simple substitution to complex formulations using techniques available in the public domain. Item: using computer analysis, no significant date or geographical coordinates have been derived from any of the transcripts. Conclusion: the intelligence has no credibility."' Warren crunched the page in his hand and threw it at the desert wastes of Babylon now hanging against the wall of his office. He returned to his desk.

'I'm deeply sorry, sir.' said Larry.

'Sorry?' said Warren, shifting in his chair. 'Explain to this imbecile, William, what happens next.'

'Your IT team will be disbanded, and your security clearance revoked. The London assignment is over, Mr Antony. Once you return to Washington, you will be subpoenaed to testify before a committee of inquiry.'

'But sir, the transcripts were marked top secret. James Ellison had the approval of his government.'

'We know, sir,' snapped Warren, 'that James Ellison is an intelligence director of Her Majesty's government. His loyalty, sir, is to the British Crown.' He leant forward at his desk. 'These people built a whole empire on deception. Their government has spent decades looking for this secret. Do you think our country will be safe if they discover it before we do?'

Larry wiped his eyes as he struggled with his composure.

'Pull yourself together, damn you,' said Warren, slamming the desk. 'While you slouched in bars, the students made a pact with the devil.'

'I don't think,' said William, suppressing a smile, 'that James Ellison knows anything more about the students' secret than we do.'

'That's right,' said Larry, glancing anxiously at his colleagues. 'That's why they were out to fool us. Like you said, sir … their James is an intelligence director.' He lowered his head, slipping eye contact with both William and his boss.

John Martin's Persian hordes, massing before the walls of Babylon, drew Warren's attention. He placed his hands together and looked down. Why did I trust this clown? Why were his parents allowed into my congregation? Warren closed his eyes. Lord, thou hast tested me and I have been found wanting. He fixed on his subordinate: 'Before I pass judgement on you, Antony, have you anything further to say?'

'Sir, the Brits are not my only source of information. I have a contact at the university.' Larry glanced warily at William as his posture steadied.

'Who?' asked William.

'An informant. In my pay.' Larry stepped closer to his boss. 'Sir, there's a new guy who has joined the students. His name is Addings, Richard Addings. I know where he lives.'

William folded his arms. 'There are lots of students in London, Warren. This sounds like another trap by British intelligence.'

'No, sir. Addings's flat is their base. The other students meet there. Rowdesley. Eggar and Shere. Even last week. On Saturday, talking about their plans. My informant … he's sure of this.'

'Then he must know their secret, too,' said Warren.

'That's right, sir. And what the satanists plan to do to our country.'

Warren switched his attention. 'Does the CIA know anything about him, William?'

William shook his head. 'Once we've made an official protest to the Foreign Office, it's time to pull out, Warren. We won't get anything else out of Whitehall.'

Warren considered his predicament. With the operation compromised, and the CIA losing interest, perhaps a direct approach would allow him to regain the advantage. His thoughts slipped back to his seminary days and his fellow warriors of truth. He looked again at John Martin's expansive scene. If Satan has been freed from the bottomless pit, he reflected, then scripture declares it is but a short while before he is recaptured for eternity. Sitting upright, he faced the others. 'I wish to speak to this young man as a matter of urgency. A sinner saved gives more joy than an army of saints praising the Lord.'

'But he's committed, sir, to Satan.'

'No matter. If his heart proves to be against us, we shall dangle wealth before him. The Foundation, gentlemen, has prepared for this outcome. If Richard knows the secret of when and where the world was created, then the sacrifices of the faithful will be redeemed by its purchase. I will instruct our board to make a transfer of bonds from our accounts in Geneva.' Warren refreshed his computer screen. 'You will receive further orders from me shortly, Antony.'

'These proposals,' said William, stepping forward, 'are outside of my remit, Warren. I will need to raise this with my superiors at Langley.'

'Then I shall speak to the president, William. The crisis in London is escalating. If the students disrupt our destiny, or the British get hold of the secret, the apocalypse will be denied us forever. The president understands this.'

'Sir, we should act quickly. I'm feeling bad about these strange things that are happening in the sky.'

'It's nothing,' insisted William. 'British scientists have linked the phenomena to unusual radiation from the sun. The rest is just fantasy and hysteria. The news channels are exploiting it. My advice is to leave these guys alone. The apocalypse stuff is just baloney.'

'I'm not so sure, sir. That isn't what I learnt in bible class.'

Warren clasped his hands. 'It is done. The bond holdings will be placed in a new account ready for dispersal. All that remains is to secure this young man's co-operation.' Warren reached for a control button on his desk. 'You must excuse me now, gentlemen, I have an important announcement to make to my congregation.' His eyes switched to the door as it opened in readiness for the departure of his associates.

William Carter and Larry Antony left the room, making their way separately to the exit fifteen floors below. The door closed behind them.

* * *

Warren followed their movements on his computer, flipping between security cameras until the two gentlemen had left the building. He reached for his phone and re-read a text from a military contact in Washington: *Missile deployment confirmed, Warren. London target configured. Countdown initiated.* Whatever Addings might reveal, he thought, Satan must still be destroyed. He rose from his chair and moved towards the private rooms that adjoined his office. He unlocked the door. 'Come, child. The others have left.'

Jonathan Saunders emerged from a dimly lit room before falling to his knees. 'I saw them eat flesh. I saw them fornicate.' He sobbed, clutching the leg of the old man's trousers.

'Rise child. Your faith has saved you. The blood feast of Satan consumes only the wicked.' Warren led Jonathan back into the adjoining apartment before they sat together on a sofa. 'Tell me what happened to our enemies. And their damnation.'

'I arrived at the Globe theatre as the sun set. I dined alone in the restaurant beneath ground level. For the sum of one thousand pounds, I gained a key that gave me access to the rest of the building. After securing a hideout on the roof, I alerted the team to join me.'

'At what time was this?'

'Six in the evening. We hid for four hours overlooking the stage, repeating the prayers that you gave us. At ten, a trumpet announced the start of Marlowe's play. Faustus appeared before the audience and scorned both the law and our holy works. After a short delay, he called on the forces of darkness. I looked towards the crowd as they chanted deliriously. Alex Rowdesley stood rapt among them, his eyes damning his soul.'

Warren reached for Jonathan's hand. 'Did you see the Beast?'

'I saw his servant Mephistopheles. Covered in slime and excrement, he brandished his penis at the crowd. I called on our saviour and threw a rope towards the stage. We landed amidst the scarlet whores of Babylon. But two of my brethren were drawn to the flames. I pleaded with them not to sin. But their spirit was weak, and they yielded. Horrified, I watched as their parts were torn from them and their faces scraped raw with knives.'

Warren shook. He placed his hands together in prayer.

'With an obedient servant, we leapt at Rowdesley and, defying the stench, we drove him towards the abyss, cursing him as he screamed, and promising everlasting damnation.' Jonathan stared into his mentor's eyes. 'We watched him fall. Into the arms of Satan as fire raged, engulfing those unwilling to flee.'

Warren knelt. 'O Lord, I am unworthy of your grace, and helpless without your love. Guide me, Lord. Guide me, so that I may serve you in this titanic struggle, for your greatest foe has surfaced here beside the Thames. Give me the strength to defeat him. And lock forever the gates of his abode.'

'Will I be forgiven?'

Warren lifted himself to his feet. 'Calm yourself, Jonathan. God is merciful.'

'But I have sinned.' His face whitened.

'You have served God well, and cast into oblivion those who are against us.'

'Thou shalt not kill, sayeth the Lord.'

'We are tools in his handiwork, child. Do not chastise yourself lest you presume on God's justice.'

'But I shot the man they called Paulo. And I pushed his body into the Thames. I have lied about my studies and deceived my friends. I am a sinner. And I have seen the abyss.'

Warren opened his arms. 'You were saved from the abyss. With your companion in Christ.'

'But I have murdered.'

'God will forgive you. Obey his command and he will shine upon you.' Jonathan and Warren embraced. 'Listen, child. The Lord has spoken to me. In six days, the world will be created anew.'

'The end of times?'

'Armageddon. When the righteous will be saved.'

Jonathan rested his head on Warren's shoulder.

'It is God's plan that hell is locked for eternity. A great thunderbolt will descend from the sky and wreak havoc upon the ground. God has asked me for your help to destroy his enemies.'

'What must I do?'

'There is one amongst us who plans to betray us to the British authorities.'

'Who?'

'Our disciple, Larry Antony, in whom our mission has placed its trust and who assisted you in your work for the Foundation. He has fallen into lustful ways and seeks the secret of the universe for himself.'

Jonathan stepped back. 'He ... he must be condemned.'

'It is God's command, child.'

'Tell me what I should do.'

'With your obedient servant, take Larry back to the site of the Globe theatre where I shall arrange for you to present a gift at their fund raising event.' Warren reached into his pocket before placing a small electronic device into Jonathan's hand. 'Take this token of our faith and keep it with you. On Christmas Eve, you will see a bright light on the horizon like an avenging angel. This is a sign from God. Hold forth the token so that He may know his own even amongst the damned.'

'Will I die?'

'In the certainty of the resurrection to come. And the destruction of Satan and all his legions. The military has assured me of this.'

'Is this lawful?'

'It is lawful if we do God's work.'

Warren and Jonathan wept.

39

'Oranges and lemons say the bells of Saint…' I couldn't get the stupid rhyme out of my head. Fiona rushed up to me holding an essay. 'Look, can you see the golden sands and crystal brooks?' 'Where, Fiona? Where? I see only fish.' She laughed, mocking my answer as she faded. The fish darted and then towards me swam. 'Can you see the sun and moon', they teased? 'But where?' I asked. They turned and fled towards a light. Be careful, I urged. It might not be real. A sly, juicy bait dangled before their eyes in the cold, murky water. Enamoured, they rushed to their fate.

A voice accosted me. 'You owe me five farthings …' I turned 'Alex, is that you?' I could see a shape … a figure edging away. I hurried over. 'Excuse me, I'm looking for Alex. Have you seen him? He's my friend but we've parted. I have to find him. It's for our destiny, you know.' The figure stared back at me. 'When will you pay me say the bells of Old …'

The image faded.

There was pressure on my lungs. And pain. I wanted to breathe, but was afraid I'd swallow water instead of air. I reached out in one last bid towards another shape. Reaching for hands that were soft, and fingers that locked with mine. To lips that sealed. Giving breath. Sweet breath. And life. I ran my hands across her face, her shoulders and her breasts as long, silky hair caressed my skin. Tingling my senses. Tensing my limbs until our bodies fused, beating as one in a slow, erotic motion.

We clung together, drifting in a deep, languorous sea.

'I do not know, said the great bell of Bow.' I opened my eyes.

* * *

I was standing in a room. The walls were white. And I was naked. Behind me were a bed and a leather armchair. Draped across the chair was a dark-blue dressing gown. I put it on but let it hang loose as I glanced around. Where was I? A rectangular window overlooked a garden that was enclosed by terraced buildings made of dark grey brick and white-painted window frames. Chimneys divided the nineteenth century rooftops made of slate. This must be Jane's flat, I thought. The one in Bloomsbury that she shared with Francis. I opened the bedroom door, and stepped quietly along the hallway, passing another room with its door closed and then past the kitchen and bathroom. There were no sounds or noises. I turned the lock on the external door of the apartment, but the door remained secure.

Where is Alex, I wondered?

I entered the lounge. The dining table was set against the limestone surround of the fireplace. A blanket and a bedsheet were folded and placed on the sofa. A print on the wall reminded me of Durer. Leaving the lounge, I headed to the kitchen but paused briefly in the hallway, listening again for sounds. In the kitchen, I found bread crumbs and nut shells strewn across the floor. A flat wicker basket lay upside down on a tabletop. Tins of food and bags of seeds lined a shelf. I returned to the bedroom, sat in the leather chair and tried to make sense of what had happened since I entered the Globe.

I recalled a pert, irritating boy who wanted to argue. An overbearing Faustus. A demonic chalk circle drawn to the sound of a Latin spell. And a lighted candelabra in a building made of wood, plaster and reeds. Then a fire. And general panic. But was this fate or carelessness? Francis said nothing about a conflagration. Nor a river in which I swam but struggled for breath. Struggle. And air. My heart raced as I rose to my feet. Someone had helped me to stay afloat. But who? Who saved me from drowning?

Returning to the lounge, I found an envelope with my name written on it. Inside was a letter in Jane's handwriting:

Richard, dear Richard. You will probably wake before we can see you. Please believe me when I say that everything is okay. We are with Otto at the British Museum, but will return soon. I am sorry about the mess. After we discovered you by the Thames, we were very frantic and not sure how things would develop in the days ahead. But you are safe. There is food in the kitchen and we will bring more soon. You may notice the occasional tremor affecting the building. And while you slept, there were flashes of light in the sky. This will continue for several days. The door of the apartment is double locked, but in the writing desk alongside, there is a set of keys, including the key to your room in Drury Lane. Please do not leave the flat unless the danger is very great. It is so important that we continue our work, especially for the sake of Alex. When we found you in the Thames, you were not alone. A young native girl of your own age was with you. You were both unconscious, but in each other's arms. The girl is in my bedroom. Francis was able to communicate with her when she revived, although she does not speak English, and is quite alarmed by her circumstances. For this reason, we secured the door. The events unfolding are quite extraordinary, but once our intervention is complete, much of what has happened in our lives will change forever as our plans are fulfilled..

I collapsed on to the sofa and cried.

I'd fallen asleep. When I awoke, the midday light had given way to a red glow from a bulb in the hallway. The apartment felt colder. I pulled my dressing gown tighter and headed to the second bedroom, where I waited outside the door. Who was she … this native girl? I gripped the handle but hesitated to enter. Would she be afraid? Would she remember? Or care? I pushed at the door and, stepping forward, reached for the light switch. I stalled: the room was empty. But on a bedside table, I noticed a framed photograph of Jane and Alex together. I headed back to the writing desk in the hallway. *Please do not leave the flat,* Jane had written. I opened the drawer and found the keys, but my attention was drawn to something else. A small bundle of feathers next to the alabaster figurine. I shut the drawer. How could this be?

A shadow shifted as the light swung gently in the hallway.

I returned to the lounge. Books, shoes and clothing caught my eye, and then a small retro-style radio like the one I had at home. I turned it on. There was no music, just messages to keep listening and others to save energy and water. I re-tuned the frequency, turned up the sound, and sat on the sofa. I could hear sirens followed by the sound of heavy trucks before a voice intervened with an announcement. Two thousand soldiers were deployed across central London, the voice said. Southwark and Bermondsey had been evacuated and access to Holborn and the City of London restricted. A fire had badly damaged the Globe theatre two days before. Flooding had closed tunnels beneath the Thames. The Millennium Bridge had collapsed. I stood up and moved closer to the radio. People recounted what they'd seen. 'As I said to the police, there was this sudden roar and huge flames rising out of the ground, but like a flash, because there was no actual fire or heat. Then when we looked across the river, St. Paul's Cathedral was alight. Just like the Fire of London.' The interviewer moved on, catching snippets, and then an elderly lady who'd grown up near the old London docks. It was like the War: I could hear the planes in the sky and bombs exploding around me, but nothing was destroyed. Another witness reported ships in the river with masts and sails. Someone mentioned the old London Bridge. And As I listened, lots of bizarre thoughts raced through my head. Had time coalesced? Were past and present somehow misaligned? Was this what Francis intended? Nothing of what I'd heard made much sense, and the thought of hanging around unsettled me. I returned to the bedroom, and, ignoring Jane's plea, got dressed and took my own key from the drawer.

I left the flat, slipping the figurine into my pocket before I departed.

40

Troy fell. Mycenae fell. And across the sun-scorched, shattered lands of the great Assyrian empire, the temples and walls of Nineveh crumbled too. Babylon, Rome and Byzantium followed. James Ellison looked down from his study into the Foreign Office compound. A headless torso caught his eye, impotent amidst the scattered debris thrown from the palace-like facades. 'Look on my works, ye mighty, and despair.' The ironic boast from Shelley's 'Ozymandias' taunted his weary eyes.

He turned sharply as his office door opened. Felix Leighton stood at the threshold. 'So, William is back,' said Felix, stepping forward.

'Yes,' said James. 'But who told you?'

'Alison. She phoned me last night.' He made his way to James's desk and settled into a chair.

'You mean at your home, Felix?'

'At nine o'clock. I'd just got in. She thought you were … unavailable.'

'Unavailable? But I was here. Until … very late.' James returned to his desk, and retrieving his tie, slipped it into a drawer. He buttoned his shirt sleeves. 'I'm sorry about the mess,' he said, waving his hand in a show of irritation.

'She thought you could … brief me in the morning. Regarding Larry Antony.'

'Brief you?'

'Yes. COBRA met yesterday. His name was mentioned.'

'I wasn't aware.' James rubbed his chin, conscious he hadn't shaved for several days. 'This student business … I'm afraid it has preoccupied me. I'll have to catch up with the foreign secretary. I'm sorry.' He reached for a pen and pad, scribbling a note to himself.

Felix glanced towards the window. 'The car park is littered with rubble. Several of the statues have fallen from their plinths.'

'Just tremors,' remarked James. 'I'm not sure we should rush to conclusions.' He drew his laptop closer and tried to logon. 'Has the password changed, Felix?'

'I don't think so.'

James leant back. 'So Alison wants me to brief you.'

Felix nodded. 'But if you need another hour, James … to freshen up. Or collect your thoughts.'

'That won't be necessary,' said James, regaining his composure. 'What you should know is that Larry Antony has been suspended. And that William Carter has been asked to stay in London until matters are resolved.'

'Do we know why?'

'Oh, something personal.' James reached for a briefing paper on the desk. 'What it means …' He paused as his attention fell on an old textbook. He moved it aside before returning to his laptop. 'Are you sure the password hasn't changed?'

'There were IT issues this morning, James. Something to do with electromagnetic waves, I believe. It's why COBRA is meeting again.'

James slammed the table. 'I should have been told of this.'

Felix remained silent.

'I'm sorry,' said James. He continued in a softer voice. 'How much of the Karlstad material have we sent to Larry's team?'

'Over six gigabytes. As you instructed, James.' Felix eased back from the desk. 'There's another file ready to go, using "The World" by Thomas Vaughan as the key to the transcripts.'

'Henry Vaughan,' said James, quietly. 'Thomas was his twin brother.'

Felix nodded.

James rose from his chair and moved to the window. 'We must suspend the intelligence operation, Felix. No more despatches. No more encryptions.'

'Have the Americans discovered something?'

'Probably. It's the only way I can explain William's return to the Committee.' He stared into the courtyard. 'The CIA must have infiltrated Antony's team and analysed the material without him knowing. Or us.'

Felix sent a short text to GCHQ on his phone. 'Does Alison know of your fears?'

'No. I shall have to tell her. There's bound to be fall-out with the White House.'

'I think, James, that Alison Farring's immediate concern is what the students will do next. That is why she and the PM attended COBRA.'

'We'll just have to prepare the public.' He watched as building services roped-off the periphery of the compound while damaged cars were hauled on to waiting trucks.

'COBRA is worried that the students have initiated their assault. There were strange reports in central London.'

'Yes. I heard some wild stories on the BBC.'

Felix placed a hand inside his jacket. 'The PM doesn't want them to have a second chance, James.'

'No, of course not.'

'His instruction is to take them into custody before Christmas. There is particular concern at the operational role of a Richard Addings.'

James turned and set his eyes on his colleague. 'And your part in this … if I may ask?'

'I shall lead a snatch squad from MI5. Earlier this morning, I took possession of a Walther P99 from the armoury.' James shrugged at the disclosure. 'Alison said that you have a contact in the university who can help.'

'Yes.' James returned to his chair and wrote a name on a scrap of paper.

'Vivien Weekes,' said Felix, reading the name.

'Medieval history, I believe. Weekes is a talent-spotter for MI5.'

Felix slipped the note into his wallet. 'There's an address in Bloomsbury and another in Covent Garden that we know about. I'm expecting the go-ahead shortly.'

'Then I wish you luck, Felix.' James re-opened his laptop. 'I'm sure … everything will go well.' He pressed a key and watched a trail of letters race across the screen.

'There is one more thing, James.'

'Oh? And what is that?'

'Alison mentioned Kalinsky on her call.'

'Really?' James looked up.

'She sounded concerned, James. And she wondered if you could be more informative about your past association.'

'And what exactly does that mean?'

Felix cleared his throat. 'I'd like you to recall your trip to Latvia and Sweden. Thirty years ago, wasn't it?'

'That's right.' James watched as Felix set his phone to record.

'To avoid any misunderstanding, James, when I brief Alison.'

'As you wish.' James rested his arms on the table, unsure of his colleague's intentions. 'It was late 1990 … I think you know that. William joined me in what was a joint operation with the CIA. We had various tip-offs … and one led us to the Baltic.' James smiled at his colleague. They both glanced at the phone before James continued. 'There were rumours about a manuscript from a Renaissance library. And a date that had significance for events in the world.

And since people were ready to kill for it, our governments were naturally curious.'

'Concerning the destiny question?'

'Yes. The destiny question, Felix.' James leant forward, resting on his elbows. He clapped his hands audibly. 'But then we lost track of Kalinsky in a snowstorm.'

'That's right. In Stockholm. But Alison was more curious about Riga, James?'

'In Latvia?'

'Yes.' Felix smiled. 'You stayed at a hotel called Neiburg's. For three nights, I believe.'

James eyed his colleague guardedly. Had Felix been briefed? he wondered.

'The hotel is opposite the cathedral, I understand. Not the Old Castle as you once thought.' Felix glanced at the phone.

'The cathedral? Yes, so it is. But, really, it wasn't much of a hotel. Grim Soviet apartments, I remember. But there was an interesting restaurant on the ground floor. One favoured by young, Latvian radicals. We were, of course, in the dying days of Russia's grip on the Baltics, Felix.' He paused, before repeating the thought. 'The dying days, Felix.'

'Is that all?'

'No. I believe the building is famous for its art nouveau exterior.'

'Yes. But the manuscript, James?'

James ran his eyes around the wall. Marcus would have understood, he mused.

'If I may, James, ask you to think again about your stay in Riga? Apropos … Dr Josef Kalinsky.'

James opened a drawer of his desk. He removed a document and placed it in front of Felix. The words 'Prague Nineteen Fifty' stood out in a Gothic typeface on the cover page. 'I photographed the original using a miniature Minox camera while its owner and, shall we say, his confidante, slept soundly in bed. This is a copy, Felix.'

'At Neiburg's?'

'Yes.'

Felix reached for the document.

'It's full of geometrical drawings, mathematical equations and strange symbols. There's also a commentary on Plato's "Timaeus" by the Greek Epicureans.'

'Does GCHQ know about this?'

'No. Nor William. But since he joined me at the hotel, I always allowed for a similar initiative on his part.'

Felix turned the pages until a statement containing an empty bracket caught his attention. He reverted to James. 'The missing value … it's the secret, isn't it?'

'The key to a new world, Felix. A set of eighteen numbers comprising a six digit date and the decimal co-ordinates of a latitude and longitude of a location somewhere in North America. Our Washington friends have always been keen to discover it before we do.'

Felix sat back. 'Hence our diversions involving GCHQ.'

James grinned. 'Who knows what mischief might arise if you could manipulate the past? The Americans have their religious anxieties, and we never trusted the Germans or the French given historical antagonisms.'

'But how did Kalinsky become involved?'

The sound of building services clambering on the roof interrupted their conversation. James returned the document to the drawer. 'Kalinsky's early career was in espionage, Felix. Initially disposed towards the Soviet regime, he was sent from his homeland to study art history in Prague. In the mid-eighties, he was involved in cultural exchanges between the West and the East, often involving obscure, alchemical texts as a bait. But his brief wasn't as innocuous as it seemed. Posing as a young, adventurous Balt, but with links to a circle of academics run by the KGB, his real role was to penetrate Western intelligence.'

'In a ruse by the Soviets?'

'Yes. We'd fallen for it before, of course. Angry intellectuals. Even orthodox priests pleading help for their congregations.' James chuckled as he spoke. 'Well, at first, the CIA weren't interested, correctly suspecting that the young man's angst at the suppression of art movements was disingenuous.' James yawned. 'But in a game of double bluff, we risked an approach through one of our people in Berlin.'

'To see if he might be turned, I assume.'

'Indeed. Or not. But as events unfolded, we became curious about a mystery he claimed to have solved. Then the fall of the Wall changed everything, and with it, a convenient shift in Kalinsky's ideological perspective.'

'Who was the British contact?'

'An officer in a signals regiment. An Oxford man called Phillip Shere.'

'Shere? The name sounds familiar.'

'And it should. He was Jane Shere's father.'

'So it was through her father that she became involved.'

'Yes. And before she introduced the other students to the mystery. But once Kalinsky realised the potential of his discovery, he broke off negotiations with us and offered his material to the black market.'

'And you said nothing of this to William Carter?'

'Not a word. We followed Kalinsky to Stockholm berated by our own service chiefs once we'd lost the trail and,' he stretched his arms, 'squandering the taxpayers' precious money.'

Felix retrieved his phone.

'Of course, whenever Kalinsky came on to the radar, I made inquiries. In 1997, he surfaced at the Bank of England.'

'As a forensic specialist in the Notes department,' recalled Felix.

'Correct. But there was always a suspicion that the missing data in the formula lay concealed somewhere in the Bank's underground fortress.'

'But Godson, I remember, didn't give it much credence.'

'No,' said James.

Felix paused as a tremor filtered through the building. 'I shall let Alison know what you have told me, James. But I suggest the document will be safer in the depository instead of your drawer.'

'I daresay it will, Felix … I dare say it will.'

Felix rose and stood by James's desk. 'There was one other matter that troubled the foreign secretary.' James looked up. 'The shooting of Kalinsky at the British Museum. Is there any news regarding an assailant?'

'The shooting? No. At least not yet. Perhaps I should visit the BM and make inquiries.'

Felix stepped back. For a few moments, his eyes lingered on James and then the disarray of his desk. He checked for his concealed weapon before turning towards the door, but a splinter of glass by the leg of the chair detained him. He placed it on the desk. 'It was on the floor.'

'Must be the tremors. An old photograph. Nothing important.'

'I understand … that Alison will be in touch, James.' Felix buttoned his jacket.

'Thank you, Felix. My diary is clear. I shall … await her call.'

Felix departed, closing the door gently behind him.

James stared wistfully at the blank space on the wall. In his mind, he slipped back to his undergraduate days at Cambridge and the fresh, vibrant faces of his youth. The lively streets. The uncensored looks. He reached once more for the book that had kept him company along the grassy banks of the Cam, the windswept lanes of the eerie Fens. On college green … and with the hand of a young lady who wasn't sure. He turned to the opening page of 'Paradise Lost' as tears trickled down his cheek.

'Of man's first disobedience …' he humbly read.

41

I stood in the old churchyard of St. Paul's, Covent Garden.

I'd left Bloomsbury an hour before, making my way to the river and then to Embankment Gardens where I lingered by the solitary Watergate, the towering tree, and the iron railings where Francis and Jane had cried for their friend. Retracing these steps helped me to think things over, and as I struggled with feelings and loyalties, I sensed it was not just my immediate predicament that needed a resolution, but things in my recent past that now craved the light of day.

I entered the church.

Plaster had fallen from the ceiling, but otherwise the interior of the building retained a quiet composure. It was known locally as the actors' church. And if all the world's a stage, I recalled, then 'exeunt', for this was their final exit. Various plaques commemorated the thespian fraternity. I read a few names, hearing echoes of their past triumphs, but no longer the applause.

Inigo Jones designed the church. But before his career blossomed as architect and surveyor, he worked with poets constructing Court masques—Jacobean diversions with perspective backdrops and prettified verse for the friends of the king. Ben Jonson was his first collaborator until they fell out over who ran the show. But the playwright, George Chapman, proved a more enduring partner. Chapman, a friend of Christopher Marlowe, had picked up earlier from the younger Kit with a continuation of his lusty 'Hero and

Leander', a minor epic about two lovers doomed on the shores of the Bosporus. Alex once quoted a line of it to me though I didn't realise it at the time.

The central aisle led me to the altar.

Inigo's brief was to build a barn. So he promised the finest barn in the country. St Paul's was the first parish church to be built in London since the early sixteenth-century, and while the Gothic had become unloved, the Renaissance, and its revived classical spirit, offered new ways to charm the intellect and please the soul. The inspiration for this was a Roman architect called Vitruvius, a guy who wrote twelve books on architecture and military encampments, and was as good on building country barns as he was on Tuscan temples. That at least lent an agrarian connection to whatever stray fancy linked St Paul's and its urban parish to rural Arcadia. As for the old man I met at the café, he promised the secrets of harmony … before getting shot at while accosting me with a few tricky lines from one of Donne's intriguing poems.

A shard of glass had landed on the altar, and as I examined it, I heard footsteps approaching me from behind. I turned. A slim, elderly lady, dressed in a dark green jacket and skirt, stood alongside me. She sported a guide badge on her lapel. In her hand was a lighted taper. 'I was curious about the church,' I said, holding the glass. 'I saw it in a drawing. It must be old.'

'It was built between 1631 and 1633,' she replied. 'At the instigation of the 4th Earl of Bedford.'

'Bedford?' The name sounded familiar.

'Frances Russell. His great-grandfather purchased the land following the dissolution of the monasteries. But the piazza and church were built a hundred years later.'

'By Inigo Jones,' I said. 'Kind of classical.' I smiled as she walked towards a stand where she lit a heavy candle. I placed the fragment of glass in my pocket.

'The church has always been involved with the local community. Visitors often ask me about its history and associations.'

'You must know about the door, then.'

'The door?'

'The forbidden door ... isn't there some sort of mystery?' I glanced behind the altar at a decorative structure fixed to the wall. It mirrored the pediment and columns on the outside of the church in the piazza, giving the illusion of access.

'You are the third person today who has asked about that.' She looked at me with curiosity. 'A young man and an American gentleman who were here an hour ago put the same question to me.'

I shrugged. My attention was still on the door. 'Could the design be esoteric? Like hiding a secret.'

Her expression soured. 'Oh, there's no mystery. Jones had proposed an arrangement quite contrary to regular practice. The Bishop of London soon put a stop to it.'

'But doesn't the church imitate a temple?'

'Very much so. But a classical temple had its altar outside. In the open.'

'Yes, of course. I'd forgotten. But maybe the sunset ... or a vision of eternity inspired him? Or death, even?'

The lady stared at me. 'There was an obelisk in the square, but it was demolished before 1790.'

A memorial plaque on the wall caught my eye. 'What about famous people?'

'Well, the wood-carver Grinling Gibbons and the composer Thomas Arne are buried here.' She relit the taper. 'Gibbons in 1721 and Arne in 1778.'

I shook my head. Too late, I thought. 'How about astronomers or mathematicians?'

'Mathematicians? You could ask the vicar. But I read that Bishop Usher preached here in the 1650s.'

Usher, I thought. And dates. 'Didn't he calculate the age of the earth?'

'From the day it was created,' she said, lighting another candle.

'When?'

'4004BC, I believe.'

I sat in a pew. That wasn't the answer, either.

After I had returned from my interview at Oxford, I never told my parents the truth. Not the whole truth about what had happened. Nor the bizarre questions I'd been asked, or the undertakings I was supposed to give to my prospective tutors. Just a modest account that must have crushed their hopes about my academic future. Nor were my friends at school pleased as they reminded me of my erratic attention in class, my distance from the world, and its issues. The very things that energised them but left me sometimes cold, or sometimes indifferent. What now? I placed my hands together in my lap, feeling tired and even forlorn. No longer a detached observer of the world's anguish, I am its inadvertent cause and the lonely judge of its fate. My thoughts drifted back and forth. I'd travelled to Oxford wanting to study T. S. Eliot and 'The Waste Land'. Poems like 'Prufrock'. And Shakespeare and Donne. But by the end of the encounter, I'd been scared away—bewildered and irritated by what I'd heard, and what I was supposed to do when I got there. And I remember … What? I remember the music. The gramophone playing as we ate. Over and over. And a song drifting across the lake. And questions. Lots of questions about me. About crossing an ocean … And I still don't know if Josh can swim. Or if Alex will see Jane again. And I remember bells. But not then. Not at Oxford. And a storm raging around me. I remember … those gentle lips that offered breath. The skin that tingled mine. I remember our embrace … and the sweet, gentle thrust of penetration. And wondering … who are you that your life is so entwined with mine?

My eyes opened. Someone was shaking me by the arm.

'The afternoon service has been cancelled,' said the church-warden, releasing his grip but not his gaze.

'Oh …' I said, waking. 'I'm sorry. Maybe I should come back.' I got up and stepped into the aisle. The candles, I noticed, had been extinguished. 'It's a … lovely church,' I said, turning to the exit. 'Kind of peaceful. Like … contemplative.'

'Yes. The crossroads of time and space. The distillation of hope and memory. Are you homeless?'

'Er, no. I live close by. In Drury Lane. I'm a student. First year. English literature.'

'Drury Lane? I believe that the poet John Donne lived there for a while.'

'Really? I didn't know.'

He smiled softly. 'Our noticeboard and website may have something that might interest you before you leave the church.'

'Thanks. But I've got friends waiting for me. I need to sort something out.' I headed for the porch. The Donne connection had unsettled me.

I left the church and stood on the steps at the rear. For another fifty yards the garden—the graveyard as it used to be—stretched west … blasted with sighs, and surrounded with tears, I fancied, recalling the poet's evocative lines. Ahead of me, two rows of empty benches lined the path towards the iron gates alongside a road that led down to the Strand. To my right, a coppiced tree, its boughs and branches aching for the sky, reached high, skeletal and bare. Forbidden to laugh, I mused. The air was cold, and a frost of several days lay on the ground … while a hurt tormented my heart. I looked around. Precipitous walls rose on either side, trapping me with my thoughts. Windows stared down like plucked, hollowed eyes. Birds watched silently. Mulling my dilemma.

I turned towards the piazza and—still restless—continued to my flat on Drury Lane.

Donne never saw the church nor its garden, or the square designed by his contemporary Inigo Jones. He died three weeks before Easter on the last day of March, 1631. So much for April, I thought. So much for the spring.

* * *

My room was just as Alex and I had left it before we joined Francis and Jane at the Globe. A bit of a mess. I picked up his bag from the floor and placed it on the bed, made myself a cup of tea and a cheese sandwich, and sat at the desk by the window. There was still the rest of Jane's letter to read.

> *Of course, we all have a nervous first time making love. An intimacy flushed with sensations and joy. Both of you looked so beautiful together. In each other's arms when we found you alongside the Thames. It seemed a tragedy to let you part. A profanation, as the poet says.*

I stopped reading and swallowed.

> *You were right to study Donne. Who else captures that fear of loss? And yet enduring presence. But you will see the young woman again. You must, for Alex's sake.*

The letter trembled in my hands.

> *We all depend on myths, Richard, for our sanity and psychological well-being. Myths that link us subtly with the cosmos, lending coherence to historical narratives. To life. To death. And as Francis and I learnt more, we became aware of a deeper meaning and how the myths*

A noise from the landing outside my room diverted me. I listened before returning to the letter.

accompanies the world at its inglorious end. But this was a necessary part of our plan. This is why we chose the play by Marlowe. And there, during the unfolding drama, we too lay naked and exhausted.

But soon the reconstitution will begin. A new age will arise from the disorder we have set underway. Everything that has been built will be dismantled and recreated from an unblemished design. New doctrines will supersede the old. And you, Richard, are part of its reconstruction, securing the return of Alex once the final, communal act is performed. An act the ancients called orgia—choreographed to the beat of drums, ritual chanting, and the scourging of flesh—just as the myths and legends describe.

And now the practicalities. The orgiastic rite will take place at an underground location linked to the British Museum, where your initiation began. You and the young woman will rebuild the world's trajectory in a naked, cosmic act of fertilisation. A new world. One that will rival the Golden Age.

Francis and I will join you soon. Your partner is safe in the museum. She is very pretty. The Helen of her world and the redeemer of ours. But there are still dangers to face. The deterministic hand of fate draws towards the shadows, ready to impose new trials upon you and further mishaps in your life. Such as those failures and reversals for which you already blame yourself. Be brave Richard. Be strong. Francis knows how it will end.

This is some sort of cult, I thought. A sect. A weird sect. I re-read some passages. 'You looked so beautiful together ... a communal act.' Francis and Jane want to watch me ... having sex. This is insane. I let go of the letter. The universe had better figure out how to handle its own destiny because I'm not sure I want to bed its beautiful future in a public orgy of creation.

I crossed my room and pulled an empty holdall from under my bed. There was enough space for whatever I needed before I headed home to talk to my parents about quitting uni altogether. I threw clothes, books and my laptop into the bag, but a knock on my door disturbed me. I paused, holding the figurine in my hand. Please say your name … so I know who you are. A louder knock brought me to my feet. I dropped the artifact into the bag.

A young guy stood facing me as I opened the door. An acrid smell of body odour hovered around him. On his arm, I noticed cuts and bruises. I eased back, unsure if he'd been injecting.

'I'm your neighbour,' he said, stepping forward. 'The gas thing on my cooker won't light and I'm afraid there'll be an explosion.' He rubbed his eyes, adding to the redness that coloured his cheeks. His finger nails were bitten.

A dim light shone from his room, but his sudden appearance confused me. My thoughts flipped back to the start of uni. He's a loner, Eddie had said. You won't see him around. So why now?

He fell suddenly towards me before I caught him in my arms. But who is he? I felt uneasy; and after lowering him to the floor, went into his bed-sit where I saw a mattress on the floor and a thick curtain drawn across the window. I checked the gas hob. The only smells I could detect were from a whiskey bottle in the sink and fast-food cartons in a plastic bag. I swung around, hearing footsteps race down the stairs, and as I headed out, the room fell dark and the door slammed shut ahead of me.

'You must be Richard,' said a voice as a blow sent me crashing to the floor.

42

My visit to Oxford, some twelve months past, began on the afternoon of a damp, early December day, three months after my eighteenth birthday. I took the train from London and arrived just as it was getting dark. On my arrival at the station, I ignored the instructions on my phone and took a roundabout route to the college that led me to the Sheepwash Channel and then to Castle Mill Stream, where the Isis Lock controlled a shallow backwater of the Thames. An iron footbridge took me to the Oxford Canal where a dusting of snow lay on the towpath. This I remember.

At the college lodge, I was directed to the quadrangle and asked to wait by the steps to the Old Library. Above my head, a eunuch moon, I recall, had pierced the wintery clouds, shedding its contorted light, like a dew, on the dark green ivy that clung to the college walls. The ivy reminded me of a wreath, though I was seeking neither a crown nor expecting a funeral as part of the occasion.

A gust of wind hurried through the cloister. Whistling. In my mind.

My interview was not far from the lake and the intervening lawn where the college porters liked to play croquet. Under a hot sun, I'd been advised. But it can't be summer already, I thought, as a shower of rain seemed to freshen my face? Reminding me of games of cricket at school … a haunting film that I'd watched with my sixth-form friends … though I still haven't heard from Simon or Becky. Or Anna, even. This, too, I remember.

A sharp-eyed cat ran across the quad and into a gaping hole by the fence. The cat reminded me of Macavity, whose true identity is unknown, of course. Once, I saw him on stage when I went to the theatre with my parents for my little sister's birthday. She was wearing a new dress, and I tried to lift her higher to see the action on stage before Mum said be careful. My sister laughed, hugging me, anyway—her arms tight around my neck. Be careful, I thought.

There is a dryness in my throat now, and my breathing is fast and short. Barely enough. That's all. And it's so easy to forget and mix up things when you are afraid. And you are surrounded by the sea and a cold, remorseless tide.

The interview was late in the evening. The tutors, I was informed, had dined earlier but were still attending chapel. This surprised me, and, as I waited, my thoughts turned to what I should say about my prospective studies. Since it was the end of term, the lighting around the quad had been switched off to enhance the moonlight so it wasn't until a college servant had lit a candelabra that I made my way to the tutor's suite behind the North Terrace's imposing façade. The Latin words 'quo vadis' were written in red ink on the door of the tutor's room. I spoke to the footman, expressing concern. The other candidates had fled, he advised. I felt uneasy as the door opened and I almost threw up.

Unlike the corridor and stairs, the room was well lit. One bright light shone into my eyes. But I have to breathe slowly, now, to remember. The ceiling was high, and the walls were a faded white. Not like my fingers or toes, with fresh blood seeping from them.

I stepped inside but halted as two attendants held the portrait of a young woman drowned in a stream, her hair adrift in the water. It was in the pre-Raphaelite style, I believe. She looked pretty. At least once, I fancied, before the attendants carried the painting away. My stomach churned.

There were three tutors sitting at a long, narrow table. One, a lady in her late fifties, with a sallow complexion, and angular features, struck me as friendly but not an older man who was called Vit or some name like Vit. Except it wasn't Vit but like Vit. The third tutor wore a cowboy hat and had his arms folded. My maths teacher, to my surprise, then rose from a high-backed chair carved from English oak and introduced me to the panel of assessors. I thanked her as she withdrew from our presence. My attention returned to the panel. An unsheathed sword lay in reach of me on the table, but I wasn't sure if I could lift it. A shard of glass, I noticed, was embedded in the pommel. None of the attendants dared to talk about my prospects.

The tutors conferred. Then Vit asked me why I had come. To discuss a poem, I said. A poem, he queried? Yes, I said. 'The Waste Land' and its elusive personae. Do you know any of them? The tutors conferred again. I was feeling more confident, and I readied myself for their challenge. The tutor with the cowboy hat said they were intrigued and wondered if I could tell them more about the poem. Well, basically, it's about sex, I said, smiling. But kind of allusive. And a bit dirty. I blushed and looked towards the window.

* * *

'Cut that crap about Oxford. Just give me the truth. Or I'll kill you.'

My head fell back. I was secured lengthwise on the metal frame of a bed in a cell without windows. Blood clotted my hair and smeared my arms and legs. My tormentor stood beside me and placed open scissors to my throat. We were alone.

'Who controls your operations, satanist?'

'I don't know.'

'Where is your base?'

'In London. Near the uni.'

'Liar. Liar. Liar.'

The scissors snapped at the air. My tormentor grabbed my feet and pressed my toes against the blades. Sweat pooled at the base of my spine.

'Who is the Lady of the Rocks? Tell me … tell me or…'

'Her name is Jane.'

'And the one-eyed merchant?'

'I don't know. He's a character … in a poem … called "The Waste Land".'

'Is it you, satanist?'

With a blade, he drew a line on my chest. My jaw trembled. 'Francis. It's Francis.'

'Who is Alex? What is his code name?'

'Alex is my friend.'

'You have no friends. No one has friends. No one. No one.' I braced as the scissors stabbed up and down between my legs until my tormentor, in a frenzy, threw the scissors to the floor. 'I hate Satan,' he screamed, ripping open his shirt, digging his nails into his chest before falling to his knees and whimpering like a child.

Oh, death, I thought. Free me from this madman.

I woke. My tormentor was wearing a dark blue suit. A towel had been thrown over my hips, covering my nakedness. An ointment had been applied to my wounds, numbing the pain. My assailant addressed the wall.

'Larry Antony, Special Forces … I mean, affiliated.' He bowed his head, before crossing the floor towards me. He was wearing sun glasses and held an antique map of Europe and North America between his hands. 'Where is the city over the mountain?' he asked.

'I don't know.'

Larry held the map closer. 'Co-ordinates and time zones, Mr

Addings. I believe you can confirm this data to the inquiry. Both latitude and longitude.'

'Co-ordinates? What are you talking about?'

'The birthplace of the modern world.' Larry spoke again to the wall. 'My intelligence team believe the city is in America. Or Greenland. Decryptions of British and Soviet data support this.' He leant over me, grinning dementedly. 'Please help the inquiry, Mr Addings. My boss is upset and wants to buy the secret from you.'

'Why? The place doesn't exist. It's a fantasy.'

Larry wet his lips. 'Then make it up in a nursery rhyme and sing it for the inquiry's approval.'

'But there's no one listening. There's no one here.'

Larry moved closer to the wall, letting the map fall to the floor. He nodded earnestly, as if agreeing with something he'd heard in his head. 'That is correct, senator. The origin of America. The first day of existence since Adam's expulsion from Eden.' Larry removed his sunglasses. 'Gentleman, the future of the Free World is at stake. Our destiny is no longer secure.'

'I need water and food,' I cried.

Larry rushed to me and slapped my face. 'Tell us the date the world began, Mr Addings. The penalty for failure is death.' He slapped me again, making the room surge and stagger around me.

'Water. Please.'

My tormentor turned to the wall. 'Phlebas, the Phoenician. If you gentlemen turn to my notes, you will find that he is mentioned in line three hundred and twelve of their manifesto. My team has linked this alias to Alex Rowdesley. The satanists use the same code words as the Soviets. As did the messages we demanded from the British.' Larry approached me. 'Who is the hanged man?' he asked, with a casual air.

I groaned, weary of his torment and delusion.

Larry straightened the sleeves of his jacket. He coughed quietly, as if to draw the attention of an invisible crowd. 'Before I play an audio as an aide-mémoire for the accused, I suggest that you gentlemen hear more of Mr Addings's visit to Oxford and the propositions put to him by his tutors. You might like to take coffee and syrup crepes as he remembers his experience.'

Larry moved around. Talking to ghosts.

* * *

I remember … a year ago, after the portrait of the drowned Ophelia was taken away, after my maths teacher withdrew, and after discussing sex, the fecund earth and mandrakes clinging to the soil, we rose from our chairs and gathered outside on the patio that overlooked the spacious lawn. A line of trees cast shadows under the brittle light of the moon. I stood beside the balustrade with a glass of sherry as the tutors recalled the summer before when the sun shone and the students frolicked, carefree, by the lake. In the background, an old gramophone played 'Love Is the Sweetest Thing' and 'The Very Thought of You'—songs I felt I knew, and in a style that sounded intimate yet far away. The singer, they stated, was a Mr Bowlly. Killed in the Blitz. I gazed towards the lawn.

As the music faded, the gentleman with the cowboy hat gestured to a dining table with uneven sides and unequal angles. The table was warmed by an old electric heater. A college servant, wearing gloves, handed us white napkins and took our orders for food. We thanked him before he returned to the kitchen with our culinary requests.

I drew a breath before sitting upright in a chair.

'Shall we start at the beginning or the end?' asked the lady tutor.

'Of what?' I asked.

'The world, Mr Addings. My understanding is that you have been sent to destroy it and start it again.'

I scratched my head. One of the servants placed a stuffed quail on my plate. But as the discussion turned to childbirth, I felt disinclined to eat. With a gesture, I waved the food away.

'Would you ask Mr Addings if he'd care for another sherry?' said the older man.

I turned to the tutor called Vit, or something like Vit, and politely declined.

I eased back and looked over to the lake, wondering if it encompassed the earth. Like the god Oceanus and his riverside daughters, I mused, who mentored the young and thirsty on their journeys across the seas. Brave argonauts and adventurers. Fishermen by the shore. But my thoughts, I recall, were suddenly interrupted.

'You must focus, Richard. And answer all the questions correctly if you want to understand your predicament.' Vit rolled his napkin into a ball and threw it into the air, making everyone laugh.

The turn of a key drew my attention. The French windows that led to the tutor's rooms had been closed and padlocked. 'I think I am ready,' I said.

A servant removed the plates before setting a box of ivory chess pieces in front of us. Each chess piece was then allotted to a notional square on the crooked table.

The lady tutor reached forward and re-positioned the queen. 'In that case, Mr Addings, we want you to go to a mystery island.'

'Why?' I asked, unsure of the invisible boundaries of the game. I countered with my knight.

'There has been a shipwreck. And the Prince of Naples has been lost.'

'How?'

'We cannot say. The intelligence services have two opinions. And neither of them is permitted by convention.' She moved a pawn in opposition to my knight.

'And what am I supposed to do?'

'Stop the conflict. Before it starts.'

'Between whom?'

'The Eastern Slavs and the Sarmatians. The German king has resigned. And the Americans are nervous.'

'I think you are mixing things up.' I moved my bishop forward, still unsure of the layout of the board.

'We don't believe so, Mr Addings. Is it not true that one thing always leads to another?'

'Yes. In a logical order. But freely, and not everything all at once.'

The man with the cowboy hat snatched one of my pawns and threw it to the floor. 'The outcome of the game must be altered,' he announced. 'There are dangers ahead of us.' He rearranged the other chess pieces, returning them to their starting positions before sitting and insisting on my attention. 'The Council has installed an hourglass at sixty-four missile sites across North America. Each site is heavily guarded. If forty-eight are blocked, and fifteen are declared false, how much time remains in your calculation?'

'I'd say … one. Which must be one hourglass.'

A servant brought the hourglass and placed it front of me, disturbing the ivory chess pieces as he did so. Should I get up and leave? I wondered.

The tutor called Vit, or something like Vit, raised his hand as if to pre-empt my departure. 'You spoke earlier about sex, Mr Addings.'

I agreed, but then yawned. 'It's quite pervasive.' I stretched my arms, letting the moonlight slip between the sleeves of my shirt and settle on my damp, shrunken belly. 'Sometimes violent and one-sided. Sometimes perfunctory. There is a belief, too, that it can be faked or even resisted,' I said, wiping my eyes with an unused handkerchief I'd concealed in the back pocket of my trousers.

The tutors rose in horror. 'But the fertilisation will fail, Mr Addings, if it isn't taken seriously.'

'Yes,' I said, as I gathered up the fallen chess pieces and placed them together in an anxious huddle.

'But this is unacceptable. The coupling of Leda and the swan was an act of necessity and compassion.'

'It's a myth. Like an allegory or a story. It's not literally true.' I reached for my knight and clutched it in my hand.

'But it prefigured the Trojan War, young man. And the birth of Helen.'

'Don't be silly,' I said. 'It's a metaphor for insemination. The re-emergence of life in a wasted land. And the precursor to the birth of the human ego.'

My words were followed by uproar. The servants hurried over and re-positioned the table alongside the balustrade. They placed a set of wooden steps at the side, allowing the tutor with the cowboy hat to rise safely without risking a fall. 'Blow the trumpet,' he declared, as his colleagues cheered and applauded.

As I stood by the electric heater, two more servants appeared from behind a screen carrying another large painting enclosed within a gnarled, decorative frame. They paused in front of me just as it snowed. 'Who are the figures in the painting?' I asked.

'Orpheus and Eurydice. Before their tragic parting.'

I touched the canvas, sensing their heartbreak. Would he? Should he … sacrifice his love to prove his fidelity? Hold me again, she urged, within the bond of one immortal look. My heart raced. And a solitary tear caressed my cheek.

* * *

My eyes opened and my mouth was no longer dry. I was sitting in a high-backed chair with my hands tied behind me by a length of sticky tape. A curtain covered the wall facing me. At my feet, my clothes were folded on top of my shoes. I was wearing headphones.

My tormentor drew back the curtain to expose a spiralling figure drawn on the wall in the colour red.

Larry stood before the figure and bowed his head in a gesture of obedience. 'The recording you will hear, gentlemen, has been played many times before. And with your permission, I would like to play it once more.' He smiled and presented the blades of the scissors, tied together by a large birthday ribbon, as an offering to the wall. I wasn't sure what he intended. 'The individuals named in this recording are now deceased, but I have arranged for substitutes to re-enact their roles consistent with the historical circumstances.' He turned to me. 'Mr Addings, please show your face to the panel.' I shifted in my chair as I tried to free my hands from the tape.

A young man cried out in the headphones: 'You are hurting me … I can't breathe.' But the sound cut suddenly. I wondered about the voice.

'I'm sorry,' said Larry, addressing the spiral on the wall. 'There's been a database error. I'll replace the recording and start again. He sent an instruction on his phone.'

Larry pressed his hands against his headphones, holding them close to his ears.

Anxiously, I listened through mine, but my wrists were almost free.

'May 1592. We put to you, Thomas Kyd, matters pertaining to the security of the State and the safety of our Sovereign.' 'Sir,' said a feeble reply. 'You are a confidant of a traitor, Mr Kyd, and privy to his contemptible ambitions.' My tormentor nodded as if in agreement. 'No!' screamed a voice in pain. I shook my head, trying to dislodge the headphones as I struggled with the binding. 'I love our Sovereign. The charges are false.' I closed my eyes. 'Your fingers are more use to you, Thomas, than they are dismembered to us,' said a sharper voice. 'Have mercy. Have mercy, sir. In the name of our Lord.' Then a fearful cry. 'You and the accused have denied Christ,

Thomas. Boasting that he lived in sin with his disciples.' Another scream assaulted my ears. 'No, sir. It was Marly. Marly wrote the pamphlets.' There was a pause. 'Hand him his confession. Your mark will save your own life but condemn your friend's.'

The recording ended, but the voices lingered uneasily in my mind.

Larry relaxed his pose. 'Thank you, gentlemen, for your patience and indulgence,' he said, addressing the phantoms in his head. 'The accused, I can confirm, was released from his confinement, having agreed to co-operate with his interrogators.' Larry returned a smile as our eyes made contact. He placed a hand to his headphone. 'That is correct, senator, the person called Marly was later eliminated in a pub brawl.'

Past and present, I thought, as my brain searched for clues about his behaviour. As for the testimony of Thomas Kyd, I knew it was forced and only carried out at the instruction of Elizabeth's Star Chamber. It wasn't a betrayal or a stich-up of Christopher Marlowe, whatever else was in my tormentor's deluded head. I glanced over at the scissors, ready to take my chances. There was still a way out. For one of us.

Larry looked pensive as he approached, stopping three feet from my chair. Warily, I watched as he unfolded a piece of paper in his hand, before reading words scribbled on the page. He stepped closer and whispered into my ear. 'Who is the Hyacinth girl in your manifesto?' he asked curiously.

I paused before answering, unsure of his mood. 'She is the young lady. She will return to her own land. And her own time.'

'Why?'

'Because she will be exchanged for Alex.'

'When?'

'At a ceremony. When I am free.'

'Where is she now?'

'With Jane … the Lady of the Rocks.'

'I want her, Richard. I want her to be mine.'

'But she must help Alex. It's the plan. The plan to change the world. And change our destiny.'

'Fuck your plan. Fuck destiny,' he said. 'I want you to kill Alex Rowdesley. Do you understand? I want you to drown the Phoenician.' Larry rose upright and pointed to the door. 'Only then, Mr Addings, will you be free.'

My tormentor swung away and fell to his knees by the wall. I freed my hands, snatched my clothes from the floor, and with my heart pounding, fled into the street outside.

43

A nunnery. Two Norman knights of yore, and a sly old trickster rising from his bed like an angry corpse. And then a sudden blow. I barely caught Martin's tale as he and Josh carried me through the narrow streets that skirt the south side of the Thames, not far from the medieval Clink and its chamber of gruesome horrors. John Overs, a miserable ferryman on the river, had been struck dead with the thrust of a single wooden oar. But I, Martin promised, would be rescued by four of them.

Within a few minutes we arrived at Overie dock—eponymous John, I fancied—and to a boat already rigged, oared and tied fast to the side. Josh threw me a padded jacket, a canvas sheet, and a flask of rum to help me settle in. 'Catch the drift somewhere in the middle,' said Martin, as Josh pushed us off, into the dark, and a lingering fog that allowed us to move, barely observed, on the water.

We headed west, and as the chill of the waves splashed my cheeks, I realised this was no dream. No delusion forced by a tortured brain or the incisions of a heartless blade. Hours before, I'd lingered near death at the hands of a lunatic. Days before, in the arms of a young woman's embrace. I was too confused to ask questions. Too scared to seek meaning. I let Martin do the talking.

'Who speaks up for the dead or dying?' he asked, sliding in his seat. 'Who hears their cries?' I lifted my head. It was three o'clock in the morning. 'Sometimes a small bird, they say. Jug, jug tereu. Sometimes a frail, whispered word.' I smiled, wondering at the lyrical turn of his words. 'What bird so sings,' he mused, sharing a look, 'her woes at midnight rise?' He asked. Well, it wasn't Donne, I thought. Or the white swans of Edmund Spenser gliding prettily towards the Thames. 'Who is it now we hear? None but the lark so shrill and clear.' I still wasn't sure, though the prospect of flight consoled me. I smiled again. Martin slid closer. 'Or just a late night call from Josh,' he declared. 'Get the boat out, he says. The boat? I said. Are you out of your mind? It's pitch black. The streets are closed. There are police and squaddies everywhere. Even the bleeding ground won't stay still.' Martin lifted his oars, leaving Josh to pull the weight. 'That's why we need a boat, he says. On the river.' He leant forward. 'So what is it, I ask? No need to, he adds. It's for a friend. A friend in need. Then you're on, I said.' Martin slid back with Josh, his big, billowing eyes saying it all.

I sipped the rum and used the canvas to keep myself dry.

'Hard on your left oar, Josh. We'd better steer clear of the abandoned piers. Our rudder's a bit dazed to do anything useful.'

We were at Blackfriars where rail and road each crossed the Thames, and where, jutting from the river bed, several bridge supports sat like ghostly stumps of time. Josh manoeuvred us on the waves as Martin held a finger to his lips. There were guards patrolling the bridge.

'Hard again, Josh,' he whispered, holding his own oars above the water. We cleared the second bridge with the help of the tide. I felt a nudge. 'I taught him that. Taught him everything he knows about the river.' He winked. 'All's well, ahoy.'

I nodded. The river moved silently about its business.

'Now, they've got a lot to answer for,' said Martin, glancing to his left.

'Who?' I asked, opening my eyes.

'The Dominicans. The bleeding friars, mate. The Black Brothers.'

I sniffed the air. Their monastery had once overlooked the Thames.

Martin slid forward. 'Dissolved in 1538,' he said. 'And that's when the fun started.'

'Fun? You mean the Master of the Revels?'

'And the Chapel Royal. Even Shakespeare lived next door.'

I looked at the riverbank. Where the world-weary had once knelt, youth was soon to strut. Richard Farrant and John Lyly wrote for the first theatre, using the Chapel's boys for music and drama. James Burbage constructed a second.

'Now, I'm not saying the Dominicans weren't clever.'

'Oh?'

'And they weren't all that fond of heresy, either,' he added. 'Mind, it was one of the Vatican Bulls that gave them cover.' He drew back, unsettling the rhythm of the boat.

'Sorry?'

'Ad extirpanda. Inquisitio. Confessio.' Martin pulled a face before his head dropped precipitously. I remained still. 'We were having this discussion on torture. Must have been my human rights module … last October, just after I met you and Josh in that fancy lawyers' pub. Remember, when Josh got an earful?'

I grinned.

'So for evidence, I mean like a confession, you could learn a few things that might otherwise escape your notice in a casual chat.'

'What?'

'Names of conspirators. Motives.' He slid away from me. 'Maybe even state secrets.'

'But it's cruel, Martin. It's degrading. And you can't call it human rights.'

'A matter of opinion, young man. Or everlasting damnation. But the real question was it any use?' Martin looked at me sternly. 'And you should know. What you've been through.'

'But I don't want to know.'

'Nobody wants to.' He pulled again.

'It's still unethical, Martin.'

'Really? Augustine was okay with it. And it was Roman law that put him up to it. Best practice. Even the witness of a crime could be tortured.'

I wanted to be sick.

'The Common law had never heard of it. But then he was a churchman. Confess, young man. Or I'll push needles under your nails. Brand you, crouch you, stretch you.' He pulled harder on the oars. 'Today they'll wire you up to electric toys … well, at least you're spared the indignity of having your dirty bits chopped off before they're stuffed in your mouth to keep the noise down. I'd rather the fires of hell, mate, than salvation.'

Martin's words belied his usual cynicism. There was nothing crafty, I thought, in his sudden outburst. Our flesh is all we have. Even when seared by anger, vanity and greed.

He slid forward, lifting his oars. 'So what did you tell them?'

'I told my tormentor everything. About everyone.'

'Don't blame you. Otherwise we'd be fishing you out of the Thames instead of picking you up at the door.'

'He threatened to … to kill me. But every time he got angry, he started crying and standing by the wall. And talking … as if people were listening and watching. I wasn't a hero, Martin. I was scared to death.'

'No one wants to be a hero, mate,' said Martin, settling into his stroke. 'I don't want to be a hero.'

'Maybe. But at least you got the boat out.'

'Yep. And Josh, don't forget.'

We took the bend ahead of Big Ben, Westminster Hall and the ancient Abbey. It was almost four-thirty. Lollard's Tower lay on the left. Millbank and MI5 on our right. Josh steered a middle path, setting the pace, pulling constantly. There's still hope, I thought: the solitary string that stirs a lonely heart. We pressed on.

Vauxhall crowded the river bank. But Pimlico stayed low.

'Head down, Richard. The denizens of Battersea might throw a few barbs at us.'

I hid under the canvas. Putney, Hammersmith, and then Barnes drifted by. But why are the Americans nervous? I wondered. The Prince of Naples didn't drown. And why did the man with the cowboy hat throw my pawn to the floor, wanting the game to start again? My pulse beat harder. Is youth's destiny to fight or fall? I wondered. Was this why I was abducted and tortured? We floated under Chiswick Bridge. And I still don't know the co-ordinates. Or the city over the mountain. Or if Alex will see Jane.

A spasm of pain shot through my legs, forcing me upright. I cried out until my face hit the water.

'The bank, Josh. Before he goes overboard.'

I was half in and half out. Martin reached forward, holding me as my arms beat the air. 'Why?' I screamed. 'I tried to help, Martin. My neighbour. He was ragged and scared. And then I was abducted. And for three days I was mocked and tortured.'

The boat swung hard to the left as Josh shifted his weight. Martin hauled me back in as flashes of my nightmare returned to me. I sobbed, wanting to flee but afraid to be alone.

'Grab the branches, Josh.'

A bough, hanging low by the river, helped Josh secure the boat before I staggered up the bank and fell on to my knees. Have I let Alex down? Have I betrayed my friend? I cried again, clutching the soil with my fingers and broken nails.

Martin jumped out of the boat. 'Give him some rum, Josh. If he sleeps, keep his head up. I'll be back in fifteen minutes with something stronger.'

Martin slipped away. We were somewhere between Richmond and Kew where the river cuts a course through a flat, rural landscape, and the city is held at bay. Only a lantern in Syon House challenged the darkness.

'What's happening, Josh?' I asked, shivering.

'We're happening. All of us.' Josh placed the flask to my lips.

I drank. 'Where are you guys taking me?'

'To friends.' He held my head. 'To people you know.'

'Who?'

'Sophie. And her dad, Richard.'

'But why?'

'To take you to Oxford.'

'To Oxford?'

'Yes. Your schoolfriend Anna—she needs to talk to you. About what happens next.'

44

Martin rowed back from the river bank, and with a final nod and glum-looking smile, headed home along the Thames. His last gesture was to hand me a wad of ten-pound notes. You might need it for the return journey, he'd said, before settling on a steady stroke, countering the tide that pushed in from the east. I raised my arm, acknowledging his help but feeling uneasy at his departure.

Josh led me to a dark green Range Rover that was parked a short distance from the botanical gardens by Kew Green. A shot of morphine, clean clothes, hot drinks, and a few biscuits helped me to get back on my feet. My attack on the water an hour before was now just a cry of anguish, while the news about Anna gave an unexpected twist to my predicament.

'You've been knocked about a bit, young man,' said Ian, opening the car door for me. Josh dealt with the seat belt as I sat back, feeling anxious and alone. Sophie joined her father at the front of the vehicle, before Ian started the engine. We moved quietly into a mist that lingered across the Green and the adjacent roads.

'Why did you leave Jane's flat?' snapped Josh. 'You were safe there. Jane wanted you to stay.'

'I wanted to find Alex. Do you know where he is?'

'No,' replied Josh, emphatically.

'Well, you knew where to find me.'

We crossed the Thames in silence. Oxford would take two hours if our journey was direct, and I was sure my rescuers had no intention of hanging around whatever else might happen before we reached our destination. We headed towards the motorway with only sporadic street lighting to show us the way and with the car's headlamps switched off to make our progress difficult to follow.

Sophie turned to me. 'After you left the flat, Richard, where did you go?'

'To my room on Drury Lane. But I stopped at the church in Covent Garden beforehand.'

'Were you followed?'

'I don't think so. I was trying to piece events together. The world was in chaos and Jane said I was part of the blame.'

'Because you didn't do what you were supposed to do, Rick.'

'No, Josh. But why does it matter to you? Why are you part of this? Why am I being cornered and abused?' The car sped up.

'Francis called me at 11 pm last night. He told me where I could find you, so I contacted Martin. The river was the safest route out of London since other routes were blocked by soldiers or the police.'

If I'd gone home to my parents … if I'd not tried to help, I thought. Or, if I had stayed by the old Watergate in Embankment Gardens, would this nightmare be just a dream? Yet wherever I go, I hear reminders and pleas like an angry chant. Am I their pawn or their hero, I wonder? Jane says I must save the world—though I'm already the cause of its demise—in a ceremony, she says, raw and naked, with drums, and dancing choreographed by the hand of Fate while my friends spin a web of intrigue around me. But who is their spider? And who is their fly? I wasn't sure. Oxford was another seventy miles, I noticed.

'How long have you known Francis?' I asked, turning back to Josh.

'Since the start of term. Just before you arrived at uni.'

The car slowed ahead of a red light. We changed lanes, ready for a sharp turn at a roundabout. 'So all that stuff about poems was bollocks, right?' My mood tensed. Innocent Josh, I thought, wanting to brush up on his poetry. And I'd fallen for it.

Sophie shifted around. 'We'd heard that there was a post-grad in your class, Richard. Francis remembered the trouble with Alex, so Josh was asked to look after you.'

'You mean Jonathan? Well, if I remember, we sparred over one or two poems, but nothing earth shattering.'

'The poetry was my cover, Rick. Jonathan has links with a group responsible for your abduction. Ian knows more about them.'

'They're a fundamentalist cult. Based in North America and the UK.' Ian paused as he shifted up the gears before we joined the motorway. 'Their basic belief is a passion for the Apocalypse. And the destruction of Satan as written in the Revelation to John.'

The Promised Land with a bang, I fancied. As if everyone didn't have enough to fret over. 'They're deluded,' I said. 'And Revelations is nuts. Even Donne shied away from it.'

'But Donne would have known the gospel Matthew and the message about things hidden, Richard. And they think you can help,' said Ian.

The Range Rover sped past the access road to Heathrow Airport. A stack of planes, like lamps in the sky, hovered on the eastern horizon. 'This is what I know. My abductor was called Larry Antony. He was from the States, and he showed me a map, asking me about a date and the co-ordinates of a place in North America or Greenland. A date when the world was created, he claimed.' I watched as a plane committed to the runway. 'Most of the time, he was confused. Or demented. A poem by T. S. Eliot completely obsessed him.' Another plane began its descent. It, too, had military markings.

Sophie reached into the glove compartment. Taking a bible into her hand, she found the reference. 'Matthew 13, verse 35. Before the parable of the weeds, Jesus declares he will utter what has been hidden since the foundation of the world. But it's not just a start date,

Richard. Once you've discovered that, you can calculate the day of the Apocalypse.'

'Then I can't help you, Sophie. I don't know any poems about it, either.' Nor was I convinced that Larry or Jonathan were harbingers of a golden future. 'Look, even if the whole cosmos started on a single day, who knows what the rest of the calculation is supposed to be? You can make up anything you want. Hidden or not.' I glanced out of the window. We were on the orbital motorway around London, still an hour and more from our destination. 'Pick a date, everyone,' I proposed.

'Jonathan's boss already has,' said Ian. 'And he intends to announce this to his followers before Christmas.'

'Then he'll be disappointed. Like other hapless prophets.'

'Take the next exit, dad.' We slowed before heading north-west on another motorway.

Maybe I told Larry about a poem. Maybe he has figured out the information he wants. And maybe Francis has too, since he knows how the cosmos will end, anyway. At least, that is how Jane put it to me in her letter. I closed my eyes. More trials, she promised. More pain.

'So long as you save Alex,' said Josh, 'there'll be a better world, because the destruction hard-coded into this one will be averted.'

Perhaps. But I was treading a difficult path. Alex—or the world as it is. Someone's going to be a loser.

'Another forty minutes and we'll arrive in Oxford,' said Ian. 'Anna is aware of what has happened and will stay with you over the next couple of days.'

'Thank you. We used to be close, you know.'

My last communication to Anna was back in early October. The last time we met, when we went to the cinema with Simon and Becky, was before the end of the summer term at school. Yes, we'd argued, but I'd tried to shrug it off with a few texts over the holidays, though without success. Eventually, the hurt gave way to resignation. And now … foreboding. We pressed on.

'How are you feeling, Richard?' asked Ian.

'So-so. A bit nauseous, actually. Can we stop somewhere? Anywhere will do. I'd like to get some air.'

'Can't stop, I'm afraid.'

Josh reached for a towel at his feet and threw it across my lap.

My eyes watered. 'I've been thinking … about what happens next.'

'We're not far, Richard. Anna is waiting for us in the college grounds near the canal,' said Sophie.

'Look, it's almost Christmas. I need to get home. To my mum and dad. And my sister. My younger sister.' We slowed as the motorway led to a roundabout on the city ring road. 'Then I want to go to the police. And to a hospital.'

'I'm sorry, Richard. We can't turn back.'

'But I've had enough of everything. All of you. Just get me home. Please.' I threw up against the seat in front of me.

'Josh, you'd better tell him why he can't go home,' said Sophie, reaching into her bag as an acrid smell filled the car.

'The guy in the flat next to yours. You said you tried to help him, Rick.'

'Yes. It was not long after I'd got back from the church. There was a hard knock on my door. He was standing on the landing and asked me for help. He looked beaten or injured.' Sophie passed me a roll of tissue paper. I wiped my mouth and my eyes. 'Something has happened to him?'

'He's dead. Strangled.'

'Dead?'

'He was found in his room in his underwear. The police want to question you. They've already spoken to your parents, and they're waiting outside your house in case you show up.'

In an eerie light, we pulled up alongside Worcester College near the centre of Oxford. I watched as Anna approached the car.

45

I t was getting light when Anna led me through the woods that fringed the college lake. The trees had thrown off the last of their autumnal colours while frost-coated leaves made a crisp mat under our feet. We crossed a narrow wooden bridge, making our way towards the quad. We didn't speak, but I think we both agonised over words running through our heads—words that shaped a conversation that we would surely have. A doorway took us from the gardens to a path alongside a row of medieval cottages that looked comically squat but strangely timeless. Fortuitous survivors, I fancied, as we headed to the chapel, skirting the green and the eighteenth-century cloister that adjoined the gatehouse. The year before, I'd waited by the porter's lodge, hoping to grasp a friendly hand as the day faded and my mood wavered, waiting, until a gentleman, holding a lighted candelabra, lit the way to the tutor's study.

Anna glanced at me, assuring herself of my presence as we reached the door of a compact but airy chapel built in 1791.

Was I at fault, I wondered? Six months before I'd left school, we'd slipped away at a sixth-form party, abetted by dance and drink, to a bedroom of our desires, and a mattress still warm from the sweat of others. Afterwards, I'd tried to play it cool with my friends. Was sex a kind of death, I thought, unsure of the sacrifice it demanded or the victory to behold? I found no answer. Nor have the poets.

We entered the chapel and paused just beyond the threshold. A rich display of colour and narrative greeted our arrival as pinks, reds and golds rioted across the walls and the lofty ceiling. We paused to capture the moment.

'Did you venture in when you came for your interview?'

'No. I'd wanted to warm up, but there was a service on. There'd been some snow, I remember.'

I glanced at the church organ to my left. A cantata by Bach sat above the keyboard. Anna moved into the aisle between wooden stalls aligned in the old monastic fashion where the choir sang and the penitent could watch each other barely eight feet apart. I stepped forward, scanning the décor, but keeping a little distance between us. 'Isn't it kind of Byzantine?' I asked, lengthening the initial vowel without thinking.

'Biz, Richard,' she countered. 'Like business,' she added, before softening her words with a smile.

'Or just Orthodox,' I suggested, catching sight of a Greek-style icon of the Christ positioned near the altar. I reached for the carved figure of an animal that adorned the end of a row of seating.

Anna stepped towards me. 'My boyfriend … says the animal carvings are very funny.' She placed her hand on the posterior of what looked like a hippopotamus.

Boyfriend, I thought. An alligator drew my attention. 'They must be something to do with the story of Creation. Or Noah's Ark.'

'There's even a dodo.' Anna pointed to a figure on the wall.

'So … not everything has survived, then.'

'No,' she said, avoiding eye contact.

I stepped away, moving along a mosaic flooring made of hexagons and squares where images of saints and scholars lay at my feet. 'The others, our school friends … are they well?'

'Yes.'

'Good. But I hadn't heard, you know.' My voice sharpened as I studied the floor. 'We're all so busy, of course. Killing and dying.'

The names Boniface and Alfred caught my eye. 'And I can't say that the last three months of my life have been … uneventful. Just busy.'

Anna closed up towards me. For a moment, she reached out, but her gesture faltered as an instinct made me recoil. But our eyes met.

'They know what's happened, Richard.'

'Do they know about the torture, then? The humiliation? Do they know about the guy strangled in his room? Or the burdens you've heaped on me since the day I started uni?'

'They knew that you'd gone missing after the Globe.'

'Missing? You nearly lost me for ever,' I said, moving to my right to avoid an elaborate stone lectern that blocked the aisle.

'Francis discovered where you were and contacted Josh. Josh contacted Martin.'

'Evidently.' I stood closer to the altar. 'And now, broken, I'm back in Oxford. Where I might have started, if I recall.' Turning to Anna, I asked: 'Where are the others?'

'In London. Simon and Becky left Durham straight after the upheaval at the Globe and are staying with Francis and Jane. They'll take part in the ceremony on Christmas Eve.'

'So they understand what's going to happen?'

'You mean … with the young woman?'

'Yes, damn it.' I swung away.

'Without your help, Richard, Alex is lost.'

'I know that.' My eyes settled on the stained glass window behind the altar. A skull lay at the foot of a crucified Christ. Death and memento mori, I knew. But if I am the world's saviour, who is mine? Or my partner's? The animal carvings offered no clue.

'The plan is that you and I travel to London tomorrow.'

'And tonight?'

'There is a guest room in the student accommodation block, Richard. There, you'll be safe.'

'And how do we get back to London?'

'I've arranged for a driver. He will take us to the British Museum. The ceremony will take place some distance from the atrium.'

'Underground, I believe. In a chamber.'

'It's about renewal, Richard. But before the … communal rites.'

'Rites! I know the details, Anna. And my testicles, if you are interested, are still in good shape.'

'Alex is your friend, Richard.'

'I have no friends. Only my conscience and my so-called destiny.' A parade of figures formed a frieze along the chapel wall, reminding me of the Parthenon marbles. Only there was no cloth. 'Do you remember when we went to the cinema? When we last met. At the end of school.'

'We were trying to get you to understand, Richard. About the world and its future.'

'Yeah,' I scoffed. 'So we head off to see a film, drenched in blood. A film about a war and a madman who'd gone AWOL. Remember? And then I'm supposed to sign up and shake the world's history free of sin. Great. Future solved.' My eyes fell on the icon before I turned back to Anna. 'But because Simon couldn't discuss politics without getting angry, you had to drag Alex into your subterfuge. Or someone … or something did.'

'Simon was trying to explain, but you were adamant. That's why our maths tutor tried to help you.'

'Help? She gave me a book. With a poem called "The Waste Land".'

'Becky suggested it, and I agreed with her.'

'Becky?' I felt pain cascading through my fingers. 'I thought Simon spoke for her. They always said the same bloody thing in class.' My voice faltered. I squeezed my fists, ready to scream.

Anna removed a tiny syringe from her bag and, standing beside me, injected morphine into a vein in my arm to neutralise the pain. 'Becky wanted to resume contact, Richard. But Simon was against it.'

'Why?' I snapped.

'Because he was … afraid of you.'

'Afraid?' I settled against a stall. 'What I wanted was for Simon to think things through. Instead, he'd make sweeping statements as if he had the final word. That's why I switched off. But it wasn't all. None of you thought I needed an explanation. You were a clique. Infatuated with instant solutions.' I paused as my eyes lingered on another stained glass window. An empty tomb and the mystery paradox, I recalled. I sat down. 'Anna.' My breathing steadied. 'The fact was … I was think- ing. About things … and about us.' Anna wiped a tear from my cheek. 'You know, I once stumbled on Simon and Becky having sex.'

'Where?'

'I'd gone to the sixth-form block at school after picking up an essay from my locker. It wasn't quite dark, and the teachers had already left. They'd put chair cushions on the floor. There was a bra and other clothes beside them. Simon looked up and Becky smiled at me. They wanted me to watch.'

'And did you?'

'Briefly. It was a clue, wasn't it?'

'They weren't teasing you, Richard, if that's what you think.'

'No. But I suppose it wasn't their first time, either. Anyway, I'm no longer the blushing boy you once knew.'

The pain in my fingers faded, though my heart still ached. Sixth form was another planet. Another world where we'd battled for grades and vied for teachers' praise. Projects. Tests. Competitions— until I asked my own questions, searched for my own voice, probed a silence as life … and friends slipped by. I filled my lungs. Sweet air, but weary thoughts. I stood up and scanned the benches of the chapel. Why are these dumb animals staring at me?

'Are you still angry with us, Richard?'

'Yes. But it's an anger tempered.' Anna offered me her arm before we walked back to the door of the chapel.

'We thought the film might help you, and prepare you for your own journey.'

'But it was brutal, Anna.' I stopped in the aisle. 'There were heads on poles. A river that went on and on until every bend was like the last and every slaughter an act of mimicry.' I studied the ceiling. A circular figure, comprising eight segments fell in towards the centre, conjuring an optical dome on its flat decorated surface. It looked real to the untrained eye. 'Events troubled me as much as the rest of you. I just wasn't clear what I could do about them.' I turned back to Anna. 'But I do understand the difference between right and wrong, and erasing this world doesn't look like an improvement whatever horrors Francis has divined for its future. Or his own personal agenda.' We continued along the aisle.

'If you turn away, you will never see Alex again. All sorts of disaster will befall us.'

'Maybe that's my burden, Anna, or my destiny, if you want to call it that. But I will go to your ceremony. And there I'll make my decision. Quietly. For you. For Alex. For the young woman who saved me from the river Thames. And for everyone who trusts my considered judgement.'

We looked at each other. I was feeling stronger. My resolve, firmer.

Anna closed her bag before placing its strap over her shoulder. 'My tutor would like you to join us for dinner tonight, Richard.'

'Dinner?'

'If you are … well enough.'

'I'm well, tell him … at least, well enough.'

'Then I shall confirm for 7.30. There are clean clothes in your room. I still remember how you dressed when we were together.'

I smiled. Even small kindnesses soften hardship, and I'd forgotten about clothes. But I did notice that her hair was shorter, and her eyes sadder. 'Does your tutor have something particular to say?' I asked as we stood by the door. 'The college has an interesting history, I've heard.'

Anna returned my smile. 'Well, you have met him before, Richard.'

'Really? What's his name?'

'Vittalli. Professor Eustace Vittalli.'

'Vittalli? He was at my interview twelve months ago.'

'That's right. And he wants to remind you of something you did before the world ends tomorrow.'

46

After a rest, I showered and had a rough shave using a razor I'd found in the guest room where I was staying. I then changed into the clothes Anna had put aside for me ready for dinner with her tutor. It was around 4pm, and the dull light of the early morning had returned as the twilight of the day. I'd slept for seven hours, grateful for the soft mattress and a warm, dry room in the students' accommodation block not far from the canal that ran north alongside the college grounds. As I got dressed, I noticed a padded envelope on the study desk under the window with my name on it. Unsealing it with a small penknife from a drawer, I let the contents fall on to the desk before examining them. There was a student ID card. A doctor's letter detailing my trauma, and an appointment the following day at a clinic in London. The photo on the ID card was mine, but the name wasn't. I checked the room and found my discarded clothes in a wardrobe, including the cash I'd received from Martin. Anna, I decided, must know more than she is saying.

With dinner still another hour, I made my way to the gardens and then the lake. The first stars were now visible. Jane, of course, enthused about them; but the winter sky, in Oxford, and summer above Delos, in the Aegean, are strikingly different. No Scorpio or Sagittarius at fifty-two degrees north. No Virgo. And yet the year, I recalled … as well as the lesser sun, had now to Capricorn run. The words from one of Donne's poems made me smile as I mused on the constellation of the Goat, while that of the Archer, part horse, part human, had shifted its place in the sky along with the calendar. Francis understood—we'd talked about centaurs in the British Museum a few weeks into the autumn term.

I'd never expected to see Anna again. Vittalli had slipped my mind altogether, and what I remembered of my interview was mostly chaotic. My parents were disappointed, and my teachers puzzled. But now I was back where I'd begun. Involuntarily, I admit, and with the world balanced on my shoulders. I edged closer to the water. The lake had frozen, and with the light dwindling away, I swung to my right and along a path that led me to the quad.

I was always unsure about Simon. We'd been in the same class for several years without getting to know each another, only to find ourselves in a much smaller study group in the two years before uni. Some of my classmates looked up to him, and by the time we'd left school, he'd become a guru to his followers. But I wasn't good at pedestal worship, and our last year proved the most fractious, with our disagreements influencing my studies, making me work harder but for more frugal results. Sometimes, I wanted him to piss off. But I lived through it, and I wasn't aware that he saw me as a threat or even a rival.

The air was crisp. Much like my thoughts. Vittalli wants to remind me of something, said Anna. Something I'd said over a year ago. The problem is that I didn't take notes, and we both know the time for forgetting is over. The world hangs. I remember the man with the hat, though. The lady with the sharply cut nose, and the attendants with works of art, hurrying one moment but pausing the next: Ophelia, who drowned, and Eurydice, who was lost. But is that my legacy? If Alex can tinker with time, can he tinker a little more? The grass crunched under my feet. Maybe an orgy is not such a bad idea, I reflected. One world ends. Another begins. Alex returns. The young lady goes home. Jane will be happy at the outcome and Francis too. But where does that leave me and everyone else—like Anna. Could we make up? Maybe Francis should draw another circle in his busy chart of cherry-picked destinies.

A church clock struck the first quarter, leaving me fifteen minutes to dash back to my room and grab my bow tie before dinner.

* * *

I entered the refectory.

'Ah, Mr Addings,' said professor Vittalli. 'Welcome to our college. I am very pleased to see you again.' Vittalli beckoned me to join him as he and Anna stood next to a large fire before he released some paperwork on to a lively flame.

The refectory was as large as the chapel. The ceiling was decorated with stucco. Grey flagstones covered the floor, while college worthies, old and new, graced the walls. The building was constructed in the early eighteenth century in a style that reflected the tastes of the age. The college was also the repository of the drawings of Inigo Jones, I'd learnt. I joined the others after straightening my tie.

'You are … well, I see.'

'In the circumstances,' I replied, flipping a glance towards Anna.

'Richard is still on morphine, professor.' She turned to me. 'I redressed your wounds while you slept, earlier.'

'Ah,' said Vittalli, glancing at my hands. 'You have done an excellent job. I'm sure your recent experience, Richard, was more than disagreeable.'

'I am feeling better, sir. My friends have been very attentive. I owe them my life.'

'Your friends have been brave, and your river journey a sensible precaution. The security situation is deteriorating in London, I believe.'

'So I understand.'

'But tonight you are safe with us, Richard.'

Vittalli was no younger than the illustrious portraits on the wall. But unlike the worthies staring down at us, he looked neither as severe nor as smug even if his watchful eyes suggested a wit ready to tease or even ensnare. 'Of course, my previous visit to your college, sir, was not … without incident.'

'Indeed,' he replied before turning briefly to Anna. 'I see the young man still has a sense of humour. You are quite right, Richard, and there is much for us to discuss over dinner, even if memory proves to be a fickle friend.'

I shrugged.

Vittalli placed his hands together. 'But first, may I offer you a glass of sherry?'

'Thank you. But a glass of water will do.' And as professor Vittalli moved to a drinks cabinet by the wall, I whispered to Anna: 'Is he joining us on Christmas Eve?'

Anna shook her head. 'He leads the team at Culham, outside Oxford, so he will stay here. But Dr Hatherleigh and Dr Arbetta will both attend.'

'Hatherleigh?' My jaw dropped.

'My dear friend, Julian,' said Vittalli, overhearing my surprise. He handed me a glass of water and Anna a glass of sherry. 'He once explained to me how to breed rabbits arithmetically, you know.'

'Oh?' I looked at Anna before changing the subject. 'There were two other tutors at my interview, I recall.'

'Two? Quite easily.'

'One was a tall gentleman. American, I thought. He wore a hat.'

'Yes. From Boston. A visiting scholar, and part of our exchange programme.'

'Also, a lady from the English department who spoke to me before things … kind of broke down.'

'Dr Martingale, Richard. She has been with us for several years.'

Vittalli turned to Anna. 'On matters pertaining to the college, we are not always in agreement. Otherwise, an astute member of the staff.'

With the fire burning lustily, I tried to recollect my encounter with Vittalli and his colleagues in a room with French windows that overlooked a spacious lawn. But why was my math's tutor there? Or were there four people interviewing me? A flame flared around the charred remnants of a book. Another awaited its fate. I sipped the water.

Vittalli glanced at the flames.

'There was a sword lying unsheathed on the table, professor.'

'Very unlikely, Richard.'

'But there was. And my math's tutor would have seen it.'

'Your maths tutor? But you were alone at your interview, young man. That is college procedure.'

I looked quizzically at Vittalli as the fire crackled. 'You asked me why I had come to your college, professor, and I said to discuss a poem.'

'Indeed. I remember.'

'Then the American asked me what the poem was about? And I said sex.'

'Yes. That is correct. My colleagues were impressed with your answer. And if matters had contrived differently, our library would have been at your disposal. We much admired your interest in poetry, Richard.'

'Really? So why are you burning books and papers on the fire, sir?' My eyes fell on some yellowed pages close to the fireplace.

'It is a precaution, young man. Tomorrow you will invoke a new world for us. But first we must return artefacts that have crossed the borders of time, lest they distort the outcome. They are of no consequence: records of the old medieval college that preceded our re-establishment in 1714 and a lost play from 1597 by one of Shakespeare's contemporaries.'

'In a fire indifferent to its fuel,' I remarked.

'Fire consumes the present. These artefacts live in the past, and so they are being returned to their proper place, as will the tokens we dispatched be to ours.'

'Oh? And what were they?'

'A book on celestial mechanics. And another on anatomy.'

'We have to swap things, Richard, to get Alex back,' said Anna.

'Things? You mean the native girl?' My pulse ticked up. The thought of purging through fire had unpleasant implications.

'But you should not be alarmed, Richard. We want Alex alive. It is through your intercession that the balance between worlds is restored, the old is revised, and the new will be sprung upon us.'

'Francis has explained the details to me. I'm just not sure of the outcome, however good the intention.'

'The chaos around us is intolerable. Our futures will be very bleak if we fail to take corrective action …' The door to the refectory opened suddenly, interrupting the tutor's flow. We turned as a trolley with dinner was pushed towards us by a college servant. 'Ah, I think we should take our places at table,' said Vittalli.

Anna gestured towards a table positioned on a platform a few inches above the flagstones of the hall. I found a place with a view of the exit and the fire. Anna and the professor sat facing me.

Vittalli leant forward. 'I took the liberty of using the college dining service as well as selecting something suitable from our cellar. A good meal always strengthens morale.'

A waiter part-filled my glass with a dark red wine after presenting the food on the table. I thanked him as Anna, conscious of my difficulties, took charge of serving the course. 'I recall, just before the start of my interview, professor, two gentlemen crossed your study with a large painting in oil.' Anna placed a piece of braised chicken on to my plate. 'They paused in front of me, quite deliberately.'

'The death of Ophelia, Richard. Romantics were haunted by her suicide in the stream. The painting by Millais is quite extraordinary.'

'But I am not Prince Hamlet, professor Vittalli. I'm Richard, Richard Addings.' I glanced at Anna, wondering if she might respond to my assertion. 'Then, after some discussion, we ventured on to the patio. There was music in the background.'

'I think that was Dr Martingale's idea. Applicants are sometimes stressed by the occasion and the gramophone has a positive effect on their concentration.'

I held my fork above my plate. 'We then ate.'

'Almost certainly. At that time of year, the staff tries to empty the larder. I suspect we had something stuffed. Probably bird, but I would need to check with the head chef to confirm that.'

'I don't remember, but it's of no consequence.' I wiped my lips with my napkin. 'The conversation then turned to politics.'

Professor Vittalli leant back in his chair, pausing as he savoured the wine. 'I have never understood why younger members of the common room are so keen to engage in all the nonsense that goes on in the world.' His eyes rested on me. 'Perhaps I should apologise, young man.'

'No, not at all. But the discussion struck me as incoherent.'

'The ability to see connections between myth, opinion and fact, Mr Addings, is a sign of maturity. What you observed then and what you recall now are not always the same thing.'

'Dr Martingale asked me if I had been sent to destroy the world.'

'That was our understanding.'

'She spoke of a conflict involving the Eastern Slavs. But it became confused with the Trojan War and the birth of Helen.'

'Then I must remind you of a little history, Richard. The Pontus Sea was well known to the mythical Argonauts just as much as to other warring factions in more recent times.'

'Pontus? Shouldn't we call it the Black Sea, professor?'

'In that case, we should be mindful, too, that Snake Island was the legendary burial place of Achilles. The incoherence of which you speak is a matter of perspective.' I watched as Vittalli folded his napkin before leaving it on the table. 'Time is indivisible to memory, Richard. Many poets have appreciated this conundrum, and some philosophers as well.' Turning aside, he gestured to the servant who had topped up our glasses.

'We played chess, I recall.'

'A good sign of spatial and temporal awareness, young man. My American colleague spoke to me afterwards about your game.'

'And then it started snowing.' I looked towards the fire. The flames had died down. 'At which point, professor, I left, not sure what was happening.'

Anna broke the silence. 'Where did you go so late at night, Richard?'

'Back to the canal, and the stream that runs alongside. It was dark, of course, and there was more snow, but intermittent. I saw a man fishing on the bank, using a lamp to attract his prey, and a net to catch them.'

'Did you speak?'

'Yes. He asked me where I was going.'

'And what did you say?'

'To London.'

A college servant removed the plates from the table. There was a brief conversation between him and Vittalli that I chose not to overhear. I stared at my hands as I set them beside my plate.

'Richard …' I looked at Vittalli. 'What did you tell your parents when you returned home?'

'I told them it had gone badly. I told everyone it had gone badly.'

'Was that true?'

'I was confused by what had happened. That's what I said.'

'Richard, I think you know what I mean. Was that true?'

'No.' I glanced at Anna.

'So what was the truth?'

'You sent me a text offering me a place. Unconditionally.'

'And you rejected it.'

'Yes,' I snapped, rising to my feet. 'I was angry. When I reached the riverbank, I told the angler what had happened and that I would ignore your offer. He said I would come back. I just laughed, crossed the bridge, and caught a night train on which I fell asleep before being woken by a stranger.'

Anna stared back at me.

'There was, I recall, some concern that you might accept our offer, at least initially. Dr Martingale thought your ego was too strong for you to spurn us. But I saw fear and anxiety in your countenance.'

'Why was I tormented?'

'Because your path is difficult, Mr Addings. Your reversals are part of your destiny. You must falter and then regret. That was the meaning in the painting you saw—the heartbreak of Orpheus for Eurydice because of an unguarded moment of vanity.' I sat down, conscious of his continuing attention. 'And now you are back where you started—wiser and ready to play your part, with your transformation almost complete.' He wiped his lips with the napkin and then turned to Anna. 'I shall remain here at the college until our new dispensation takes effect.'

Professor Vittalli rose from his chair and walked briskly towards the door of the hall, where he collected his coat from an attendant. The door closed firmly behind him.

Can truth save us? I wondered.

Anna reached for my hand. 'Tomorrow, we should meet outside the gate house at 6 a.m. The porter can call you earlier, if it helps, Richard.'

'No. There's a clock in my room with the other things you left me. I'll be ready.'

'We can have breakfast here, but we'll be alone, of course, since it is Christmas Eve.'

'End of term,' I said, flicking a glance towards the portraits on the wall. 'I'll wear something from the clothes I found in the wardrobe. But not this.' I unclipped the black tie, letting it hang loose around my collar.

Anna and I left the table. As we passed the fire, I noticed the flames had barely consumed a book that lay, like a log, resistant to the flames. For a moment, I was tempted to record its name for posterity, but a little bird, I fancied, whispered 'no'. We left the hall and paused outside in the adjoining cloister. There was still one more question on my mind—one of a more intimate nature. 'Anna,' I said, forcing eye contact, 'your boyfriend … what year is he in?'

'He's a second year.'

'Oh.' I shrugged. 'Is he travelling with us tomorrow? To London, I mean.'

'No. But you will see him later in the day.'

'At the ceremony, I suppose?'

'Yes. But you know him, already, Richard.'

'How? Who is he?'

'It's Alex.'

Stunned, I stepped back, unsure what to say. 'Does … does Jane know?'

Anna shook her head.

'I think … this complicates matters.' Turning, I headed back to the room. And another nightmare.

47

Oxford wasn't so far, after all. Not when you're driven at eighty miles an hour at four o'clock in the morning. Earlier, I'd sneaked out of the college grounds and made my way to a service station on the edge of the city looking for a lift. I'd made up a story about a disagreement with a friend who'd stormed off in his car with my Christmas presents. All because of a poem, I'd explained, to two middle-aged guys who'd stopped for petrol. They'd asked me my name before offering me a lift. Giles, I'd told them, showing my new identity card as proof. We hit the motorway back to London on a full tank of petrol.

My chance companions were both scientists with a weapons technology background. For the next hour, they talked about everything from handguns to the sky above our heads. I listened as they discussed cloud cover, electrical discharges and changes to the earth's magnetic field. They mentioned torrential downpours, violent auroras, and banshee-like winds as though the earth had become unhinged. Demeter in tears, I proposed. What are you studying, they asked? Art history. But the classical allusion washed over them, and after a nod, their curiosity faded.

I was dropped off in Trafalgar Square. The Strand led me to Drury Lane, and a little before 6 a.m. I arrived outside my accommodation block near Covent Garden. I paused in the courtyard and looked up. My room was never much of a home to me, I thought. More a halfway house between one existence and another. Sometimes a refuge and sometimes an uneasy trespass. A room in which I'd read poems by John Donne and puzzled over others by T. S. Eliot. A room where Fiona had called but wouldn't stay. Where Alex and I had laughed and wrestled, and where I'd been unsure … and alone. And yet, on my first day, I'd reached out. Thrilling at the encounter with Francis and Jane, hearing their story of Maximillian and his strange, pompous arch. It was a glorious start, even if the rest of my journey has proven more brutal, and must still reach a decisive end. My eyes settled on the common doorway. Daring. Warning me … until a consoling thought prompted a smile. There was more than one portal in Durer's engraving, I remembered. And more than one way to march brazenly through it.

The usual access code got me into the downstairs hall, where I paused and listened for voices. I closed the door behind me, unsure what might lie ahead. My alibi, if cornered, was that I was heading home at the end of the term, but that I'd been at Oxford for a few days before returning to collect a present from my room for my younger sister. No, I'd say, I don't know anything about a killing. Or any secrets. Or plans to overthrow the world. And that I intend to return to my parents for the Christmas break.

Avoiding the light switch, I went to the stairs and reached for the handrail.

'Richard,' said a whisper.

My heart raced as I turned. A torch shone at the floor before flipping to a familiar face. 'Eddie,' I said, as he reached forward to keep me on my feet.

'Listen, there are three guys in your room waiting for you.'

'The police?'

'Not sure. Just follow me.'

We crept outside and hugged the unlit side of the courtyard for cover. A locked entrance led us to the rear of an adjacent building, and a set of keys secured our escape. I jumped into the back of Eddie's cab before a maze of local streets took us back along the Strand.

Eddie glanced into his mirror. 'Half the security services are looking for you. And the police want you for murder.'

'I killed no one. I was abducted and tortured. That's the truth.'

The cab skipped a red light, before swinging into Northumberland Avenue where we drew up at a taxi rank by Hungerford Bridge. Eddie switched off the engine.

'Otto wants to see you, Richard. At the British Museum. Today.'

I leant against the leather upholstery. 'I was supposed to travel with Anna. From Oxford. She was minding me.'

'And I was supposed to be your driver, young man.'

We were close to the river and Embankment Gardens where Jane and I had talked until Francis, and death, caught up with us, in what was a blow to them but a glancing sadness to me. But now, I was no longer the innocent naïf or the bystander to others' heartache. The world was closing in, and I was ready to fight back. 'I'm not going anywhere, Eddie, until I get answers. Or I walk.'

'The doors are locked.'

'So? Otto needs me more than I need him. Sooner or later, you'll have to open them.'

Eddie scanned the street. 'Okay. I'll talk as I drive. You've got twenty minutes. I'll tell you what I know. Scouts honour.' We swung away from the curb, reversed in the road, and headed towards Trafalgar Square. The gushing fountains had frozen during the night.

'The students in my block … what can you tell me about them?'

'What I told you. First day. Ask again.'

'There was a guy on the second floor I spoke to. What was his name?'

'George. Does history. Works for me.'

'Works for you?'

'Yeah. Small jobs. Taps the router in your block.'

'I kind of interrupted him once. With his girlfriend.'

'None of my business. Next question.'

We turned into the Mall and towards Buckingham Palace. 'There were two guys I never met on the first floor.'

'A law student called Gideon Davies. An informer for MI5. Vivien Weekes is his contact at the uni.'

'Weekes? The guy with the ponytail?'

'That's him. The other lad disappeared at the beginning of term.'

'And the student next door to me … is dead.'

'You should never have left the flat in Bloomsbury, Richard.'

'So everyone says. But I wanted to get away.'

At Hyde Park Corner, we turned on to Park Lane by Wellesley House. A bronze statue of Achilles rose heroically by the junction, reminding me again of myth, and Jane, and those squabbling male egos she liked to disdain. Daylight staggered into the dawn as we flitted by.

'And when you got home, you walked into a trap.' He changed gear.

'And a guy called Larry Antony abducted me.'

'He did. And he reports to a guy who thinks he's a prophet. Warren Dudley. Bloody charlatan, if you ask me.'

'He thinks I know the secret.'

'So does MI5.' At Marble Arch, we joined the Edgware Road before passing a convoy of military trucks parked along the road.

'You know a lot, Eddie.'

'Contacts. Money. But remember, I grew up around the old market. We had networks, and could figure out things for ourselves when we had to.' He flipped a glance to the mirror. 'Not like some of you youngsters.'

'I'm doing my best.'

'Look, Richard, sometimes we have to start again. You've heard it from Francis and Jane. And now you've got to help your mates.'

'I've got to destroy everything I see around me. In a ritual.'

'Talk to Otto.'

We picked up speed along the Marylebone Road. Baker Street wasn't far away. Nor the elegant terraces of Bloomsbury and their genteel charm.

'There's a girl involved. Someone real.'

'We're all real. Even your next-door neighbour was real. But that didn't save him.'

'How did he die?'

'Choked to death. Did it himself.'

'He wanted my help.' I shut my eyes, overwhelmed by his wretchedness. 'Everything's sordid and unfair, Eddie.'

'If you'd stayed where you were ….' Braking suddenly, he cut his words. The cab swerved as a stone hit the windscreen. We spun around and turned into another street. Behind us, a mob hurled missiles as we fled.

'What's happening?'

'Nutters, Richard. They think the world's coming to an end.'

Angry groups patrolled the pavements. Abandoned cars burned in the street ahead. If we were stopped, we'd have no chance to run for it. A guy with an axe leapt towards us before we knocked him aside. We weren't taking hostages. And neither would they.

'My job's to get you to Otto.'

'Alive, Eddie.'

'No problem, I know the streets.' We screeched to a halt, ready to turn. I leant forward only to be thrown back as the pace changed again. 'Dead end, he explained,' hitting the gas. A woman holding a brick targeted us as we passed. 'Keep your head down, their greetings don't always bounce off.'

We raced along Malet Street and pulled into the forecourt of Senate House. The rear entrance of the museum was across the road, but time was short.

Eddie turned to me. 'Use the steel door at the bottom of the ramp. Here's the password. Go to the staircase by the Enlightenment gallery. Part way up, there's an office. But check the bookshelves. The boss is waiting for you.'

Otto was the great tarantula at the centre of this intrigue, I knew. Like the petrifying Medusa waiting for her ill-prepared adventurers, or the ravenous Minotaur devouring the best of Athens's youth. But where Perseus had his mirror to deflect the monster's stare and Theseus his string to retrace his steps, all I had were my convictions. I read the piece of paper in Eddie's hand. 'Thanks,' I said, remembering the code.

'It's up to you now, Richard.'

I got out with the engine still running. 'There's one more thing on my mind, Eddie.'

'Tell me. But be quick.'

'In my bedsit, there's a small figurine in a bag. Made of alabaster. It's a present for my little sister. I mean … if I don't make it home.' Eddie swallowed as our eyes met. 'For Christmas,' I added, my voice faltering.

'I'll … talk to George. Don't worry, son, we'll sort something out.'

'Tell the others, I'm going in because I want to.' I stood back, watching the cab pull away. Eddie had looked after me, I thought. And he'd always told me the truth. I owed him, I knew, but all I could do was make a simple gesture. I left the money Martin had thrust at me on the seat of the cab. The sixty pounds would cover the fare—the fare he'd paid three months before, when a short ride from the campus proved to be the start of a longer, and more fateful, journey. A journey that was now approaching its end.

48

Eddie didn't want me to hang around, so once past the security door, I made my way to a small auditorium overlooked by a flight of steps that gave access to the floors above. Debris, bricks, and smashed pots littered the stairs. I retrieved a section of a mosaic. A pagan god stared back at me. I continued to the next level of the building and the entrance to the Pacific and Oceanic department. There were no signs of damage or disarray. Ancestor spirits, I presumed—hurrying through.

In a smaller gallery, where the lighting was subdued, a black and red ceramic bowl drew my attention. To the Greeks, it was called a kylix. A saucer shaped container for drinking wine. A winged goddess of ancient Greece decorated its centre. The goddess Eris, I noted. Patron of strife and discord. She was grinning. But I was in no mood to return the smile.

A spotlight fell on an Etruscan mural depicting a parade of figures from the Trojan War. In faded hues, three supplicants, led by Hermes, and looking clumsy in their curled, pointed boots, approached Paris, the son of Priam and king of Troy. Who is the fairest? The goddesses asked. My eyes switched to a disconsolate Helen—the ambivalent prize in this grim tale of disaster. I shrugged. So who was next?

I had not been to the museum since the shooting of Kalinsky, since Francis's explanation about the Parthenon marbles, the aborted Q and A, and Josh's text about joining him in the pub for a lunchtime pint. I glanced back at Paris, trembling at the anxious smiles of Hera, Athena, and Aphrodite. Poor lad, I thought. If only he'd kept his mouth shut … if only Josh had called me another day.

A sound broke my concentration.

It can't be Eddie. But it might be Otto … lurking and watching. Testing me. I'm not hiding, I whispered. Brazenly, I moved to the centre of the room and stood alone by the prostrate figure of Achilles, his smooth muscular frame glistening in a sharp, crystal light. I'm not afraid, I said, daring the silence with an uncertain swagger.

The shadows stayed still. My pulse beat stronger.

The fate of every hero is death, my teacher warned. Tragic. Early. And foredoomed. He'd rattle off examples to us in class. Theseus. Perseus. Odysseus. Even the stubborn Achilles, he said, yielded to a destiny foretold. I glanced at the ankle where an arrow, laced with poison, and stuck fast in his heel, delivered the final blow. I removed it. As a weapon, it was as good as any Bronze Age dagger, I fancied. I'm not afraid, I said, raising my voice, hearing my words as I spoke them.

Clutching my prize, I moved on.

Eddie must have told Otto by now. He must know that I am looking for him. And for the young lady. I left the exhibition on Troy and the Mycenaean Greeks, and entered the museum's vast and airy atrium, heading for the white, limestone staircase that ascended the rotund library at its heart. Above me, a roof of translucent glass, undulating like the sea, flooded the space with blue-tinted light, bleaching the walls and making the floor shine.

He must know that I'm here.

I raised my arm, and holding the arrow aloft, fixed on a small window cut into the wall above the atrium's temple style entrance. 'Otto, I've made my decision. I know what I shall do.' My voice echoed across the chamber. 'There's no need to hide. Show yourself.'

Otto appeared, and looking down, called out to me: 'It's Alex or the girl, Richard. Choose this world or the one we have planned for you.'

'Destiny has no hold over me. Tell Francis that the stars mean nothing...'

A sharp crack sent me diving behind a wall as glass splinters pierced the air. For a few minutes, I stayed low and then lifted my head. Otto had gone. I listened as the commotion outside grew louder, and the sound of gunshots was followed by screams. How long, I wondered, before the crowd storms in? I dashed down the staircase and crossed the floor to the entrance of the gallery only to find that the large door providing access was locked. I found another, but it, too, was locked. I paused. Was I supposed to retrace my steps and turn back? Or was I supposed to fall here? I called out: 'For god's sake, Otto, stop playing games.' But to no answer.

The atrium, I noticed, had already been plundered. A horse rider lay toppled from his plinth, but his severed limb and a discarded wooden box suggested a solution to my dilemma. I dragged the box to a large rectangular window overlooking the atrium, and standing on it to gain height, I hurled the remnant of a leg at the glass, covering my head as the window shattered around me. I scrambled through, a mixture of morphine and adrenaline still cruising through my veins.

A walkway, eight feet above the floor, looked down on the Age of Enlightenment. The large, elongated room was empty, but broken vases and another toppled statue suggested the earlier disturbance. A dark pool of blood ... something more sinister. I lowered myself to the floor. Undaunted, I moved towards the exit and the staircase that would lead to Otto's office.

The room, I'd heard, had once housed the library of George the Third. But today, only faux bookshelves lined the walls—a remembrance, perhaps, to the gentleman's love of science and astronomy whatever else Eddie was thinking of. I passed a cabinet emptied of its contents, but then another untouched by the intrusion. Puzzled by the random violence, I paused thinking of the eerie quiet that must have befallen Troy after its destruction by the Mycenaeans … until a lifeless foot unsettled the fancy. Warily, I approached and, turning my head, looked down. Behind the pristine display, and like a sheep slaughtered in a field, a museum official lay butchered on the floor. I swung away, stunned by his dismemberment.

'Well, well, well,' declared the voice of his blood-stained assassin. An unshaven youth, no older than me but shorter, stood armed a few feet from where I was standing. 'If it isn't the poet lover from Covent Garden,' he teased. 'Remember me, pretty boy?'

My heart pounded. Confronting me was the guy who had mocked me to his mates. The guy who had demanded my name and my obedience at the start of the autumn term. Filled with rage, I returned the compliment. 'Still learning to read, dickhead? I see your friends are not here to applaud you.'

'This is my friend,' he said, running his finger along the shaft of Achilles' arrow. 'I found it on the steps in the atrium. Tut, tut,' he added with a frown. 'You have a habit of leaving things around, Richard. Like that weird book of poems you study. I reckon it's you who needs a lesson.' He feigned a stab at me as he stepped forward.

I stood firm. 'Fuck off. And get out of my way.'

'Only the dead pass me,' he said, gesturing to the corpse.

We circled a display case. Maybe a machete lay within reach, I thought. Maybe the ghastly tool he'd used on the guide, or even a sword. But as my attention darted, he lunged fast at me. I felt the tip of the arrow slide off my collar and graze my neck. I snatched at the weapon, trying to divert another thrust, and as my balance shifted, he swung towards me until we fell together, locked in a frantic embrace. Alex, I yelled, grabbing my assailant's hair, pulling his head down as the arrow hovered before my face. With a scream, I shoved my knee into his groin, and beat his head against the floor, still struggling with his outstretched arm, and an arrow poised to fall—its stab fatal, its shaft warmed by our sweaty hands, and our faces by desperate tears.

We rested. Amidst a memory of our first, unequal encounter. In a café with a balustrade. I sighed and closed my eyes. But oh, self-traitor, I recalled … I've brought the spider love. I let go of the arrow, lifted myself clear, and staggered towards the exit.

49

A crow swept low over the crowd, looking for food. A fox scampered for safety under an abandoned car. In the sky, a flock of birds, hesitating as they swarmed, shifted left and right, turned, and soared far above the frozen earth. A tree stood. Shattered. Its leaves shrivelled and crushed underfoot. A wolf howled on Hampstead Heath, and another in a far-off, snow-covered glen. A bison grazed by a bank of the Thames, and across the Plains, the buffalo herded, loitered and roamed. The ice came. The ice departed. The rains came. The flood departed. A raven searched for his friend, and in the darkness, a turtle shook mud from its ageless shell. A shrub lent cover to a sly, solicitous snake, blushing as the creature shed its skin. The great auk forgot to fly and died.

* * *

Otto rushed from his desk and stared down at the mob howling below his window. Soon you idiots will be swept away, he thought. Even the very streets you strut will vanish and return to fields. He closed and barred the window's stiff, protective shutters and returned to his desk. In front of him, lay a diagram of a new space-time configuration of the cosmos. Satisfied with the consequences, he phoned his associate, Eustace Vittalli, in Oxford.

'Vittalli, your report, please.'

'Richard is back in London, Otto. He left the college in the early hours and travelled by car along the M40 motorway.'

'Yes. Just as we expected. Eddie picked him up at his flat before MI5 could snatch him. He is now somewhere in the museum. Unfortunately, the tremors have stopped the monitors from working, but I have agents posted around the galleries. Have Culham completed their checks on the planetary alignments?'

'Last night. As Richard joined me at dinner, we made a trial projection of his encounter with the void. The presence of Anna allowed us to simulate the act of coitus prior to the opening of the portal on the Intermediate Zone.'

'Was he co-operative?'

'Sufficiently. I reminded him of his debt to his parents.'

'Good. So far the augurs are favourable. But we must track his progress through the IZ to be sure he is committed.'

'We can do this through a trace of iodine that we concealed in his food, Otto. This allowed us to follow Richard to London and keep Eddie informed of his movements. In the IZ, his presence will create a disturbance in the space-time construct and from this we will calculate his co-ordinates. We have already confirmed Alex's position.'

'Thank you.'

'Have the other young people joined you, Otto?'

'Francis and Jane arrived last night. The native girl is safe and eager to return to her homeland once the ceremony begins. Simon and Becky have performed their ritual cleansings and are guarding the caesium isotope.'

'And the rest of the assembly? Are they prepared for the end?'

'All thirty-four members of the assembly have been briefed. Events will unfold like a drama, and they will marvel at what they hear and see.' Otto turned to the diagram. 'In which part of the sky will the portal be opened?'

'In the constellation of Taurus, Otto. The star cluster of the Hyades is the doorway to other dimensions. In ancient times, it was known as the Golden Gate of the Ecliptic.'

And in legend, emblazoned on the Shield of Achilles, Otto reflected. 'Run through the path, Richard will take through the cosmos. There are certain rites I will perform in mimesis of his journey.'

'Once the threshold of the IZ is crossed, he will continue along the winding course of the constellation Eridanus—the river of the abyss—skirting the constellations of Orion, Lepus, Caelum and Horologium to his right, and Cetus, Fornax and Phoenix to his left. At this time, the world will be plunged into darkness and the cold will intensify. During his journey, he will pause at the star Epsilon Eridani and send a signal comprising the words of the poem that haunt him most.'

'The Nocturnal?'

'Yes. The very lines he heard on the steps of the British Museum.'

'Good. But I shall ask him to say the words before he begins his journey as a test of his resolve.' Otto paused, remembering the collections of poetry still on his bookshelf. His thoughts returned to Richard's journey: 'And then at the end, at the river's end, Vittalli?'

'Yes. Between the constellations of Horologium and Phoenix, Otto. There he will reach the star Achernar. A binary. And there he will meet Alex before leading him back to us along the same tortuous path. The native girl will return to her land. And the changes that Alex has wrought in our destiny will unfold.'

'And the bull will be slain.' Otto drew a deep breath.

'The Minotaur, indeed. But if Richard teases us or walks out, what should we do?'

'There is an alternative …' Otto paused as his eyes strayed along a crack in the ceiling of his room. He wondered about the crowd and the safety of his agents.

'Who?' asked Vittalli.

'Simon,' replied Otto, his attention returning to the diagram. 'He is a fit young man and will take Richard's place if he challenges us.'

'And not Francis?'

'No. I have had enough of the nonsense that obsesses him. This evening's outcome will be very different to what he is expecting.'

'Is Alex aware of this?'

'No. I have decided that Francis will follow his own brother into oblivion. The details have been coded into the new specification without his knowing that he will perish.' Pausing, Otto fixed his eyes on the door to his office. He listened before resuming the conversation. 'We cannot solve every personal mishap or social angst when ridding the world of its lazy expectations.'

'I agree. Things should be simpler, Otto. As they were when the colleges were founded.'

'And as they shall be, Vittalli. There is no place for Francis's social theories or political calculations in my scheme. Delusion is at the root of modern alienation and Francis's ambitions are typical of the condition. Those who survive the ceremony will understand that.'

'So Francis will be our sacrifice?'

'At the end of the penance. Simon will dispatch him during the second humbling once I give the word. He is popular with the Thirteen Elders who are already aware of my intention. Once the new space-time has crystallised, the Elders will take control of the world under my direction.'

'And Jane, Otto?'

'Yes, Jane … she will survive. Though she must learn to live with her predicament. Her disdain was always too cultured. I was never sure she truly understood what we intended even when she played her part.'

'And she never did get close to Richard, I believe.'

'No. It appears not. I think we underestimated Richard's loyalty to Alex. But if he falters, Simon will take his place. The specification permits this.' Otto rose as a roar erupted from the crowd. 'The crowd is hysterical, Vittalli. They will destroy everything.'

'You must leave, Otto. Let Richard find his way. That is his destiny. Or Simon's if he fails.'

'You are right, Vittalli. His garments and instructions are ready and placed in the chest. He has only to access the spiral staircase and follow the trail that I shall leave for him. Once hooded and attired, he may enter our assembly as an initiate and celebrant, and will remain silent and masked until we hear from him the words of the poem.'

Otto ended the call. From an unlocked drawer, he retrieved a leather pouch and checked the contents. He rose from his chair, turned, and removed three books before placing them on his desk. A small panel behind the bookcase concealed a switch. He waited as the shelves edged back and opened on a spiral staircase behind the wall. Clutching the pouch, he made his way towards the basement of the museum.

At the foot of the steps, he uttered a prayer to Aphrodite, born of the sea, mother of Eros, and lover of gentle Adonis. From the pouch, he removed a large handful of shells and arranged them on the ground in a circular pattern. Proceeding further, he followed a brick-lined passage that wound its way below the floor of the museum's atrium until he entered a small chamber with planets and stars painted in reds and golds across its arched ceiling. Ahead of him, three doors exited the chamber. At the first door, on his left, he placed the tooth of a whale, and at the second, on his right, he pinned the paw of an arctic hare. Between these two, he placed a ceramic tile on which the outline of a boat was etched. He uttered a prayer to Persephone, the abducted one, the mother of the Furies, and the restless breath of spring. After making his choice, he passed below the museum forecourt and south under the streets of Holborn towards the centre of London. The brick changed to steel. Old pipes and cables cluttered the way. At a juncture, he entered another chamber. Before the door on his left, he placed a small pot hollowed from a ball of clay, and before the door on his right, he placed a bronze-aged chisel. He lit a candle and placed it in the pot. Between the clay pot and the chisel, he poured sand from the pouch, and with his finger, traced the shape of a water snake on its undulating surface. He uttered a prayer to Hermes, messenger of the gods, protector of travellers, merchants and thieves. Otto descended deeper, approaching the complex where his associates and friends sang and chanted, burnt scented oils, and savoured erotic wines. At the end of the way, he stopped by a ladder that shimmered brightly in the colours of a rainbow. Above and below, the ladder gave access to secret domains. At one side, he placed an hourglass filled with sand, and by the other, a bird feather wrapped in the dried skin of a pomegranate. Raising his arms in salutation, he honoured the god Dionysus, the god of fertility, madness and ecstasy, discarded the pouch and hurried to his destination.

50

'Behold. I shall come like a thief in the night!' Felix fell back as the crowd rushed towards the iron railings of the British Museum. Another blast from the public address system attacked his ears: 'I will give him power over the nations, and he shall rule them with a rod of iron.'

A roar greeted the words as Felix pushed his way across the street and entered the smashed-up premises of a local pub. He pulled a headband from his forehead and reached for his gun. 'Jesus loves you,' he shouted, surprising two looters as they robbed the till. They fled at the sound of his greeting.

Slipping behind the bar, he crouched low, and phoned the COBRA control room in Whitehall. The foreign secretary answered the call.

'Where are you, Felix?'

'In a pub. Great Russell Street. Just opposite the museum.'

'Can you see Warren Dudley?'

'No. But I can hear him.'

Felix raised his phone without revealing his presence. The voice of the preacher greeted his ears: 'Come. Come, faithful. Behold the rider with a bow. Behold the rider with a crown.'

The crowd roared in unison: 'Let him conquer. Let him conquer.'

Felix withdrew his arm and shifted suddenly as bottles of spirit crashed to the floor. He waited as a tremor shook the building before returning to the call. 'The words are from Revelation, Alison.

The opening of the scroll and its seven seals. He's whipping up his followers with promises from the bible.'

'Are you able to get closer to the museum?'

'No chance. The crowd is delirious. '

'Well we need you inside. Fast. The PM wants Addings and the rest of them alive. And he wants the secret before Dudley or his mob gets there first.'

Felix raised his head, checked the two exits of the pub, and a plate-glass window that had escaped the fate of three others. He ducked as a small group of Dudley's followers swept by, animated by the exhortations of their preacher. With their leader's words echoing in his head, he removed his gun from a concealed holster. He felt for a stun grenade in an outside pocket of his jacket. 'There must be other entrances. At the back or the side, Alison.'

'Six. But they're all blocked, and the windows are boarded up from inside.'

'How big is the crowd?'

'The police estimate is over two thousand, and growing. We're watching live footage in the control room. They've dug a pit in the forecourt and are holding hostages from the museum at its edge.'

'Or victims, Alison. Can we do anything to stop them?'

'The police will attack with tear gas once their reinforcements are in place.'

'They'll need armoured vehicles. The mob are stockpiling petrol bombs for their finale.'

'Whatever. But we have to get you inside, Felix.'

'Can you get a rescue team on to the pub roof? I can hold the crowd back on the stairs.'

'OK. We'll get a SWAT team in and then switch you to the museum. Once there, search the tunnels under the galleries that lead south towards Covent Garden. There's a chamber where they will hold a ceremony. We'll dress you up before you join them …'

Alison paused, hearing the crash of a plate-glass window. 'Felix. Are you ...?'

'Still here. But I might have to shoot my way out.'

'If you do, we'll try to give you cover from the air.'

'Alison, there's another way into the tunnels. The abandoned tube station. Between Holborn and Tottenham Court Road. It was shut in the 1930s.'

'We've already broken in. But we're not sure where the students are. It's a labyrinth. With multiple levels and booby-traps from the days of the Cold War.'

'If you can, draw the mob away from Russell St., I could make a dash for it. But you'll need to kill their PA system. He's driving his followers crazy.'

'Keep your ears open. We're about to rejig it. Their saviour will have something to say to them shortly.'

Hallelujah, thought Felix. 'Alison, James thinks the secret comprises eighteen digits. It was part of the Kalinsky material I sent you. How can I be sure of the number, if I find it?'

'We think they are using an atomic clock as the count-down to their space-time upheaval. The digits are embedded in an isotope of caesium-137. Hold them off until the technical team arrives. They're likely to be armed, so do whatever is needed.'

'How long have we got?'

'Five hours, if they wait for sunset.'

Another roar interrupted their call.

'Hold on,' said Felix, raising his phone to catch the PA.

'A pale horse. And its name is Death,' thundered Dudley to his followers.

'That's The Four Horsemen, Alison. He's opened the fourth seal on the scroll.' He reached for his headband, wearing it so that its mark covered his forehead.

'What does it mean?'

'It means they'll wait until the seventh seal is opened and the seventh trumpet is sounded before they execute their prisoners.'

'Should I get the Bishop of London to talk to them?'

'If she can play the Lamb of God. But right now, you need trumpeters on the roof of the museum. It'll grab their attention before Dudley pulls the same trick as Revelations. There's still fifty or sixty verses of the text to go.'

'We can get the household cavalry if we have to, Felix. But we need you inside the tunnels, whatever happens to their prisoners. The SWAT team has your co-ordinates.' More glasses and bottles fell from the shelves. 'The secret … can you hear me?'

'Yes.'

'The secret is more important to the PM. And national defence. But there's a complication.'

'What?'

'We picked up some intelligence on Dudley's sidekick this morning.'

'Larry Antony?'

'Yes. He's inside the museum or trying to break in. We arrested a young man at the Globe theatre earlier today. He had an art work under his arm and was detained on suspicion of theft … Are you there?'

'Yes. Who is he?'

'His name is Jonathan Saunders, and he claims to be a post-grad at UCL in Addings's class. He broke down after his arrest and told us everything he knows.'

'Does he know where the students are?'

'No. But he thinks Larry Antony and an accomplice are trying to join them for their ceremony.'

'Larry? Whose side is he …?' He paused as a light fixture crashed beside him.

'Felix?'

'Don't worry. Some plaster from the ceiling. Just a few cuts, but stinking of gin.'

'OK. Listen carefully: the PM's orders are to shoot him dead on sight.'

'Why?'

'He's carrying a homing device for an ICBM missile. Warren Dudley's plan was to destroy the Globe theatre with Saunders, his accomplice, and Antony in it. The Foundation believes it is the gateway to Hell, and he wants to super-charge the Apocalypse.'

'Hold on, Alison.' Felix turned his ear to the commotion outside the pub.

'And in the East, a portent appeared in heaven; behold a great red dragon with seven heads and ten horns … and his tail swept down a third of the stars of heaven and he stood before the woman with child that he might devour the child.'

'Felix?'

'Sorry. Just catching up with Warren's sermon. He's halfway through the last book of the New Testament. The war in heaven is about to break out.'

'Well, whatever happens, we have a ship with anti-ballistic missiles in the Thames. Plus others west and east of the UK.'

'If Dudley is following his script, it'll be from the east. And from below the waves.'

'We're covering the Russian arctic and the eastern Mediterranean. According to a CIA source, Dudley has a fanatical cell on a US submarine.'

'Or the Black Sea. You'd better alert Moscow in case they misinterpret the launch.'

'The PM has called the hot line. But NATO forces are on standby in the event of conflict.'

Felix removed the grenade from his pocket. And I saw a beast rise out of the sea … with seven warheads, he thought, listening out for the preacher. 'I have to get out of here, Alison, otherwise we are all going to hell. Where is the SWAT team?'

'Felix?'

'Sorry. I'm on my feet. I've got customers.' Felix released the phone from his left hand and reached for the grenade. He placed his finger on the trigger of his gun. If these guys stop moving … His eyes flicked left and right as three spaced-out delinquents stared back at him. One held a machete. The others, iron bars. 'Sorry. We're closed. For renovations.'

'Who are you, stranger?' asked one of the three, stepping forward.

'A friend. A friend of the chosen.'

'Take care, brothers,' said another. 'There is a strange mark on his headband.'

'I think the day of judgement has come,' said Felix, eyeing his opponents as they shifted around the bar.

'Only the preacher knows the day of judgement, stranger,' replied the third.

Felix chose his targets. Two dead might scare off the third and still leave a present for Larry. He flicked a glance towards the door.

'Behold!' thundered the preacher. But the blast of a grenade drowned the PA and sent the intruders flying unconscious to the floor.

Felix leapt up from behind the bar and escaped into the street. The SWAT team raced after him.

51

Ahead of me, a marble staircase led to the oak-panelled door of Otto's office. It was now Christmas Eve: I brought a promise to the world, but no gifts. I was wanted by the police, set-up by my friends, and was the target of an angry mob. Nothing had prepared me for this, nor the decision that I knew would soon follow. Defiant, I pushed open the door and entered a large rectangular room. In the gallery below, I'd left two bloodied corpses.

'I've met death, Otto, and I'm no longer afraid.' I scanned the room. I was alone. A wooden chest sat askew in front of Otto's desk. As I approached, I noticed a sequence of carved panels on its side. I lifted the lid. The chest was empty. Is Otto playing games? I returned to the door and closed it, but the deceptive silence, I feared, would soon break. Aware of an icy draught, I checked the shutter protecting the window, and as I turned away, a silver coffee pot on the desk caught my attention. Where is he?

I sat in his chair and tried to open the drawers of his desk, only to find one of them locked and another empty. I flicked a glance around the room. Close to the architrave was a wooden stand, and at its base, fragments of a broken vase. Alongside that, a fireplace with a limestone surround. In its grate, there were ashes, but no embers like those I saw burning at the college in Oxford. Behind me, a row of bookshelves lined the wall. I looked again at the chest before my eyes settled once more on the coffee pot. It was cold. I felt my pulse: strong but wary. Was I supposed to wait here? Or just die? I pressed my lips. I'm not giving up, Otto, if that's what you're thinking.

In front of me, lay a map of the cosmos. And where Francis had once placed his finger, there was now a world sketched in a hand quite different to the rest of the drawing. Along the margins, and in the same hand, I read a list of treaties and familiar historical events. Some, I noticed, had been crossed out while others were underlined. History was up for grabs, I remembered. Shifting my eyes, I lingered on three books placed together in a small pile on Otto's desk.

Plato's 'Timaeus' sat on top of the pile. I checked the map but could find no sign of Atlantis. Nor had Francis mentioned it when he explained the cosmos to me before we headed off to see 'Doctor Faustus' at the Globe. I shrugged: it was just a fable. A myth like Shangri-La or an imagined loss like the Golden Age—the one my school teacher was so fond of invoking. He'd also forgotten Hades and its underworld. So much for young Persephone, I thought. I set Plato aside and reached for the 'Songs and Sonnets' by John Donne. With a smile, I landed on a poem I knew well: 'A Valediction Forbidding Mourning'. And two loving souls like the stiff arms of a compass. As one leant, the other turned … amidst the trepidation of the spheres, observed the poet. I shut the book—another memory dislodging the lines. A memory of an evening spent laughing and talking in a pub, and Alex arriving late. My pulse beat faster as I reached for the poems of Robert Frost, and a loose slip of paper that I found inside the book's cover. I read the following words: *To Richard. From Alex. Because only you will understand.* I swallowed, remembering our antics in the square, Jane's anguish and her friendly rebuke. And how, as the evening ended, I'd held my hand aloft until we'd parted … our fates somehow aligned and confused. I let go of the book. Why, my friend? Why did you write this for me?

I jumped to my feet, hearing a stone hit the window to my right. Turning to the bookshelves, I wondered if they hid as much as they revealed, and then with greater force, I tried again to pull open the locked drawer of the desk. Still determined, I went back to the chest, and grabbing the frail, wooden lid, ripped it free. I used the long spine of a hinge as a wedge and, with repeated blows from the coffee pot, I broke open the drawer. Inside, I found a loaded handgun. But where was Otto? My mind was racing as fast as my heartbeat.

I shifted around … past the windows, and then on to the stairwell holding the gun. Emboldened, I returned to the room, locked the door, and stared ahead. I could see books. Lots of them lining the shelves. If the answer was buried there, I was running out of time. O little bird, must I join you … aloft?

I scanned the room—a shuttered window, a fireplace, a chest and a coffee pot scarred with random dents. And a space on the bookshelf for Donne, Plato and Frost. Eddie's words came back to me. I flew towards it, shifted the other books aside, and found a small panel enclosing a switch.

As the bookshelf edged away from me, I slipped through the gap and down a flight of steps that spiralled to a lower basement level. A faint light illuminated my way, but the circular movement as I descended induced a sudden nausea in my head. I paused at the foot of the stairs and held the rail. Looking down, I could see shells on the floor like those I'd found in Jane's flat. Some had been crushed, as if trodden on. I looked ahead. The passageway, brick-lined and poorly lit, veered into shadows on its left, obscuring what lay beyond. I let go of the handrail and followed the passage. The young woman was now on my mind.

As the light improved, the passage hit a chamber that lay lengthwise across its path. Three doors offered egress from the elongated room. Lamps illuminated the walls, and also an arched ceiling decorated with pagan symbols where planets and constellations invoked the night sky, and where a comet stole a solitary path across a backdrop of the heavens. What goes on here? And why underground?

I examined each of the doors. Pinned to the exit on my right, I could see the severed foot of an animal, its white fur standing out in the light. To my left, a large tooth of another creature was propped upright against the wall. Between these, lay a broken tile with markings. Which exit should I take? And would one prove to be a trap—like an interview I'd once attended but never quite escaped? One, two or three, I mulled, before stepping forward and choosing the door with the broken tile. I entered a tunnel that sloped away. I had to go deeper.

The Greek hero Theseus, I fancied, would have struggled to find his way around central London. But below ground, he might never have been seen again. Of course, he too was a myth and part of the tease that my friends and tutors enjoyed playing on me. But in the story, he returns to Athens, while the bull—the Minotaur he confronts—he slays. Perhaps Otto and Francis have something else in mind. Jane only told me about how I would make love. If I choose, that is. And if the young woman, whom I shall embrace, chooses to be my partner.

Francis, though, would insist that there was no choice. That every step was already fated, every thought, every passion, bound in an unbroken chain. That I was here because of what had happened since I was born, along a course fated since the beginning of time—or the birthing of one of his new worlds if his cosmic secret was true. Even Alex told me that will in us is overruled by fate. A line from Marlowe. But if Alex was here now, I'd tell him he was wrong since his fate, my fate, the world's fate is still in the balance. I'm not the only stakeholder in this stripped-down ritual that Otto's chums are expecting.

I re-checked my wound. What had felt irritable was now starting to burn. It wasn't helping my mood, either. I continued along a tunnel made of steel. Cables and piping lined the walls. After about twenty minutes, I arrived at a second chamber and another set of doors. Wearily, I studied each, but saw nothing that might guide my progress. No signs, no animals and no ceramics.

If I'd not gone to uni, would I be standing here, puzzled where to go? Maybe the doors all lead to the same place, so it matters not which one I take. But if I turned back, wouldn't that change the course of events? I recalled the trick I'd played on Jenny and her friends in Covent Garden. A trick that loaded the outcome of her silly game. And if she'd gone out with me after we'd danced, she wouldn't have lost out to those guys wanting to paw her. Or if Fiona had stayed the night, would that have changed my fate? Anna changed her mind, of course. About me. At school. And now, if I and the young woman make love as Francis wants, and if the world dissolves, and if Alex returns … then he too must choose. Between Anna and Jane. And as the title of his favourite poem declared, he must choose one or the other. And choose a road … a road not taken.

Bloody hell, I thought. Frost's poem, and Alex's note. Impulse and doubt, he'd said. That's the clue. He's quitting. No IZ. No exchange. He's not coming home whatever I say, think or do. So, Francis—servant of destiny—will this upend your cosmic plans? I pushed open a door without caring. Soon, my friend, we'll find out how much of the future you really do control.

52

Standing six feet high, in an underground chamber a hundred feet long and fifty wide, a cylinder-shaped omphalos made of red obsidian lava, stood upright on a pedestal of Athenian marble. Carved near its base, a string of numbers recorded the nativity of the modern age, detailing its date of birth and the geographical co-ordinates of its incarnation. At the heart of the omphalos, a caesium rod decayed, casting a dull light on the hooded costumes and barbarous masks of its followers. In the middle of the chamber, a rectangular block of granite with a depression cut into its surface, lay like a graveyard tomb bathed in icy moonlight. And around the chamber's periphery, the soft beat of drums echoed the pulse of a dying cosmos.

At the tinkle of a bell, Dr Hatherleigh stepped forward and knelt before the omphalic sculpture. He opened a wooden box and released two serpents, coaxing them to rise and embrace the stone. 'This is how the world will end,' he whispered. 'This is where we will die.' He bowed and returned to the assembly.

Lionel Arbetta stepped forward. At the tinkle of a bell, he filled his lungs and in a rhythmic chant sang of the end of time and the destruction of matter. He returned to the assembly.

Francis and Jane joined hands and approached the upright stone. Together, they set eyes on the serpents. 'We call upon the gods of creation. We call upon the sky and the sea. We call upon the sun and the moon, and Hecate, goddess of the cross-roads. We call upon

415

Protogonos, egg-born from the coupling of Time and Fate. We call upon Pan, goat limbed, servant of passion and author of seductive song. We call upon the Muses for our inspiration.'

The congregation responded, fusing their voices in ascending and descending cries that ran and swelled like an ocean tide above the soft beat of drums that marked the end of eternity and dissolution of the dying cosmos.

Francis and Jane retreated, and retracing their steps, joined the young celebrant couple whose desire and intercourse would lead Alex home, would ignite a new cosmic order, and change forever the destiny of the modern world.

Boy to girl and girl to boy, they reached for the hands of their silent partners.

'There is no law but the truth,' said Francis to his companion.

'Aletheia!' cried the crowd.

'There is no sin but forgetfulness,' said Jane to her companion.

'Mnemosyne!' cried the crowd.

Francis and Jane embraced their partners before stepping aside.

Otto addressed the gathering. 'We have hastened without thought,' he declared, 'and we have idolised distractions. We have languished in ignorance and stunted growth. We have caressed the beast and tasted its blood.' He paused as the notes of a solitary reed pipe filled the air, evoking the beauty of swans, the flight of birds, and the glimmer of a breaking dawn. 'Let us now proceed to the first humbling,' he directed.

Simon led Francis to the omphalos. Jane followed and knelt beside her friend as he lay next to the pedestal. She placed a strip of leather into his mouth, and lifting his garment, exposed his soft flesh ahead of his ritual chastisement. Settling closer, she held his hand, and rested her head close to his.

Simon administered the first blow. 'In expiation of your arrogance, I lash you, Francis, servant of pride.'

'We have scorned humility, and banished shame,' said the congregation.

'In expiation of your wantonness, I lash you, Francis, servant of lust.'

'We have exalted sensation, and we denied death.'

'In expiation of your deceit, I lash you, Francis, servant of hypocrisy.'

'We have hidden the truth and mocked virtue.'

Francis bit deeper as blood splashed from his wounds, staining the step with his pain and fortitude. 'Jane, hear me. There is something I want to say.' Jane squeezed his hand. 'I was selfish, Jane. And I abandoned Robbie, my brother, to his fate.'

Her grip tightened. 'But you tried to save him, Francis. Before he drowned. When Alex should have helped him.'

'No, Jane. It was not … not Alex's fault.' Francis lurched suddenly as the lash cut into his skin before the shadow of an outstretched arm fell again across his torso.

'In expiation of your passivity, I lash you, Francis, servant of indolence.'

'We have stood aside, and we have closed our eyes to misfortune,' said the congregation.

Jane wiped his tears. 'But Alex was there when he struggled. You said that. To me.'

'No Jane. It was too late. My brother was dragged deeper and I must suffer for his loss.'

'No, Francis.'

'Yes. Because … because I'd mocked his timidity, Jane, when he was afraid.'

Jane cried out as the lash struck again.

Otto gestured to Simon. 'Cease the humbling. Jane and Hatherleigh. Remove Francis and bathe his wounds. He may rest before we continue with his penance for this dying world.'

The assembly bowed their heads.

Simon stepped back, and turning from the wounds he had

inflicted, nodded discreetly to Otto.

'It is through loss that a new future is won,' declared Otto.

'It is through sacrifice that promise renews,' responded the congregation.

'Let us wipe clean the past,' said Otto.

'Let us start again without its heavy burdens,' said the gathering.

A tremor struck the chamber. The glow of the omphalos intensified. Shadows fell on the walls, hinting at forms and embryos, at the shape of a leaf, the petals of a flower, and the soft cranial form of an unborn child.

'Jane,' said Otto, 'we must continue with the second humbling.'

With the help of Julian Hatherleigh, Jane lifted Francis and returned to the obsidian sculpture. As they made their way, they showed Francis's wounds to the grateful congregation. Jane removed the hood of his garment and placed a cup of water to his lips. After he drank, she wiped tears from his face.

Otto raised his arms. 'Let the human sacrifice be scorched above one eye. Simon. Prepare the rod of iron. Make it shine with fire.'

Francis reached for Jane as his body trembled. 'Listen to me. I was confused, but now I see clearly. I called out to Alex, but the sea was unforgiving.' Choking, he paused. 'Jane, my failure is great. And my heartbreak is my reward. I loved my brother, but I … I failed him.'

Jane moved closer. She touched Francis's cheek and stroked his hair. 'Soon your grief will be over, Francis. Alex will be with us. And Robbie will live again.'

'Jane. I have studied everything I can. But I worry that the stars have deceived me. That I have misread their intentions. That I have believed blindly.'

'No, Francis. The myths are elusive. Do not lose faith in them.'

'But I followed their clues, Jane. And yet Richard failed us at the Globe.'

'But you said that was his destiny.'

'Because I still believed. And still hoped. Yet now … now I feel helpless.'

Jane looked away. 'We can't go back. Not now, Francis.'

Simon lifted the rod of iron into the air, exposing its bright anger to the humbled crowd. He grabbed Francis by the hair, pulled back his head, and held the rod like a dagger above his face.

Jane fell to the floor.

'Now, Simon,' shouted Otto.

'Now!' echoed the congregation.

And as the iron flared, a single shot cracked the air. Simon spun violently, falling to the ground as a bullet struck his shoulder. The assembly threw itself down and stayed silent.

Felix Leighton removed his mask. 'This is an illegal gathering,' he declared, training his gun around the chamber.

'Get up,' demanded Otto. 'Seize this intruder.'

Another shot whistled across the chamber. Felix shifted to the block of granite. 'If anyone moves, your two lovers will die.'

'Who are you?' said Otto.

'I am a member of the security services. Your meeting is surrounded. Your secrets are now the property of the Crown.'

'What secrets?'

'The day, month and year the modern world was created.'

'Fool. The date is carved on the great stone in front of you. Look for yourself.'

Felix edged towards the omphalos. 'I want the list of events that you intend to alter.'

'Surely, you can guess them.'

'But not those of the future. Or the mechanism for changing them.'

'Then learn them. The stone is yours. The map is carved on its surface.' Otto addressed his followers. 'Lock all the doors. Let the celebrants rise. Let them be naked!'

'Stay still … all of you.'

'Rise!' I say. 'Let the celebrants embrace. Let them enjoy their passions.'

The assembly rose to their feet.

'This is grotesque. Your ritual is forbidden.'

'Our ritual will renew the world.'

'You are deluded. The world is not yours to dispose of. I am the legal authority at this meeting. And I will shoot to kill.'

'You are one. And we are thirty-five.'

Felix studied the chamber as the light from the stone intensified. Along the walls, primeval creatures stirred with life. Bones softened and twisted into shapes. Stick men and women marched under the gaze of many suns. He turned his head as the gathering moved closer, their closely fitting masks fixed with eerie smiles. 'This is … this is …' they taunted.

'Stand back,' said Felix, threatening the lovers once more with his gun.

The assembly stalled.

'You, celebrant. Go to the stone and read the numbers at its base.'

The celebrant remained still.

Felix pointed his gun.

'She is unfamiliar with your language,' explained Otto.

Felix lifted her mask, exposing the face of a young lady with light brown skin, dark eyes, and silky, black hair.

'This is how the world ends,' whispered the crowd. 'This is where we die.'

'Does her partner understand?' snapped Felix.

'Yes,' replied the celebrant alongside her.

'Read the number. Now.'

'Stay where you are, Richard,' said Otto. 'You have your own instructions and tasks to perform.'

Felix turned to the stone, entranced by the serpents coiling at its peak. He watched as their heads darted and tongues flashed until a sudden blast of light overwhelmed him. He screamed as one of the serpents slithered around his neck. Hatherleigh rushed forward and snatched the gun from his grasp before pulling the snake from the inside of Felix's garment.

'Drag him away,' ordered Otto. 'This intruder will be our sacrifice.' Otto turned to Jane. 'Francis is reprieved. Arbetta, give Simon morphine. I shall perform the humbling in his absence. Proceed with the ceremony. Let the celebrants be naked!'

The congregation retreated. 'But who is this intruder?' they asked. 'This armed man who has forced his way amongst us?'

'He is an imposter,' replied Otto. 'And an enemy of our cause.'

'But his actions … have they disturbed our plans? Will his presence hurt our future?'

'Silence—those of you who question destiny. Francis has been spared. Are you not satisfied with the outcome?'

'We are ready. But we have doubts. We hope Richard agrees with your plans.'

'Let the Thirteen step forward. Let the musicians prepare their instruments.'

Julian Hatherleigh led the Thirteen Elders to the side of the rectangular block. To assist movement and copulation, they poured scented oils into its shallow depression and sprinkled a cascade of soft petals to temper the harshness of its rock. They loosened the cords of their garments, lowered their masks, and to the beat of a drum, synchronised their breathing.

'Richard,' said Otto. 'Neophyte and celebrant. After a journey of trials and setbacks, you must now decide the fate of this world and the fate of your closest friend. But let us first hear the words of the poem that began your journey and your intimations of remorse in preparation for the judgement of our cause.'

'Is it this world or the next?' asked the Thirteen. 'Is it your friend or your partner?'

A tremor unsettled the ground.

'Give us your answer, Richard,' said Otto.

'Say the words,' said the Thirteen, 'that we may remember the beginning and experience the end.'

The vibrations intensified.

'Fuck you, Otto. Fuck all you satanists.' The celebrant ripped the mask from his face and thrust a small object above his head. 'This is how your world ends. This is how you losers die.'

'Who are you?' said the crowd.

'His name is Antony, Larry Antony,' said Felix, struggling free of his guards. 'The device he holds controls a warhead. Kill him. Before he activates it.'

'Give me the girl,' demanded Larry. 'She's mine.' Jane rushed to the young lady, but a blow sent her to the ground as Larry seized his prize. 'Open the doors!' he screamed. 'Open the doors or you all die.'

'Otto. Let him flee,' said Hatherleigh. 'We are lost.' He fell as masonry crashed down from the ceiling.

'Kill him,' shouted Felix, as he crawled towards the stone.

'Stop him,' shouted Otto. 'He must be sacrificed. Arbetta, seize him ...' But his voice failed as the light intensified, and the walls shook around him.

A piercing scream drowned the cries of the assembly. And as the walls heaved, the bolted entrance to the chamber sprung open. A young man appeared on a stepped platform, fearless before the frightened assembly.

'Where is the native woman?' demanded Richard Addings.

'With Antony' shouted Felix.

'Release her,' said Richard, scanning the mayhem before him.

Larry Antony stalled. His eyes fixed on Richard as he thrust his head forward. 'But you're not real. You're dead. You're just a phantom.' Larry poked out his tongue.

'It's your killer who lies slaughtered, Antony.'

'Liar. Liar. Pants on fire.'

'Save us, Richard. Or we die.'

Richard pulled a gun from his pocket and from the steps pointed the weapon with both hands. 'Release her. Now, damn you.'

'No,' he roared. 'She's mine. Mine, mine, mine.'

'Shoot, Richard,' cried the crowd.

Larry Antony pushed his hostage aside and climbed on to the petalled bed of granite. Still clutching the device, and laughing hysterically, he took aim at the omphalos.

'Stop him,' pleaded Otto.

'It doesn't matter,' said Hatherleigh. 'The omphalos is transforming.'

And as the crowd's attention shifted, and the piercing whine from the stone fell away, Richard sent round after round into his adversary's tormented ego. Larry fell—the shallow depression of the petalled bed trapping his fall … catching the blood that coloured his borrowed garments.

The air stilled, and the ground settled. The walls of the underground building faded. Images of the past drifted by like fragments from a forgotten tale. And as the assembly studied the strange projections—the images of conflict and suffering, of joys and heartbreak—a thin skeletal figure appeared alone on a distant horizon.

Jane lifted her arm 'It's Alex,' she said. 'Look everyone. Look Francis. He's coming home.'

The assembly knelt.

Richard led the young lady towards the unfolding scene. Together, they watched as the figure struggled to make progress, unsure of its path but drawn to the light that shone steadily from the chamber. They turned to each other, and with a smile, their eyes met like greetings to the morning sun. They embraced. Their lips touched in one last, remembered kiss. And as their hands parted, the stranger from a far-off world vanished into the cosmic void.

'Otto,' whispered the assembly, 'have our hopes come true?'

'No,' said Francis.

'But Alex is returning,' said Jane. 'Look, he will soon be amongst us.'

'No,' repeated Francis, kneeling beside the granite block as he reached for Larry's lifeless hand. He stood up. 'It's not Alex, Jane. It's my brother. He's calling to me. He wants my help.'

Jane, transfixed, stared at the youth as he waved frantically for assistance.

'I'm coming,' said Francis. 'I will save you, Robbie. Please god, I will save you.' Francis rushed into the abyss, taking Larry's apocalyptic device and its threat of destruction with him.

The cosmic pathway closed around him. And as the ethereal images of past and future faded, the omphalos fragmented and broke apart, returning its coveted secret to the cosmos, and the hopes of its followers to the grave.

Richard surveyed the carnage around him. But before he turned and left for home, the words of a poem that had once eluded him slipped back into his mind. 'At the next spring,' he recalled, 'for I … I am every dead thing.' He smiled as a small wicker basket caught his eye, and reaching down, remembered one more line from the poem's troubled verse: 'In whom love … has wrought new alchemy.'

He threw the gun to the floor and without a backward glance, headed out of the chamber and towards the light that beckoned another day.

END